Virapoj Asavajarn

Jake Needham is an American screenwriter who is married to a Thai-born concert pianist. They have two sons, and live in San Francisco and Bangkok.

THE BIG MANGO

THE BIG MANGO

A Novel By

JAKE NEEDHAM

ASIA BOOKS

Published and Distributed by
Asia Books Co. Ltd.,
5 Sukhumvit Road Soi 61,
PO Box 40,
Bangkok 10110,
Thailand.
Tel: (662) 714 0740-2 ext. 221-223
Fax: (662) 381 1621, 391 2277

Typeset by COMSET Limited Partnership
Printed by Darnsutha Press Ltd.

ISBN 974-8237-36-2

For Aey, James and Charles.
But then, everything is for them.

"I would be glad to know which is worst: to be ravished a hundred times by pirates, to have one buttock cut off, to run the gauntlet among the Bulgarians, to be whipped and hanged at an *auto-de-fen*, to be dissected, to be chained to an oar in a galley; and, in short, to experience all the miseries through which every one of us hath passed, or to remain here doing nothing?"

"This," said Candide, "is a grand question."

Voltaire
Candide, 1759

PROLOGUE

*O*n *April 21, 1975, late in the afternoon, Nguyen Van Thieu
abruptly resigned as the president of the Republic of
South Vietnam, abandoning what was left of his weary and
wasted country to the North Vietnamese.*

*Just before dawn the next morning, a C-118 belonging to
the South Vietnamese Air Force rolled unnoticed down a
darkened runway at Tan Sun Nhut. The plane was heavy;
crammed with boxes and crates that had been trucked to the
airfield from the Presidential Palace during the night. Gaining
altitude and turning its back on the approaching dawn, the big
cargo plane crawled slowly into the moist, early morning
darkness, and lumbered away.*

*Four nights later, on April 25, an aging DC-6 provided by
the American Ambassador slipped Thieu and nine of his
confederates quietly out of Vietnam. Each of them was carrying
a document, personally signed by President Gerald Ford,
authorizing his entry into the United States.*

*By daybreak on April 26, the rumors were already spreading
through Saigon—Thieu and his cronies had fled, but they had
not gone empty-handed. The vaults of the Bank of Vietnam, so
the whispers went, were bare. Thieu had taken all the bank's
currency and gold reserves, and had spirited them secretly out
of the country before he left.*

*It made a good story, but it wasn't true. The C-118 that flew
out of Tan Sun Nhut in the morning darkness of April 22
carried only a few personal possessions belonging to Thieu,
and government archives that he hoped might win him*

sympathetic treatment from future historians. The Bank of Vietnam's gold and foreign currency reserves were still stored safely in South Vietnam.

The rumors did have one thing right, however. The reserves were no longer in the vaults of the Bank of Vietnam. They were in the basement of a nondescript warehouse on Phan Binh Street—a narrow, shell-cratered road just north of the American Embassy compound. The reserves were there, and not still in the bank's vaults, because a secret operation had been mounted by the CIA to get the money out of the country before it fell into the hands of the North Vietnamese.

A United States Marine Corps captain who was trusted by the CIA chief of station in Saigon had been assigned the task of preparing the contents of the vaults for shipment to safety several weeks before—and he had done his job well. That was no surprise to the station chief. He knew the officer to be a reliable man—a bit of an oddball as marine captains usually went perhaps, but he was well-educated, intelligent, and resourceful. It was even said by some that he wrote poetry, but the station chief had never read any of it himself, and he had never asked.

That the captain did have an interesting intellectual bent was apparent, however, from the code name he selected for the project. He chose, for some reason, to call it Operation Voltaire. No one ever asked him why.

A total of almost 20,000 pounds of currency—mostly American dollars, but also some German marks, British pounds and Japanese yen—together with a small amount of gold bullion cast into 10kg ingots, had been packed and sealed into watertight, steel containers by six American employees of Saigon's CIA station. The embassy maintenance staff—local men who had no idea what was in the containers—then boxed them up in ordinary, wooden shipping crates, and trucked them to the warehouse on Phan Binh Street. The captain organized a small detachment of marines to guard the building, and then *settled back to wait for orders to fly the crates out of the country to safety.*

Those orders never came.

As the noose around Saigon tightened, the CIA pressed what was left of the South Vietnamese government to approve the implementation of Operation Voltaire, and ship the money to Switzerland. But the frightened men abandoned by Thieu dithered. They clung to their daydreams, like drowning men to driftwood.

Maybe the North would accept a negotiated settlement, they hoped against all reason. If that happened, then letting the Americans fly the Bank of Vietnam's gold and foreign currency out of the country would suddenly seem like a very bad idea. After the North Vietnamese took over the South, they would undoubtedly tag any South Vietnamese who had been rash enough to endorse such a thing as a traitor—a label that would undoubtedly prove fatal.

Then April 30, 1975, came—and it didn't matter anymore.

North Vietnamese artillery pounded the city remorselessly. Saigon began to burn, and the population spiraled into an ugly panic. The Department of State ordered all Americans remaining in Saigon evacuated, but it took a cordon of American marines on the walls of the embassy compound— bayonets fixed to their M-16s, and thump guns popping canisters of tear gas into an angry mob of Vietnamese—to make it possible.

By the time the last helicopter-load of Americans lifted off the roof of the gutted embassy building and clattered through the dense smoke to the aircraft carriers waiting offshore in the South China Sea, the crates of currency and gold stored in the warehouse on Phan Binh Street had turned into 20,000 pounds of excess baggage. Operation Voltaire was forgotten.

As the years passed following the fall of Saigon, those few people who had known about the existence of Operation Voltaire either retired, or died—and most of the informed speculation as to what happened to the Bank of Vietnam's money disappeared along with them. After little more than a decade, the colorful story of a vast hoard of gold and currency abandoned by the fleeing Americans in the flames of Saigon had become part of Washington folklore. Only half-believed at most, it was tucked away somewhere between Deep Throat and the grassy knoll.

Then, in 1995, reconciliation became the flavor of the day, and Vietnam and the United States resumed diplomatic relations. They reopened their embassies and exchanged diplomatic personnel.

The newly-appointed second secretary at the American Embassy in Hanoi—a position reserved in many embassies for a senior CIA official—was a man who had begun his career, not coincidentally, with a brief tour in Saigon in 1975. That posting had been minor—he had been listed on the embassy personnel roster as nothing more than a junior cultural attaché—but nevertheless, he was one of the few people still in public life who knew for certain that the story of tons of money and gold left behind in the ruins of Saigon was not folklore. And he had not forgotten.

As far as the second secretary knew, no trace of those 20,000 pounds of currency and gold had ever surfaced anywhere; so the first time he found an excuse to travel from Hanoi down to Saigon—now called Ho Chi Minh City in what, he thought, was a particularly graceless brutalization of history—his curiosity naturally led him to take a stroll around to Phan Binh Street.

The warehouse was gone.

The second secretary glanced at the overgrown vacant lot; he took in the mounds of broken concrete and the twisted, rusting rebars that marked the place where it had once stood; and he walked on without stopping.

As nearly as he could calculate with any certainty, the ten tons of gold and currency he knew were in that warehouse in

April, 1975, would now be worth at least 400 million dollars. Since plainly the money was no longer where it had been left, the second secretary thought he should ask around— diplomatically, of course—to find out what the North Vietnamese had done with it after they rolled into Saigon.

And imagine his surprise when he discovered that the North Vietnamese hadn't done anything with it.

Because they didn't have it either.

1

Fourteen months as a marine grunt in Vietnam had left Eddie Dare with at least one staunch conviction: he'd been born for better things than crawling around in the mud with a bunch of stoned assholes. However, when he reflected on the subject now—which was something he tried awfully hard not to do—he had to admit that practicing law in San Francisco had a lot of the very same qualities.

Pushing that unhappy assessment aside, Eddie folded open the *Chronicle* sports section to a story about the Warrior's latest loss, and propped it up against a stainless steel napkin holder.

The Buena Vista Café was way down at the end of Hyde Street, right on the bay where the cable cars from Union Square turned around—and a stool at the counter there was Eddie's favorite place to begin a day. Three fried eggs, crispy bacon, that thick-cut patty sausage that you almost couldn't find anymore, hash browns swimming in catsup, and two slices of sourdough toast soaked with enough butter to cause little rivulets to form and run down his fingers every time he lifted a slice. Eating breakfast like that wasn't fashionable anymore, Eddie knew—but he figured he wasn't fashionable anymore either, so to hell with it.

The waitress eased over with a fresh pot of coffee. Blond and athletic-looking with a light dusting of suntan, she looked like the runners in Golden Gate Park who could only manage to put in miles on weekends. As she refilled Eddie's chunky ceramic mug, she tossed out her most dazzling smile—but Eddie was tough to dazzle before the caffeine kicked in.

"Anything else, handsome?"

"No thanks, Suzie. Got to get to the office."

"Hey, new client, maybe? My tips going to get better?"

Suzie had been flirting mildly with Eddie ever since she started working days at the BV instead of nights. Eddie noticed she'd made a point of telling him she changed shifts because she was sick of the yuppies and tourists who piled into the place every night to slurp Irish coffee and check out the action; that she liked more mature, more stable men— guys who had *lived* a little. Eddie didn't take long to get the idea, but it didn't really excite him all that much once he did. Suzie was okay, but Eddie was already up to his ass in okay. 'Okay' was the story of his life.

Christ, is that what it's going to say on my tombstone? He chewed on a piece of toast and wiped the crumbs off his upper lip. *'Here lies Eddie Dare. He was okay.' Oh, man.*

"Did that woman ever call? The one I gave your number to?"

"I don't do divorces, Suzie."

"Well, you know . . . I figured with all the experience you'd had yourself . . ."

Eddie winced.

So I've been married a couple of times without it taking. So what?

"This woman looked like she had pretty good money."

"I just don't do divorce work, Suzie."

Suzie rubbed at a spot on the counter that was invisible, at least to Eddie, then she tossed the towel away and sloshed coffee around in the pot.

"So, you still working on that case for the dog?" she finally asked, mostly just to keep the conversation going.

"It's not a case for a dog, Suzie. It's a case that happens to involve a dog."

"I thought it was two dogs."

"Okay, two dogs."

Eddie had represented Eric Ratmoski on and off for five years. Breaking and entering a half dozen times; extortion, of course; a couple of assault charges; a concealed weapons beef; and an interstate gambling conviction. All that was pretty much business as usual for Eric, but now he had plunged headlong into the porno business. That by itself probably wouldn't have bothered Eddie all that much, but Eric's fixation with German Shepherds was pretty far over the line.

Two dogs that Eric said he particularly loved—and Eric's choice of words there was something Eddie wasn't about to reflect on too closely—had been taken away and locked up at the San Francisco Animal Shelter. Eric had been onto Eddie every day to get them back, and Eddie had been trying. He hadn't managed it yet, and he figured that if he had to sit through one more meeting with the vice squad and listen to all their doggie sex jokes again, he was going to puke. Probably he should tell Eric to get himself another lawyer. Maybe one who liked dogs.

"I don't know, Eddie," Suzie mused. "Seems to me that talking to people about divorces isn't any worse than watching videos of dogs humping."

Eddie was still trying to figure out what to say to that when a customer down the counter waved his coffee cup for a refill. Suzie wandered off, and Eddie jumped at his chance. He used the last crust of his sourdough toast to sop up a stray bit of egg, dropped a ten on the counter with a wave to Suzie, and headed outside to grab a cable car back over Russian Hill to his office.

People who lived in San Francisco claimed that only tourists rode cable cars, and generally it was true. A real San Franciscan normally couldn't manage to wedge his way onto one, even if he wanted to. The flip-flops and camcorders and kids wearing T-shirts with stupid slogans gave no quarter; but it was still pretty early in the day for little hooligans to be out and about their business of ruining the city, and Eddie usually had no difficulty getting on a car back over the hill after breakfast.

It had been several years now since he'd moved up to the better end of Grant, just west of Market. He shared a small, vaguely Victorian building with a restaurant on the ground floor and something on the third floor called Pacific Century Import Company—which apparently opened only occasionally, and usually very late at night. That was odd, even for San Francisco, but Eddie had made a point of not asking too many questions. That was *not* odd for San Francisco.

Eddie had started out as an uptown guy in a flashy, bronzed-glass office tower—then worked his way down to a one-man office over a Chinese restaurant. Most people usually tried to get that the other way around, he knew—and he would have preferred that approach himself—but you had to play the cards you were dealt, and he figured he'd done the best he could with his.

His first stop after he left Wren & Simon—the big downtown firm where he had started right out of law school—had been two dingy rooms over a grocery store in Chinatown. After Eddie took a few days in the silence of his new office to contemplate the stark fact that he didn't have any clients—not one—he hit upon a marketing strategy that was designed to get him some as quickly as possible.

The idea was straightforward enough. Mostly he hung around the criminal courts at the Hall of Justice, wore a good suit, and radiated a willingness to work cheap. It turned out to be a remarkably effective plan because Eddie had one important thing going for him: he was pretty fast on his feet. That gave him a useful edge over the other lawyers who cruised the courthouse in search of a living, most of whom in

Eddie's eyes were only a step or two from swapping lives with their clients anyway.

When he managed to cut a few guys loose, even if he wasn't exactly sure how he had done it, he began to develop a reputation among a particular clientele as a good man to know. Almost before he realized it, he was on a roll; and it wasn't long before his client list was reasonably impressive— that is if he stuck strictly to contemplating its quantity and didn't worry too much about its quality.

Sometimes it occurred to Eddie that he didn't know much about actually practicing criminal law, since he had done nothing after school except banking and finance work. But then most—if not all—of the people who hired him were guilty as hell anyway, so he figured maybe it didn't matter all that much that he knew so little. Sometimes he wondered if doctors knew any more about medicine when they started out on their own, than he knew about law. That thought always scared the crap out of him, and it caused him to swear that he'd never go to a doctor who wasn't really old.

Eddie jumped off the cable car when it slowed at California Street for the brakeman to lock-up for the steep crawl down Nob Hill. He let the car's momentum carry him into a gentle jog onto Powell, and he angled off just enough to make the turn toward Grant without slowing down. It was a slick-looking move if he did say so himself, and he felt a momentary stab of disappointment that some woman he wanted to impress hadn't been around to see it. Good moves were good moves anyway, he reassured himself, even if no one was around to admire them.

He climbed the stairs and heard the clicking from Joshua's keyboard even before he opened his office door. Eddie had known Joshua since he had been his first paralegal at Wren & Simon—although why Joshua had given up the security and prestige of a big, commercial firm to go with him to Chinatown, Eddie had never really understood. Joshua lived with a retired fireman on a houseboat in Sausalito, and he was Eddie's most loyal employee. Actually he was Eddie's only employee. He was very thin, and with his full head of long, silver hair, and his rimless glasses, he looked like he'd come straight to the office from a Grateful Dead concert in 1968 and hadn't left since. Eddie didn't know for sure how old Joshua was, and frankly he didn't think Joshua knew either.

"If you're thinking of giving me anything else to do, you can forget it."

As usual, Joshua didn't look up—or stop typing—before he spoke, and Eddie always wondered how he knew who had come in.

"I'm still doing the discovery motions in the Wong robbery."

"How about starting on the Wright robbery instead?"

"I don't remember any . . ." Joshua's fingers stopped moving, but he kept his eyes fixed on the computer screen. "Was that a joke? It was, wasn't it?"

Before Eddie could say anything, Joshua began to shake his head. Then he started typing again, very fast. "That was pathetic, Eddie. Really pathetic. You're no Al Gore, are you, man?"

"Any messages?"

"Michael called from Seattle."

That was odd. Eddie's son had just turned fourteen and didn't call him all that often.

"Really? What about?"

"Didn't tell me. Said he'd call back later."

Joshua had recently begun to resent Michael a little, and didn't try very hard to keep it hidden. He and Eddie had never talked about it, but Eddie knew that Joshua thought Michael treated Eddie disdainfully—almost like he was ashamed Eddie was his father.

Joshua had Mike's attitude diagnosed about right, Eddie knew. And he didn't like it much either. But he also knew that being a father and an ex-husband was a complicated thing, and you had to make allowances. Joshua hadn't had any experience trying to be either—at least not that Eddie knew of—so he just let the whole thing slide, and they didn't get into it.

Eddie had still been at Wren & Simon when he came home late on a wet Tuesday in November and discovered that his wife had taken Michael, as well as most of what they owned, and moved out. Before he could get a grip on what was happening to him, Jennifer surfaced in Seattle and filed for divorce, as well as custody of Michael. She told Eddie that it wasn't his fault really. It was just that she didn't want to be married anymore; that she wanted to have her own life, not be an extension of his. Eddie didn't really know what to say to that—actually it sounded pretty reasonable to him—so when the divorce papers came, he signed them and sent them back.

It was while Eddie was still trying to decide how he felt about being single again, that what he later took to calling 'the disagreement' occurred—and he abruptly parted company with Wren & Simon. That made two divorces in the same month. It had been almost ten years ago now, but he could still recall every minute of the day when the firm's management committee called him into the conference room and fired him. He could remember every word they had said. His memory of the other divorce was less vivid.

"No other messages?"

"Nothing you care about."

Bless Joshua, Eddie thought. Everything always under control. He, on the other hand, wasn't really certain he'd had *anything* under control since about 1960. That had been the time at his fifth birthday party when he socked Becky Schulman in the nose. She'd been seven and had stuck out her tongue at Eddie and called him a ninny—so he'd drawn back his little fist and popped her right in the snot. Becky had bled all over the carpet, and Eddie's mother had spanked him hard—although whether for hitting Becky or for getting blood on the carpet he was never absolutely certain—but he hadn't yelled because it had been worth it. He'd cold-cocked the little bitch, and even now he thought she'd deserved it. But he also figured that was probably the very last time in his life that he'd been fully in control of anything.

"Could you bring me some coffee, Joshua?" Eddie asked as he headed into his office.

"Right away, oh master of mine."

Come to think of it, Eddie reflected, Joshua was starting to remind him a whole lot of Becky Schulman.

Eddie flopped into his low-back chair that was upholstered in nondescript brown cloth—he hated those high-back, black leather thrones that lawyers usually sat in—and dumped his briefcase on the floor. He rummaged half-heartedly through the mail, and was mildly pleased to find a couple of real letters along with the usual junk. The first bore the engraved return address of Martin, Fletcher & O'Brien—a famously-stuffy, commercial firm that occupied about half of the Bank of America Tower—and Eddie threw that one back onto his desk unopened.

The other envelope had no return address at all, and Eddie held it up and looked it over curiously.

It was an airmail envelope, one of those old-fashioned ones with a bright red and blue border and the words *Par Avion* printed in big letters underneath two exotic-looking stamps. It crossed Eddie's mind briefly that he hadn't seen an envelope like that in a long time, and it even surprised him a little to see that they still existed.

This one had been addressed by hand. Very neatly and carefully, someone had printed in black ink: MR. EDWARD DARE, ATTORNEY-AT-LAW, 469 GRANT STREET, SAN FRANCISCO, CALIFORNIA 94108, UNITED STATES OF AMERICA.

The envelope wasn't very heavy, and when Eddie ripped into it he thought at first that it was empty. But then he turned it up and shook it, and a single snapshot slid out onto his desk, face up.

It was a photograph that must have been taken at least twenty years before, he realized immediately. The picture had caught a bunch of young marines in a moment of horsing around with some Asian girls. From the uniforms and the look of the kids wearing them, Eddie knew the picture had to date back to the Vietnam War era, but other than that, nothing about it hinted where or exactly when it had been taken.

There was one thing about the picture that got Eddie's complete and undivided attention, however—and it caused him to pick it up slowly, and then to sit and stare at it for a long time.

Someone had drawn a bright, red circle on the snapshot with a sharp-pointed pen, and they must have wielded it using considerable force. The line was angry-looking, and etched deeply into the surface of the photograph. It had even ripped through the paper entirely in one place, almost decapitating one of the young marines.

Eddie carefully studied the fresh, open face in the center of the red circle. The face studied him silently in return, oblivious to the deep slash yawning just below its chin.

There was no doubt in his mind at all—the loopy, slightly lopsided stare he met there was his own.

The violent slashes framing his face added a deeply unsettling element to Eddie's surprise at seeing the photograph. It bothered him, too—he had to honestly admit—that the young Eddie gazed so guilelessly out of the picture at the middle-aged Eddie slumped in a cheap chair in a crummy office over a noodle shop. That was a swipe far subtler than the harsh, red circle, of course—but for all its slyness, it dug into him almost as deeply.

Eddie fumbled for some sensible explanation for the photograph—some obvious interpretation that would match the innocence of his cockeyed, young face—but nothing came to him.

As he sat and thought about it however, he began to feel the unmistakable sensation of a cool breeze on the back of his neck. It was gentle but persistent, and as Eddie raised his head from the photograph to take its measure, all in a rush he knew.

Something was coming at him; something straight out of a cloudy, forgotten corner of his past. He couldn't imagine what it was, but of one thing he was absolutely certain.

Whatever it might turn out to be, it was about to dump all over him.

2

Eddie wanted to forget about the picture entirely, to tell himself it meant nothing at all. He wanted to write it off as a prank by someone he hadn't seen in years, and throw it away. He wanted to do all of that, but he couldn't.

In Eddie's experience, weird things that happened to him seldom meant nothing. Weird things, he had found, almost always turned out to mean *something*—frequently something not too good. Every time he tried to ignore weirdness until it went away, he would eventually find it tattooed onto his butt. No, it was always good policy to take on weirdness before it took him on, Eddie had decided a long time ago—to meet it out in the street before it got inside his house, popped open a Coors, and made itself at home on his couch.

The problem was, he wasn't certain how to apply his policy in this particular case. For the life of him, he couldn't work out what the point of the photograph was supposed to be.

Maybe it was a threat, but he really couldn't think of any-body who would want to threaten him at all, much less in such an obscure way. Certainly none of his clients were the sort to go in for that kind of subtlety. If any of them had a problem with him, they were the kind of guys who'd come around to his apartment one night with a hockey stick. But if the photograph wasn't a threat, then what the hell *was* it? A joke?

Eddie stared at the other men in the photograph—and at the women, too—threading them back and forth through his memory. No matter how hard he tried, he couldn't recall any of the faces. He might even have sworn he didn't know anybody in the picture at all, but there he was right in the middle of them, so he guessed he must have seen them at least that once. Surely no one would have gone to the trouble of faking such an innocuous picture. All of which brought him back full circle again to wondering why anyone would send the picture to him at all, even if it *was* real.

The best idea Eddie could come up with off-hand was to show the picture to someone else he'd been in the marines with, and see what they made of it. Only one possibility came to him readily, but it was a good one, so he tucked the photograph into a jacket pocket and headed for the door.

Joshua was on the telephone as Eddie came out of his office. He quickly put the call on hold, twisting around until his eyes caught Eddie's.

"Must be family day for you."

Eddie was about to say something impatient—he was already up to his ass in subtlety and couldn't face any more—when Joshua laid it out.

"It's Kathleen." He tilted his head toward the telephone.

Eddie had given marriage another shot three or four years after Jennifer left him. Her name had been Kathleen Strong—not Kathleen Dare, Kathleen Strong—and she had been an assistant district attorney in Marin County. He always had to stop and think to work out exactly when they had been married and when they got divorced, so he seldom bothered. It hadn't lasted very long, and thank God they hadn't had any children. Eddie flinched a bit every time he realized he was thinking that. But if they had, Kathleen would probably have hung the unfortunate kid with some idiotic surname like Strong-Dare—and that was a future too horrible to wish on any child.

Actually Kathleen had been okay, if a little strident and overly prone to sneak attacks. At least Eddie had thought of her that way, until one day she announced that she'd decided to leave him and move to Alaska. Kathleen failed to mention then that the reason was not a new-found love of elk crap and the NRA, but rather that she was screwing a federal judge in Fairbanks at the time.

Eddie hadn't really minded all that much finding himself single again—actually he hardly noticed any change in his life at all—and he figured that anybody who ran off to Fairbanks to sleep with a federal judge probably had enough trouble already, so he didn't make a fuss when she filed the papers. That meant the divorce was—what else?—okay.

"She's calling from Alaska?"

"No, from Tiburon. I gather the judge is history and she's back."

"Oh, Christ." Eddie thought for a minute. "You didn't . . ."

"No, I said I thought you'd just left."

Eddie wiggled his eyebrows a couple of times and then cut Joshua the biggest wink he could manage as he ducked through the door. That damned picture was already giving him heartburn. Kathleen would just have to take a number if she wanted to make him miserable today.

He covered the few blocks down Grant to the Transamerica Pyramid in a brisk walk, cut through the plaza underneath it, and turned north on Columbus toward the bay. Maybe he'd get lucky and sort this thing out quickly.

Heluska Jones had been the endlessly good-natured guy in his platoon—the volunteer for whatever might be going. There seemed to be one in every outfit. Lusk always claimed to be a full-blooded Apache Indian whose name meant 'great warrior'—until deeply stoned one night, he admitted that he actually came from a tribe named the Winnebagos, and that Heluska really translated as something more like 'little fairy sent by the gods.'

From then on of course, Lusk was Winnebago Jones for life. They would have tried out Little Fairy Jones for a while, but then they saw the look in his eyes and decided that screwing with an angry Indian was probably riskier than screwing with the VC. Anyway, 'Winnebago Jones' had something. You could almost dance to it.

Winnebago and Eddie rotated back to Camp Pendleton together in 1975 and were discharged within a few days of each other. Eddie was hitching up the coast to San Francisco to get himself into college, and since Winnebago had nowhere to go but back to the hard-scrabble of Northern Arizona, he just tagged along. As it turned out, Winnebago quickly found the old beatnik ghetto around Columbus Avenue—or it found him—and he was home.

A hippie Indian named Winnebago was just the right thing for San Francisco in the mid-seventies, and for a few years he worked in a bookstore and wrote what he insisted was poetry. But as a decade slid past, and Columbus Avenue turned from a hang-out for aging beats into a tourist attraction, Winnebago just went with the flow and became a tourist attraction, too.

Even now, after more than twenty years, he could still be found in the same little bookstore on Columbus—wearing what he thought was an appropriate costume for a hippie Indian in San Francisco—selling a few books and a lot of unspeakable garbage to tourists.

When Eddie pushed open the door, a bell on the back tinkled, and Winnebago glanced up from a paperback he was reading propped against the cash register. He was wearing a shirt with a beaded front that he'd bought at a garage sale in San Jose—because it reminded him of the one Tonto wore in the Lone Ranger movies, he said—and his shoulder-length, black hair was tied back off his face with a red and white beaded headband that announced, FULL-BLOODED AMERICAN INDIAN.

Eddie had once tried to tell Winnebago that he wasn't supposed to be an Indian anymore; that somebody had gone and made him a Native American when he wasn't looking. It had something to do with preserving the dignity of his race, Eddie explained, but Winnebago said he didn't really care too much about that since he already had all the dignity he could use in San Francisco anyway. He was an Indian; he'd always been an Indian; and he intended to stay an Indian. That seemed to settle it, and Eddie never brought the matter up again.

"Hey, Eddie, my man!" Winnebago closed the book and scraped his stool back slightly. "How long's it been?"

"Two weeks. I was here two weeks ago Thursday."

Winnebago thought about that as he reached for the pack of unfiltered Camels he always kept close at hand.

"Yeah?"

"We walked over to North Beach Pizza."

Winnebago seemed to strain a moment, trying to remember as he shook a cigarette from the pack. He gave up quickly however, struck a match, and lit the cigarette, exhaling in a long, steady stream.

"Well, if you say so, Eddie. Can't remember a damned thing about it though."

"You must be getting old, Winnebago."

Winnebago tapped one finger slowly against the side of the cash register and considered the proposition. Eddie waited for him to decide what he thought, but when it became obvious that it might take a while, Eddie went ahead and fished the picture out of his pocket and put it on the counter. Winnebago took another toke on his cigarette and shifted his weight slightly on the stool so that he could see it more clearly.

"Hey, that's you, Eddie! Damn, you look so young!" He lifted the picture from the counter and peered at it. "Why'd you draw that circle around your head?"

"I didn't. It came that way."

"Your head? Came that way?"

Winnebago apparently was not having one of his better days, Eddie reflected.

"No, the picture. The picture came that way."

"What do you mean? Where'd it come from?"

Eddie told him.

Winnebago just shook his head slowly after he heard the story. "Ain't that the weirdest thing, man? Ain't that the weirdest?"

"Do you recognize anyone?"

"I recognize you, Eddie."

Winnebago had times like this; times when all the foreign substances he had poured and sucked and snorted into his body over the years held a convention in his brain all at once. On the other hand, Eddie knew there were also times when Winnebago was so penetrating and insightful that he scared the hell out of most people. When the magnetic fields in his brain overlapped just right, Winnebago sounded like an Old Testament prophet who had suffered the bizarre misfortune of emerging from reincarnation as a hippie Indian in a San Francisco bookstore.

"No, Winnebago, anyone else. Do you recognize anyone else in the picture?"

Winnebago looked hard at the snapshot, tilting it from side to side to study the faces more closely. The smoke from his Camel formed a little wreath around his head and caught the light in such a way that it made Eddie think for a moment of some bizarrely vandalized Renaissance painting.

"Isn't that guy behind you somebody from our squad?" Winnebago laid the photograph back on the counter and twisted it toward Eddie.

"Maybe. You can't see him well enough to tell."

"There's something about his ears. They look familiar."

"You can't remember we had pizza together two weeks ago and you recognize the ears on a guy you haven't seen in twenty years?"

"Man, I remember every minute of twenty years ago. Don't you?"

"Well," Eddie admitted, "a lot of it, I guess."

Eddie and Winnebago stood together in silence for a moment, each contemplating the mute relic of their past that had suddenly elbowed its way into their present. Finally, Winnebago took a last puff on his cigarette and stubbed it out in an ashtray already overflowing onto the counter.

"Who do you think sent it, Eddie?"

"Beats the hell out of me."

Winnebago just nodded a couple of times, then looked up and studied Eddie carefully. "I look at that picture, I gotta tell you, and I get a real bad feeling."

"Meaning what?"

"Meaning I don't see why anybody would send it, except to say they had some sort of business with you. And don't you think this is a pretty strange way to say that? Unless a guy was a little off, wouldn't he just call you up and say, 'Hey, Eddie, how's tricks? Maybe you don't remember me, but I've got some business with you.' Wouldn't he just do that?"

"You'd think so."

"Yeah, well, that's what gives me a bad feeling."

Eddie decided that Winnebago was just being inexplicably logical for once, rather than measuring the pulse of the unseen.

"How about the girls, Winnebago? Can you remember any of them?"

"No. I'm ashamed to admit it, but all them little chickens always looked pretty much the same to me. Besides, I was only in Thailand a few times." Winnebago tapped the snapshot with his forefinger. "This is that place in Bangkok where we used to go on R&R."

Eddie picked the photograph up and looked at it again. "How do you know that?"

"Those are Thai girls, man. Couldn't be anybody else."

"I thought they were probably Vietnamese."

"Shit, Eddie." Winnebago sounded disgusted. "How could you forget? We'd get off the R&R flights, not even get a room, just go straight to the bars. Usually slept on the floor of one of them." He shook his head a few times. "Those girls may have been whores, but they were nice girls. They saved my life more than once, I'll tell you. Those are absofuckinglutely Thai girls. You can bet your ass on it, man."

Eddie looked at the picture some more and felt the memories start to stir. "Maybe you're right. I didn't see that before."

Winnebago snorted. "You see today better. I see yesterday better. I'm not sure who that makes worse off."

The bell on the shop door tinkled and a very fat woman came in with a very skinny man. They were wearing matching, polyester jogging suits in phosphorescent blue with white stripes running down both legs, and they stood looking around uncertainly until Winnebago bounded out from behind the cash register.

"Welcome, welcome! Just have a look around folks. Hasn't changed a bit since Allen Ginsberg and I started the place in '65. Got first editions of Ginsberg's books up there." He pointed to the rickety staircase. "Every one autographed by him personally!"

Eddie gave Winnebago a long look. The couple nodded tentatively and started up the stairs as Winnebago settled back behind the counter on his stool.

"Sometimes commerce demands you stretch a point or two," he mumbled, carefully avoiding Eddie's eyes.

Eddie pushed the picture back into his pocket. He now knew something about the photograph he hadn't known before, but it wasn't much, and off-hand he couldn't see what use it was to him anyway.

"Okay, Winnebago. See ya."

"Later, man."

As he left the store, Eddie heard the fat woman and the skinny man coming back down the stairs.

"Who the fuck's Allen Ginsberg?" the woman was asking the man, but he wasn't answering.

3

Eddie waited near Judge Rybeck's court at the Hall of Justice trying to make himself as comfortable as possible on the hard mahogany bench. He hoped it wouldn't be long before they got to him because he was just there to enter a plea. He could do that in his sleep. As a matter of fact, he usually did.

His client was a man named Dante Bauer who was in the limousine business. Dante had been busted for living on the earnings of a prostitute after his girlfriend Shalynn had offered to go down on a plainclothes cop in the men's room of the St. Francis Hotel for a hundred bucks. Shalynn said it was all just a misunderstanding. Dante said he didn't know Shalynn was a hooker, and besides, no one could live on the shit money she made giving 100-dollar blowjobs.

"Actually in court today, huh, Counselor?" Kelly Wuntz wedged his way onto the bench next to Eddie, glaring at a gangbanger in a baggy, red and gold 49ers jacket until the kid slid over and gave him some room. Wuntz was a vice cop who worked the old Tenderloin district, and he had accumulated more nauseating stories about people than Eddie ever really wanted to hear.

"I thought big-time criminal mouthpieces just cut cozy deals for their clients and then hung out at the golf course the rest of the day, Dare."

"Yeah, Wuntz, you got it. That's exactly what big-time criminal mouthpieces do."

"Why are you always so hard on yourself, Dare? Myself now, I think you're an okay guy. If my ass were in a crack, you're exactly the fella I'd want wiping it for me."

"That's disgusting, Wuntz."

"Don't mention it."

A silence fell and they sat for a while, contemplating the courthouse crowd together. It had taken Eddie a while to understand where he had landed after he was kicked out of his big, uptown office: the one with the indirect lighting, the glistening hardwood floors, and the expensive oriental rugs. He eventually worked out that he had crossed over an invisible line; one he had never before known existed. As quietly as a spy, he had slipped through the border that divided the orthodox world in which he had always lived his life from an angry, corrosive realm whose citizens reveled in being at war with everybody else.

Lawyers were like priests in that world, Eddie soon discovered—the secular priests of the Other Side. In the privacy of their lawyers' offices, people often told stories of deeds, failures, and betrayals that were too horrible to mention even in a real confessional. People came into Eddie's office and told him what they thought about when they couldn't sleep at night. They told him sad stories, disgusting stories, brutal stories, occasionally even funny stories. But they were always stories of misery, greed, fear, and stupidity. They were stories that would break your heart, if you let them.

Some lawyers Eddie knew had crossed the line deliberately, so romantically enraged at the random idiocy they encountered every day that they were determined to change things. But they never did. At least not that anyone could tell. Before long, even the craziest of them stopped worrying about how the universe was screwing their clients, and started worrying instead about how it was screwing *them*. The Hall of Justice was a mean and unforgiving world. It cut no slack for good intentions.

"You hear about Judge Bono?' Kelly suddenly asked.

Eddie shook his head.

"We busted the bastard last night. He was parked down in the Presidio in his big Mercedes swabbing out some 16-year-old's throat with his shriveled little weenie."

"Nobody cares about that garbage anymore, Wuntz. It'll probably end up getting Bono appointed to the Supreme Court or something."

"Really?"

Wuntz savored his tales and liked to string them out. This time he really had the look in his eye. Eddie saw it, so he was half prepared when Wuntz eased in his punch line.

"I know we're politically real righteous around here and all that good shit . . ." Wuntz looked away and Eddie couldn't make out the expression on his face any longer. "But even in San Francisco . . . don't you think it might've been better for Bono's career if he'd been tonsil humping a *girl*?"

Wuntz turned back to Eddie, roaring at his own story until he was almost choking. A few heads tilted toward him, distracted briefly from their own private miseries by the sight of an overweight man in a wrinkled, polyester sports coat laughing himself into a fit. The Hall of Justice was not normally a place where people found very much to laugh about.

Eddie was even smiling a little himself when his telephone rang.

"Dad?"

Eddie heard his son's impatient voice before he got the telephone completely up to his ear.

"Hey, Michael. This is a surprise."

Michael, as he usually did when he and Eddie talked, got right to the point.

"Mom said I had to apologize to you before she'd give me my allowance."

"Apologize for what?"

"She said I was rude when you called last week."

Eddie considered that. "Do you think you were rude?"

"No. I was watching the Lakers game. I just didn't want to talk to you."

"Then don't apologize."

"Okay, I won't." The boy paused for a moment and Eddie could almost hear him thinking, weighing exactly where that left him. Then he made up his mind. "So here's Mom. Would you tell her to give me my allowance anyway?"

Eddie listened to the telephone receiver scrape against something as Michael handed it to Jennifer.

"Hello, Eddie. I'm sorry about that. Michael's getting a little hard to deal with these days and I just thought it wasn't fair the way he talked to you when you called last week, so I insisted he apologize. Anyway, don't make too much of it. I'll give him his allowance. You know how teenagers are. I hope we didn't catch you at a bad time."

Jennifer always talked a lot when she was working herself up to telling Eddie something she thought he wouldn't like to hear—so he just waited.

"Eddie? Hello? Are you there, Eddie?"

"Yes, Jennifer, I'm here."

Eddie glanced up and noticed that Wuntz was trying hard not to look like he was listening.

"Look, Eddie, there *is* one other thing."

At least she isn't going to take any longer getting to it.

"Franklin and I are going to Australia next month."

Jennifer had married Franklin Pierce, a spectacularly successful developer of shopping malls, a few months after she left Eddie. While the timing was rife with unhappy implications, Eddie had never dwelled on it, preferring to keep in mind instead that Franklin was a pleasant enough man, and that Michael could certainly have done a great deal worse for a stepfather.

"Franklin wants to go diving on the Barrier Reef."

"Uh-huh."

"Well, you see, since Michael's school holidays are next month, we'd like him to go with us."

So that's what Franklin's latest kick had to do with him. He had been just about to ask.

"The problem there of course is that Michael won't be able to come to see you this vacation. There's the problem." Jennifer paused a moment to let that sink in. "He really wants to go with us, Eddie. If you don't mind, that is."

I damned well do mind.

"I wish you'd talked to me about this first, Jennifer. I can't tell Michael now that he's not going to Australia because he has to spend his vacation with me."

"Well, It's such a great opportunity for him, Eddie. I knew you'd want him to go."

"Yes, but I'd also like to spend some time with him, Jennifer."

"Next vacation, Eddie. Promise."

Eddie clicked his tongue against his teeth a couple of times while he thought—although he supposed there wasn't all that much for him to think about.

"I gather Michael doesn't mind not seeing me for a while."

"I wish you wouldn't put it that way, Eddie. This is just such an exciting opportunity for him, that's all. So, is it all right with you?"

Eddie took a deep breath. "Whatever he wants, Jennifer."

"Wonderful. I really do think that's the right thing to do."

Eddie knew the conversation was over after that, so he drifted politely along with the small talk until Jennifer thought a decent enough interval had passed, and she broke off and hung up.

When Eddie slowly folded up the telephone and pushed it back into his pocket, he realized that Wuntz was looking at him.

"Your ex busting your hump, partner?"

"One of them. And the other's waiting her turn."

Oh Christ, Eddie suddenly remembered, *I never called Kathleen back. That's going to cost me.*

"You haven't had much luck with the family thing, have you, Dare?"

Eddie tried not to think of it that way. He figured that if he let it get too deeply set in his mind that he was just plain unfortunate when it came to his personal life, he'd do the sensible thing. He'd fold his cards and stop trying to have one. And he really didn't want to do that.

"Is it Jennifer again, or the kid?" Wuntz persisted.

"It's no big deal." Eddie tried to shake him off. "Mike's just going through a phase."

"Don't take any crap from him." The emotion in Wuntz's voice was plain, and it startled Eddie. "My kid was ashamed his old man was a cop. Started calling me a Nazi when he wasn't even fifteen. Screaming '*Seig Heil!*' when I tried to keep him in line. Crap like that. I figured it would pass, so I ignored it. I let him piss all over me. Tried not to think about it too much."

Eddie could see the memory of it working in Wuntz's face.

"That was a long time ago, but nothing's changed. He still thinks his old man's nothing but a fat jerk." Wuntz chewed on his lip a moment, and then the corners of his mouth slipped down into a shrug. "He doesn't know a fucking thing about me. That's my fault, I guess, mostly. But it's too late. I don't see him much anymore."

Wuntz's outburst left Eddie momentarily confounded. It was as if a cloud had passed over them as they sat there on that hard bench at the Hall of Justice. He had known Wuntz for five or six years, but they'd never gotten all that personal with each other before, and he wasn't sure he wanted to start now. What was it about the few casual words he'd exchanged with Jennifer and Michael that had popped open Wuntz's floodgates like that?

Wuntz looked at the floor between his feet while Eddie shifted his weight uneasily on the bench.

"Kids make you look at stuff whether you want to or not. Stuff about yourself." Wuntz spoke so quietly that Eddie almost missed it. Then he looked up with more hurt in his eyes than Eddie could stand. "Do whatever you have to do. Just don't lose your kid like I lost mine. Once he's gone, he'll never fucking come back."

Wuntz's hurt stuck in Eddie, but before he could work out exactly where, Judge Rybeck's clerk came out of an unmarked door carrying a pile of papers and headed straight for him.

"Sorry, Mr. Dare. There's no way the judge can take your plea today. Everything except this freaking Carnotolli case has been put over to Monday."

Pissey Carnotolli was a flamboyant Italian who owned a chain of stores around the Bay Area called Hide-A-Bed's Galore. A local celebrity from his late-night TV commercials in which he wore nothing but a very large diaper, Pissey had been charged with killing his wife—and the *Examiner* had hinted that he'd brought in hired muscle from New York to do it. Eddie figured if Pissey had used local guys, he might never have been indicted. San Francisco was an awfully insular place.

"Anyway, wait a second." The clerk pawed around in the papers he was carrying and pulled out an envelope. "Joshua sent this over a couple of hours ago. Said he thought you'd want it right away."

It was another of those airmail envelopes like the one in which the photograph with the red circle had come. Eddie hesitated a moment, not sure that he wanted the damned thing, but then took it and slowly turned it over. It was addressed to him in the same careful printing, and it carried the same kind of exotic-looking stamps.

Eddie tore off one end and dumped a single photograph into his palm, remembering this time to fold away the envelope and put it in his pocket.

Wuntz—recovered from his outburst—leaned over and took a look. "What the fuck's that?"

Eddie didn't answer, but he knew of course.

It was another picture of him and the same young marines with the same girls. This one had apparently been taken at about the same time as the first one, but from a slightly different angle, because now the guy who had been standing behind Eddie in the other photograph was fully visible.

And this time it was *that* guy who had a red circle around his head.

Eddie lifted the photograph and studied it carefully. But he didn't really need to. He knew immediately.

It was Winnebago.

4

"No wonder I thought the ears looked familiar." Winnebago held the photograph in both hands, his elbows propped on the bookstore's counter as he shook his head slowly back and forth. "What about the envelope?"

Eddie took the crumpled airmail envelope from his pocket and smoothed it out.

"I told you those were Thai girls," Winnebago said as soon as it saw it. He tapped his forefinger on the envelope. "It's from Thailand. Says so right on the stamps there."

Eddie picked up the envelope and squinted at the stamps—but they were small, and the printing looked like hieroglyphics to him. How did Winnebago know that?

Winnebago held the picture up, twisting it around to catch the light. "It sure as all shit beats me, but I really don't like the look of that red circle around my head."

"Who else was with us those times we were in Bangkok? Can you remember anybody?"

Winnebago reached under the counter for his cigarettes. He lit one, taking his time about it.

"That kid we called Donkey might've been there." Winnebago pointed at one of the men in the background. "Is that him?"

They both stared hard at the face, willing it to speak to them; to spell out to them whatever message they were supposed to be getting. But it didn't.

"What was his real name?"

"Damned if I can remember." Winnebago pondered a moment. "Isn't there some place you can call about old military records?"

"Yeah, well, I can just see myself calling up a personnel office at the Pentagon and saying, 'Excuse me, but would you have anything on a guy named Donkey,' and then listening to some NCO say, 'Hey, pal, we're *all* called Donkey around here.' No way."

Winnebago thought some more. "Maybe you can find the captain somehow. That might be easier."

"Jeez, Winnebago, I wouldn't have the first idea where to start looking."

"I'll bet he's become a real successful guy. He was just the type. Shouldn't be all that hard to find him."

"Maybe you're right. Probably did do something to get himself noticed after he got out."

"Yeah." Winnebago nodded. "That sounds to me like the way to go. I'll bet you Captain Austin made a real big splash somewhere."

Eddie slogged away dutifully at this and that for the rest of the week, but he couldn't get the photographs out of his mind, and his concentration was all over the place. By four o'clock on Friday afternoon he gave up and started the weekend.

The House of Shields was a saloon on New Montgomery Street, just south of Market. It was comfortable as old loafers, and still smelled a little of cigars and cigarettes stubbed out in what Eddie was sure were better times. In spite of its name, the place had nothing to do with medieval warfare, at least not unless you counted the screeching done by some of the old bags who hung around there most of the day with a snoot full. A guy named Shields, so the story went, had opened it near the turn of the century. He hung a big sign over the front door . . . ENTER THESE PORTALS, AND TIME AND CARES ARE FORGOT.

Eddie liked that—even if they had taken the sign down a decade or so ago when most cares just got too big to be forgot anymore—and he liked the fact that a middle-aged woman in a taffeta prom dress and way too much make-up was usually there playing things like "Our Love Is Here To Stay" on a scarred, old Steinway. When it was slow, and sometimes it was very slow, Eddie would spread his papers around on the bar to make it look good, sip a beer or a diet soda, and whistle quietly along with the piano, easing his way out of another week.

San Francisco did that kind of thing to you, Eddie knew. Maybe some other places, too, but San Francisco sure as hell did .

When Eddie finished law school he was looking to burn down the world. But then he discovered all that good California wine at a few bucks a bottle; cracked crab straight off the boats at Fisherman's Wharf, at least back before all the real boats disappeared and the place turned into a tourist trap; the taste of warm sourdough bread as it came out of the ovens over at Sammy's Bakery on Powell; the musty, used-book store up on Fremont that smelled like his grandmother's attic; and the sun dusting the city with magic as it eased gracefully into the Pacific beyond the orange-red towers of the Golden Gate.

Almost before he knew it, twenty years slipped away. Gone like a goddamned bullet, it had. *Oh, Lord,* he'd begun sighing to himself whenever he thought about it. *What the hell happened?*

"Hey, fella. You know who you look like?"

The voice behind him shook him out of his reverie.

"That actor. You know . . ."

Eddie had noticed the guy in the brown leather bomber-jacket eyeing him before, so he wasn't particularly surprised when he started in. Whenever Eddie saw someone doing that—and it was way, way too often as far as he was concerned—it eventually came down to the same thing.

"You look a little like . . ." The man wiggled his left index finger at Eddie and tossed in a little finger popping for punctuation. "You know . . . that actor . . . *snap, snap, snap . . .* Clint Eastwood! Yeah, that's it—Clint Eastwood! Anyone ever say you look like Clint Eastwood before, man?"

The guy grinned triumphantly at Eddie, and then he twisted around toward a thin woman with a pinched face and tiny lips who was waiting for him at a table and grinned some more.

Big deal, Eddie thought as he always did. *Big damned deal.*

He arched his eyebrows steeply, and—keeping his face otherwise expressionless—nodded very slowly a couple of times over his shoulder before returning his full attention to his Diet Coke. That just made things worse, he knew—it was exactly what Clint Eastwood had done a hundred times in the movies—but it was still a look that Eddie particularly favored whenever the subject came up. The ambiguity of it appealed to him.

When he heard the stool next to him scrape back a few moments later, Eddie glanced over and was surprised to see Kelly Wuntz sliding onto it. It had been three days since Eddie asked Wuntz if he could do something through SFPD to get a line on Harry Austin, and he'd heard nothing from him since. He figured that was a write-off—especially since his own efforts to locate Captain Austin had come to exactly nothing either. As far as he could tell, Austin had vanished cleanly off the face of the earth after he left the marines in 1975.

Wuntz had an odd look on his face, but before Eddie could say anything about it, he held a finger up to his lips and shook his head vigorously to indicate that Eddie should remain silent. Eddie looked around the bar, but there was no one near enough to overhear them; and besides, he'd only started to ask Wuntz how he was doing.

Wuntz eased up off the bar stool and walked away, gesturing for Eddie to follow. Even for Kelly Wuntz, that was peculiar behavior, so—half out of curiosity and half just to humor him—Eddie did. He trailed along behind as Wuntz went up the stairs at the end of the bar and disappeared into the men's toilet. When Eddie went inside, Wuntz had just finished checking under the stall doors to make sure they were alone.

"I've got something on your old captain," Wuntz said very quietly when he was satisfied. "But first I have to ask you a couple of questions."

"Shoot," Eddie answered, immediately regretting his choice of words a little.

"When was the last time you saw Austin?"

"I don't know." Eddie thought about it. "Certainly not since I was discharged."

"Have you heard from him?"

Eddie just shook his head.

"You sure?"

"Of course I'm sure. What is this, Wuntz?"

Wuntz was still looking at him in a funny way, and Eddie started getting a bad feeling.

"You asked me to check on this Austin guy for you and I did. There's this DEA fruit I busted a few months ago in a gay cat house over in the Castro and then cut loose, so I figured he might be just the guy to poke around with the feds for me."

"If you're going through all this just to tell me that Austin's gay, I don't really care. I just want to talk to him, not sleep with him."

"Look, Dare, you want to hear what I've got or not?"

Eddie nodded vaguely, trying not to look too excited—which he found was fairly easy based on how the conversation with Wuntz had gone up to that point.

"Then shut the fuck up for once in your life and listen."

Wuntz cleared his throat a couple of times, giving himself a build up.

"Okay, the guy says he'll see what he can do, and then today he calls me back. He sounds nervous and at first I don't get it. I'm not looking to bust anybody's balls here. I'm just asking this pansy to check around and see if he can get a current address on some guy who was a run-of-the-mill marine captain something like twenty years ago. Then he tells me that this Austin has a DEA file and I start to pay real close attention."

"Harry Austin was a *drug dealer*?"

"I don't think so. This guy says a file was opened on a routine investigation of Austin several years ago for some reason he didn't know anything about. Apparently it turned up zip. That's not the point."

"Then what *is* the point, Wuntz?"

"My guy says the file was closed permanently two weeks ago."

"Because they didn't find anything?"

Wuntz blew air into his cheeks, puffing up like a chipmunk that had just found a particularly nice acorn. "This guy faxed me a copy of the last document in Austin's file. You want to see it?"

"Sure, let's have it. After all the dramatics, I just hope I'm not disappointed."

"You won't be."

Wuntz was giving him the eye, Eddie noticed.

What the hell's going on here?

"So all you wanted to do was to talk to your old CO, huh?"

Eddie realized that was an introduction, not a real question, but he nodded anyway. More important, he realized Wuntz had just switched into the past tense.

So when Wuntz reached into an inside pocket of his jacket and handed Eddie a single sheet of paper folded lengthwise, Eddie was pretty sure what he was going to see on it—although he had no idea as to what form the details would take. He unfolded the sheet and studied the smudged photocopy of a newspaper clipping, while Wuntz walked around behind him and stood looking over his shoulder.

The clipping appeared to be from an inside page of some newspaper—the right side just above the fold. It was obviously a foreign paper, since it was printed in some bizarre-looking language that Eddie couldn't even hope to make any sense out of.

Of course, he had been right about what to expect. Both he and Wuntz stood silently for a few moments, looking down at the copy of the clipping, and contemplating the blood and guts photograph that took up the entire top half of it—a man's battered body sprawled lifelessly somewhere in a muddy street.

"Jesus Christ," Eddie finally said in a voice that was much smaller than he would really have liked. "Look at that."

The head of the man in the picture seemed perfectly normal on one side. A dark eye stared fixedly into the lens of the camera, and you could almost imagine it was about to blink. The other side of his head was something else again. It distinctly resembled a ripe pomegranate that had been dropped onto the street from a very great height.

Recognizing Harry Austin after twenty years would probably have been hard enough anyway—the thought came suddenly to Eddie as he examined the clipping carefully—and having only half a head to work with didn't make it any easier. Maybe this wasn't him. Then Eddie noticed two words in Western script that stood out quite clearly among the monotonous lines of unfathomable print below the picture. They read, 'Harry Austin.'

"After everything he lived through, he walks down the wrong street on the wrong day and dies in an accident. It doesn't seem right." Eddie looked up and caught the strange look on Wuntz's face. "What?"

"You're assuming this was an accident."

Eddie quickly glanced down at the clipping again to see if he was missing something—but nothing jumped out at him and he shifted his eyes back to Wuntz.

"It wasn't?"

"My guy says DEA thinks maybe it wasn't."

"Why would they think that?"

"He didn't know. He'd just heard around that some people thought your man Austin was taken out."

"I thought you said he wasn't a drug dealer."

"He wasn't."

"Then why would anyone want to kill him?"

Wuntz rolled his eyes. "I look like the Amazing Randy to you or what, Eddie? How the fuck would I know?"

"I thought maybe your DEA guy told you."

"Well, he didn't."

Eddie blew air out between his teeth as he studied the clipping some more. "This is sure a hell of a coincidence."

Wuntz reached over Eddie's shoulder and tapped his finger on a date that had been stamped on the bottom of the clipping.

"DEA logged this in three weeks ago, just before those pictures started showing up in your mail. Still think it's a coincidence?"

Eddie didn't much care for the way the conversation was developing—or for what he gathered Wuntz was suggesting. "Do you know what the story with the picture says?"

"There was no translation in the file. Maybe one of those Asian hoods you call clients can read Thai."

Eddie's eyes flicked up to Wuntz, but he was still looking down at the clipping. "This is from a Thai newspaper?"

"Yeah."

"That's where Captain Austin was killed?"

But Eddie knew, of course, what the answer was going to be before he finished the question.

"Yeah. In Bangkok," Wuntz replied, right on cue.

Eddie's reaction must have been easy to read.

"Bangkok," Wuntz repeated, giving Eddie a long look. "You know, the place with all the little broads and the big massage parlors. That mean something to you?"

Eddie quickly shook his head. He knew Wuntz didn't believe him, but he let it go for some reason anyway, and Eddie was grateful to him for that.

He didn't really want to talk anymore right then—and even if he had, he couldn't imagine what he would say.

5

Eddie was walking slowly along Market Street, still trying to get his mind around the conversation he'd just had with Kelly Wuntz, when his telephone began tweeting. He hated that sound. Every time he heard it, he wondered why nobody could make a mobile telephone that just rang instead of making a noise like a canary with gas.

"Get back here now," Joshua snapped even before Eddie could say hello.

"Hello, Joshua. How are you?"

"I said get back here now."

"I heard you."

He gave it a second, but Joshua didn't add anything.

"We having a fire or something?" Eddie prompted.

"There are some men here to see you."

Joshua sounded a little strange.

"I don't have any appointments this afternoon."

"Eddie, I'm telling you there are some people here to see you, and you have to come back right now."

"'People,' Joshua? I thought you said 'men.' Now which is it? 'Men' or 'people?' You know that might have a very significant effect on whether I come back because . . ."

"Eddie," Joshua interrupted. "Cut the shit and get back here."

And then he hung up.

When Eddie walked into his outer office a few minutes later, he half expected to find Joshua tied to a chair with a gag in his mouth, but everything looked normal enough. Joshua gestured toward the closed door of Eddie's office with a tilt of his head, and went right on typing without looking up like he always did. Eddie opened his door with a shrug and went in.

There was quite a crowd waiting for him: three men and a woman. At least they looked like a crowd all squeezed at once into Eddie's office. He had only two straight-backed chairs for visitors, and one of the men and the woman sat in them at his desk, while the other two men leaned against the wall. The expressions of bored contempt on their faces tagged them unmistakably as cops, particularly to anyone who'd been around the Hall of Justice as long as Eddie had.

Wondering what kind of roust this was going to be, Eddie moved around his desk at what he thought was a stately enough pace to suggest a complete lack of interest, and then settled slowly into his own chair. No one spoke, and he studied the man and woman facing him while he waited for something to happen.

Eddie could work out who was in charge of the raiding party without much trouble. The seated man wore the same kind of costume as Frick and Frack over against the wall, but he was older and had a look that made his authority clear. With his short hair, wiry build and rimless glasses, the man made Eddie think of an astronaut who had retired and taken up running a used-book store.

The woman had close-cropped, blond hair, and a very fair, slightly ruddy complexion. She looked Irish, Eddie thought. Not bad really, for a cop at least. But then he spotted something considerably more interesting about the woman than her complexion. She had a pair of headlights on her that would freeze a moose.

He remembered in college some woman telling him that the great tragedy of her life was being born with big breasts, because men wouldn't take a woman seriously who had really huge ones. He had cooed and comforted her, saying how wrong she was, but he would have said anything just to get her to shut the hell up and take off her bra. Eddie wondered for a moment if the big headlights ever got in this woman's way, professionally speaking of course.

"What can I do for you, Detectives?" he finally asked when no one seemed inclined to break the silence.

"We're not from the police, Mr. Dare," the seated man responded slowly without any change in his bland expression.

Uh-oh.

The man took a slim, black wallet out of his coat pocket, laid it on the desk, and flipped it open.

"I'm Agent Shepherd. United States Secret Service." He indicated the other two men and the woman by inclining his head slightly toward each with an economy of movement that Eddie found a little scary for some reason. "These are Agents Booth, Evans and Sanchez."

Shepherd returned his identification wallet to the inside pocket of his coat and resumed his inspection of Eddie. "You know, you remind me of somebody."

Oh, Christ. Not now.

"Yeah, you look a lot like . . ."

Eddie held up his right hand, palm out. "Sure. And that's Julia Roberts outside doing the typing." He smiled, but no one else did.

"We're investigating a situation, Mr. Dare," Headlights said in a voice so toneless that it sounded synthesized. "And we think you can help us."

Eddie tried to look her in the eye, struggling hard to avoid the obvious alternative. "That's an interesting expression."

Shepherd and the woman glanced at each other.

"What expression is that, Mr. Dare?" Headlights asked, shifting her gaze back to Eddie.

"Situation."

"What do you find interesting about it?"

Eddie saw this was going nowhere good, so he worked his face into a blandly pleasant expression, shut his mouth, and waited for developments.

Another glance between the two agents, then Shepherd took over again. "Is it because you already know why we're here, Mr. Dare?"

Teasing Headlights was one thing, Eddie quickly decided, but Shepherd was another matter entirely.

"Maybe we could start over." Eddie accompanied the *mea culpa* with his most sincere smile. Still, nobody smiled back.

"No, I don't know why you're here," he went on anyway. "I assume you're going to hassle me about one of my clients. After that, I'll probably tell you some stuff you already know about the lawyer-client privilege, toss in a little speech about the Constitution, and then wish you a nice day."

Shepherd's eyes tightened and he leaned forward slightly. "You seem to be real good at talking. How are you at listening, Mr. Dare? You listen as good as you talk?"

"Yeah, I can listen."

"That's good." Shepherd nodded seriously. "Maybe I can hold your interest for a few minutes here then, Eddie."

He noticed that he'd suddenly become Eddie instead of Mr. Dare. That was not, in his experience, a good sign when you were talking to cops.

"I'm all ears."

"You mean as opposed to all mouth, which I gather you usually are."

Shepherd grinned around at the other agents—as if he'd said something funny—and they all grinned back right on cue. Eddie could have sworn he even saw the headlights blink, but he might have been mistaken.

Shepherd shifted his full attention back to Eddie. "You were in the marines, weren't you?"

"You going to tell me what this is all about?"

Eddie had been rousted plenty of times before, but these jokers weren't playing by the rules.

"Were you in Vietnam in April, 1975?"

Eddie looked at Shepherd without answering, determined to wait him out.

"Yes, you were in Vietnam in April, 1975. You were in Saigon. We know that."

"Then why did you ask me?"

"What was your assignment?"

"Do you already know that, too?"

"Do *you*?"

To hell with this.

"I took pap smears for bargirls."

He was sure of it this time. The headlights definitely blinked.

Shepherd just kept on rolling. "You were a tech sergeant in Company A, Fifth Battalion. You were assigned to assist with the evacuation of the American Embassy in Saigon, and you went out on one of the last choppers from the compound."

Eddie's irritation was suddenly swept cleanly away by a swiftly rising tide of anxiety. First the two pictures of the groups of marines with the red circles on them, then the clipping out of the DEA file about Harry Austin's death, and now this.

"What do you remember about Operation Voltaire, Eddie?"

Eddie almost laughed out loud. "Operation *what*?"

"That was your last assignment before you were evacuated from Saigon, wasn't it?"

"I never heard of Operation Voltaire. I was never involved in anything that sounded remotely that intelligent."

Shepherd made a dismissive gesture. "You were assigned to Operation Voltaire all right, Eddie. But just to refresh your memory, that was the exercise to rescue the Bank of Vietnam's currency and gold reserves before the North Vietnamese took over. You were in charge of the guard detail for Operation Voltaire, weren't you?"

What in God's name is this guy talking about?

"We secured the perimeter of the embassy compound and protected the evacuation," Eddie answered carefully. He was hearing alarm bells going off all around him, but he couldn't for the life of him figure out what they meant. "That's all I remember."

Shepherd obviously didn't really care what answers Eddie gave him. He couldn't have been stopped with a howitzer. "All the bank's money disappeared during the evacuation. We're looking for it."

That was interesting, Eddie reflected through his wariness, even if he still couldn't work out what it had to do with him.

"How much is missing?"

"Using today's values?"

"By all means, use today's values."

"A little over 400 million dollars."

Eddie started to laugh, but then he noticed that none of his visitors looked even slightly amused.

Christ on a damned crutch! These people are serious.

His mind raced, trying to remember anything that might connect to what Shepherd was talking about. "You're telling me that someone just got around to noticing all that money was missing?"

"It was always assumed the money had been abandoned in the panic and that the North Vietnamese eventually got it," Shepherd answered with a half smile that Eddie found vaguely unsettling. "When diplomatic relations were restored last year, we discovered the Vietnamese didn't have it. A task force was formed at Treasury to account for it."

"Well, if you're looking for 400 million dollars around here. . . ," Eddie gestured at his modest office, ". . . you're flat out of luck."

"Maybe not." Shepherd leaned forward very slowly and rested his forearms on Eddie's desk. "Pentagon records say that on April 27, 1975, you were the ranking NCO in a squad assigned by Captain Harry Austin to secure a warehouse about two blocks from the American Embassy in Saigon. That was where Austin had stored the Bank of Vietnam's money—sealed in containers, and crated up—all ready to be flown out to Thailand."

Shepherd was so close to his face that Eddie could smell the peppermint tic-tac he'd popped just before he came into the office.

"You and your squad were the last people we know of who had that money."

Eddie was still drawing a complete blank when Shepherd suddenly reared all the way back in his chair, spread his arms, and smiled broadly.

"We just want you to tell us what you did with it, Eddie."

6

Winnebago sucked hard on the butt of his Camel and then flicked it cleanly across the sidewalk into a dark green garbage bin without breaking stride. "So what did you tell them?" he asked Eddie as they crossed Union Street against the light.

"The truth. I told them they had bad information. We were on the embassy walls kicking people down until we lifted out, not guarding crates full of money."

"Did they believe you?"

"Of course not."

Eddie had gotten to the bookstore just as Winnebago was closing, and they'd walked down Columbus toward Washington Square together. The Friday night throngs were already filling North Beach—the fiercely Italian quarter of the city that surrounded the square—and they jostled for space on the crowded sidewalk.

"What do you mean? It's true, Eddie. We weren't guarding any damned money."

"You sure of that?"

"Of course I'm sure. I know what money looks like."

"Somebody sure as hell thinks we know something about it."

"Yeah, so?"

Eddie shoved his hands deeper into the pockets of his leather jacket as they crossed the square toward the wedding-cake towers of St. Peter and Paul Cathedral.

"Maybe they're right, Winnebago."

"What the hell does that mean?"

"I'm just saying that maybe we do know something about it. Sometimes you know things you don't know you know."

"Oh, for Christ's sake. That didn't even make sense to me."

Eddie watched a few tentacles of fog licking at the foot of Columbus where it ended at Fisherman's Wharf. Out in the middle of the bay, Alcatraz was already lost in a cotton-candy swirl. In another hour or two, Eddie suspected, a lumpy flood would submerge the city's famous hills, leaving only the tops of buildings poking out here and there; marker buoys posting the hazards in a diaphanous sea of white.

Eddie had always thought that its famous fogs suited San Francisco perfectly. The city was a wispy, fragile place; a watercolor world, where everything was always slightly indistinct, just out of focus. When Eddie looked at it that way, he figured San Francisco was exactly the right place for those damned pictures to turn up.

"We were only grunts, Winnebago. Half the time we didn't know where we were, and the other half we didn't know what we were doing there." When Eddie continued, he lowered his voice. He felt silly doing it, but he just couldn't help it. "Maybe we *were* somewhere around that money without knowing it."

Winnebago started to say something, but Eddie waved him off.

"Think about it. First somebody sends me those two pictures. Then, a couple of days later, the Secret Service shows up in my office and asks me what we did with the 400 million dollars we were guarding when Saigon collapsed. That can't just be a coincidence. It's all got to be connected somehow, and if it is . . . ," Eddie reached across with his forefinger and tapped Winnebago on the shoulder, ". . . then somebody other than the Secret Service thinks we know something about that money, too."

They reached the other side of the square, and Eddie led the way to an empty bench facing the cathedral. They sat in silence for a while, but then Winnebago scratched the back of his neck and cleared his throat. "Maybe that wasn't really the Secret Service. Maybe those guys were the same people who sent the pictures."

"Yeah, I wondered about that at first, too. But what sense would it make?" Eddie looked at his watch. "Anyway, Wuntz can probably find out. He said he'd be here by nine."

"Are you sure you want to tell him about this, Eddie?"

Eddie glanced over at Winnebago. "When did you develop such a suspicious streak?"

"The minute I saw that red circle around my head."

Eddie thought back to what he'd seen in Wuntz's face when he talked about his son. He'd never thought much before about how far he'd be willing to trust Wuntz if he ever had to, but now he knew. He just couldn't work out how to explain it to Winnebago. "Don't worry about Wuntz. He's okay."

Eddie fell silent again—not sure he'd said enough, yet not knowing what else to say—but Winnebago didn't seem to mind.

"You think that maybe it's all just bullshit?" Winnebago asked after a while. "How could that much money just disappear anyway? It would have to weigh a ton."

"More like ten."

"Ten tons? *Of money?*"

Eddie nodded, and Winnebago gave a low whistle under his breath.

"It's a real shame about the captain," he went on after a respectful pause. "He could've straightened all this out, I'll bet."

Eddie had been trying not to think too much about Austin, but the picture of his caved-in skull and broken body dumped in a Bangkok mud-hole kept coming back to him with unhappy clarity.

"Say, Eddie, you don't think the captain might've been killed because . . ."

Eddie turned his head very slowly and gave Winnebago a dead-eyed stare.

"Oh, man, like I really want to hear that kind of shit," Winnebago mumbled, looking quickly away.

A dirty, brown Ford pulled into a handicapped parking slot a little off to their left, and Wuntz blinked his lights at them. He got out, ambled slowly over to the bench, and sat down.

"You're not handicapped," Eddie observed.

"Sure I am," Wuntz replied, smiling pleasantly. "I'm a cop."

Eddie looked thoughtful, and Wuntz jabbed a thumb toward Winnebago. "Who's he?"

"He's the guy who was circled in the second picture."

Winnebago leaned around Eddie, offering Wuntz his hand. "Winnebago Jones."

"You a half Chinaman or something?" Wuntz asked as they shook.

"I'm a Native American," Winnebago replied, and Eddie gave him a long look.

"So let's have whatever this hot news is," Wuntz said as he leaned back and laced his fingers together behind his head. "The night's passing and I've got hookers to harass."

While they all pondered the twin towers of St. Peter and Paul's—glistening so whitely in their bath of powerful floodlights that they seemed achromatic—Eddie told Wuntz the story his callers had told him.

"No shit," was all Wuntz said when Eddie had finished. "No fucking shit."

"Do you think you could find out if these guys were kosher, Wuntz?"

"Didn't their ID look real?"

"Sure it did, but so does that Russian passport I bought in Hong Kong last year."

"You sure you don't know anything about the money they were asking about?"

"I've never lied to you before, Wuntz."

"No, but we've never talked about 400 million dollars before either."

"We're not talking about 400 million dollars now. We're talking about some people who claim they're the Secret Service and who *think* I know where 400 million dollars might be. Which I don't."

Wuntz looked hard at Eddie, but he didn't say anything. After a moment he pulled a telephone from the inside pocket of his jacket, pushed himself to his feet, and walked across the square out of earshot while he dialed.

Winnebago lit a Camel and smoked silently. Eddie slouched down on the bench, stretched out his legs, and crossed his ankles. Neither spoke while they waited for Wuntz to make his call. Winnebago finished his first cigarette and was most of the way through another before Wuntz came back.

"It's illegal to smoke almost everywhere in San Francisco these days." He settled back onto the bench and returned his phone to his pocket.

"Then naturally I'll put this out right away," Winnebago replied as he offered Wuntz a cigarette. Wuntz took it and bent forward so Winnebago could light it with his old Zippo. Inhaling deeply and savoring the taste as he let it go, Wuntz gave out with a deep sigh that seemed to chase the smoke away.

"Your visitors were legit. This guy Shepherd's in charge of some kind of task force in the Treasury Department that no one seems to know much about. They gave it a really weird name though. Why would they name a federal task force after an old Dean Martin song?"

Eddie looked puzzled. "What do you mean?"

"Volare, it's called. Task Force Volare. You know . . ."

Wuntz tilted his head back, and—to Eddie's complete astonishment—began to sing in a remarkably rich and vibrant baritone . . .

> *Volare . . . oh oh . . .*
> *Da da da . . . oh oh oh oh . . .*
> *Da da my happy heart sings . . .*
> *Your love has . . .*

An elderly Chinese woman shuffling past swiveled her head and stared at them. Wuntz slid into a chastened silence.

"It's Voltaire, Wuntz," Eddie offered quietly.

"No, man. I've heard the song a thousand times. It's Volare."

"Not the song. The name of the task force. It's Voltaire."

Wuntz looked baffled. "What's a Voltaire?"

"Jesus," Winnebago grunted. "Don't cops read anything but comic books? Voltaire was a French writer noted for his satire who was the soul of the eighteenth-century French enlightenment."

Wuntz looked hurt. "Myself, I don't think the French are all that enlightened *now*," he grumbled. "Christ knows what they must've been like in the eighteenth century."

Winnebago tried to catch Eddie's eye, but Eddie was chewing his lip and looking off into the night.

"Anyway," Wuntz went on, clearing his throat. "What's Voltaire or Volare, or whatever the fuck it is, supposed to mean?" He addressed the question to Eddie, conspicuously ignoring Winnebago.

"Shepherd said the plan to get the money out of Vietnam before the North Vietnamese took over was called Operation Voltaire."

"It was, huh?" Wuntz thought about that for a moment. "And who was doing this planning?"

"A marine captain."

"Not . . ."

"Yeah, him."

Wuntz was silent for a moment and then raised a question Eddie had already asked himself. "Voltaire doesn't sound like the name of a military operation to me. What's it mean?"

"No idea."

Winnebago leaned across Eddie, getting as close to Wuntz as he could. "Voltaire wrote Candide in 1759, one of the masterpieces of . . ."

"Shut the fuck up," Wuntz snarled.

"Can you ask your DEA guy if he knows anything about Shepherd's task force?" Eddie asked Wuntz, quickly changing the subject.

"I think I've squeezed all the juice out of the little fruit I'm going to get. So to speak."

"I was almost hoping the feds would turn out to be phonies. If they're real, the pictures must've come from somebody else."

"Yeah, that's the way I figure it, too," Wuntz said, bobbing his head around a little. "I'd say it's a sure bet you've got someone else on your ass about the same deal."

"Like who?" Winnebago demanded, stubbing out his cigarette.

"You want to get something to eat?" Wuntz asked suddenly, continuing to ignore Winnebago. He scratched himself and sniffed the air. "Fuck, that pizza smell down here always drives me crazy."

"Why would anybody who thought I might know where the money is send me those pictures?" Eddie asked as if Wuntz hadn't spoken at all. "I don't see the point."

"It's not all that hard." Wuntz sniffed half-heartedly at the air one more time, and then sighed in resignation. "What would *you* do if you wanted to find out where something was, and the guy who knew wasn't about to tell you?"

"I guess I'd get someone to slap the guy around a little. Beat it out of him."

Winnebago's eyes went glassy, and he reached for his cigarettes. Wuntz shook his head firmly.

"Nah, that never works. At least not if the guy has enough incentive to keep his mouth shut and just take the beating. And I think we can agree here that the whereabouts of 400 million dollars is a hell of an incentive."

"Then how would you get somebody to give up something like that?"

"You'd have to get into some serious torture to have any chance at all. Metal pins under the fingernails, lighted cigarettes on the nuts, that kind of thing."

Winnebago broke out in a fit of coughing as he exhaled.

"Then why send pictures to put me on guard? Why not just drag me away?"

"Because they're not going to torture you."

"I'm glad you're sure of that."

"I am."

"Then what are they going to do?"

"Nothing."

"Nothing?"

Wuntz nodded solemnly. "Nothing."

"For Christ's sakes, Wuntz, stop the damned riddles. Just spell it out for me."

"I think they're trying to spook you."

"Then they're doing a hell of a good job so far."

"I'm not joking, Eddie."

Eddie raised his eyebrows skeptically. "You mean they think the pictures will scare me so badly that when they come around and ask where the money is, I'll just tell them?"

"I thought you didn't know where it was."

"I *don't*. I *can't* tell anybody." Eddie cut his eyes at Wuntz and saw that he was smiling one of those cop smiles that said he knew a liar when he heard one. "But they won't just go away quietly when I tell them I don't know anything, will they?"

"Probably not, but I wouldn't worry about it. I don't think anyone's planning to show up and ask you anything either."

Eddie just waited for the rest of it this time, and let Wuntz preen a little before he went on, spinning out his theory.

"They're trying to make you run."

Eddie obviously still didn't get it, so Wuntz went on, slowly.

"Look, if you thought that after all these years somebody had finally put you together with the missing money and they were coming to put enough hurt on to make you give it up, what would you do?"

"You mean, what would I do if I actually knew where the 400 million dollars was?"

Wuntz shrugged. "Okay, we'll play it your way."

"I'd grab as much as I could carry and find a nice warm beach in a country without any extradition treaties."

"Exactly." Wuntz steepled his fingers, pursed his lips and tried to look professorial. "You'd run, Eddie. You'd run straight to the money."

"Give me a break, Wuntz. Even if I did know where the money was, it sure as hell wouldn't be buried in a box in my backyard. We're talking about maybe ten tons of gold and currency. It'd be in bank accounts, invested in stocks, bonds, and real estate. Stuff like that."

Wuntz looked unimpressed. "Doesn't make any difference. The principle's the same." He held up his open hand when Eddie started to interrupt. "If you feel threatened enough, you'll check the money to be sure it's safe, whatever form it's in. That's human nature."

"And of course if I did that . . ."

"Yep." Wuntz nodded vigorously. "Whoever it is would be right behind you. He's probably got people watching you now."

Winnebago glanced around quickly and rubbed at the side of his face. "Oh, Jesus."

"Maybe he even has a way of checking your bank accounts, seeing if you move money from one account to another—shit like that," Wuntz went on. "I'll bet he's all over your ass right now and you don't even know it."

"You think that's it, huh? You think that's what the pictures are all about?" Eddie mused.

Wuntz clicked his tongue against the roof of his mouth a couple of times. "That's sure as shit the way I'd do it. More effective than torture. Neater, too."

The more Eddie thought about Wuntz's theory, the more sense it made; and the more sense it made, the better he felt.

If Wuntz was right, all he really had to do was sit tight and this would eventually go away. When he didn't do anything out of the ordinary, whoever was behind the pictures would eventually get sick of watching a garden-variety San Francisco lawyer go about his daily business, realize that Eddie didn't know anything about the money, and give up.

And what could the Secret Service do to him? After all, he didn't know anything about Operation Voltaire, and he couldn't tell them where the money was, no matter how many times they asked him. After a while they'd have to give up, too.

Yeah, Eddie concluded, Wuntz was giving him good advice. All he had to do was keep his nose clean, go about his business, and in a few weeks this would all turn into nothing but a story he'd tell some woman one day when he was trying to make his life sound interesting to her. Wuntz was a pretty savvy guy.

And Eddie kept thinking that for a long time after they left Washington Square that night and went their separate ways. In fact, he kept thinking that all through the rest of the weekend, and all the way up until he walked into his office on Monday morning and saw the look on Joshua's face.

Joshua held Eddie's eyes while he tilted his head slowly in the direction of the inner office's closed door, and pursed his lips into a long, silent whistle.

'Secret Service?' Eddie mouthed the question.

Joshua replied by shaking his head vigorously and allowing his eyebrows to begin a slow migration toward the ceiling.

All in a flash, Eddie was as sure of one thing as he had ever been of anything in his entire life—Kelly Wuntz was about to turn out to be one really dumb son of a bitch after all.

7

"Mr. Rupert, he said his name was," Joshua stage whispered. "Marinus Rupert."

"And you believed that?"

"No, but what do I care? How about that Chinese guy last week who kept insisting we call him O.J. Simpson?"

"Do we at least know what this Mr. Marinus wants?" Eddie asked with a hint of irritation.

"Mr. Rupert. Marinus is his first name."

"As long as *he* remembers. What does he want?"

Joshua gave him a tired look and went back to typing, so Eddie took a deep breath and opened the door to his office.

The man turned out to be not at all what Eddie had expected, although when he thought about it later, he realized he wasn't sure what he *had* expected. Marinus Rupert could have passed for fifty, but Eddie guessed he was probably a lot older. He was a handsome man, trim and well-dressed, with a patrician face that made Eddie think of Henry Cabot Lodge, Jr. as he had looked in the sixties. The man certainly didn't strike Eddie as the kind who went around using a phony name. Maybe his name really *was* Marinus Rupert. Poor bastard.

"Thank you for seeing me without an appointment, Mr. Dare."

Eddie offered his hand. "No problem."

The man's voice was deep and smooth, with authority to it. His accent tagged him as English possibly, maybe a colonial of some kind. As they made small talk, Eddie looked Rupert over carefully. More than anything else, he looked rich: a suit that was obviously custom tailored; small, gold links glinting against the cuffs of his snow-white shirt; a wristwatch so exclusive that Eddie couldn't immediately identify the make; and expensively-barbered, dark hair, graying in perfect symmetry at both temples.

"So, what can I do for you, Mr. Rupert?" Eddie asked when he got bored with sizing the man up.

"I'm sure you realize Rupert isn't my real name, Mr. Dare, and I know you realize it, or I wouldn't be here." The man looked mildly amused. "Nevertheless, why don't we just continue to use it for a while. Just between us."

This is interesting.

"Okay. And you can use the name Eddie Dare for me, since that really *is* my name."

The man smiled broadly, as if he found Eddie's response delightfully witty. "No, actually it's not, sport. Rupert Edward Dare is your real name. Eddie is just the charmingly American diminutive you began using when you became a voice for the criminal classes. I'm sure your usual clientele likes it, but then I'm not your usual clientele, am I?"

"I see," Eddie said. But of course, he didn't see anything.

"That's why I selected Rupert as my surname for this meeting. I thought it might amuse you."

"I'm amused all to hell. What about the Marinus part?'

"That was my mother's maiden name."

"Really?"

"No, of course not."

The man smiled again—an automatic-looking flicker at the corners of his mouth—and then briskly changed the subject. "I know quite a lot about you, Mr. Dare."

"Well, I don't know anything about you."

"And you won't. Not unless I want you to. Not a thing."

Eddie looked at the man and waited for him to continue,

but he seemed in no hurry. He just sat and flicked his smile on and off a few times.

Finally, Eddie leaned back in his chair, folded his arms across his chest, propped his feet on the desk, and crossed his legs at the ankle.

"Okay, buddy, I give up. You've got the floor."

Rupert nodded as if he were satisfied, and rose from his chair. He walked to a window and stood there quietly looking down at Grant Street, his back to the room.

"I need your help to collect some money, Eddie. I may call you Eddie, may I not?"

Eddie made a vague gesture of some kind.

"Good." He spoke again without turning from the window. "It's quite a lot of money actually."

Eddie wondered for a moment if the man was looking at anything in particular, or if he was only letting his eyes drift over the throng of people down below that was surging in and out of the little shops along Grant. It was a crush that always made Eddie think of Hong Kong: a vast swarm of mostly elderly Chinese, pushing and shoving; filling the sidewalks and, eventually, the street; overwhelming—with sheer numbers—even those motor vehicles that were foolish enough to challenge them.

"Do you ever miss the old days at Wren & Simon, Eddie?"

The question felt like a slap, and Eddie immediately realized that was exactly how it had been intended.

"That's none of your business."

"When you tried those two big money laundering cases back in . . . '87 was it?"

"'88."

"Whenever. It looked like you were really going places then."

"I did go places."

"So you did." Rupert chuckled, looking around. "So you did, Eddie."

He briskly turned away from the window and returned to his chair. He settled himself again, taking his time about it, and then began to tap his right forefinger slowly against his cheek. It was a stagy gesture of a man who wanted to look like he was thinking, and—Eddie thought—it appeared ridiculous.

"They should never have kicked you out of the firm, you know."

"Why are we talking about this?"

"You were doing the best you could to keep a very greedy and quite stupid banker out of jail. As I recall . . . he worked for . . . who was it now?"

Eddie stayed silent. He knew the man didn't really expect him to answer.

"It doesn't really matter. Anyway, you did what good lawyers always do, didn't you, Eddie? Good lawyers always represent their clients to the best of their ability. Everyone understands that. It's just that sometimes they have to get their hands a little dirty to do it, don't they?"

"My hands didn't get dirty."

"Some of your partners thought they did."

"Well, they were wrong." Eddie abruptly swung his feet back onto the floor and leaned toward the man, his forearms resting on the desk. "That's all I'm saying about that. You can change the subject or get the hell out of here. I don't really care which."

Rupert raised both hands in mock surrender. "Easy, Eddie. No offense. I'm on your side here."

"Then that makes two of us. Tell me what you want or take off."

"Whatever you say." He nodded pleasantly. "I'm here to become one of your clients."

"I'm not sure I want you for a client."

"Oh, I think you do. I'm really a very interesting guy when you get to know me."

Eddie searched the man's eyes for some clue as to where this was going, but he found none. "Before we even get close to anything like that, there're still a few formalities to deal with. You know . . . little things like who you are and what you want me to do."

"I already told you. I want you to help me collect some money. We'll get to the rest of it later."

The man was putting on a performance that suggested he needed something a little less routine than foreclosing a second mortgage on a strip mall he'd sold to a syndicate of proctologists in Palo Alto. Was he talking about hot money of some kind? The man didn't look the sort for laundering drug money, but then Eddie wasn't absolutely sure what 'the sort' looked like when you got up to what was obviously this guy's level. Most of Eddie's recent clients had been a lot lower down the food chain. Embezzlement, maybe? Bribery? Arms smuggling?

"The amount involved is roughly 400 million dollars."

Some people seemed to believe in coincidence as a major force in their lives, and some didn't. Eddie had never thought much about it one way or the other. Until now.

What were the chances of two conversations in his office on two consecutive days each being about a *different* 400 million dollars? What was the possibility this was just a coincidence? Eddie did the math and easily came up with what he knew was the right answer.

Zero.

He eyed the man for a while without saying anything. Rupert just smiled blandly.

"I don't know anything about the money you're looking for," Eddie finally said.

"If you don't know anything about it, how do you know what money I'm looking for?"

"Because a Secret Service agent sitting right there on Friday was looking for 400 million dollars, too. He even told me a little story about it. Just enough for me to be able to tell him the same thing I'm telling you. I don't know anything about it, and I can't help you."

Eddie thought he saw a quick flicker of uncertainty in the man's eyes, and he pounced. "By the way, what was the point of sending me those photographs?"

"Photographs?" Whatever Eddie thought he had seen before was gone now. The man's voice was level and untroubled, if clearly puzzled. "What photographs are you talking about?"

"Never mind." Eddie mentally kicked himself for bringing up the pictures without thinking more carefully. His increasing bewilderment was making him stupid. "It doesn't matter."

Rupert nodded absent-mindedly several times—apparently thinking of something else entirely—and then, to Eddie's relief, let his mention of the photographs slip by without comment. Instead, he asked something that immediately made it clear what was on his mind. "What exactly did you tell the Secret Service?"

"That I couldn't help them."

"Anything else?" The man was trying hard to sound casual.

"I told them I was in Saigon in '75 and my company was assigned to support the evacuation. I had nothing to do with the Bank of Vietnam or the money they're looking for."

The man was silent, and Eddie noticed he'd stopped smiling. He wondered what that meant.

"We rode shotgun on the last convoy out to Tan Sun Nhut before the North Vietnamese started shelling it and flight operations were stopped. After that we helped with the helicopter evacuation from the embassy and were lifted out off the rooftop pad. I didn't have any 400 million dollars with me when I went off that roof, and as far as I could tell, neither did anyone else. That's it. I just can't help you."

The man began nodding slowly, as if he were a teacher drilling an exceptionally dim pupil; one who simply needed some gentle encouragement to come up with the right answer.

"We've looked into your background thoroughly, Eddie. We know you couldn't possibly have what we're looking for."

"If you already know I can't help you, then what are you doing here?"

"Because you *can* help us, Eddie. Just not the way you think."

We? Us? Who are we talking about here?

"This is our proposition." Rupert bent forward and lowered his voice, although there was no particular reason for it. "We understand that you and your company commander were pretty close. We want you to talk to Captain Austin for us. That's it, really. Just talk to him."

Boy, is this guy in for a surprise.

"We think Austin either has the money himself, or he knows who does. We also think that most of the money is still intact."

"Why do you think that?"

"It's impossible to get that much money into circulation quietly, unless of course you possess technical knowledge and means—which we are confident Captain Austin couldn't." Rupert watched Eddie carefully. "That's why we want you to offer Captain Austin a deal. We've established a completely legal structure for moving the entire amount very quickly into the international banking system without attracting any attention whatsoever, and we want to form a partnership with him for that purpose."

"What you're saying is that you can launder 400 million dollars."

"Yes."

"You've got a big laundry."

"The biggest."

"Why not just call Austin up and tell him that yourself?"

"We think that's a bad risk. Put yourself in Austin's position, Eddie. Some stranger rings up one day and says, 'We hear you probably have ten tons of currency that once belonged to the Bank of Vietnam and we wonder if you'd like to make a deal with us to launder it into bank deposits and legitimate investments.' What's he likely to do then? What would *you* do? If he panics and runs, we might never find him again. To minimize that possibility, we think that someone should contact Austin whom he knows and trusts. We think you're the perfect guy."

The man's story made more sense than Eddie had expected it to. It might even have been moderately persuasive, if he hadn't known that Captain Austin was dead.

"I am here, Eddie, to offer you a fee of 100,000 dollars for contacting Austin and trying to convince him to do a deal with us. Your fee will be paid in advance. Even if you fail, or if it turns out that Austin has nothing and knows nothing, you keep the money. What have you got to lose?"

A hundred grand? Eddie's mind raced. If he just told the man right now that Austin was dead, there it went. If he didn't tell him—if he took the fee, crapped around a while, and then announced that he'd stumbled upon a small problem putting his case to Austin—he'd get to keep it. Wouldn't he? That was what the guy just said. He got the money whether he was successful or not.

On the other hand, if he took the guy's money knowing that he couldn't come up with anything, that was the same as stealing from him. Before he could figure out what to do, the man added one more thing.

"Furthermore, if Austin enters into an arrangement with us, we'll pay you an additional one million dollars."

For a moment Eddie wasn't certain he had heard right.

"How much?"

"A million dollars."

"*A million dollars*? Are you goddamn *kidding*?"

"You'll never meet anyone more serious than I am, Eddie."

Eddie pushed himself out of his chair and walked slowly to the window. How many times in his life was somebody going to walk through his door and offer him a million dollars to do anything, let alone something that he might easily be able to do? Or could, if Austin were alive. The captain being dead and all did raise the bar somewhat, Eddie had to admit. Raised the *crap* out of it actually.

Eddie studied the people down below his window in Grant Street. He wondered briefly what all those people were rushing toward? Maybe more to the point, what was rushing toward *them*? What was already out there waiting for each of them, a few minutes or a few days into their futures, the son of a gun already cocked and aimed right between their innocent, bovine eyes?

Maybe one was about to stumble on a curb and break his leg; maybe the bus another was catching would crash and he'd be dead before he could get home; maybe somebody was about to walk up to a third and offer him a life-altering bag of money for doing something that sounded simple but was actually impossible; or maybe nothing at all was going to happen to any of them.

"There's something you should know," Eddie said to the man as he eased himself back into the chair behind his desk.

"Yes?" Rupert's voice was empty, waiting.

"Austin's dead."

The man didn't really look all that surprised, Eddie noticed. Not exactly the reaction he'd been expecting.

"Well, that may make things more difficult." Rupert spoke slowly in a low voice, almost to himself.

Suddenly, he bolted from his chair. He pulled an over-sized, brown envelope out of the inside pocket of his jacket, and dropped it onto Eddie's desk.

"I am still prepared to retain you under the same terms regardless. If you wish to accept my offer, you must come to

Bangkok immediately. In this envelope is an airline ticket, a hotel confirmation, and funds for your expenses. The day after you arrive, 100,000 dollars will be wired to whatever bank you designate." The stiff set of Rupert's features suddenly broke, and a surprisingly soft smile spread across his face. "I do hope you will accept my proposition. Bangkok can be rather fun, you know." Then he winked, swung open the door, and was gone.

Jesus H. Christ. What the fuck was that?

First the guy wants to hire him to find Austin and make a deal to launder ten tons of money Austin may never have had. Then, when Eddie tells him that Austin's dead, he just nods and says that might make it more difficult—but he still wants to hire Eddie anyway.

And then there was Bangkok again. It was hanging out there like a tenth planet, generating a gravitational field all its own. It seemed to Eddie like he was riding in a little space capsule that was locked into an orbit whirring endlessly around the place.

No matter how many times he made the damned circle, no matter how he tried to get away, eventually the pull would be too strong and Bangkok was going to reel him right on in. It was starting to seem utterly inescapable.

On top of all that, there was the way the guy had left his office. Eddie almost laughed out loud. He couldn't keep the almost-forgotten lines from rolling through his head, repeating themselves over and over . . .

> "And laying his finger
> Aside of his nose,
> And giving a nod,
> Up the chimney he rose."

Well, shit a goddamned brick. He shook his head slowly. *Who* was *that masked man?*

8

Eddie had his feet on the desk and was poking idly with one chopstick at the remnants of the moo shu pork he'd gotten from the Chinese place downstairs. Joshua had offered to get it for him, but Eddie had gone himself because he thought it might loosen him up a little to get out of the office— even just to walk down one floor.

Ever since the man who had called himself Marinus Rupert left that morning, Eddie had been mostly just sitting around trying to decide what to do. Almost the entire day had passed now, and other than choosing steamed rice over fried, he hadn't made any particularly decisive moves. He'd even gone Chinese in the first place because he was hoping his fortune cookie might give him a subtle nudge in the right direction; but Chung had forgotten to put one in the bag this time, the bastard.

Was there some kind of hint for him in that? Eddie had considered the possibility for a while. Perhaps he should see himself as a man without a fortune. Eventually, however, he decided that was stretching Chung's pedestrian oversight way too far, and he let it slide.

Joshua pushed his head into Eddie's office. "It's Jennifer on one."

Eddie shifted his eyes and glanced at the white light blinking rhythmically on his telephone.

"No calls means no calls, Joshua."

"She said it was urgent. Anyway, I told her you were taking a deposition in the library."

"We don't have a library, Joshua."

"Take the call or not. Makes no difference to me."

Eddie twirled the chopstick in his fingers for a moment, and then arced the white take-out carton toward the trash can with his left hand. It hit the rim, bounced into the air and fell back into the center with a deeply satisfying plop.

"That's okay. I'll talk to her."

Joshua nodded silently and clicked the door shut, but Eddie didn't immediately pick up the telephone.

The brown envelope had laid untouched on his desk all day—left exactly where Rupert had put it that morning—and now Eddie imagined that it was regarding him with a baleful gaze, impatient for him to make up his mind. The 100,000 tempted him a lot, he had to admit, and frankly so did the chance to figure out why so many people thought he knew what happened to the Bank of Vietnam's money. But the picture of Harry Austin's head split open in a Bangkok street—still vivid in his mind—was keeping temptation under a tight reign.

Finally, Eddie sighed and picked up the telephone, stabbing at the blinking button. "Hello, Jennifer."

"Sorry to bother you, Eddie. I tried you at home first and you didn't answer, so I thought you might be at the office. I guess if you're working late like this you must be busy, so I'm sorry to . . ."

"Jennifer," Eddie quickly cut into her stream of consciousness before she got up to critical mass. "I don't mean to be rude, but I've got a lot on my mind. Why are you calling?"

"I want you to talk to Michael."

"I do talk to Michael, Jennifer. I talk to him all the time. I talked to him just a few days ago."

"No, I mean right now. I want you to talk to him now."

"Has something happened?"

"No. Well, yes."

"Okay. Which is it?"

"He's got a gun, Eddie."

For an instant, Eddie flashed on a picture of Jennifer and Franklin sitting rigid on the sofa while Michael waved a pistol at them and announced his demands.

"I don't understand."

"He's got a *gun*, Eddie. Some kind of pistol. A black one. I found it in his room yesterday."

"You searched his room?"

"Of course not." Jennifer hesitated. "Well, he's been acting funny lately, so I was just looking around. I thought maybe he was trying out drugs. You know, I just didn't know what to do so . . ."

"You searched his room," Eddie finished.

"Don't be a fucking lawyer with me!" Jennifer snapped. "I don't need a warrant. I'm his mother." She stopped talking and Eddie could hear her breathing. "And you're his father," she went on after a moment in a calmer tone. "I want you to talk to him."

"Have you asked him about it?"

She exhaled heavily. "He said it's no big deal; sometimes he takes it to school."

"He's taking a gun to *school*?"

"That's what he says. He claims a lot of the kids do."

"I have a little trouble believing that very many kids in the Seattle suburbs carry handguns in their backpacks, Jennifer."

"I don't know how to tell you this, Eddie, but we live in the real world up here, not in San Francisco. It's probably true."

After Jennifer had moved away, she got in her digs about San Francisco whenever she saw an opening. Still, the thought gave Eddie pause this time. Maybe he really *was* losing touch with whatever was happening out in the normal world, over there on the other side of the wall.

"Is this some kind of gang thing?"

"No. At least I don't think it is. Michael's too much of a loner for that. I didn't think I'd ever be grateful he inherited that trait from you, but I guess I am now."

Jennifer wanted to blame somebody for this and was trying hard to target Eddie, even if she didn't quite know how to do it so that it made sense. He didn't bite.

"Where is the gun now?"

"Michael took it somewhere. He won't tell me where."

"Well, for Christ's sake, Jennifer, if you can't do it yourself, get Franklin to take it away from him."

There was a long pause. "Franklin's in France. He won't be back until Friday."

"Wonderful," Eddie said as much to himself as to her. "Is Michael there now?"

"He's upstairs. I'll get him."

While Eddie waited, he tried to think things through. Was this nothing but idle teenage posturing and blossoming machismo? Or was it something else? And if it was something else, how was he going to get Michael to tell him what it was? The father-son thing had been drifting a while now for reasons he was already having difficulty understanding. It seemed an impossibly tall order to find out why Michael had suddenly decided to cart a gun around while he was coping with everything else, too.

"Yeah?"

The deep resonance of the voice startled Eddie, and for a moment he even wondered fleetingly who had picked up the phone. Michael used to sound like his mother over the phone when he was younger. Once, to his great embarrassment, Eddie had mixed them up when he called, and Michael's feelings had been badly hurt by it. At least, he guessed, it wouldn't be hard to tell them apart from now on.

"I hear we've got a problem, Mike."

"I don't have a problem. You might. But I don't."

"Carrying a gun's dangerous, Mike, not to mention illegal."

Jesus. A half dozen words and I'm already sounding like a damned lawyer.

"Those scumbags you work for do a lot worse. So if they arrest me, maybe you could work for me, too, Dad. How would that be?"

"I don't work for those guys, Mike. They're my clients."

It was a distinction that Eddie had always treasured, but suddenly it sounded embarrassingly lame. There was a sullen silence from the other end of the line, and for once, he was grateful for it.

"So where did you get the gun?" There was no answer. Eddie realized that it had been a stupid question to ask, and worse, pointless. "Okay, let's try this a different way. *Why* do you have a gun?"

This time he allowed the silence to go on, determined to wait Michael out.

"I just keep it around." Eddie could hear the shrug in his son's voice. "Most of the time it's not even loaded."

"So why do you have it?"

"Just . . . you know . . . protection."

"No, I don't know. Protection from what?"

"From stuff. Whatever."

The silence started up again and Eddie let it go on until Mike broke it.

"I figure I'd better start looking out for myself. Who else is going to do it? You?" The cruelty in his voice was unmistakable.

It was a finger straight in the eye, but Eddie blinked it away. "Is there something you're not telling me here, Mike?"

"Look, let's just cut the father-son bullshit, huh, Dad?" Michael's voice was steely and distant, and Eddie started to feel a little numb. "I just want to be sure my ass is covered. You ought to understand that. You spend enough time covering yours."

Eddie was fighting back his increasing anger at Michael's wild swings when, with a sudden flash of horror, a thought dawned on him. Had some former client of his been harassing Mike?

"There's nothing going on, honest," Michael answered the question before Eddie could ask it. "I just want to take care of myself if I have to. You're sure as hell not going to be around to help."

The conversation rattled around a little after that, but essentially it was all over. Mike had said his piece, and Eddie was left with no real response other than to get angry and hit back—and he was not going to do that. If that was what his son thought of him, that was what his son thought of him.

The gun wasn't the issue, Eddie knew. *He* was the issue. The gun would no doubt disappear in a few days—maybe it already had—but he wouldn't. Jennifer could worry about the gun. Eddie was going to worry about why his son thought he was such a jerk.

After he hung up, Eddie replayed the conversation in his head several times, searching for subtle meanings and thoughtful insights he might have missed the first time around. He found none.

Okay, maybe he wasn't any big deal—he hadn't done all that much with his life, he supposed—but why did his son see him as such a loser? It certainly wasn't true. Was it?

As he thought about his conversation with Michael, Eddie idly picked up the envelope Rupert had left on his desk and toyed with it, sliding it absent-mindedly from hand to hand. Forgetting his vow not to open it until he had decided whether to accept Rupert's offer, he slipped his forefinger under the back flap, ripped it open, and shook the contents out onto his desk. He sat for a long time looking at what spilled out, and he could feel the sting of Michael's words being shouldered aside by a growing sense of foreboding.

There was nothing particularly sinister or even surprising about what was in the envelope—it was exactly what Rupert had said it would be—but looking at everything spread out across his desk, Eddie thought he could feel the very air around him start to grow heavy.

He was certain that at the very moment he opened the envelope, the atmosphere began to give off a restless, distinctive odor. He could smell it. Oxygen was being burned into ozone somewhere nearby; the first forewarning of an approaching storm. It was a vivid premonition. Bolts of lightning, still too far away to be seen, were coming closer by the minute. Soon, he felt absolutely sure, they would be slashing the sky around his head.

He cautiously picked up a rectangular red and gold folder and opened the cover. Inside was a ticket for a San Francisco to Bangkok flight on Singapore Airlines leaving Wednesday, just before midnight. It was a round-trip ticket, with an open return. At least, Eddie noted, it was first class.

There was cash, too—hundred-dollar bills, ten of them—and a letter from the Oriental Hotel in Bangkok confirming that a suite had been reserved for Mr. Rupert Edward Dare for an indefinite stay. The letter begged to thank Mr. Dare for the 5,000 dollar cash deposit to his account.

A suite at one of the most famous hotels in the world and a first-class ticket on Singapore Airlines would normally be fine with him, Eddie reflected. But there was something about the open return and the 'indefinite stay' part of the letter that bothered him a lot.

When he thought about it later, Eddie realized he had acted unconsciously after that. He dug around on his desk until he found the remote control, and then punched on the little Sony that he kept in the office for watching sports when he was pretending to work on weekends. He had only been going to check out CNN, as he remembered. Just to see what the weather was like in Bangkok. Purely out of curiosity.

"Anything else before I leave, Eddie?" Joshua was standing just inside the door, and Eddie registered the concern on his face even in the fading twilight of the office. He had no secrets from Joshua, so he'd told him about Marinus Rupert and about the Secret Service. He'd told Joshua what he knew—but that hadn't taken long.

"I'm okay, Joshua." He hesitated and then decided to take the easy way out. "The call from Jennifer was no big deal. A problem with Mike. Nothing I can't handle."

Joshua nodded, but his expression remained the same as he watched Eddie closely.

Eventually he tilted his head toward the television set. "I've always liked that movie, too."

Eddie rotated his chair slightly and saw that the set had come on to a channel that was playing some old western he didn't recognize. A man dressed all in black was galloping on a sleek, white horse through the dusty streets of a small, western town while its awe-struck residents gazed up at him with a mixture of respect and admiration.

"I wasn't watching . . ."

"You know, Eddie, I've always thought that's what America is really all about," Joshua interrupted, pointing his forefinger at the television set.

"About riding horses and shooting people?"

Joshua hardly even noticed Eddie's smirky ripostes any longer, at least not that he let on.

"It's about people who're willing to go out over the next horizon. Those are the real American heroes. Men who aren't afraid to step right off into the future, to make something good happen."

Eddie smiled slightly. So that was what Joshua's sudden interest in western movies was all about.

"I don't want to be an American hero, Joshua."

Joshua watched him without expression for a moment, and then slowly smiled in such a sweetly melancholy way that

Eddie felt the goosebumps start to rise on his forearms.

"Oh yes, you do," Joshua murmured in a voice that was like the wind rattling dead leaves high up in an oak tree.

Then he slipped out the door, closing it behind him without another word, and was gone.

9

When Eddie walked into the bookstore the next morning and told Winnebago about Marinus Rupert and his proposition, Winnebago looked exactly like someone who didn't want to hear a word of it.

"Forget it, man." He rapped his open hand on the counter next to the cash register for emphasis. "Just forget it."

"This will get us two business-class seats." Eddie held up the red folder with the first-class ticket in it. "We're covered on the hotel and have a thousand bucks in cash. What have you got to lose?"

Winnebago regarded Eddie with amazement. "You're kidding, right?" He took off his glasses and leaned forward until his face was just inches from Eddie's. "What have I got to *lose*? My fucking *life* is what it looks to me like I've got to lose."

"Don't worry so much, Winnebago. Everything will be fine."

"Oh, sure it will. We'll just fly 10,000 miles around the world, I'll get the trots from the food, emphysema from the air, the clap from the girls, and my ass handed to me in a bag by somebody who thinks I know where 400 million dollars is. Oh yeah. It'll be fucking fantastic, it will." He folded his arms. "No goddamned way."

Eddie exhaled slowly and studied a tall bookcase labeled with a neat sign tacked to the top shelf. It was hand-printed in black ink: FETISHES—HARDBACK.

"Why do you *really* want to do this, Eddie?"

"Too many people think we know something about the Voltaire money."

"Yeah. So?"

"Well, we *were* there, somewhere. If I take this guy's money and we use it to poke around a little, maybe we'll remember things; start to put it all together." Eddie waited, but Winnebago didn't say anything, so he spelled it out. "Maybe we can find out what happened to that money."

"Did it ever occur to you that someone probably doesn't *want* anyone to find out; that maybe they're getting rid of anyone they think knows anything?" Winnebago's eyes had shifted away from Eddie, but now they shifted back. "That's probably why Captain Austin ended up with his head busted open, and you can bet your sweet ass that's what those big, red circles around us on those pictures are supposed to mean."

"I don't think so." Eddie shook his head. "If someone wanted to kill us, why put us on guard like that? The pictures have to mean something else. We just haven't figured it out yet."

Winnebago didn't have an answer for that, but his skeptical expression remained unchanged. "You haven't been to Bangkok in twenty years. You've got no chance screwing around out there, man. No fucking chance."

"I've been to Bangkok since we were there." Eddie's voice sounded a little defensive, even to him. "A couple of times."

Eddie had loved Bangkok in the seventies, when he and Winnebago had taken their R&R there. He'd been back twice since: once on a banking case when he was still an uptown lawyer, and again about a year ago getting an unlucky druggie, whose father owned half of Santa Cruz, out of jail. He had to admit that Bangkok had changed a lot over twenty years, and he was less certain what he thought about it now.

"Look, Winnebago, I've never asked you for anything before, but I don't want to go out there without someone covering my butt."

"Then don't go, Eddie."

"I've got to go."

"Bullshit. Don't risk your life in some fucking crazy treasure hunt, man."

"It's not the money."

"Not the money?"

"No."

"Then maybe you can explain to me what I'm missing here."

Eddie looked down at his feet, inhaled deeply, and made little popping sounds with his lips as he blew the air out again. The question was more than fair. He knew Winnebago would ask it—he'd asked it of himself over and over since last night when he'd decided what he was going to do—and he'd been thinking all the way over to the bookshop about how to explain the answer sensibly.

Everyone he knew daydreamed about trading in their old life for a new one. Everyone said that someday they would really do it. Now Eddie's someday had walked right up to the door and knocked. He was staring straight into a gaping exit hole from the scattered debris of his life, and an unshakable conviction had taken control of him. He *had* to crawl through that hole.

Maybe Winnebago had nailed it. Maybe it *was* a treasure hunt. But what would the treasure turn out to be? The Voltaire money? Maybe. But perhaps it would be something else; something entirely unexpected.

The more he thought about it, the less he figured there was any real difference. The truth was, he just wanted to hunt for treasure before he got too old to know what it looked like when he found it.

That was it, really. That was what mattered.

'Here lies Eddie Dare. He was okay.' Fuck that shit.

Eddie tried to explain everything, but the more he talked, the more ridiculous he thought it sounded. Finally, he just trailed off.

"I'm going to Bangkok, Winnebago," he finished up, his voice dropping. "Maybe I can't make you understand why, but I'm going, and I'm asking you right now to come with me."

Winnebago tapped a Camel out of a nearly empty pack and took his time about lighting it. "You don't have the first damned idea what you're going to do when you get there, do you?" He was still shaking his head, but Eddie got the feeling that he was coming around.

"Sure I do."

"And that is . . ." Winnebago made a little gesture with his hand.

"If we can find out what Captain Austin was doing in Bangkok—who he knew there, what he did, things like that— we can put that together with what we already know, and I'll bet you then we'll have something."

"And how are you going to do all that?"

"I'm not sure yet," Eddie admitted. "But I got a place to start. I know a guy in Bangkok."

"Oh well, you know a guy in Bangkok. The population there's . . . what? Six, eight million?"

"About ten, I think. Give or take."

"And you know *one* guy. That's just great. I can certainly see how that solves everything."

Eddie was sure he had Winnebago going. He could see it in his eyes. "Yeah, but you're going to come with me anyway, aren't you?"

Winnebago leaned back as far as he could without falling off his stool, put his hands together over his eyes, and sighed deeply. "Man, I know I'm going to regret this."

Eddie knew that might well be true, so he kept his mouth shut.

"When are we leaving?" Winnebago dropped his hands and shook his head a little more, still not quite believing what he was doing.

"Tomorrow."

"*Tomorrow*? I can't take off like that, Eddie! I've got to find someone to watch the store."

"No one's bought a damned thing here in six months. Just lock the door."

"That's a slight exaggeration," Winnebago grumbled, but he opened the drawer beneath the cash register and began scraping around anyway, trying to find his keys.

Eddie walked over to Mason to catch a cable car back to his office. The morning fog had turned to rain while he was inside the bookstore, and a few big drops were splattering Columbus Street as he headed down a block and turned west on Vallejo. There was an odor in the rain that he had never noticed before—the smell of salt from the Pacific and ... something else; something that just eluded him.

He had spent half his life in San Francisco and he always thought of it as like living inside a huge theme park. From outside the wall, somewhere over in the real world, he could hear the thuds and crashes and the sounds of smashing furniture—but he'd made his life there inside, safely away from all that. He had let the stars spin past and the planet whirl inexorably under him for almost twenty years, and he'd never worried all that much about what things might be like out there beyond the wall.

Yet now here he was, about to hurl himself across the Pacific Ocean. He was about to fly halfway around the world, on board his personal red-eye.

Something was waiting for him in Bangkok—he knew that it was—and he was ready to trade his present for whatever future it might offer. Just like that.

Eddie didn't blame Winnebago for being skeptical. It all must have sounded unbelievably stupid when he tried to explain it, but he knew he could do it. He could make the trade, and he could make it stick. He *did* know a guy in Bangkok, and what's more, the guy he knew was quite a guy.

Eddie could sense the bargain being sealed even as he trotted toward a green and yellow cable car that was just rattling up Mason.

As he breathed in the sweetness of the San Francisco breeze, he reached for a brass pole and pulled himself up onto the car's worn steps. The high-pitched singing of the cable in its metal groove beneath the street had never sounded quite so distinct to him, or so loud.

Glancing back over his shoulder at North Beach, he saw it as if he was peering out over a great distance, watching as it receded further and further into his past.

That was when Eddie felt it for sure. He was edging across an unmarked border. He was creeping toward a new world; one that was unknown to him certainly, maybe even unknowable.

It was wonderful.

10

Bar Phillips was a New York boy who headed west in the fifties, searching for the golden life like everybody else. But somehow he just slid right on through California without grabbing hold of anything solid, skidded all the way across the Pacific, and didn't stop until he ended up in Bangkok. From the Big Apple to the Big Orange to the Big Mango. It still had a kind of nutty logic to it, even when he thought about it now, almost forty years later. He *had* headed west, hadn't he? And Bangkok, he was certain, had to be as far west as he could get without falling completely off the edge of the world.

On the other hand, sometimes Bar figured that was exactly what he *had* done. What was it about the place that held him there? Bangkok was so polluted you couldn't breathe; it was grid-locked with cars and crazies; hardly anyone spoke English; it was hotter than hell; half the year the streets were flooded, and the other half they were full of rabid dogs. No, he couldn't see for the life of him what kept him there. He could only see that he would never leave.

Bar had tried going back to New York once in the late seventies, just to see if he was missing out on anything. The whole place had turned fat, ugly, mean and crazy, he quickly decided—and it scared the hell out of him.

He ended up in some tourist hotel on Forty-Seventh Street, down almost to Eighth Avenue, just sitting in his room day after day, eating pizzas he had delivered from Ray's, and flipping slowly back and forth through 68 channels of cable television. He was too bewildered and browbeaten by the city even to go outside much, and after a week of that, he decided he was done. He took a cab straight to Kennedy and sat in the Pan American terminal until somebody got him into a seat on a flight back to Bangkok. That was that. From then on, he knew, he was a lifer.

Bar slurped down the last of his tomato soup, ran some water into the bowl, and dumped it in the sink. As he walked past the only real window in his tiny condo, he stopped and contemplated the streaky, orange twilight that he thought was the nicest thing about Bangkok.

Some people said there was so much crud in Bangkok's air that you should walk on it instead of trying to breathe it, but Bar loved the way it made the sky glow just after sunset with a luminescent, mango-colored haze. Maybe that wasn't the reason why some of Bangkok's foreign residents called the place the Big Mango, but Bar always thought it should have been. Bangkok's twilight radiance was what kept him believing there was magic in the world. If the only price he had to pay for that was sucking up a little crap with his air, he'd pay it, gladly.

From the window he could see all the way across the city to the Chao Praya River; its dusky surface turning to pewter in the fading light. A long train of broad-beamed teak rice barges was drifting slowly downriver toward the Gulf of Thailand, looking like a child's wooden toys embedded forever in a river of tin.

Part Oriental alchemy, part Western jazz—John Coltrane played on instruments from another planet—there was something about Bangkok that defied time and disdained reality.

That might be a romantic way to look at a city that hardly anyone else ever thought of as romantic—either before or after sunset—but that was the way Bar Phillips wanted to look at Bangkok, and that was the way he *had* looked at it for most of his almost forty years there.

◐━◐

An hour later, Bar got out of a taxi on Silom Road just across the street from the Dusit Thani Hotel—a cavernous old barn favored by airline crews and Taiwanese tourists. He gave the driver a 100-baht note and ignored him when he demanded 200. Ducking down a narrow alley, Bar by-passed the long rows of carts where the street vendors were setting up the night market. Slipping past the first wave of grazing tourists, he made for the Crown Royal.

Izzie Schultz had opened the Crown Royal in the early seventies, following a couple of years as an observer with the Canadian Army in Vietnam—although Izzie doubted that what he had spent his time observing was exactly what the Canadian Army had in mind when they sent him there. He had declined to re-enlist when he found out he was about to be sent back to Canada. With all the warm, sticky delights of Saigon and Bangkok beckoning, he couldn't think of even one good reason to go back to freezing his ass off in some God-forsaken, crappy little Canadian town.

Izzie hadn't been much interested in politics back then, but he'd observed enough on his rounds among the massage parlors to know that Saigon wasn't much of a bet for long-term retirement. That left Bangkok, so he had used the money he saved to buy into a bar there with some friends. In a part-ing salute to his heritage, he'd convinced his partners to name the place the Crown Royal. *Good-bye Canada, you ice-cold bitch. Hell-ooo, Bangkok.*

The Crown Royal was dark and woody, comfortably smoky. No loud music, no go-go girls, just a place where a serious man went for a serious drink. Over twenty-odd years, it had become a Bangkok institution. Although Izzie had long ago bought out his partners, everything else was pretty much the same as it had always been.

Bar settled into his usual seat in the last booth at the back, facing forward. A local never sat with his back to the door in Bangkok. Those were the seats the tourists got. They didn't know any better.

"Hi, baby." A dark girl wearing a short, red dress and pretty good counterfeit Gucci pumps put a sweating Carlsberg in front of Bar and squeezed onto the seat next to him. She began to massage the back of his neck with more energy than skill, and he reached around and gently removed her hands without looking at her.

The girl effected a hurt pout. "You no love Noi no more. You treat Noi bad."

A large man wearing a T-shirt and khaki shorts flopped into the booth opposite Bar and banged down a bottle of Singha. He was balding and fleshy, his long jowls hanging down over his collar, and he twisted his body around on the seat until he was in a position to flick his eyes comfortably back and forth between Bar and the front door.

Bar had some long-ago night christened the man Sydney Sidney, since he claimed to be an Australian named Sidney and no one seemed to know what his last name really was. Sidney said he was an undercover agent for ASIO, the Australian intelligence service, but no one really believed him, and Bar had stopped trying to catch him out years ago.

Frankly, Bar didn't even think Sidney was Australian, but what the hell difference did it make? Bangkok was the kind of place where, if you were foolish enough to ask anyone who they were and what they did, the only thing you could be certain of was that they would lie to you. Even if it didn't matter—and it almost never did—they would still lie to you. Bangkok just did that to people.

"You seen Flippo around tonight, mate?"

"Nope. Just got here."

Flippo Kurtz had worked diligently for 17 years on the assembly line of a Mercedes plant in Stuttgart until he won a package tour to Bangkok in a union raffle. After three days, he decided he'd be out of his mind to go back to Stuttgart, and he started a business in Bangkok making T-shirts for tourists. Discovering a previously unknown genius for devising smutty epigrams, he had prospered hugely.

"He come and he go," Noi offered.

Sidney nodded slowly and finished his beer with a thoughtful expression, as if he was contemplating the philosophical nuances in Noi's observation.

Bar's eyes drifted to a girl stacking glasses behind the bar. She was young—probably not more than twenty—and had huge, brown eyes that played hide-and-seek with him from behind straight bangs that swung rhythmically from side to side whenever she moved her head. When she realized Bar was looking at her, she giggled and quickly raised an open hand to her mouth. It was a gesture of spontaneous innocence that Bar thought was so charming, he briefly contemplated the possibility of falling in love.

"New?" he asked Sidney, nodding toward the girl.

Sidney twisted around and looked where Bar's eyes were pointing. When he turned back he was grinning. "Mine, mate."

"Really? That what she says?"

"She'd better. Besides, you're too fuckin' old for her. What are you? Sixty?"

Bar ignored Sidney as he studied the girl. In Bangkok a man's age didn't count for nearly as much as it did out in the real world.

"What's her name?"

Sidney hesitated just an instant. "Meow."

"Bullshit," Bar scoffed. "You never even saw her until I did."

"I fuckin' did too." Sidney seemed genuinely indignant. "I fuckin' *did*."

"Tell you what, Sidney. Don't worry about it. She's yours, old man. I'll stay completely out of the way."

"Piss off," Sidney snapped, but he was smiling. "Anyway, who you calling old, you fuckin' fossil?"

Sidney rapped his empty Singha bottle against the table. Noi shifted her eyes slowly toward him, and with a little pout, snatched up the bottle and slid out of the booth to get him another.

"Everything okay at the paper?" Sidney asked Bar as he followed Noi's twitching rump with his eyes.

"Yeah . . ." Bar searched for exactly the right word, but nothing came to mind so he settled for the obvious. "Okay."

The paper was the *Bangkok Post*, the city's primary English-language daily, and the mouthpiece for the local establishment—whatever that might mean from time to time in Thailand. The *Post* had been around for a long time, surviving coups and other lesser events remarkably intact. It wasn't the *New York Times*, but Bar thought it was still a pretty good paper. On the other hand, he had to admit that it did publish some awfully strange things sometimes—and Bar himself was personally responsible for one of the strangest.

His weekly column had been spread over a full page each Saturday for nearly thirty years. It was called 'Bar by Bar'—a little cute maybe, but he liked it—and although few of them would admit it without making excuses, almost every expatriate in town, and most visitors, read it every week. Bar was the ranking expert on Bangkok's nightlife, and that was a subject in which almost every Westerner was more than a little interested.

'Bar by Bar' was more than just a newspaper column. Over the years, it had become a kind of bulletin board for all the shipwrecked expats who had washed up on the great dirty beach of Bangkok; a flotsam and jetsam of lost souls who were happy as hell to be lost, and only hoped no one would ever find them again.

In some places a man's past could foretell his future, but in Bangkok the rules were different. It was *all* future. The past didn't exist. All kinds of people regularly disappeared into Bangkok and emerged entirely recreated. It was a sort of Bermuda Triangle for discarded lives.

Growing old anywhere was shit, but drifting along Sukhumvit Road on a sticky Bangkok Saturday night with a graceful, young Thai girl on their arm, a lot of middle-aged men suddenly saw life from an entirely new perspective. When they'd been stuck back in Kansas City, spending their weekends at the Red Lobster, the future hadn't looked nearly so promising.

The door to the Crown Royal swung open and six Japanese in nearly identical gray suits tumbled in. They took seats around the one empty table, first carefully organizing themselves in what Bar surmised was the appropriate order of rank. The bargirls moved quickly to stake out the newcomers, wary eyes flashing warnings at potential competitors.

Noi glared resentfully at Sidney as she slammed his beer down. Since she had been behind the bar getting it, she'd lost out on grabbing one of the Japanese for herself.

"I stay with you. I no butterfly. I luv you," she said to Bar as she slid back into the booth next to him, but she knew it didn't matter what she said because Bar was never good for a touch. Not only had he heard all the bargirl stories before, he'd probably helped make most of them up.

"Look at that, Bar." Sidney stared with hard eyes at the table of Japanese. "Fuckin' Nips think they own Asia."

"They *do* own Asia, Sidney."

"They don't own *my* part of it, mate. Fuck 'em."

Sidney shook his head, but his heart wasn't in it. He and Bar had been having the same conversation for about twenty years. It just wasn't any fun crapping on the Japs, Sidney had noticed, unless he was totally shit-faced. Then he could really do a number on the little bastards. Somehow, stone cold sober, he found the whole subject way too depressing to think about.

They sat in silence for a while, Sidney shooting hostile glances at the Japanese every time he heard anything that suggested one of them might be having a good time.

Suddenly he brightened. "I almost forgot, Bar. A guy was in here looking for you. Must've been about an hour ago."

"Who was it?"

"I dunno. Just some guy. A Yank, I reckon."

"You didn't know him?"

Sidney looked disgusted. "If I knew him, Bar, I'd have fuckin' told you who it was, wouldn't I?"

"Did he know me?"

"Seemed to."

"What did he want?"

"Didn't say. Just asked were you coming in tonight."

"And you told him . . ." Bar prompted patiently.

"I told him I didn't know. Sometimes you did, sometimes you didn't." Sidney shrugged. "Probably just some fuckin' tourist wants you to autograph your column and tell him where to get laid cheap."

Maybe, Bar thought. *And maybe not.*

When you worked the night scene in Bangkok, you always kept an ear open for footsteps. You never knew who you might have pissed off—and when you pissed off people in Thailand, they didn't have their lawyer call your lawyer.

The going rate for a hit in Bangkok was usually no more than five thousand baht, about 200 American dollars. Sometimes, of course, *farangs* cost a little more to do— foreigners could be messy and conspicuous—but the price seldom went over ten thousand, regardless. Unless, of course, it was during an election, and all the hitmen were booked up.

Bar couldn't think of anything he had written recently that might cause anyone to want him popped, and he was even pretty sure he hadn't been dinking the mistress of any Chinese drug peddler lately either—at least not that he knew of for sure.

Maybe he *was* getting old, he reflected briefly; not much of a candidate anymore for a double tap behind the ear with one of those little .22 revolvers the local pros favored for close-in work. The thought left him with strangely mixed feelings.

"Was the guy a Thai?" Bar asked Sidney.

"No, a *farang*. I already told you. Probably just some tourist looking for a bit of action."

Bar let it go. "Yeah, probably," he agreed, and took another long pull from the Carlsberg.

But he made a mental note of everything Sidney had said, and filed it carefully away.

When you'd been around Bangkok as long as Bar had, you lived by the local rules. One of the most important of those was that you weren't usually interested in being found by anyone who was looking for you.

Bar figured he'd better watch his step for a few days, just to be on the safe side.

11

When they emerged into the arrival hall of Don Muang International Airport—blinking to get their bearings in the harsh fluorescent lights of the cavernous room—Winnebago nudged Eddie and pointed to a man in the crowd that was waiting for arriving passengers. He was wearing a crisp, white uniform with brass buttons and dark shoulder boards, and he was holding up a large card on which was printed in block letters, WELCOME TO MR. RUPERT EDWARD DARE, ESQ.

"Go get him, Rupert, baby," Winnebago snickered.

Eddie narrowed his eyes at Winnebago, and then dragged his luggage trolley over and gave the man a weary smile. "That's me, Admiral."

"Welcome to Bangkok, Mr. Dare." The man's voice was formal, but not unfriendly. "I am here to drive you to the Oriental Hotel. May I, sir?" He took Eddie's suitcase off the luggage cart without waiting for an answer, and bowed slightly. "Please follow me, Mr. Dare."

"I got a bag, too. You only work for certain races or what, little buddy?"

"He's with me," Eddie explained. "He's an Indian, but it's not his fault."

"Native American," Winnebago corrected.

"Are you still on that kick?"

"I think I'll just try it on for size while we're here. See how it goes."

"I don't know." Eddie looked at the driver. He was still punchy from the 22-hour flight and knew he wasn't making much sense, but it didn't particularly matter to him. "What do you think?"

The driver was starting to wonder what he'd gotten into. Who were these deranged morons? His wife always said white guys were crazy. He put on the blandest expression he could manage, and switched into his humble coolie routine. "I just driver, sir. I not understand."

Winnebago held out his suitcase. "Just take it away, man, and we'll all live happily ever after."

The driver quickly grabbed Winnebago's bag with his free hand, and—giving a little bob with his head—he scuttled off.

◒◼◒

The dark blue Mercedes edged out of the airport garage and turned its three-pointed star toward central Bangkok. Within minutes it was edging slowly through the worst traffic Eddie had ever seen. The road in from the airport looked like a freeway inexplicably converted to a temporary parking lot. It was marked with four lanes, but no one seemed particularly impressed. Vehicles of every possible kind jostled for space, and added up to at least six lanes, if not more. Calling this a traffic jam, Eddie thought to himself, was like calling a lump of coal a dead plant.

Even inside the big Mercedes that was chilled down to the temperature of a berserk Fridgidaire, Eddie could already smell Bangkok—a mix of automobile exhaust, jasmine blossoms, burned grease, drifting incense, and raw sewage that was like the smell of no other city he'd ever known. It was something that the strongest rain would never wash away; a scent that even the hot, heavy Bangkok air could never smother.

The massed assault on his senses was starting to kick-start Eddie into a second wind. He knew a place where Bar Phillips hung out most evenings, and had thought during the flight about stopping there on the way in from the airport. He could always call the *Bangkok Post* and leave a message, of course, but Bar wasn't a guy who put much effort into returning calls, and Eddie thought the sooner he could find him the better. Maybe he'd get lucky if they just dropped by the Crown Royal.

"You feel like making a stop on the way in?" He glanced sideways at Winnebago.

"Fuck." Winnebago tilted his head back against the seat and closed his eyes. "What I feel like is hammered sheep shit on a flat rock."

Visibility through the gathering darkness and the rancid air was terrible, but Eddie could make out lines of shophouses along the roadside; street stalls with dented aluminum pots of food stacked on wooden tables; and junkyards piled with greasy, used automobile parts. In one place, a bunch of kids and dogs were just standing by the freeway watching the traffic not move. They looked to Eddie like fishermen gathered on a riverbank, waiting to cast a line out into the traffic and haul in an old tire, or maybe a whole Toyota.

The car's windows were tinted so darkly that no one could see in. Eddie looked straight into the eyes of people outside without them realizing he was there. It was a creepy feeling, watching people that way as they crawled along, but there was something oddly familiar about it, too. It was like being on a ride at Disneyland, he finally decided, sitting with the other tourists in a little car being towed slowly through a make-believe world. Here he was in Third World Land; a place of chaos and squalor, but boasting stunningly life-like animatronics.

The Mercedes edged along until they came upon a pack of street kids wearing shorts without shirts and working the roadway selling garlands of flowers. Suddenly, an old man leaned up against the window and Eddie jumped back a bit in spite of himself. The man was a skinny, shrunken fellow wearing a baggy Oakland Raiders T-shirt, and he thrust out a rooster that looked even more skinny and shrunken than he did. Jesus, Eddie wondered, who'd buy a rooster in the middle of a traffic jam? But then the car began to edge forward again, the old man fell behind, and Eddie never found out.

They didn't have any trouble locating the Crown Royal after Eddie asked the driver to stop there, but Bar Phillips wasn't around, and no one seemed to know whether he was coming in any time soon. Eddie briefly considered waiting, but he was just too beaten up from the long flight, so he went back to the car and they drove on to the hotel. Besides, there really wasn't all that much of a rush, he told himself. He'd get some sleep and see what the next day brought.

An assistant manager dressed in a frock coat and gray, striped trousers was waiting when their car finally pulled up to the Oriental, and he gave Winnebago the same kind of look that the driver had. Followed by two uniformed porters, each carrying one suitcase, he escorted Eddie and Winnebago directly to a suite near the top of the hotel facing the river. After assuring them that the formalities of registration had already been taken care of, and politely wishing them a pleasant stay, he bowed his way out of the suite.

"That was real nice," Winnebago said. "All except the part when he asked if you needed a small room for 'your man' here."

Eddie stood at the big windows and looked at the Chao Praya River down below. It was a lazy looking bastard, he thought; wide and still, twisting aimlessly back and forth through the city. Here and there, lights winked on small boats dodging through the darkness, darting like water bugs in shifting patterns that made no more sense to Eddie than the meandering of the big river itself.

When he heard the two sharp taps, he walked over and opened the door. For a moment he wasn't able to decide if the figure standing there was a small boy, or a midget with weird dress sense. Decked out in a spotless, white uniform with a pillbox hat tilted to the side and tied under his chin with a red ribbon, the caller wordlessly thrust out a silver tray containing nothing but a single, white envelope. Eddie took the envelope, and the apparition wheeled sharply and vanished through some almost invisible door in the hotel corridor. With a shrug, Eddie closed the door and tore open the envelope.

"Who was that?" Winnebago asked.

"I wouldn't know how to tell you."

Eddie scanned the single sheet of paper.

"According to this, we won't be seeing our benefactor until noon tomorrow. Thank God. What I need is a shower and about twelve hours of sleep in a real bed."

Winnebago couldn't believe what he was hearing. "*What? We're in Bangkok, man! Sleep?* Let's get some action!"

"I thought you were all done in, Sitting Bull. If that's what you have in mind, you're going to need more energy than either of us has left tonight. You're a lot older than you were the last time you were here."

"Maybe you, white man," Winnebago snapped, slapping an open palm against his chest. "Maybe you, but not *this* Native American."

Eddie responded with a sound that was appropriately ambiguous, kicked off his shoes, and lay back on the couch. There was a copy of the *Bangkok Post* on the coffee table and he picked it up, idly flipping the pages.

Winnebago lit a Camel and examined the tray of crystal glasses on top of a large, intricately-worked teak cabinet under the windows. "Nice glasses, but why so many?"

"They go with the bar." Eddie lowered the newspaper and pointed toward the cabinet's twin doors. "Probably in there."

Winnebago ditched his cigarette in an ashtray and bent over, pulling them open. "Wow! Look at this, Eddie! There's even an ice box!" He pulled on the door and the little refrigerator rattled open. "You want something?"

Eddie shook his head. "Neither will you when you find out how much that stuff costs in a place like this."

"Isn't our bill being paid by this guy who gave you the ticket?"

Eddie reflected on that for a moment. "Sometimes, Winnebago, I fail to credit you for the simple wisdom you bring to life's larger dilemmas."

Eddie cracked open a bottle of Tanqueray—pouring a generous measure into one of the glasses and dropping in a couple of ice cubes—while Winnebago brought a can of Carlsberg and a bag of chips over to the coffee table. He popped the tab on the can and ripped open the bag, scooping out a handful of the chips and stuffing them into his mouth.

Putting his feet up and sinking back into the soft cushions of the couch, Eddie sloshed the gin around in his glass. He watched the clear liquid bounce between the tiny blocks of ice and collide with the crystal walls of the glass, making little pools and curls as it swirled around the sides. Then he looked up, and—for the first time—fully absorbed the elegance and refinement of their surroundings.

Is some yo-yo really going to show up here tomorrow and hand me 100,000 dollars?

It sounded too good to be true, and in Eddie's experience, it was axiomatic that anything that *sounded* too good to be true always *was*. He took a hit of the gin and thought about how good it tasted; about how good *everything* tasted right then.

What the hell. Have fun while it all lasts.

He flipped a few more pages in the *Bangkok Post* while he sipped at his drink, and then folded over a page and held the paper out to Winnebago. "Here's the guy I've been telling you about."

Winnebago glanced at the tiny picture at the top of the column.

"He looks kind of old."

"Well," Eddie admitted, "he's not young, but neither are we anymore. Bar's been around Bangkok forever. He's the guy to call if you want to know where they bury the bodies."

"Oh, man," Winnebago sighed and waved the paper away. "I wish you'd put that some other way."

"Yeah." Eddie took it back and looked at the picture some more. "Sorry."

"So what now, Eddie?"

"You do what you want. I'm going to crash."

"Oh, come on. Let's at least get some food first, huh?"

Eddie took another hit on the Tanqueray and felt his resolve to be sensible start to weaken.

"What do you feel like?"

"Poontang!"

As Eddie began to laugh, he realized that a sort of giddiness was threatening to engulf both of them; a lightheadedness that might just have been jet lag, but he didn't think so. It was too much like a feeling he remembered clearly from a long time back.

When he'd been in law school, he would sometimes hitchhike down to LA on weekends and sleep in a cheap motel on Hollywood Boulevard. At night, about nine or ten, after napping all day in his room with the drapes closed, he'd walk out into the hard, sweet-smelling desert air. He remembered how much he had loved it then, just standing there, doing nothing but breathing deeply in and out, getting a little buzzed on the inexhaustible adventures drifting on the night; wallowing in the limitless possibilities that stretched out in front of him.

He'd thought so many times that feeling would never come to him again, but suddenly it had. Against all understanding, here in this bewildering place halfway around the earth, it had come to him again.

12

Promptly at noon the next day, the suite's doorbell sounded a chime so discreet that, for a moment, Eddie couldn't figure out what it was supposed to be. When he finally worked it out and opened the door, he found a young man of about thirty carrying a leather briefcase. He was probably European, Eddie decided immediately, mostly from the cut of his dark, expensive-looking suit.

"Mr. Dare?"

Eddie nodded noncommittally.

"My name is Geoffrey Morse. May I come in?"

Eddie waved the young man toward a couch in front of the big windows overlooking the river, and then settled into a chair opposite him. Morse's accent was obviously English, Eddie reflected—as Marinus Rupert's had been—but he had no idea what significance that might have.

"Nice suite," Morse said after a moment. "Wonderful view."

"I don't deserve any credit. You're paying for it."

"Only in a manner of speaking." Morse reached into an inside pocket of his jacket. He produced a business card and was about to hand it to Eddie when Winnebago walked in from the second bedroom. Morse stopped—the card suspended in the air—and looked at Eddie. "I wasn't told you were traveling with anyone, sir."

"Until two days ago I wasn't told I was traveling at all."

Winnebago took an empty chair, and Morse played with the business card, rubbing it between his fingers. He was obviously uncomfortable that something unexpected had occurred, and wasn't sure what he should do.

Everyone just sat and looked at one another for a while, waiting, until Morse finally broke the silence.

"I'm only following instructions, sir. I had no idea anyone else would be here. I've been asked to brief you—and only you—on the situation."

That expression had a familiar ring to Eddie.

"The 'situation?'"

"Yes, sir."

"You don't happen to work for the Secret Service, do you?"

Morse looked bewildered. "I'm sorry, but I don't . . ."

"Never mind," Eddie interrupted. Leaning back, he folded his arms.

Morse shifted his weight uncomfortably in the chair and cut his eyes at Winnebago again. He hesitated another moment and then flicked the business card out toward Eddie.

"I'm an associate in the Bangkok office of Fairfields."

Eddie took the business card and examined it.

When he didn't say anything, Morse added helpfully, "You have heard of us, haven't you? We are the largest firm of solicitors in the United Kingdom."

"Of course you are."

"Then you *have* heard of us."

"No."

"I was told you were a lawyer in America."

"I am."

"You're a lawyer, but you've never . . ."

"No. Never."

"Ah."

Morse let the single syllable hang there in judgment of Eddie's apparent stature in the world's legal community. Eddie had never liked English solicitors very much, and just then it was clearly coming back to him exactly why that was.

"Anyway. . . ," there was something like a shrug in the young man's voice, ". . . we represent the General."

"The General?"

"Yes, sir. The General."

"General who?"

"I'm sorry, but I can't talk about that. Anyway, you may not believe me, but I couldn't tell you even if I was ethically permitted to. I really don't know."

"You're right," Eddie said. "I don't believe you."

Morse looked at Eddie and then at Winnebago, both of whom gazed back patiently. He inclined his head slightly toward Winnebago, but spoke to Eddie. "I mean no offense to your traveling companion, Mr. Dare, but what I have to tell you is extremely confidential."

Eddie just nodded. "No problem. Go ahead."

Morse examined Winnebago carefully again, and then returned his eyes to Eddie.

He cleared his throat unnecessarily. "As you wish. The General has asked us to make arrangements to wire the amount of 100,000 dollars immediately to whatever bank you designate."

The young man unsnapped his briefcase, extracted a single sheet of paper, and handed it to Eddie. "If you would just fill in your account information at the bottom of this transfer instruction, the funds will be sent by the close of business today."

Eddie took the piece of paper, but he didn't look at it. "What's your connection with the man who came to my office?"

"Who was that?"

"Marinus Rupert was the name he used."

The young solicitor looked genuinely puzzled. "Is that a code or something?" His eyes twitched nervously and he licked his lips, wishing he was somewhere else. "I don't know anyone by that name."

"Then let's get back to who this general is."

"I already told you that I can't talk about that, and even if I could, I don't know what I would tell you." Morse sounded exasperated and embarrassed at the same time. "Look, I was instructed by our Hong Kong office to bring you this wire transfer order to complete." He gestured at the paper Eddie was holding, still unread. "And I'm also to give you a message. That's all I know about whatever is going on here—and it's all I want to know."

"What's the message?"

"The General wishes you to join him for lunch today at the Regent."

When Eddie didn't react, the young man added helpfully, "It's a hotel."

"I know it's a hotel," Eddie said. "I'm a lawyer, not an idiot. At least in America, they're not always the same thing."

There was another Mercedes waiting for Eddie when he went downstairs. The driver looked like a local, and apparently didn't speak any English, since his only response to Eddie's greeting was a vague smile. Eddie leaned his head back against the butter-soft, black leather and closed his eyes as they drove at a stately pace from the Oriental up Silom Road, under the massive Rama IV overpass, and past the parched, dusty space referred to—with a remarkable show of local optimism—as Lumpini Park.

A white-uniformed doorman wearing a pith helmet waited at the top of the Regent's long, arcing driveway. When the Mercedes glided to a halt, he opened the rear door with a snappy salute, and Eddie stepped out. It all happened so smoothly that Eddie didn't realize until after the car pulled away that no one had yet told him where he was supposed to go.

He strolled between the two ponds covered with floating lilies, entered the Regent's vast lobby, and took a couple of laps around it to see what struck him. He couldn't see anyone he recognized, and no one seemed to be paying the slightest attention to him either, so he sat down in a lounge area and ordered a San Miguel.

Eddie scanned the crowds drifting constantly in and out of the lobby, and finished his beer without seeing anything remotely interesting. When he thought about it, he wasn't even sure what he was looking for. He guessed he was half expecting Marinus Rupert to appear suddenly in a puff of smoke—maybe dressed as Beelzebub and wearing a red suit and carrying a pitchfork. When nothing happened and no one appeared at all—let alone Marinus Rupert in a puff of anything—he waved down a waiter and ordered another San Mig.

"Mr. Dare?" The soft voice came from just over Eddie's shoulder. "The General asks if you would please join him in his private dining room."

When he turned, he saw it was the man who had driven him from the Oriental. Eddie was very impressed that his English had improved so quickly.

"Will you come this way, sir?"

Eddie left his beer and followed the man through the crowd to an elevator manned by a uniformed attendant, who didn't appear to have anything to do except push the lighted buttons for each floor—which he did very competently. The elevator whisked them quietly to the top floor, and the man led Eddie down a long, teak-paneled hallway past several doors, finally stopping at one, knocking softly, and then swinging it open. He gestured for Eddie to enter.

The room was not large, but it was opulently appointed. A walnut dining table set with china, crystal, and crisp linen stood in the middle of the carpeted room. Along one wall, there were several cushy-looking chairs; and in front of two of the others, white-jacketed attendants stood in rigid and respectful silence awaiting instructions. The room's fourth wall was mostly glass, and it looked out on a terrace where two large and comfortable chairs flanked a wicker table on which a bar had been arranged.

The man who, in San Francisco, had called himself Marinus Rupert was standing alone on the terrace. He was near the railing, watching something through a pair of large field glasses, and when he noticed Eddie, he waved him out.

"Are you a racing man, Mr. Dare?" He didn't offer his hand.

"No."

"Ah . . . pity. I love thoroughbred racing more than almost anything."

The man gestured toward a large racetrack that was across the street from the hotel. Eddie saw that the grandstand was packed; a mob of Thais jammed along the white railings that separated the raw concrete of the public areas from the expensively-watered, unnaturally green oval of the grass track. The sound of the crowd drifted to the terrace through the humid afternoon air, and Eddie could see the bright silks of the jockeys as they maneuvered their mounts onto the track for the next race.

The man nodded toward the bar. "Anyway. Drink?"

"Just beer, thanks."

An attendant who had followed Eddie outside stepped forward and slowly filled a tall glass with San Miguel.

"That's the real stuff. From the Philippines. Not that shit they make in Hong Kong, like you were drinking downstairs."

Eddie raised his eyebrows, sipped at his allegedly genuine San Mig, and settled himself into one of the big chairs.

"Calling you Mr. Rupert seems a little awkward."

"Why is that?"

"You've already told me that's not your name."

"Just General will do then, if you like."

117

The man returned to studying the track through his glasses.
"And are you a general?"

The man lifted his right hand without taking his eyes away from the field glasses, and wiggled it in a gesture that could have meant anything.

"On whose side?"

The General lowered the glasses and smiled at that.

"On *my* side, Eddie."

There was a sudden roar from across the street as a race went off, and the General lifted the field glasses again to watch it. Eddie stayed where he was, and when the race was over, the General settled into the other chair and looked intently at him.

"You don't have much to say."

Eddie lifted his right hand and wriggled it in a close approximation of the General's own gesture.

The General laughed. "Fair enough, Eddie. I'm all yours. Ask me anything you like."

"I want to know who you are and what this is all about."

The General nodded thoughtfully a couple of times and then cleared his throat. "It's about this. I want you to find out for me what Captain Harry Austin did with the 400 million dollars he smuggled out of Saigon in 1975."

"Austin's dead. I already told you that."

"All the more reason why I need your help, Eddie. Harry Austin may indeed be dead, but—as they say—he certainly didn't take it with him."

Eddie watched the gray clouds dancing off in the distance and decided that the rains were coming soon, as they often did in the afternoons in the tropics.

"You understand that this is all a little hard to take seriously."

"Yes, of course. That's why I had my solicitors bring you the wire transfer order today—100,000 dollars—exactly as promised." The General looked at Eddie and dropped his voice a little. "Isn't that serious enough for you?"

"It doesn't change what I told you in San Francisco. I can't help you. I don't know anything about any money, and I never saw Harry Austin after 1975."

"All I ask is that you draw on whatever resources you have to do your usual thorough job of representing a client to the best of your ability, Eddie. No one can ask more of you. I certainly do not."

The General pursed his lips and thought for a moment. "For example, bringing Mr. Jones along on this trip with you shows admirable foresight. I'm sure he'll be very helpful."

"Is there anything you don't know?"

"Not a great deal."

"Except where Austin stashed the money."

"Exactly."

"If he ever had it."

"Oh, he had it. He had it all right. We're sure of that."

"Even though you know Captain Austin's dead, you still think I can find the Voltaire money for you?"

"Absolutely. I don't think there's a better man for the job."

Eddie mulled that over while the General waited patiently. He didn't even have the first idea who this guy was, let alone where to start looking for any 400 million dollars. And that was assuming Austin ever had the Voltaire money in the first place. Then again, what did he really have to lose here? Couldn't he just walk away any time things got sticky and go back to San Francisco?

"I'd have to ask a lot of questions before I agreed to anything."

"I would certainly think so."

Standing abruptly, the General stepped around Eddie's chair and held open the door that led from the terrace back inside to the dining room.

"Shall we have lunch?"

13

Somewhat to Eddie's surprise, the General didn't say another word about Harry Austin, the Bank of Vietnam, or the missing money until after dessert was served and the coffee had been poured.

As Eddie forked his first strawberry, the driver who had escorted him upstairs slipped quietly back into the dining room and ushered the attendants politely outside. It wasn't until the door had closed firmly behind the last of them, that the General began to talk.

"Please listen carefully, Eddie. I want to tell you exactly what happened in Saigon in 1975." The General sounded like a man who was hearing his own voice from somewhere else—like it was coming out of a radio. "Do you remember those shuttle flights from Tan Sun Nhut to U-Tapao Airbase in Thailand; the ones they were running every few hours right up until Saigon went down the crapper?"

Eddie nodded and the General went on.

"You and your squad were on one of those flights two days before you were shifted to guard duty at the embassy. You did escort duty for a shipment of embassy archives. Remember?"

"Sure," Eddie nodded. "When we got to U-Tapao, we turned the whole load over to the Air America guys."

"And after that . . ." the General prompted.

Eddie tried to remember.

"I think we went straight back on the next . . ." He stopped and reached back to a time more than twenty years before. "No, the guys wanted to go to Pattaya and get laid instead of sleeping at the base, but Austin came up with a van somewhere and insisted we all drive to Bangkok."

"Go on."

"That was about it. We all got pretty much wiped out in Patpong and slept wherever we could find a spot that hadn't been puked on. Nothing special happened."

"I meant the following day."

"We drove back to U-Tapao the next morning and took the first Saigon shuttle. Then. . . ," Eddie reached back again, ". . . we were transported to the embassy and turned right around again to ride shotgun on another convoy out to Tan Sun Nhut. I think it was the last one before the airport was closed."

"Then you went back to the embassy again?"

"No, Austin sent us . . ."

The General's face relaxed into something that was almost a smile, and his eyebrows started to ease up.

"That was it, wasn't it?" Eddie was beginning to see how this was coming together. "It was that warehouse Austin sent us to after we left Tan Sun Nhut. The Operation Voltaire money was there."

"I never mentioned the name Operation Voltaire to you."

"No, but the Secret Service did. That *was* it, wasn't it? That's when we had the money."

The General seemed to think about it for a moment, and then he spoke very softly.

"Not exactly. There were crates in the basement of that warehouse Austin sent you to—you're right about that—but the currency and the gold from the Bank of Vietnam wasn't in them. The crates you were guarding were just decoys."

Okay, so I'm not beginning to see how this is coming together.

"The crates containing the money and the gold had been in the warehouse all right, but they'd already been taken out before you got there."

"And of course, you don't know how the real crates got out of the warehouse or where they went."

"Oh, yes." The General smiled. "I know *exactly* how they got out—and even, to a point, where they went."

Eddie said nothing. He waited, tilting his head back and closing his eyes.

"They were all in the load you flew to U-Tapao the day before. They were the crates marked as embassy archives."

Eddie opened his eyes. He should have seen it coming, but he hadn't.

"Only two people knew that," the General continued in the same crisp tone. "A CIA guy named Sterling—and Harry Austin. Even the ambassador didn't know. Sterling was afraid that the South Vietnamese would stop him if anybody knew he was moving the money."

The General's left hand went off on a little expedition of its own, made a fist, and knocked twice against the dining table.

"You used two planes. Remember? Sterling was in the first, and you and your squad were with Austin in the second. Sterling only took a few crates on his plane so he could make secure storage arrangements in Thailand. Austin had most of the money in the plane you were on."

Then something came back to Eddie, distantly.

"Sterling never made it to U-Tapao, did he?"

The General sat looking at Eddie, as placid as a Buddhist monk.

"His plane went down in the Gulf of Thailand. There were no survivors."

"That's right, Eddie. That's exactly right. When Harry Austin landed at U-Tapao and found out Sterling's plane had crashed, he just arranged for Air America to store the crates you were carrying and didn't tell anyone what was in them."

"Well," Eddie offered the benediction in a respectful tone. "Son of a bitch."

He briefly glanced away, letting everything settle, then he looked back at the General.

"That's why Captain Austin chose to stay in Thailand after the evacuation instead of rotating back to the States with the rest of us, wasn't it? Because he knew where the money was, and nobody else did."

The nod of the General's head was barely visible.

"How did he get it out of U-Tapao?"

The General shifted in his chair, pursing his lips.

"It wasn't hard. He commandeered a big truck, got some guys to load up the crates, waved some pieces of paper, and drove out the gate."

"You mean Captain Austin just loaded up a truck and drove away? With *ten tons* of money?"

"Yeah. That was about it. The evacuation from Saigon had turned the base into chaos. Nobody gave a rat's ass about paperwork."

The General took a cigar from his inside jacket pocket. A cutter and some matches lay on the table, and he busied himself clipping and lighting the cigar without looking at Eddie.

"I want you to find that money for me, Eddie. None of it was ever accounted for. None of it. Austin still had most of it hidden somewhere when he died. We're sure of it."

"Now I understand why you're willing to pay me the hundred grand."

"No, Eddie, I doubt you do." The General consulted the ash that was forming at the tip of his cigar. "I paid you 100,000 dollars purely to ensure that you'd come to Bangkok. I wanted to make certain you understood that I'm an honorable man who meets his commitments."

The General let a small silence fall, clearly meaning for it to feel significant to Eddie.

"If you can find out where Austin hid the money, you'll receive the full one million dollar bonus we spoke of in San Francisco. All of it."

Eddie took a deep breath and considered that in silence while the General puffed contentedly at his cigar.

"You're telling me that Harry Austin just loaded up a truck and drove away with all the gold and currency from the Bank of Vietnam?" It was an unnecessary question and the General didn't bother to answer. "You're telling me he stole the entire contents of the Bank of Vietnam, and now you want me to find it for you."

The General drew on his cigar, inhaling a tiny portion of the smoke, and then he exhaled slowly and deliberately.

"Harry Austin didn't steal anything."

"Oh, they *gave* all that money to him?"

The General didn't bother to respond.

"If you say he didn't steal it, what would you call it?"

"It was abandoned property. I think 'salvaged' is probably the correct term."

"Give me a break," Eddie snorted. "Austin stole it."

Eddie's concerns didn't appear to worry the General, but when he spoke again, Eddie thought that the words came more quickly than they had before.

"Let me walk you through this. Let's just say you're in Saigon in April of 1975. The city is falling apart right in front of you. Panicked mobs control the streets; overloaded Jolly Greens are pounding out of LZs all over town, even snatching people off rooftops; the communists are shelling Tan Sun Nhut; and their ground troops are less than five miles from where you stand. Let's also say you control the security arrangements for all the Bank of Vietnam's cash reserves, *and* have the means to get them out of the country immediately. What would you do?"

"I'd send them somewhere like I was supposed to. I wouldn't take them. The money belonged to the Vietnamese government. "

"The Vietnamese government?" The General drew on his cigar again. "Which Vietnamese government would that have been, exactly?"

"The South Vietnamese government of course."

"But South Vietnam effectively ceased to exist before you ever touched the money."

Eddie could see without much difficulty where all this was going.

"Then I'd have just gotten the money out and let the State Department or someone else straighten it all out."

"You'd have turned the South Vietnamese money over to the United States government?" The General raised an eyebrow thoughtfully. "And if you *had*, what do you suppose they would have done? Maybe give it back to the Vietnamese, who were now of course the *North* Vietnamese?"

"No, of course not."

"Then what do you think they would've done with it?"

"Probably just kept it."

The General nodded a few more times, almost as if he was thinking everything through for the first time himself.

"Did that money belong to the United States government?

"No."

"But you concede they would have just kept it anyway—although they plainly had no right to it."

Eddie didn't say anything.

The General nodded a couple of times anyway—exactly as if Eddie had answered—suggesting that he was in collegial agreement with whatever it had been. Then he rose and started toward the terrace.

Passing behind Eddie, he stopped and leaned over until his lips were right next to Eddie's ear. Eddie could smell the flakes of heavy tobacco clinging to them.

"Then why the *fuck* would you just give it to them?" he hissed.

The General straightened up, took another puff on his cigar, and strolled outside.

Eddie could hear the crowd from the race track roar for a moment as the door to the terrace swung open, and then when it closed again, the roar was gone.

14

Eddie called the *Post* as soon as he got back to the hotel, but Bar Phillips wasn't there and no one seemed to know when he might be.

That didn't surprise Eddie—not from what he remembered about Bar—so he just left a message. The rest of the afternoon, Eddie and Winnebago lay around the pool at the Oriental, dozing away their jet lag in the sun, and letting the pool boys bring them brightly-colored drinks with tiny, purple and white orchids floating in them.

Eddie spent the time wondering what to do about the General's pitch on the Voltaire money. Winnebago shrugged off the whole thing as none of his concern and invested his afternoon in chain smoking Camels and ogling three busty Scandinavian tourists in string bikinis who were ogling the pool boys. The pool boys kept the drinks coming, and ogled each other.

Shortly after nine that night, Eddie's call not having been returned, they left the Oriental to take another shot at finding Bar Phillips. Sprinting across New Road through a break in the traffic, they walked up Silom, heading for the center of town. Although it had been dark for almost three hours, the heat and humidity still smothered the city. Eddie could feel the night all over him; a heavy, liquid thing that pressed against his body from every direction at once. Pools of sweat formed in his hair and began dripping down his neck before they had gone more than a couple of blocks.

The street around them pulsed with life. It was all sound and smell—the sizzling of cooking fires; drifting clouds of bus exhaust; pirated cassette tapes pounding from loudspeakers on a street vendor's cart; and the mingling odors of hundreds of slowly shuffling bodies.

They turned down a broken-up sidewalk and edged their way through the narrow opening between the vendors crowding both sides of it. The ranks of carts faced each other like two tiny freight trains stuck on parallel sidings—each loaded down with fake Rolexes, home-made copies of video cassettes, plastic Louis Vuitton luggage, T-shirts, belts, socks, and stuffed animals. There was food, too—sliced fruit, rice wrapped in banana leaves, bits of grilled chicken on wooden sticks, and other things that neither Eddie nor Winnebago recognized.

A sea of people swirled around them. Street-hardened touts, school children in blue and white uniforms, sweating tourists, office workers in suits, saggy-faced drunks, chubby Chinese housewives, and *farangs* with embarrassed grins and half-naked teenage girls hanging off their arms. No one looked worried about being mugged. No one pushed or shoved. The crowd bubbled and throbbed with an internal rhythm that was both graceful and amicable.

Some neon tubing dangling from a T-shirt vendor's cart caught Eddie's attention, and he traced the patterns it threw against the mirrored surfaces of a sleek office tower. Nearby, a street vendor swirled a huge wok filled with roasting chestnuts over a charcoal fire built right on the sidewalk. It might be almost the twenty-first century for everyone else, Eddie mused, but Bangkok didn't seem entirely sold on the concept.

It was a loud, smelly, sweaty mess. Still, there was something about it that cast a kind of spell over Eddie. The sounds, the odors, and the heat all combined to brew up a kind of magic potion; one that left him feeling a little drunk, overwhelmed, and staggering in a swirl of possibilities.

Somehow, in a way Eddie couldn't really understand, it all came together to make him feel strangely innocent and young again. It even—he had to honestly admit—gave him something like half a hard-on. But then everyone got wised up in Bangkok eventually, he figured, even when they were half hard; and he doubted that anyone stayed young there for very long.

"Where we going, Eddie?"

"The Pong. It's just up ahead, I think." Eddie pointed over the crowds, further along Silom Road.

The Pong was what the American soldiers on R&R in Bangkok during the sixties and seventies had christened Soi Patpong, undoubtedly the most famous street in Bangkok. Patpong had been little more than a narrow, bumpy alley that ran for a couple of hundred yards between Silom and Suriwong Road—until somebody opened a tiny bar there, and hired young Thai girls to go-go dance to American rock and roll. Within weeks there were fifty bars just like it up and down the street, all wall-to-wall with lithe, beautiful girls. None of them were very good dancers, but they wore very small bikinis and very high-heeled shoes, so nobody cared much.

In the eighties and nineties, however, it had all gone way downhill for the Pong. The American military went home, and left nothing behind but a motley band of sad and bedraggled misfits—burned-out Peace Corp types, drunken old Air America pilots, glue sniffers, thinner addicts, left-over hippies trying to score cheap dope, and hordes of German and Scandinavian tourists in baggy shorts, leather sandals and nylon socks. The Pong had a slightly wistful air about it now, Eddie thought; a sense of time having passed too quickly, and for too small a purpose.

"Is this a joke or something, Eddie?"

Eddie glanced over his shoulder. Winnebago had stopped in front of a Chinese restaurant and was reading some menu pages that had been xeroxed and stuck to the inside of the front window.

"I mean, do they really eat this stuff? Fried chicken knuckles? Chicken feet salad? Fish sauce? What the fuck is fish sauce? You squeeze the fish and the shit that comes out of it is sauce? You think maybe that's fish sauce?"

Winnebago read on.

"Oh, man, I don't believe it. *Sliced bull's penis?*"

"The Chinese believe it's good for your virility."

"It didn't do much for the poor, fuckin' bull's, did it?" Winnebago muttered, shaking his head.

❍❍❍

The man following Eddie and Winnebago was caught out in the open because they walked away from the restaurant so quickly.

He scrambled back into the crowd—suddenly conspicuous—and then watched from the shadows as Eddie grabbed Winnebago's elbow and pointed up Silom. It looked as if Eddie was pointing a long way up, so the man doubted it had anything to do with him. But then Winnebago nodded vigorously and they began walking straight toward him.

He looked around quickly for some place to duck out of their way. This part of Silom Road was a canyon of darkened office towers, none offering much promise to a man seeking to blend unnoticed into the background—so he took a chance. He stepped off the sidewalk and, while pretending to search for a taxi, examined his prospects further up the road

He was relieved to spot a 7-Eleven almost immediately. It was just a few doors past the next cross-street, and its façade glistened so whitely among the other dim, gray buildings lining Silom that it almost hurt his eyes.

The man lowered his head, stepped back onto the sidewalk, and made for the 7-Eleven at what he hoped was an inconspicuous pace. Once there, he slipped inside and pretended to browse the shelves while he kept an eye on the street through the big window at the front. Sure enough, as he lingered over a display of flashlight batteries, he saw Eddie and Winnebago walk past.

He edged carefully back outside to see where they were going. By the time they had covered another fifty yards, he had worked it out.

Popeye's Fried Chicken appeared to Eddie out of the Bangkok night like a hallucination. It was outlined with tubes of neon—red, blue and yellow streaks of color—and the light from the spotless dining room flooded out onto the Silom sidewalk through a glittering curtain of glass.

Several dozen people, mostly *farangs*, sat scattered among its fifty or more red, plastic-topped tables, benignly watched over by a six-foot effigy of the man himself; yellow corncob pipe clinched in his teeth and a sailor cap cocked rakishly on his head.

After they spotted Popeye's, Eddie and Winnebago quickly hit a half dozen of the bigger go-go bars in Patpong. Eddie put some cash around among the waitresses and bartenders, and accompanied it with a promise of more for anyone who sent Bar Phillips to meet them at Popeye's within the next hour. Crossing back over Silom, they grabbed a table and loaded it down with food.

"This is a hell of a lot more like it." Winnebago bit into a greasy drumstick. "I'm still so fucked up from the flight I could eat a horse."

"I can arrange that."

Winnebago gave Eddie a dead-eyed stare and changed the subject. "What are you going to do if you find this newspaper guy?"

"Ask him what he knows about Captain Austin. Bar's probably met every Westerner in Bangkok at one time or another. Maybe he can tell us what the captain was doing here. At least that would give us a place to start."

"So you're going to do it? To look for the money for this general guy?"

"I don't know." Eddie poked a french fry into a smear of catsup. "I figure we're here and he's paying for it. It couldn't hurt to ask around a little."

"You're going to tell a *reporter* what you're doing?

Eddie tilted his head toward Winnebago and raised his eyebrows.

"I didn't think you were completely stupid." Winnebago tossed a chicken bone onto a paper plate and grabbed a fresh piece. "Then what *are* you going to tell him?"

"I'm just going to say that Harry Austin's family hired me to find out what really happened to him. I think that ought to fly."

"Is this reporter some big buddy of yours?"

"No, not really. I met him when I was down here on a case once for the Bank of America. He wrote a magazine piece about some dentists from San Diego who ripped off the bank and spent the money building a porno movie studio in Bangkok. It was great human interest stuff."

Winnebago gave Eddie another long look, but he ignored it and went on.

"Anyway, he's a smart guy—tough and mean as hell—and as far as I know he's fairly honest. At least for a reporter."

"If he's not a buddy, why would he go to any trouble to help you find out about Austin?"

"I doubt it'll be any trouble. Bar can probably tell us what Austin was doing and who he hung out with right off the top of his head."

"And if he can't?"

"I'll offer him 10,000 dollars to find out."

Winnebago chewed pensively at the bone of his third drumstick while he examined a man standing out on the sidewalk who appeared to be eyeing the crowd inside Popeye's. If it was Bar Phillips, he figured they were in real trouble.

The guy looked to Winnebago like some geezer from a Tallahassee retirement home who had fled to Bangkok to draw his final breaths in—mostly imagined—debauchery. He must have been at least sixty, and wore a black shirt and pants, white belt and shoes, and a bicycle helmet with a skull and cross-bones stenciled on the front. Maybe he wasn't really sixty, it occurred to Winnebago. Maybe he was closer to thirty and Bangkok just did that kind of thing to you.

Then Bar Phillips did something that put an end to Winnebago's speculations. He came inside, walked directly to their table, and sat down.

"Hey, man," he greeted Eddie. "I would've known you anywhere. You still look exactly like . . ."

"Don't start," Eddie interrupted.

"*This* is the guy?" Winnebago asked, cutting his eyes back and forth between Bar and Eddie.

Eddie nodded.

"You got a problem of some kind, friend?" Bar glanced at Winnebago without moving his head.

"I was just wondering what the helmet was for."

"You haven't been in town very long, have you?"

Winnebago rolled his eyes and went back to his fried chicken.

"So." Eddie looked Bar over. "I see you're still writing for the *Post*."

"Yeah." Bar leaned forward and helped himself to a large cup of Pepsi sitting in front of Eddie, sloshing it around slightly to make sure it wasn't empty. "You mind?" he asked, holding it up. "It's hotter than hell out there tonight."

"I saw your column in a paper back at the hotel," Winnebago spoke up.

"You liked it, huh?"

"I said I saw it."

Bar finished the Pepsi and returned the cup to the table. "Okay, so much for the small talk. Was that you asking around the Crown Royal for me last night?"

"Yeah," Eddie answered.

"And tonight you've been waving money around and leaving messages for me all over the Pong?"

"Uh-huh."

"Jesus, man. Subtlety still counts for something. Even in Bangkok."

"I'm looking for someone who used to live here and I need your help."

"Who is it?"

"A guy I served under in the marines. Harry Austin."

"Never heard of him. You say he used to live here?"

"That's right."

"He's left Bangkok now?"

"He's left everywhere now. He's dead."

While Bar went back to playing with the empty Pepsi cup, Eddie told him about the newspaper clipping, and ad-libbed a story about Austin's family hiring him to find out what had really happened—which he thought sounded pretty good, even if he did say so himself.

"You got a picture of this guy?"

Eddie pulled a copy of the clipping out of his shirt pocket, unfolded it, and put it on the table.

Bar glanced at the photograph, and Eddie noticed he didn't flinch at the blood.

"Don't know him. He was probably never here or I would."

"He was here all right, for a while at least. I don't know exactly how long."

Bar gave a shrug and Eddie thought he seemed to be losing interest in the conversation.

So Eddie brought up the 10,000 dollars.

"Let me get this straight. You're going to give me 10,000 bucks just to help you find out about some clown who got himself run over somewhere in Bangkok?" Bar didn't even try to keep the skepticism out of his voice.

"Uh-huh."

"You going to tell me the rest of it now? Or do I have to wait a while?"

"There's nothing else. You know everything I know."

"Bullshit." Bar said it without inflection, like a man counting trees. "If that was all there was to it, you wouldn't have some guy outside following your ass around town."

"There's someone following us?" Winnebago quickly put down the last of his chicken.

"Looks that way."

"How do you know?"

Bar gave him a tried look. "This guy has his eyes locked on you and Eddie like you were two naked girls doing the dirty. He's pretty hard to miss."

Eddie glanced involuntarily toward the door, although he didn't really expect to see anything. "What's he look like?"

"Fat, obvious, and clumsy."

"A cop?"

"Not that fat." Bar smiled slightly. "Besides, he's a white guy. There're no white cops in Bangkok."

"A fed? The FBI or something like that?"

"Maybe. I'd guess CIA, but in Bangkok you always guess CIA."

"*CIA?*" Winnebago couldn't believe what he was hearing. "You think the fuckin' *CIA* is following us?"

"Could be." Bar's voice was gratingly cheerful. "Now, you want to tell me the whole story, or should I just head on back across the street where the naked girls are?"

Eddie toyed with a white plastic spoon, twirling it between his fingers. He didn't want to tell Bar Phillips any more than he had to—he didn't know the guy that well—but he figured the chances of going it alone in a strange city were getting lousier by the minute. Maybe he'd give Bar a little more. A little more, but certainly not all of it.

Bar listened carefully while Eddie told him about the pictures with the red circles, his visit from the man who called himself Marinus Rupert, and his lunch at the Regent with the same man, now calling himself the General.

But Eddie gently eased past the part about the 400 million dollars. After all, someone could have a lot of other reasons for wanting to find out about Harry Austin, couldn't they?

"That's it," he finished, catching Winnebago's eye. "Whoever this guy really is, he's paying me to find out what happened to Austin."

"Why you?"

"I guess it's because I used to know him. Apparently he thinks that's an advantage."

"You have no idea at all who this guy is?"

"No, none."

"You think the pictures were some kind of threat?"

Eddie nodded.

"Threatening you about . . . what exactly?"

"About trying to find out about Captain Austin, I guess. What else could they mean?"

"No idea who sent them to you?"

Eddie shook his head.

"We could go and ask the guy waiting outside," Winnebago suggested. "Maybe it was him."

"Nah." Bar looked off toward Silom Road out beyond Popeye's front windows. "Nobody subtle enough to pull that picture gag would do such a stinking job of tailing you."

"Military records are easy enough to get," Eddie suggested. "A lot of people could've tied us to Austin. But I still can't figure out what anyone thinks the two of us know that makes us worth threatening."

"Three," Bar said quietly.

Winnebago looked puzzled.

"Three of you," Bar repeated. "Not two. Both your heads were circled in the pictures, you said. And then there's Austin."

"Yeah, but he's dead," Winnebago said.

Bar nodded slowly. "My point exactly."

That brought a very long silence all around.

"This guy who's calling himself a general has got to know more than he's told you," Bar finally said, breaking it. "There's something else. He knows what he's really looking for, even if he hasn't told you."

"He doesn't know Austin's dead." Eddie tapped his fingers on the table.

"Yeah." Bar leaned back in his chair. "I don't get it."

"So, can I count on your help?"

Bar turned his head away and looked out the big windows toward Silom Road.

"I need to know," Eddie pressed.

"Let me think about it." Bar flicked his eyes sideways for a moment and then back to Eddie. "It looks to me like you boys may be about to step on your dicks here, and 10,000 dollars isn't really enough to get me to risk mine."

"You mean you want more money?"

"No, man, that's not what I mean." Bar's face relaxed into something that was almost, but not quite, a smile. "Just let me think about it for a couple of days. I'll call you."

"Would you tell me a couple of things before you go?"

"Sure."

"How can I find out what happened to Austin's body?"

Bar reached out and picked up the newspaper clipping that still lay on the table, studying it silently for a moment. "If he was killed where this says, it was in the Thonglor police district. Any cab driver can find the Thonglor station. Go over there tomorrow and ask for Lieutenant Sirapop. Tell him I sent you and he'll probably be reasonably helpful."

"Does he speak English?"

"Enough. Just don't try to discuss Spinoza with him." Bar thought a moment and then added, "There's one other thing. You'd better understand how things are done here if you're going to fuck around with the local cops." He lifted his eyebrows at Eddie, making a question out of it.

"You're telling me he's dirty and that information will cost me."

"They're all dirty, but Sirapop's pretty harmless as these guys usually go. He might help you out just because I sent you around, but if you don't give him 5,000 baht or so, he'll lose face. And if he loses face, I lose face. Give him the 5,000."

"Okay," Eddie nodded.

"So what's the other thing?" Bar asked.

Eddie shot a quick glance at the blackness outside the big plate glass windows, wondering again exactly who was waiting for them out there.

"You think this place has a back door?"

"Shit, man." Bar grinned. "The whole goddamned world's got a back door."

15

When Winnebago woke up, he could have sworn he had the echo of a loud explosion rattling around in his head, but other than the low hum of the room's air conditioner, he could hear nothing at all. He decided that he must have dreamed the explosion, and so he just lay there in bed wondering what time it was, and trying to sort through everything that had happened the night before, when they slipped out the back door at Popeye's.

He and Eddie had wandered around the Pong for several hours before coming back to the Oriental; that much he remembered clearly. He was also pretty sure they had dumped the guy who was supposed to be following them, but he wasn't certain. Actually, he didn't know why it mattered. Anyone following them would surely know where they were staying. Besides, all he and Eddie had done was go to a couple of bars in the Pong, put away a few drinks—quite a few, he winced as he felt his stomach pitch up—and fooled around a little with the girls. He couldn't imagine who'd care very much about two guys doing nothing more than that.

The first place they went to had been pretty raw, Winnebago recalled now that his head was starting to clear a little; so much so that it had made him uncomfortable, or something close to it.

When he and Eddie pushed through the heavy curtain hanging over the doorway, a pleasant young man in a white shirt and tie had quickly seated them on stools at the bar and gotten them bottles of Singha beer. On a narrow, raised runway just behind the bartender, there were a dozen or more girls dancing to ear-splitting disco music. They all looked pretty young to Winnebago—mostly teens and early twenties, with maybe one or two who might have been thirty—and in spite of the lethargic way they were shuffling their feet in no readily discernible relationship to the music, they all seemed to be having a good enough time. The whole bunch of them were smiling, giggling and touching, chattering away to each other like girlfriends out together for an afternoon at the mall.

It embarrassed Winnebago a little that that he and Eddie were looking up at the girls from such a sharp angle that he could have seen right up their skirts—that is, he could have if they'd been wearing any. Of course, since they were all completely naked—except for shoes that ranged from gleaming red stilettos to towering platforms worn with schoolgirl knee-socks—he'd decided that worrying about whether his view offended the girls' sense of modesty was pretty much a waste of effort.

They were good-looking girls, mostly, but it had never crossed his mind before that having a bunch of naked women wiggling around right in front of him could be so monotonous. There he was, so close to their most private parts he could have given them a pelvic with a swizzle stick, and he was half yawning himself to sleep.

Winnebago rolled his head around to confirm that it was still attached to his neck. Maybe he really *was* getting old. Finding himself first embarrassed and then finally bored witless by a room full of naked young girls—not to mention getting completely wasted on only a few drinks—was not an encouraging sign.

He was slowly raising his wrist to check his watch when a fusillade of noise crashed into the room. Winnebago started to duck until he realized it was only thunder, and it was probably what had waked him in the first place. It sounded like Bangkok was about to get hammered by one of those rainstorms that he remembered so well from Vietnam; the kind that hurled down sheets of water and lightning until you felt helpless, and you just sat very still until it stopped.

He was trying again to read his watch, hoping its face would swim into focus, when he realized that there was another sound in the room; something other than the dying echoes of the thunder. It was a tapping noise, and—after a moment of intense concentration—he finally identified it positively as a persistent knocking on his bedroom door. He called out something that he gathered was intelligible because the tapping stopped. Slowly sitting up on the edge of the bed, he collected his wits. When he finally made it across the room and got the door open, Eddie stepped inside and closed it behind him.

"Are you alone?" Eddie's eyes worked their way quickly around the room, finally coming to rest on Winnebago, whom he regarded dubiously for a moment. "You look like shit."

Winnebago was certain that under other circumstances he could have said something that would have been heart-stoppingly funny—but a sort of grunt was the best he could manage right then. He took a couple of faltering steps and sat back down heavily on the edge of his rumpled bed.

"What time is it?"

"A little after nine."

"Why are you here, man?" Winnebago shook his head, willing it to feel smaller.

"To wake you up."

"But didn't we just go to bed?"

"I got one of the girls at the front desk to call that police station. This Lieutenant Serpico . . ."

"Sirapop," Winnebago corrected Eddie, startling himself with his clear recall of what Bar Phillips had said the night before.

"Right. Anyway, this guy's supposed to be coming in at ten, and I want us to go over there and catch him before he leaves again."

Winnebago tried to absorb that. "Over where?" he finally managed to ask.

"Thonglor police station. The girl downstairs said it wasn't far. I'm going back to my room to make a call while you get yourself together. We'll grab breakfast somewhere on the way." Eddie took another close look at Winnebago. "You really do look like shit. How much did you drink last night?"

Winnebago didn't bother to answer. Pushing himself reluctantly off the bed, he tossed off a salute and stumbled away in the general direction of where he thought the shower was.

Eddie went back to his own bedroom and tried to work out the time difference between Bangkok and the West Coast while he dialed.

Making calls across the International Date Line still left him feeling muddled no matter how many times he did it. He was reasonably certain this time that he had it; that nine o'clock on Monday morning in Bangkok was six o'clock the previous Sunday afternoon on the West Coast. If he was wrong and it was really four in the morning or something like that, he was confident Jennifer would tell him all about it as soon as she answered.

"Hello."

Eddie was mildly surprised when Michael picked up the phone instead of Jennifer, but he wasn't sure why he should have been.

"Hey, Mike."

"Dad?"

"Yeah. How are you?"

"Okay."

Michael didn't say anything else, and they both sat and listened together to the hum of the international connection for a moment.

"This line sounds funny. Where are you?" Michael finally asked.

"I'm in Bangkok."

Eddie wondered what Michael's reaction to that would be.

"Oh."

That's it? Your father tells you he's calling from some unimaginably exotic city halfway around the world and all you can say is, 'Oh'?

"Listen, Dad. Could you talk to Mom? She's messing me around about my allowance again."

Eddie lifted the telephone away from his ear and let it sag slightly. Who was this person he was talking to? If this was really his son—and he had always lived by the assumption that Michael was indeed, even if he sometimes wondered how that might be—how could he have so little interest in his father that he wouldn't even bother to ask what he was doing in Bangkok? Was life in Seattle so endlessly fascinating that his father being in Bangkok seemed perhaps, by comparison, commonplace?

"In a second, Mike. I just called to tell you about Bangkok." Eddie juiced himself up a little and tried to add the right note of between-us-guys to his voice. "This is a really weird place. You've never seen anything like it."

"That's cool, Dad, but would you talk to Mom now. I gotta, like, go out pretty soon and I need my money."

And with that Eddie heard the telephone receiver go clattering onto a tabletop.

Okay, so much for the father-son crap.

He fidgeted for what felt like a minute or more, waiting for Jennifer to pick up. Feeling defeated and subdued from Mike's complete disinterest in him, he'd just decided to hang up when a male voice came on the line.

"Eddie, it's Franklin. Jennifer can't come to the phone right now. Could she call you back?"

"I'm calling from Bangkok, Franklin."

"Where?"

"Bangkok."

"Oh . . ." He seemed to think about that. "Then maybe you should call her back, huh?"

"Fine, Franklin. Tell her I'll do that." Eddie hung up quickly, before he said anything he might be sorry for later, and leaned back in the chair.

Man, oh man. Is that it?

Michael was his son and Jennifer was . . . well, she was his ex-wife of course, and married to someone else now, but Eddie still thought of Jennifer and Michael as his family anyway, since it was the only one he had. On the other hand, maybe the time had come to rethink that. If *that* was the extent of his family's interest in him, maybe he had things all wrong.

With a long sigh, Eddie pushed himself to his feet.

Of course he had things all wrong. Jennifer and Michael both had new lives now, and he wasn't a part of either of them. He was an ex-husband—twice, he reluctantly reminded himself—and now it looked like he might be well on his way to becoming an ex-father, too.

He had gone into the bedroom with some vague idea that he was calling home; not that anyone else apparently thought of it that way. When was he going to stop being so surprised about that? Clearly his whole concept of 'home' required fundamental reappraisal.

With a shake of his head, he jammed his hands in his pockets and went out to the living room to wait for Winnebago.

16

The Thonglor police station was on Soi 55, out off Sukhumvit Road past the Sheraton Hotel. On the way from the Oriental, Winnebago spotted a McDonald's just opening up, and Eddie waved the taxi driver to a stop.

Splashing through the rain that had been falling steadily all morning, he and Winnebago ran inside and had some surprisingly passable coffee and a couple of Big Macs. Winnebago bought a second round and carried it back outside where they flagged down another cab. Eddie gathered Winnebago was slowly returning to a state that was reasonably close to normal—at least for Winnebago.

"I didn't remember that these were so good," Winnebago said, wiping a bit of mayonnaise from the corner of his mouth.

"Don't get carried away. You're probably still in shock from last night."

"Damn, man." Winnebago shook his head, thinking back. "Too much of that shit could put you off pussy forever, couldn't it?"

By the time they stopped and their driver pointed out a nondescript, two-story building composed primarily of cracked, gray concrete, the rain had slowed to a drizzle. They got out and paid off the taxi.

Eddie put a hand on Winnebago's arm. "Let's double check how this conversation's going to go before we head inside. I want to make sure we've got our stories straight."

"It'll go like always, won't it? You'll do all the talking and I'll keep my mouth shut."

"That's pretty much what I had in mind."

"What do you think this cop's going to tell you anyway?"

"Maybe nothing. But if someone identified Austin's body or claimed it for burial—and he'll give us a name—we'll have a place to start digging around."

"You really think he's going to do that?"

"I don't know, but whatever he says, just keep smiling. Being a hardass doesn't play well with Thais. Smile even if it's killing you. Got that?"

Winnebago made a noise of some kind, but Eddie wasn't sure what it meant.

Inside the station, three scarred, wooden desks were scattered around in no apparent order. In one corner, a bored-looking young policeman sat pecking slowly at an old, manual typewriter, one key at a time. A second cop—leaning against the wall across the room—read a newspaper with one hand, while the other rested on the wooden grips of a .45 automatic riding high up on his hip in a black holster with no safety strap. Both men wore their brown uniforms stretched over their bodies as tightly as spandex. The color of the fabric reminded Eddie of the inside of a baby's diaper.

As the two cops registered Eddie and Winnebago's presence, they shifted dark eyes in their direction and regarded them both with a degree of curiosity. The appearance of two *farangs* in the Thonglor police station—on a purely voluntary basis at least—was unusual.

"I'm looking for Lieutenant Sirapop." Eddie smiled, taking his own advice.

Neither policeman moved or gave any hint that they knew Eddie had spoken.

"Lieutenant Sirapop?" Eddie repeated slowly.

"Why you want him?" the cop with the newspaper asked in a toneless voice.

"I have some questions for him. Bar Phillips told me to see him. Lieutenant Sirapop is a friend of his."

The sound of a throat being cleared drifted from an open door to their left, and shortly a voice followed it. "I know him—yes—but 'a friend'? Not so sure."

The two policemen returned instantly to what they'd been doing before—as if Eddie and Winnebago had suddenly ceased to exist.

"Who are you?" the voice continued.

"My name is Eddie Dare. I need some information about an accident that happened near here."

"Information?" The voice toyed with the word as if it was entirely novel, suggesting delights heretofore unimagined.

"Look, may we come into your office?" Eddie was still smiling, but he felt ridiculous talking to a disembodied voice.

"We?"

"I have a friend with me. Mr. Jones."

Winnebago raised his right hand to shoulder level and gave the room at large a little wave. Neither of the policemen paid any attention.

"I'm very busy." There was a short silence before the voice came again. "Okay, okay. Quick, quick."

The first thing Eddie noticed when they entered the office was the posture of the man in the chair behind the plain, metal desk. It was a slump that made his attitude unmistakable—although whether it was an attitude about *farangs* in particular, or about the world in general, Eddie couldn't guess.

The man's face was long and narrow for a Thai, with a nose that looked like it had been broken several times. He wore the same tight, brown uniform that the other two cops did, but his version was embellished with a white plastic Sam Browne belt.

"Lieutenant Sirapop?"

His nod was barely visible.

Eddie looked the man over carefully. He was very short, probably not much over five feet tall—although Eddie couldn't tell exactly, since he hadn't bothered to stand when they came in—and he wore heavy sunglasses in spite of being indoors. They were so dark, he looked like a tiny, blind man.

Still smiling, Eddie nudged the office door closed behind him, and he and Winnebago sat down in the two straight chairs that faced the desk.

Eddie pulled a stack of 500-baht notes from his trouser pocket and fanned ten of the purple bills onto the desk, keeping his hand on them.

"I'm very grateful for your time, Lieutenant, but I'd be even more grateful for some information about a man I knew. Bar Phillips says he thinks you can help me."

The lieutenant's head remained stationary, but Eddie got the impression that his eyes flicked down to the money spread out over the desk—even though he couldn't see them through the dark glasses.

"Who is this man?" the lieutenant asked after a moment, still not moving.

"His name was Harry Austin. He was killed in an accident near here about a month ago."

The lieutenant said nothing for a few seconds. Finally, he pushed back in his chair slightly and folded his arms. "Yes."

"Do you remember the name?"

"Maybe."

So this is how it's going to be.

"I've been hired by this man's family in America to find out about his death," Eddie ad-libbed. "They wonder if the newspaper reports they have seen might not be correct."

"Not correct? How?"

"In calling it an accident."

The lieutenant nodded slightly, and then tilted his head unmistakably toward the stack of notes under Eddie's right hand. Eddie lifted his hand away and folded his arms, mirroring the lieutenant.

"*Aow fam kong farang tee tuk kaa tee Little Princess maa si!*" the lieutenant called out loudly.

The young policeman who'd been typing in the outer office came in so quickly that Eddie wondered for a moment if he'd been waiting right outside the door the whole time. "*I puak nee pen krai?*" he asked the lieutenant as he handed over a thin, green file folder, shooting expressionless looks at both Eddie and Winnebago.

"*Kae farang,*" the lieutenant answered him.

Eddie didn't much like the short, barking laugh the young cop gave as he left the office.

The lieutenant slowly flipped through the file without removing his dark glasses. Eddie wondered if the man could actually see anything that was in it.

"Death certificate here. Say heart stop."

"By accident?" Eddie kept smiling, "Or did somebody stop it for him?"

The lieutenant lifted his head sharply.

"He dead anyway. Why you care?"

Eddie noticed that the man's English seemed to be growing distinctly worse, but he wasn't sure what that meant.

"He killed by truck, I think." The lieutenant seemed to consider for a moment. "Maybe bus. I not remember."

"Then you're saying it *was* an accident."

The lieutenant stabbed with one finger at the open file. "Heart stop."

"Who claimed the body?"

Sirapop consulted the file again. "Friend."

Eddie's patience was running out, but he kept smiling.

"A man or a woman?"

"Man."

"A Thai?"

"No, *farang.*"

"What was his name?"

"This name." The lieutenant pulled out a sheet of paper from the file and pushed it across the table toward Eddie. He leaned forward and pointed with his forefinger at the last line on a page of incomprehensible Thai characters—below which, an illegible signature was scrawled.

Eddie had no real hope of learning anything else, but he figured he'd paid for it, so he tossed out one more question anyway.

"Did you see this friend?"

To Eddie's surprise, the lieutenant nodded, and he felt his hopes rise.

"He come here." Sirapop pointed to the chair where Winnebago—not knowing what else to do—was grinning maniacally. "He sit there."

"What did he look like?"

The lieutenant thought about that for a long time as Eddie studied his own reflection in the man's dark glasses.

"Like you," he eventually said with a shrug. "Like *farang*."

"Young? Old? Tall? Short?"

The lieutenant thought some more.

"Like *farang*," he repeated, and this time Eddie thought he saw a smile flickering around the corners of Sirapop's mouth.

"Where is the body buried?"

"Buried?" The lieutenant seemed genuinely puzzled. "What you mean?"

"Didn't this friend take the body and arrange for burial?" Eddie gestured to the floor, miming a man digging.

"Ah." The lieutenant nodded in understanding. "No . . . bury. Burn. This Thailand. We burn."

"You mean the body was cremated?"

"Cremated. Yes."

The lieutenant stood, and with his right hand, he swept the stack of purple bills off the desk top and into a drawer in one smooth motion. Eddie got the impression that he'd had a lot of practice at it.

"Okay. Finish now. You want any more question you ask Little Princess."

Eddie didn't know whether he was supposed to laugh or not.

"Who's Little Princess?" he asked as he pushed himself to his feet.

"Not who," the lieutenant answered.

He walked around his desk and opened the door for Eddie and Winnebago, encouraging their rapid departure. Winnebago tilted his head toward Eddie and lifted his eyebrows, but he was still smiling.

"Little Princess is massage parlor on Soi 31. Big place. Many room. Many girl. Thai not go, only *farang*." The lieutenant held his open hands about a foot apart, as if to illustrate something. Eddie couldn't imagine what it was, but surely, he told himself, it couldn't be the first thing that popped into his mind when he saw the gesture.

"What's the Little Princess got to do with Harry Austin?"

"Body in street there. Outside Little Princess. Maybe he go there sometime. Maybe *farang* friend go there."

As Lieutenant Sirapop ushered Eddie and Winnebago out of his office, Eddie decided that the visit had been about as much fun as a root canal—but he'd probably gotten his 5,000 baht worth anyway.

Now he might be able to begin putting together a picture of Harry Austin's life in Bangkok.

At least he had a place to start. The Little Princess massage parlor. On Soi 31.

17

It had been hot already when they went into the Thonglor station. When they came out, it was hotter still—and the humidity from the morning's rain made it feel even more oppressive than it was. As they walked in the general direction of Soi 31, sweat soon began to roll down their faces.

Eddie doubted there'd be anyone at the Little Princess at that hour—as far as he knew, most massage parlors in Bangkok weren't open during the daytime—but he thought it wouldn't hurt to go by and at least check the place out. Soi 31 wasn't far from where they were, and ten minutes with Sirapop had left him longing for fresh air, even Bangkok's peculiar version. So he figured they'd walk it, in spite of the heat and humidity.

"You sure you know where you're going, Eddie?"

Eddie briefly toyed with the philosophical implications of Winnebago's question, but let it go with a literal answer.

"Yeah, sure."

After twenty minutes of dodging along broken-up sidewalks, trying not to fall over anything, Eddie realized that the building he'd been using as a landmark wasn't getting all that much closer; and—prompted considerably by the sweat accumulating under his shirt and around the waistband of his trousers—he decided it might be better to give up the idea of walking to the Little Princess and find a taxi. He had just turned his head to tell Winnebago, when he noticed something that bothered him a lot more than either their slow progress or the sweat in his pants.

He noticed that they had picked up a tail.

Eddie's first thought was that it had to be the same guy Bar Phillips had spotted the night before outside Popeye's. But it wasn't going to be that easy. This was a local guy, and Bar Phillips said the man following them last night was a *farang*.

Having a Caucasian following somebody in an Asian city was about as subtle as tailing them across Los Angeles in a float from the Rose Parade. That had been the point of course, Eddie gathered last night—for him to know they were being watched. He could understand that game and figure out how it worked. Now, either he was dealing with somebody else entirely, or the script had been changed.

When they stopped at the next traffic light, Eddie—keeping his eyes straight ahead—spoke in a voice just loud enough for Winnebago to hear. "There's somebody following us."

He glanced over without turning his head, and saw Winnebago go very still.

"Don't worry about it. It's probably nothing."

But Eddie knew it was *not* nothing. Picking up a local tail clearly suggested that somebody was getting more serious about them. That didn't, off the top of his head, seem like good news.

The guy wasn't too bad and Eddie wasn't too good. It had just been a coincidence that he'd spotted the man. He'd probably never have made the guy at all if he and Winnebago had known exactly where they'd been going; but since they'd been less than certain, their tail's job had been a lot tougher.

Eddie had started down a small side street, and then—realizing it went nowhere—had turned back in the opposite direction, actually bumping into the man as he came up behind them. That alone meant nothing of course, but when Eddie accidentally spotted the same man behind them again fifteen minutes later—and way too far up Sukhumvit to be a coincidence—he knew immediately what was happening.

The man may have guessed he'd been made, Eddie realized, but he probably didn't care. It was Eddie's experience that Asians usually thought *farangs* were all more or less equally hopeless outside of their own countries. He figured that the guy assumed they were just the usual Caucasian idiots, lost and confused on the streets of an Asian city, and—even if they thought they were being followed—there still wouldn't be anything they could do about it. From Eddie's point of view, there was only one problem with their new friend's reasoning. He was absolutely right.

He had to find a way to dump the guy, or give up the idea of going anywhere near the Little Princess right then. That was his only lead to Harry Austin, and he damned sure wasn't ready to give it away just like that.

"What are we going to do, Eddie?" Winnebago hissed the question out of the side of his mouth like a gangster in a B-movie, and Eddie almost laughed out loud. "Try and lose him?"

Eddie nodded.

"How you gonna do that?"

"I'm not sure," he admitted. "All I know about losing a tail comes from Tom Clancy novels and late-night TV."

But then a light rain started to fall again, and just as the big drops began to hit his shoulders and splash into the puddles on the sidewalk, something suddenly came to him. He ducked into a doorway to avoid the rain, and pulled Winnebago with him. Out of the corner of his eye, he saw their tail do exactly the same thing.

"Why don't we just get a taxi back to the hotel, Eddie? If somebody wants to follow us to the Oriental, it's fine with me."

Eddie scanned the street in both directions as subtly as he could. When he didn't see anyone else making a similar move, he decided their shadow was working alone. Either somebody was short of manpower or they just thought Eddie was too much of a jerk to need the full court press. He hoped, if that was the reason, that somebody wasn't right.

"I want to check out the Little Princess. Nobody's going to scare me off that easy."

Ducking from doorway to doorway, trying to stay as dry as they could, Eddie and Winnebago worked their way up Sukhumvit until Eddie found what he was looking for. The office building across the street and up a block on their left was plain-looking and about a dozen stories high. It was perfect. Waiting until the traffic was at its heaviest, he grabbed Winnebago's elbow. "Let's go!"

Dodging together across the street, they headed straight into the building's lobby. As they shook off the rain, Eddie glanced quickly around and saw that he couldn't have hoped for better. The lobby was empty and there were only two elevators. One was just opening in front of them, while the indicator showed that the other was nearly at the top of the building.

Quickly pulling Winnebago behind him, Eddie trotted into the open elevator. He let the door slide shut behind them and then hit the switch that turned it off. Fumbling in his pocket for something to work with, he found nothing of much use except his room key from the Oriental. Fortunately the key was attached to a flat brass plate about three inches across. It looked sturdy, and—luckily—was diamond shaped.

Slipping one point of the plate under the bottom edge of the control panel, Eddie twisted it in a little and then pushed down on it as hard as he could. Somewhat to his surprise, the makeshift pry bar worked just fine, and the panel popped out far enough for him to get his fingers under it and give it another tug. When he did, the whole thing came out in his hands. He pulled it toward him, turned it over, and examined the back.

"I got it!" Winnebago shouted so loudly that Eddie put a finger to his lips and gave him a hard look. "I saw this in a

Disney movie once ... Flipper or Son of Flipper or some fucking fish movie. That's it, isn't it?"

Eddie nodded without taking his eyes away from the back of the panel.

"The good guy got into an elevator, shut it off, and then turned the lights on and off on the little thing outside to make it look like he was going up." Winnebago sounded like he was getting into it. "When the bad guy went up in the other elevator, Flipper—or whoever the Christ it was—turned the elevator back on, and ran off."

"Flipper was a fish."

"Whatever ... but that's still what you're gonna do, isn't it?"

"Yeah." Eddie continued to examine the back of the control panel. "What do you think?"

"I think you've got no goddamned chance."

It had seemed simple enough in the movie, but maybe Winnebago was right. Perhaps he'd been tired or drunk or something, because now that he had the plate out, all he could see was a mass of wires. He didn't have the first idea what to do with any of them.

Eddie figured he had a couple of seconds at most to think of something smart, because the man who'd been following them would soon be standing in front of the elevators looking at the indicator lights, if he wasn't already. He still had his room key in his hand, and having no better idea what to do with it, he stuck it against the back of the bottom button just to see what would happen.

Eddie was so delighted when the light clicked on, that he almost dropped the key, but he didn't. He could only hope that the light outside had come on just the same way.

He pulled the key out and stuck it against the back of the next button, and it too clicked on. After repeating the process all the way up to the top floor, Eddie held the key against the back of the last button for a time, giving their pursuer a chance to take the bait and get himself well upstairs. Then he pocketed his room key and pushed the panel back into place after a fashion. Taking a deep breath, he turned the elevator on.

The doors opened onto an empty lobby, and they stepped out and looked up at the indicator lights blinking over the other elevator. When the light reached the top floor, and stopped flashing, they both laughed out loud.

"Well, son of a bitch." Eddie grinned and punched Winnebago on the shoulder.

"You're a *god*, Walt Disney." Winnebago intoned respectfully as they walked briskly across the lobby toward the street. "You are a motherfuckin' *god*."

18

The rainy season in Bangkok begins sometime in June and doesn't end until at least November. During those six months everyone survives from day to day, never knowing when the heavens will open and the city slosh into chaos.

Bar scratched at his cheek, watching the rain from the library on the fourth floor of the *Post* Building. It was falling so hard that the crashing of water against the windows hurt his ears. The salvos of thunder made Bangkok seem like a city under siege.

The rains never bothered Thais as much as they did the foreign residents of Bangkok. Thais just took off their shoes, pulled pairs of rubber thongs from their bags, rolled up their pants, and went about their business as if having surf in the city's streets was the most natural occurrence in the world.

It was the Buddhist thing that caused Thais to accept the annual rains so stoically, Bar firmly believed. If Christianity could be summed up in one line, it would be, 'Do unto others as you would have them do unto you.' If Thai Buddhism could be summed up in one line, it would be, 'Shit happens.'

Bar had been paging through recent copies of local newspapers for almost three hours looking for any mention of the name Harry Austin, but so far he had drawn a complete blank. He could always just ask around at the *Post* of course, but Eddie Dare's whole story had such an odor that he didn't want to get close to it until he knew more; at least enough to guess what Dare was really up to. Right now he didn't know anything.

Ten grand was ten grand, but living in Bangkok had taught him to be cautious of foreigners who showed up touting grand schemes and dangling enticing propositions. He'd seen a pretty good truckload of them over the years. These guys floated in and out again—and resident *farangs* rash enough to get involved with them were sometimes left to clean up a mess with the locals, which frequently got a little touchy.

Bar had to be careful, he knew, but still. . . . He glanced out the windows again and saw that the rain had eased off, so he pushed the stack of newspapers away with a sigh. Gathering his things and taking the elevator down to the lobby, he headed out to the crowd of motorcycle taxis that was always gathered in the street in front of the *Post* Building.

As he walked down the steps, he saw a slim woman in a yellow silk suit talking to two men. She saw him at the same time, gave a quick wave, and bounced toward him, her high heels clicking on the pavement.

Her name was Worawanna Subhasawasdikul—improbable though that might seem to anyone other than a fellow Thai—and she had recently been assigned to Bar as his assistant. She had graduated from the University of Delaware only the year before, and sometimes it bothered him a little that her English was not only better than his Thai, it might even be better than his English. In spite of that, Bar had quickly developed the same sort of easy relationship with her that he had with most women he wasn't sleeping with—which included most of them.

"Mr. Bar, did that messenger boy find you?"

He loved that. Wor had called him Mr. Phillips at first, but he insisted she just call him Bar. She wasn't comfortable with that, she said, so they finally settled on Mr. Bar.

"What messenger boy?"

"I told him you were in the library. He said he knew what you looked like." Wor giggled. "You're a very famous man, I think."

"Don't worry about it. It was probably just some press release."

The Thai postal service was so unreliable—and motorcycle messengers were so cheap—that everything, even junk mail, was sent around Bangkok by hand.

"Okay, Mr. Bar. Anything else I can do before I go?"

"Not unless you've heard of a guy named Harry Austin."

Wor made a thinking face and Bar watched, enjoying it.

"Does he work here?"

"No. He's dead."

"Oh." She looked startled for second. "Then I don't know him. I don't know anybody who's dead."

Yeah, that'd be right, Bar thought, briefly considering how indecently young this woman was. Sometimes he thought *most* of the people he knew were dead, or at least looking pretty close to it.

He watched Wor as she clicked off toward a bus stop, wondering what she did when she wasn't at the *Post*. She was Thai-Chinese, attractive, energetic and well-dressed. Other than that, he knew practically nothing about her; not if she was married, or had children, or spent her evenings jerking off Japanese tourists in a massage parlor. Well, he doubted that.

Bar sometimes rode buses himself, but the most efficient way to negotiate Bangkok's clogged streets—sometimes the only way—was on the back of a motorcycle. A skilled rider could weave one of the whining little beasts between larger vehicles tangled in the gridlocked streets and arrive at almost any destination long before a car. On the other hand, there was a downside. You still got stuck in the traffic sometimes anyway—and sitting on the back of a motorbike in 95-degree heat, sucking on the exhaust pipe of a clapped-out Chinese bus, was not everyone's idea of a good time.

Bar selected one of the motorcycle boys who didn't look overly stoned on paint thinner that evening, gave directions, and swung onto the bike behind him. It coughed and sputtered the first couple of times the rider tried to start it, but on the third try it caught with a deep roar, and the boy bumped them over the curb and wedged his way into the passing traffic. The rain was much lighter, but the drops that were still falling were big and heavy. Occasionally one would splatter against Bar like a huge, well-aimed gob of spit.

He enjoyed taking motorcycle taxis most of the time. Their seats carried a fair cross-section of the city. He had seen them occupied by chubby, red-faced *farangs* clutching *Asian Wall Street Journals*; by Thai mothers collecting their children from school, sometimes two or three stacked up like tiny packages between her and the rider; by deliverymen balancing improbable towers of boxes on their laps; and even by policemen, hats pulled low, and opaque, black glasses masking their eyes as they headed off to do whatever cops really did in Bangkok.

Bar's favorite sights by far, however, were the Thai office girls. They usually rode side-saddle, balancing on the back of the weaving machines with breathtaking grace and perfect nonchalance. Bangkok had unquestionably the best looking office girls in the world, he was convinced. Certainly the best dressed. They never seemed to wear anything but brightly-colored, cheerful suits, with straight, tight skirts that ended a few inches above their knees. Their well-cut jackets—always buttoned—emphasized small waists and perfect hips, and their smooth, bare legs flowed down to tiny feet clad in business-like pumps.

The light on Rama IX changed, and the pack of bikes that had edged its way past the cars and buses to the front of the intersection howled off in a deafening roar. That was the moment that every motorcycle taxi rider lived for. When the light changed, there were sometimes a couple of hundred yards of open road across the intersection.

Allowing a motorcycle ridden by a Thai onto a road without traffic was suicidal. Even showing them a few hundred yards of it was pretty risky. Bar could never believe how fast they got the bikes going in so little space, nor how quickly they slowed them down to squeeze back between the lanes of traffic stalled at the next traffic light.

But Bar was paying less attention to the death race this time than he usually did. He was still thinking about Eddie Dare and his doubtful yarn.

The whole thing worked at him, although it wasn't his problem and he couldn't see for the life of him why he was getting so caught up in it. This was just a little research job on the side, wasn't it? Whoever was trying to intimidate those guys probably didn't even know Bar existed. No reason to worry, he told himself again. None at all. *Just take the ten grand and do the job.*

Having gotten a running start when the light changed, Bar's rider managed to shoot clear of the pack and make a clean little move between two lines of buses all the way to the next light. When the other bikes caught up, a big Yamaha with a passenger behind the rider pulled up alongside.

The passenger slowly turned his helmeted head and looked at Bar, his face invisible behind a greasy, black visor. When he didn't turn away after a glance, Bar became a little wary; and when the passenger reached inside a canvas bag slung over his shoulder, still without turning his head, Bar almost shit himself.

The most popular method in Thailand for conducting a contract hit was to do business from the back of a motorcycle. It was a handy arrangement. The rider could get the gunman in close to the target without arousing his suspicion, and both the rider and the shooter wore helmets that rendered them completely unidentifiable.

Unlike a gunmen working up close, a motorcycle hitter usually favored a .45 caliber automatic with soft point slugs, rather than the much smaller .22 revolver. The point was to make sure the victim was messed up enough to kill him, even if the shooter was not particularly talented—which he almost never was.

Everything Bar had heard about contract shootings from motorbikes—and it had been a great deal during his almost forty years in Bangkok—ran through his head in the moment he saw the passenger on the Yamaha push his hand deep into his bag. He had always wondered what he would do if he saw this coming—and now he knew.

He froze.

The hand slowly emerged from the canvas bag, Bar's eyes bolted to it. He pleaded with himself to move, but his body was locked rigidly in position. Only his eyes still seemed to be working. The hand continued its movement, and Bar began to resign himself to the inevitable.

Maybe he'll miss. Yeah, that's it. Maybe the little fucker will miss.

The hand appeared, and Bar clinched his eyes shut, bracing himself as it was thrust toward him. When nothing happened, he cracked his eyes back open, making tiny slits of them, and he almost laughed out loud.

The passenger was still there, and his arm was stretched out, just as Bar had thought it would be, but his hand didn't hold the .45 which had grown so large in Bar's imagination that its muzzle had taken on the dimensions of the Lincoln Tunnel.

It held an envelope.

The hand waved the envelope at Bar, gesturing for him to take it. When Bar hesitated, the waving became more frantic.

Well, what the hell? Bar reached out and took it.

All he had time to see, before the light changed and the bikes roared away again, was that it was an ordinary airmail envelope with his name neatly printed on it in black ink. Just that, and nothing more.

19

When Eddie and Winnebago bolted out of the lobby of the office building, they turned left along Sukhumvit and melted into the sidewalk crowd—at least as well as a tall, white man being followed by an American Indian could expect to melt into a crowd anywhere in Bangkok.

"That was great, man! That was fuckin' great!" Winnebago laughed as they sloshed through puddles from the rain that had stopped falling as suddenly as it had begun.

"Don't get too excited. He won't have any trouble finding us again whenever he wants."

"Any idea who . . ."

"Not a clue," Eddie cut him off. "None."

Eddie waved his hand toward a passing *tuk-tuk* and it veered immediately, heeling up unsteadily on two of its three tiny wheels as it swung to pick them up.

"Soi 31," Eddie instructed as he and Winnebago ducked under the fringed canopy sheltering the contraption, and scrambled onto the orange plastic bench over its rear wheels.

The young Thai piloting the battered vehicle twisted around and quickly sized up his prospects. "Hundred baht," he announced, holding his index finger up to Eddie to emphasize the number. Eddie waved him on.

The *tuk-tuk* lurched away from the curb with the deafening, high-pitched throb that gave it its name. Paying scant attention to the road, the driver focused mostly on adjusting the transistor radio that dangled from the rearview mirror. Cutting off a bus, the *tuk-tuk* driver couldn't believe his luck when he looked up from the radio and found himself in a lane that was momentarily clear of traffic. He hunched forward and floored it.

The screeching of the tiny engine rose alarmingly, and Winnebago lurched over the edge of the seat. He wrapped both hands around the contraption's twisted railing to keep himself from falling into the street, fixed his eyes straight ahead, and hung on.

It was less than five minutes before the boy made a right turn off Sukhumvit into a small *soi*, and slowed suddenly.

"This Soi 31. Where you go?" He turned his head back toward Eddie.

"The Little Princess. Do you know where it is?"

The driver grinned. He let the *tuk-tuk* coast as he racked the engine and weighed the opportunity that had suddenly been presented to him.

"No girl now. Close."

Eddie nodded, but said nothing.

"I know good place. Many girl. Very nice. Very sexy. I take you. Okay?"

"No girls. Just take us to the Little Princess."

"Close, boss. Little Princess close."

"Maybe." Eddie pulled a red banknote from his pocket and held it up. "But we're going there anyway."

The boy shrugged and turned away, gunning the *tuk-tuk* on down the *soi*. That's another crazy *farang* story he'll have for his friends, Eddie thought. When the *tuk-tuk* boys are drinking their beer together after work, I wonder what they'll make of the two *farangs* who insisted on going to a closed massage parlor.

The *soi* was narrow and there was no traffic. A short distance off Sukhumvit, the food vendors thinned out and the high-rises became houses, largely invisible behind high concrete walls topped with broken glass. Sleepy looking security guards lounged in sling chairs in front of some of the gates, and flies buzzed around packs of scabby dogs dozing in whatever shade they could find between the concrete trench of the road and the unbroken panorama of walls.

The *tuk-tuk* swung out to pass a group of young girls in identical dark blue skirts, white blouses, white socks, and black Mary Janes. They were bunched up against a wall near one of the gates, smoking and gossiping—ducking out early from one of the expensive, private schools in the neighborhood, Eddie guessed. As they whined by, the girls stared at the two big *farangs*, and one of the bolder ones flashed a smile and waved. Eddie waved back, setting off a fit of giggles.

They suddenly cut right into a narrow lane with a heavily-potholed surface. Water filled most of the holes, and they splashed through a few before jerking to a stop. The *tuk-tuk* boy let the engine idle and pointed to his left without bothering to turn around.

"What the fuck is that?" Winnebago leaned across Eddie to get a better look.

An empty parking area fronted the side *soi* where they had stopped. Across it was a large, two-story concrete building that looked like an abandoned military installation. The mottled, gray surface of the structure was cracked and pitted, and there were no windows—only regularly-spaced circles that had once been some shade of brown, and which marched in ranks across the façade like painted port holes. The edges of the building were outlined with strings of tiny, white lights. Those that weren't burned out, blinked on and off irregularly.

"Little Princess," the boy shouted over the engine, revving it impatiently. "Nobody here. Tell you, close."

They climbed down and Eddie paid the driver. He stared at them briefly, then roared away.

"Nice fella," Winnebago observed. "Real helpful."

They crossed the parking lot toward what Eddie assumed to be the entrance. There was a tiny canopy over a single door, with a pile of cardboard Singha beer boxes stacked on one side, and an empty metal stool on the other. Two scrawny dogs that had taken shelter from the sun in the tiny sliver of shade thrown by the canopy hauled themselves up and eased away from the approaching men. It wasn't even midday yet, and Eddie could already feel the heat in the concrete through the soles of his shoes.

He pushed at the door and rattled the handle. Locked. He banged half-heartedly a couple of times, but it was heavy, and the sound was too muffled to carry, even if anyone had been inside.

While Winnebago stood with his hands on his hips surveying the empty parking lot, Eddie stepped back, shading his eyes with his hand, and looked up. He scanned the front of the building for a minute, but then realized there was nothing to see. He dropped his hand and moved back into the shade.

"Suppose this is it?" Winnebago asked.

"I don't know."

"It doesn't look like a massage parlor."

"No, that's what it is all right. I just don't know if it's the right one. What were you expecting a massage parlor to look like?"

"I don't know. Something a little more . . . you know, sexy."

Bangkok's massage parlors were made for darkness, Eddie understood. In the vampire hours they were crystal palaces where throngs of graceful, young girls—wasp-waisted in long, brightly-colored silk sarongs—smiled and giggled to each other as they reclined on carpeted risers behind huge, plate glass windows, each wearing a small badge with a number. In a world that spun too fast, the parlors offered asylum to weary males. They were sanitariums of the night; safe houses for the seriously battle-fatigued; sanctuaries for those who had made one too many patrols into the sexual jungles of the West—the dark places where the real massacres in the war of the sexes took place.

In daylight, however, massage parlors were shabby structures that looked like derelict warehouses. You could almost smell the spilled beer, stale cigarette smoke, and industrial-strength disinfectant through the pitted concrete walls.

Eddie scanned the street. Could it be the same one he had seen in the picture; the place where Harry Austin's broken body lay in a shallow, muddy hole? He supposed it could be; but then so could half the streets he'd seen in Bangkok. One mud hole looked pretty much like another.

"I got an idea," Winnebago suddenly said. "Come on."

Eddie watched as Winnebago set out across the parking lot with a purposeful stride. Glancing back once at the locked door, he followed. By the time he caught up, Winnebago had reached the street.

"Where we going?"

"Find some folks. See what they can tell us."

"Even if we're in the right place, Winnebago, it's been a month or two. No one's going to know what we're talking about."

"Bullshit! How many dead foreigners do you suppose they find in the streets around here?"

That wasn't a question Eddie wanted to dwell on too much, so he just nodded vaguely at Winnebago and let it pass.

The narrow lane wasn't very long, and they could easily see where it ended up ahead. There were several shophouses in a straight line on one corner—apparently the local version of a strip mall—and what appeared to be a restaurant on the opposite side. Between where they were and the end of the *soi*, there was nothing but more high, concrete walls topped with broken glass.

The first two gates they walked past were solid iron—huge, black plates that looked as if they could stop tanks—but the third was a little friendlier. It was made up of round bars about three inches apart, and they stopped and peered through.

There was nothing to see except a vacant lot. A few scraggly palm trees—fronds half brown from the brutal sun—clung to life along what once might have been a shell driveway. The house that it had led to was gone, and nothing but junk and weeds now covered the lot. There was a mound of folding metal chairs, several old tires, a scattering of cardboard cartons, and even the rusted-out frame of what had once probably been a small pick-up truck. At the back of the lot, a large animal that looked like a misshapen cow grazed contentedly on the tufts of grass growing through the garbage.

"Jesus," Winnebago muttered. "It looks like an Indian reservation with water buffalo shit."

The next two gates were also solid, and firmly closed, but just before they got to the row of shophouses, Winnebago found one that was half open. Poking his head inside, he saw a manicured lawn with a driveway of crushed, red rock that led to a sprawling house elevated slightly above the road. Just inside the gate, an old man in a gray safari suit was swishing a long feather duster over a dark green BMW with blacked-out windows. The car was parked facing toward the gate, as if it was ready for a quick getaway.

"Afternoon!"

The old man looked up, confusion spreading over his face as he examined Winnebago grinning in through the half-open gate.

"Could I ask you something?"

The old man glanced over his shoulder toward the house, and then back at Winnebago again. After that, he turned his back and resumed dusting.

"He probably doesn't speak English," Eddie suggested.

"Good point." Winnebago chewed on his lip briefly, and then screeched, *"Hoh yee mahn néih yat goh mahn tàih ma?"*

The old man stiffened visibly at the noises coming from Winnebago. He slowly turned around and stared—goggle-eyed. He looked like someone who had just encountered a talking horse.

Eddie was almost as dumbstruck as the old man. "What the hell was that?"

"Chinese. The Cantonese dialect. The guy looks more Chinese than Thai, I figure."

"How do you know that?" Eddie looked from Winnebago to the man and back again. "And where the hell did you learn Cantonese?"

"I read a lot." Winnebago gave Eddie a stern look. "At the store. Now do you want to take over here, or shall I go on?"

Eddie stepped back, and—with a slight bow—gave him the floor.

Winnebago nodded encouragingly at the old man. *"Ngoh yauh geen sih séung cheng gaau néih je."*

The man took a hesitant step toward the gate. *"Nèih séung dim ah?"* The sound was all spit and gargle.

Eddie had no idea what the old man was saying, but it was obvious he wasn't offering them a tour of the premises.

"Nèih ji uhm jidou yáuh goh baahk yàhn hai ne tinh gaai bei sai ge sih ah?" Winnebago pointed over his shoulder toward the road. *"Kéuih bei che jong sei ge."*

"Ngoh den ni geen sih yat deah doh ng ji bo." A scowl, and another mouthful of spit and gargle.

Winnebago made an effort to keep the conversation going in spite of the old man's unfriendliness. *"Néih haih uhm haih juh haih ni jóg an ge?"*

"Ngoh dim ji je!" The man suddenly rushed toward the gate with surprising nimbleness and began to push it closed. *"Ján ah neih! Ngoh uhm joi tung náh gong lah! Ngoh me yeh doh uhm ji ah!"*

"Ngoh uhm haih seung gaau sib . . ." Winnebago tried to keep talking, but the gate clanged shut in his face, and he trailed off.

"You going to give me the play by play on all that?" Eddie asked Winnebago after a decent interval.

"I just asked the old bastard if he knew anything about a white man being run over around here."

"And he said?"

"Exactly, or just approximately?"

"Approximately is good."

"'Fuck you,' approximately."

Eddie nodded, anything but surprised. "So now what, Charlie Chan?"

"Just a second." Winnebago cupped his hands around his mouth, and screamed over the closed gate, *"Loh yeh, dill néih loh mei!"*

"Did that make you feel better?"

"Fuck yeah."

Eddie and Winnebago examined the shophouses carefully as they walked on to the end of the lane. The first was completely empty, a large, English-language FOR RENT sign covering the entire front. Through the window of the second, they could see what looked like a hairdressing salon, but the lights were out and there was no one inside. The third and fourth units had been joined together into a single space, and it was stuffed full of Asian furniture and sculpture. Winnebago tried the door, and when the knob turned in his hand, he and Eddie went inside.

"This is real good stuff," Winnebago said, looking around.

"And you would know that exactly how?"

Before Winnebago could answer, a tall man materialized between two standing Buddha figures as quietly and unexpectedly as if he were performing the grand finale to a magic trick.

"Vat may I do for you, gentlemen?"

Eddie immediately decided that the man's German accent suited his appearance perfectly. He was lean and taut-looking, despite seeming well into his sixties. Steel-rimmed glasses rested on the end of his hawk-nose, and his hair had been shaved so closely over his skull that only a gray fuzz remained.

"Is that the Little Princess massage parlor up at the other end of this *soi*?" Eddie asked.

The man stared unblinkingly at Eddie, like a stuffed owl. "Are you looking for a massage?"

"No, I'm investigating the death of an American who was killed here a few months ago. I'm a lawyer from San Francisco."

"I did not zink you ver a buyer of Asian antiquities."

And why the hell not?

Eddie forced a smile. "I represent the man's family. We understand he was hit by a car in front of the Little Princess massage parlor."

The man continued to stare at him, but now Eddie thought he looked amused for some reason, although he couldn't think of anything he'd said which was at all funny.

"Perhaps you knew the man. His name was Harry Austin."

"I vould not know anyone who vent to a place like that," the German responded in a voice offering little hope the conversation would go on for much longer.

Eddie glanced around for Winnebago—hoping for some help—but he was out of earshot. Over the German's shoulder, Eddie could see him peering closely at a big, gold-lacquered Buddha. The figure was seated with its legs curled under it, and had huge, sad eyes outlined in black. Gently, Winnebago reached out and ran a finger along the figure's arm, tracing it slowly down to an open palm that was curled gracefully into its lap.

"Now if you vould be good enough to go on your vay and let me get back to . . ."

"Ist das Sukhothai?" Winnebago called out in German.

The man looked over his shoulder, eyes narrowing as he examined Winnebago. He had the expression of someone who was certain he was about to be made the butt of a cruel joke.

"It is from the Sukhothai period, yes."

"Fünfzehnte Jahrhundert?" Winnebago ran his finger back up the image's arm to its shoulder. "No, not fifteenth, fourteenth. Fourteenth century, isn't it?"

The German shot Eddie a look. Eddie smiled back blandly.

"You know Sukhothai figures?" the man asked Winnebago, unable to keep the astonishment out of his voice.

"Oh, sure. They're much more peaceful looking than those from the Lanna period, don't you think?"

The German stared at Winnebago. Eddie tried not to.

"I've always particularly loved this form of the seated Buddha," Winnebago went on in a soft voice, ignoring both of them. "It's the gentleness of the open hand. That gets me every time. Don't Thais call this position the *bhumisparsa mudra*?"

👄👄👄

When Eddie and Winnebago came out of the German's shop a half hour later, they knew something they had not known before—at least not for certain. They were unquestionably standing in the *soi* where Harry Austin had died.

Ignoring Eddie completely as they toured the shop, the German eventually told Winnebago what he knew about the foreigner who'd been killed in front of the Little Princess.

"It's a shame he didn't actually see the accident," Eddie mused.

"Yeah, but he saw the body, and he saw the man who dragged it inside."

"The description wasn't very helpful. Caucasian, forties or fifties, average height, average build. Christ, Winnebago, that fits most of the Western men in Bangkok."

"Somebody at that massage place knows something." Winnebago nodded earnestly at Eddie. "I guess we better come back tonight when the place is open and do a little research, huh?"

"I was thinking of something else you could do tonight that might be even more constructive."

"Yeah?"

"Maybe your pal Fritz could remember something else if you asked him again in a more social setting." Eddie kept his tone as neutral as he could.

"Forget it, man."

"Well, he did ask you to have dinner with him and . . ."

"No fuckin' way, man. You have dinner with him."

"I don't think he liked me as much as he did you."

Winnebago gave Eddie a look he would have had some trouble putting a name to—but Eddie knew exactly what it meant.

20

The American Embassy in Bangkok always made Bar think of a particularly prosperous prison—all blast-hardened concrete, slit windows, high walls, and iron gates. The huge compound was about halfway between Lumpini Park and Ploenchit, sprawled along both sides of Wireless Road.

Bar loved the name Wireless Road. The sound of it fairly reverberated with intrigue, and it reminded him of a black and white television series from the fifties called Foreign Correspondent that had riveted him as a boy. He could never say Wireless Road without hearing off in the distance the sound of an old BBC radio broadcast—the background all hissing and static, and an earnest-sounding voice shouting out dispatches from some remote corner of the empire in an exaggerated British accent. Of course, the BBC still sounded like that most of the time, and he figured that was probably why everybody watched CNN now.

Bar didn't like going to the American Embassy, and he avoided it whenever he could. The place made him jumpy as hell. He had this terrible fear that once he was inside the gates, they might never let him out again.

Americans had always been keenly suspicious of those among them who voluntarily chose to live in another country. After all, half the world seemed to be clamoring to move to California and work in a 7-Eleven. So what the hell was with this guy who wanted to live in Bangkok? Must have done something. Yeah, that was it. Committed a crime or something. If he wasn't a drug dealer, he had to be a tax dodger, or owed child support to a penniless ex-wife on welfare back in St. Louis. Bastard. Low life. Had to be. Otherwise he'd want to live in America, like everybody else.

This was one of those times, however, when Bar knew he had to suck it up and go around to the embassy. He couldn't work out on his own what the photograph inside the envelope the motorcycle messenger had passed to him meant, but he didn't like the look of it one bit. He knew a guy at the embassy he was sure could help him. So he swallowed his misgivings and went to see him.

Chuck McBride was DEA—one of a dozen agents posted to Thailand and working out of American diplomatic facilities. Bar met him one night at the Crown Royal and they had become friends, in spite of Bar's usual policy of avoiding all Americans in Thailand—particularly government guys.

Bar had never thought of Chuck as anything at all like the rest of those arrogant, prissy jerk-offs who passed for US government employees abroad. He looked more like a semi-pro jock from some Alabama football team that had never met with much success. He had a neat, blond crew cut; a fleshy face that couldn't seem to organize itself into a chin; and no neck—at least none that anyone had ever been able to find.

Chuck and Bar spent a lot of time fooling around town together, and more than once Bar had left Chuck sitting on a curb somewhere trying to get sober enough to throw up and hit one more place before calling it a night. Bar liked cruising Bangkok with Chuck for two reasons—he was good company, and he carried a really big gun. Both of those things, Bar thought, were pretty important when you hit the local streets on a Saturday night, although you could probably get along without the company if you really had to.

It took less than ten minutes in Chuck's office for Bar to tell him everything he knew about Eddie Dare and Winnebago Jones. He recounted the story Eddie had told about being hired by the General to find out what happened to Harry Austin, and he described the pictures with the red circles that Eddie claimed he had gotten in San Francisco. Finally, he related his own encounter the night before with the motorcycle messenger, then he pushed the airmail envelope across the desk to Chuck. After that he sat back, folded his arms, and waited for the verdict.

Chuck pondered, running his hand back and forth through his crew cut so that Bar would see he was thinking and not asleep. "You sure that's it?" he asked after a moment.

"So help me. The whole story."

"The guy on the bike just handed this to you?"

"Yep."

"No shit?"

"No shit."

Chuck slowly picked the envelop up by its edges, compressed it slightly so that the end Bar had already torn off popped open, and then dropped out the single photograph inside. He examined it curiously while Bar sat quietly and watched.

"Nothing else in the envelope when you opened it?"

"Not a thing."

The picture was a snapshot of some young American marines. A few of the men were in combat gear and the others in fatigues, but they were all standing in a ragged group, their arms flung haphazardly around each other's shoulders, mugging for the camera. Oddly, one man was off a little from the rest of the group. He was straddling what had once apparently been a straight chair, but was now little more than some broken sticks of wood. Looking off into the distance, away from the photographer—watching something with what seemed to be great care—his face was largely in shadow.

What got Chuck's attention about the photograph was the same thing that had scared the bejesus out of Bar when he first saw it. Three bright red circles were scrawled on it—two around the heads of men in the large group, and the third around the man in the chair; the man whose face couldn't quite be seen.

"You say that Dare and Jones got shit like this?"

"They said they got photos with circles around their heads, but I didn't see them. Maybe they were different."

"And you're sure you don't recognize any of these guys?" Chuck held up the snapshot in his left hand so that Bar could see it, and tapped the back of it with his right forefinger.

"I think the two guys with the circles in the big group are Dare and Jones, but I'm not sure."

"How about the guy in the chair?"

"I can't see his face. I don't know."

"Maybe he's an officer," Chuck suggested. "Somehow the prick looks like an officer."

"Well . . . maybe it's Austin."

Chuck blinked, but he didn't say anything. He ran his left hand through his crew cut again, and then looked up at Bar. "This picture scare you?"

"No."

Chuck looked skeptical, and Bar reconsidered.

"Okay, maybe a little, but mostly it pisses me off. I don't like being threatened, and I especially don't liked being threatened by some cowardly fucker who hides behind a dark visor and then comes at me when I'm minding my own business riding down the street."

"Meaning . . ." Chuck rolled his hand in a gesture that suggested Bar still hadn't gotten to the point and Chuck would be grateful if he'd hurry.

"Meaning I wasn't sure whether I was going to help Dare or not, but this. . . ," Bar pointed at the picture lying on the desk, ". . . more or less puts us in the same boat now. So I guess I'm in."

"In the same boat? How does it do that?"

"Well . . . the picture's obviously a threat." He waved a finger toward it. "If that's Austin in the chair—and I'd bet you it is—we know he's dead. And it's not too hard to guess that the other circles mean Dare and Jones are next if they don't stop poking their noses in where they don't belong."

Bar chewed on his lip for a moment.

"Don't you get it, Chuck? Whoever sent me this picture is warning me that I could be on his list, too."

"So what. You're not involved."

"*So what?* It pisses me off, Chuck, that's so what. I'm not going to sit here and be threatened in my own home."

"I thought you were on the back of a motorcycle."

"Don't be such a literal bastard. You know what I mean."

"You sure it's not just the ten grand that's got you all revved up?"

"It doesn't hurt. But no, that's not it. Not anymore."

Chuck suddenly seemed to lose interest in Bar's state of mind. "You want to get a drink somewhere?"

"It's not even lunch yet, Chuck."

Chuck shrugged, not seeing the point of Bar's sudden concern with the time of day.

Bar thought about it and then realized he couldn't see the point either.

"Sure. Why not?"

The Texas was their favorite hangout during the day. No women, just a real saloon with drinks that didn't taste too strongly of Bangkok's pungent tap water. Ping, the day-shift bartender, wasn't any more honest than the other bartenders in town, but at least he was smart enough to water his drinks with bottled stuff. That was a touch of class Bar liked.

Bar also liked the small sign over the door at the Texas that announced in four languages, NO FIREARMS. When he and Chuck had first started going there, he allowed for the possibility that the sign was supposed to be a witticism— something like the signs at the Hard Rock Cafes that said, NO NUCLEAR WEAPONS—but after they'd been in the Texas a few times and he'd gotten a close look at the people who hung out there, Bar realized that the sign probably wasn't meant to be a joke at all.

Chuck had a beer to warm up, then switched to Johnny Walker Black in a tall glass with a lot of ice and a little soda. He had downed half of it before he mentioned Bar's story again.

"That's a real strange story, man."

Bar could tell that Chuck was working himself up to something, but he wasn't sure exactly what it was. Finally Chuck snorted a couple of times and cleared his throat. Here it comes, Bar thought to himself.

"This Austin guy you mentioned. He was a captain you said?"

"Yeah."

"And he was the CO of these guys, Dare and Jones?"

"That's what they said."

"This guy who hired Dare, the one who said he was a general, was he Austin's CO?"

"I doubt it. Dare told me he didn't know the guy and I don't see why he'd lie about it."

Chuck considered that—weighing the implications— although Bar couldn't off-hand see why.

"Did either Dare or Jones see Austin again after they got out of the marines?"

"They said they didn't."

"Ever hear from him?"

"Not that they mentioned."

Chuck drew little slashes with his forefinger in the condensation on the side of his glass. "And you didn't know him?"

"Harry Austin?"

"Yeah."

"No, I didn't know him."

Bar caught Chuck's slightly raised eyebrows, but was still working on what they signified when Chuck drained his drink and waved the empty glass at Ping.

"He was a local. I thought you knew all the local *farangs*."

"Well, if he was, I didn't know this one. Did you?"

"He kept to himself, mostly, but I had him under surveillance for a while."

"DEA was *following* this guy?"

Chuck rolled his head around a little before he answered.

"We had a brief interest in a guy named Harry Austin who was a retired marine captain with a couple of tours in 'Nam." Chuck did the thing with his head again. "It's got to be the same guy. How many Captain Harry Austins could there have been around here?"

"How long did he live in Bangkok?"

"For a while. I don't know for sure."

"Was he dirty?"

"Maybe." Chuck shrugged. "Maybe not."

Bar didn't push. It always took Chuck a while to get a whole story out—but eventually he'd do it in his own way.

"So you didn't know him?" Chuck asked Bar again.

Something was beginning to work at Bar. Maybe he had known Harry Austin and didn't realize it. Maybe the guy had been using a different name; something not that unusual for foreigners in Bangkok.

"This isn't that big a place, if you're a white guy," Chuck prompted.

"Look, Chuck, I'm sure I never met anyone here, or any place else, called Harry Austin. Now, if he was using some other name . . ."

"Nope. As far as I know he was just plain old Harry Austin. We put him on our watch list because he seemed to live pretty good without any source of income. Finding an American like that in Bangkok usually leads to something interesting, when you look close enough."

Chuck took a long hit on his drink and rattled the ice cubes a couple of times to get Ping started again.

"He had a penthouse in a big condo on the river. But we couldn't find any bank accounts in his name anywhere, or any other sources of funds. So, when we finally got around to doing a bag job on his place . . ."

"Bag job?" Bar interrupted.

"Yeah." Chuck looked a little defensive. "You know. He was out one day. We went in and looked around."

"You broke into his house? The DEA broke into a retired marine captain's *house* in Bangkok because they wanted to know where his money was coming from?"

Chuck looked annoyed. "It wasn't a house. It was a condo. I already told you that."

"And in your mind that somehow makes a difference?"

"You want to hear what we found or don't you, you sanctimonious prick?"

"Oh, sure. You being a law enforcement officer for the United States government and sworn to uphold the law and all that, I guess it's okay for you to tell me what you found in this American citizen's house that you broke into for absolutely no reason. I guess that would be okay, wouldn't it?"

Ping put a fresh drink in front of Chuck and he took a hit. "Damn straight. I say it's okay, it's okay."

Bar tilted his head back and waited.

Chuck grinned. "Porno. A bunch of it. Mostly local girls."

"So he was in the porno business?"

"I don't think so. It looked more like a hobby to me." Chuck cupped his left hand and made the traditional pumping gesture over his crotch.

"Seems a little hard to imagine a guy living in Bangkok and jerking himself off," Bar observed.

Chuck nodded, almost sadly. "Yeah. That's what I thought, too."

Bar waited a moment, and when Chuck offered nothing else, he asked the obvious question.

"So, what business *was* he in?"

"None that we could find any evidence of." Chuck made a show of scratching his head. "Still don't know where his money came from, but he had a pretty nice apartment and a couple of expensive cars. Sure didn't buy them out of his marine retirement pay."

"Maybe he inherited a pile."

"Oh yeah, I'm sure that was it." Chuck raised his eyebrows. "Unless of course he was just walking along one day and *found* it. *That* might be where he got it."

"Why didn't you just ask him?"

"I would have, but he was killed before I got around to it. Hit and run, the cops said. Driver fled the scene."

The last part didn't surprise Bar at all. In fact he would have been astounded if Chuck hadn't added that. After every traffic accident that occurred in Thailand the driver *always* fled the scene, usually accompanied by any police who might have had the misfortune to witness the incident. 'The driver fled the scene' was a phrase rife with local poetry. It represented nothing less than an honored and solemn ritual deeply ingrained in Thai life. It was a 'driver fled the scene' kind of country.

"But it *was* an accident, wasn't it?" Bar put the question cautiously. "You're not telling me that Austin was murdered, are you?"

Chuck pulled a couple of different faces while he pretended to think, but neither one gave much away.

Bar wondered why he bothered. It was obvious that Chuck had long ago made up his mind exactly what he thought about the demise of Captain Harry Austin.

"I don't know. We pulled the surveillance off before it happened, and nothing's turned up since. At least not until you came waltzing in this morning with that picture and your cockamamie story about Dare and Jones. Anyway, file's closed now."

"Then I guess that's that."

"Maybe not." Chuck sloshed his drink around. "I may know someone who can tell you something about the good captain. You interested?"

Bar nodded.

"I could probably arrange for you to buy Lek and me a couple of drinks one of these days."

"Just tell me when and where."

"How about the Stardust?" Chuck pondered for another moment, then he apparently made up his mind. "You know how to reach Dare and Jones?"

"Yeah. They're at the Oriental."

"They would be," Chuck grunted. "Anyway, bring them along, too. Tonight okay?"

"Who's Lek?"

"Be patient, man. Let's just go one little step at a time here."

"What's the big mystery, Chuck?"

Chuck ignored the question. "About nine. Okay?"

Tossing off a quick little salute, Chuck dropped a purple banknote by his empty glass, and was out the door before Bar could ask him any more questions.

21

Eddie had been planning for them to go back to the Little Princess that evening—and Winnebago had been particularly enthusiastic about the idea—but after Bar Phillips called, he changed his mind.

Bar told them about the motorcyclist and the snapshot, and he related the story Chuck McBride had told him about the DEA's interest in Harry Austin. After that, Eddie quickly agreed that they would meet him at the Stardust at nine instead.

Charlie Wang had owned the Stardust almost as long as Bar had been in Bangkok. It was in an old mansion near the beginning of Soi Suan Phlu, just past the corner at Sathorn Road. Local legend had it that the place had been the home of some deservedly-forgotten general who found himself on the wrong team in a military coup and wound up shoveling snow in Copenhagen. Regardless, Charlie owned it now, and over the years had built it into the Bloomingdale's of Bangkok's nightshift.

They met Bar in the Thai restaurant on the second floor. While he ordered *paad thai* and Carlsbergs all around, Eddie took in the expensive furnishings, the fresh-cut flowers, the wood-paneled walls, and the subdued lighting. But his eyes lingered longest on the elegant hostesses who seemed to be everywhere.

Their drinks arrived quickly, and Bar pointed toward a wide staircase carpeted in a deep, burgundy-colored pile.

"There's another dining room on the third floor. Very plush. Serves what Thais think French food is supposed to be. Then there's a karaoke bar on the fourth floor, and a barbershop, a steam room, and a massage parlor downstairs."

"Sounds real good to me," Winnebago nodded.

"Yep." Bar wiggled his eyebrows. "I'd bet this is the only place in the world where you can eat *escargot*, have your hair cut, sing 'Feelings,' and get your dick sucked—all at the same time if you really want to."

While Winnebago was still trying to work out what to say to that, the food arrived. Bar wolfed down half his plate in a few bites, belched in satisfaction, and then waved his spoon around. "I like this place a lot better than the restaurant upstairs."

"Yeah, I guess Thai food in Bangkok must be pretty hard to beat," Eddie agreed.

"Food's got nothing to do with it." Bar chewed thoughtfully on a noodle. "Charlie insists on having men wait the tables up there. He thinks it's more sophisticated or some crap like that. Look around here."

The women working in restaurant were all dressed in sarongs. They glided effortlessly from table to table, placing their high-heeled feet as gracefully as ballet dancers in silken slippers. Their inky-black hair glistened in the light, and as they turned this way and that, their waists looked so small, Eddie thought it had to be some kind of an optical illusion.

Bar kept one eye on the door, watching for Chuck and his guy to turn up, while Eddie and Winnebago eyed the hostesses and finished their food. When Chuck finally did make his appearance, he was with a woman—Bar was surprised to see—rather than a man.

That was a problem with Thai nicknames, Bar knew. Many of the most common names—like Lek—were used interchangeably for both sexes, and a few even covered the cases that fell in between; cases that Bar was certain could be found nowhere else but in Thailand.

He picked up his Carlsberg and shook it at Eddie and Winnebago to get their attention. They followed his eyes and watched Chuck McBride and his companion cross the room.

The woman wasn't much more than five feet tall, and she was very slight. Like so many other local women, she seemed at a glance to be a decade or two younger than she really was—but before she and Chuck had reached the table, Bar realized she was much closer to forty than twenty.

"This is Lek." Chuck looked Eddie and Winnebago over as he pulled out chairs for himself and the woman. "Which one of you is Dare?"

Eddie lifted his right hand and wiggled his fingers.

"Should've known," Chuck grunted.

"What's that supposed to mean?" Winnebago asked, leaning forward.

Chuck ignored him.

"So you say you've been hired to find out what happened to this guy Austin, huh?"

"That's right."

"Who hired you?"

"If I knew, I probably wouldn't tell you. But I honestly don't."

"Bullshit." Chuck fixed Eddie with an unblinking gaze. "Lawyers don't get involved in things without knowing who they're working for, even if they won't tell you when you ask them."

"I didn't intend to. It just worked out that way."

Chuck nodded a few times, but Eddie knew it had nothing to do with signifying agreement. "Bar told me a cock-and-bull story about you meeting some guy after you got here who claims to be a general. He's supposed to be this mysterious client of yours, is he?"

"He *is* my client." Eddie figured that was stretching things only slightly.

"You had lunch with him in a private dining room on the top floor of the Regent?"

"Uh-huh."

"That's a crock." Chuck leaned back and laced his fingers behind his head. "Look, Dare, I know this shithole as well as any white man ever could, and let me tell you something— there *ain't* no dining rooms on the top floor of the Regent, private or otherwise. There's nothing up there but regular rooms and a couple of suites."

"Then I don't know what to tell you. That's where I had lunch with the man who paid me to find out what happened to Harry Austin." Eddie tried to return Chuck's stare, but now Chuck was looking off somewhere across the room and he couldn't catch his eye. "You're a real hard on, aren't you?"

Chuck just grunted again.

"I read your column every Saturday, Mr. Phillips." Lek changed the subject in a voice so soft that, at first, Bar wasn't sure she had spoken at all. "And so did Harry."

Bar gave Chuck a long look, but he was still staring across the room and didn't seem to notice.

"Did you know Harry Austin well?" Bar finally asked Lek.

"Reasonably well," she nodded. "He was my husband."

Bar just bobbed his head a little and sipped at the dregs of his Carlsberg as if he knew she was going to say that. Winnebago cut his eyes at Eddie, but Eddie was watching Lek.

"I said I'd bring somebody who could tell you about Austin, and like Mandrake the fucking Magician, I bring you his wife." Chuck made a little two-handed flourish in Lek's direction.

"Widow," Eddie corrected.

"We'll get to that later. Anyway, I think a little gratitude's in order here." Chuck pointed at Bar's empty Carlsberg. "One of those will do fine for me. I'm a cheap date." Chuck tilted his head toward the woman and she nodded. "And one for Lek, too. But she's certainly *not* a cheap date."

Bar raised a hand at one of the waitresses, nodded toward his empty bottle on the table, and made a whirling motion in the air with his index finger. He had never known exactly what the hell that was supposed to mean, but it always seemed to get more drinks brought to the table—frequently even the right ones—so he kept on doing it.

"So you're suggesting we juice up the grieving widow with a little cash before this goes any further?" Bar gave Chuck a weary smile.

"No, Mr. Phillips." Lek's voice was much stronger now, and it had a distinct edge. "He is *not* saying that."

Bar made a gesture with his hands that he thought was appropriately apologetic, but he didn't say anything.

"I'm not surprised you assume that I am just a bargirl who met Harry a few times and is now trying to make some quick cash. I'm not surprised, Mr. Phillips, but you are quite mistaken."

Bar had, of course, assumed exactly that, but he knew he was wrong by the time Lek had said a half dozen words.

"I'm sorry if I offended you."

"You didn't offend me, Mr. Phillips. Most Thai women eventually get used to it. Men always seem to think with their peckers around us, don't they?"

She had him there, Bar thought, so he just bobbed his head noncommittally and leaned back.

"Where did you meet Captain Austin?" Eddie hadn't taken his eyes off Lek since she sat down at the table.

"We met when I worked in the international section of Bangkok Bank. My job was to coordinate our relationships with the international correspondent banks."

Bar flipped his eyes toward Chuck, who returned his glance with an insufferably smug imitation of a smile.

"Harry had quite a lot of money invested through us. Mostly term deposits in various currencies and some other very conservative stuff. Something was always getting fouled up, and I helped him sort things out several times." She stopped for a moment. "Anyway, the rest of the story is really none of your concern. The point is that eventually we fell in love and got married. After that, Harry insisted I quit working at the bank."

"Tell them why," Chuck prompted encouragingly.

"Harry worried about me. He said there were people who'd eventually come looking for him; that they wanted something from him. He said as long as I worked at a bank, it would look like I knew about it and I'd be in danger." She hesitated again, selecting her words carefully. "He never told me exactly what he meant, but I thought it was obvious it had something to do with where his money came from."

Chuck glanced at Eddie. "Bar showed you the picture, didn't he? The one the motorcycle guy gave him?"

Eddie nodded.

"Two of those circles were around your heads, and Austin was the third circle. He was the guy in the chair, wasn't he?"

Chuck made a question out of it, but Eddie didn't bother to answer. They both knew it was true.

"What the fuck's going on here?" Winnebago snapped in exasperation. "If you got this all figured out, man, just tell us, huh?"

Chuck shook his head. "I really don't know what to tell you."

Eddie noticed that Chuck aimed the answer straight at him, not at Winnebago.

"I've been trying to put a few pieces together for quite a while," Chuck went on after a pause. "Harry Austin was one, and now I seem to have found me some others. You guys know better than I do what they all add up to."

"Harry didn't die in any accident," Lek broke in. "I'm sure of it. Somebody killed him."

Winnebago pushed back in his chair. "Oh, Sweet Jesus."

"Who identified the body?" Eddie asked Lek.

"I don't know. I didn't find out what had happened until the *wat* called asking for a donation to pay for his cremation."

"The 'what'?" Winnebago asked.

"*Wat*. Not 'what,'" Bar explained. "It's the Thai word for a Buddhist temple."

"Do you know who made the cremation arrangements?" Eddie watched Lek closely.

"I guess the police must have. I didn't."

Eddie started to ask her if she'd ever heard of the Little Princess, but something made him hesitate and he was still thinking about it when Chuck took over the conversation again.

"Forget all that shit." Chuck was smiling and Eddie wasn't sure he liked that. "Here's where I'm going with this. Harry told Lek very little, but she gathered from one thing and another that everything was connected with the time he spent in 'Nam."

Bar raised his eyebrows a notch, wondering if he was overlooking something obvious. "I thought you were investigating Austin. How was it you came to be such a close friend of the family and all?"

Chuck shrugged off the implication, and Eddie noticed he didn't flinch. He made a mental note that Bar's suspicions about Chuck and Lek were probably off the mark. If there had been any personal involvement between them, Eddie would bet he could have seen it in Chuck's face when Bar popped him with the jab.

"We didn't turn anything up on Harry, so I just called him one day and introduced myself," Chuck continued. "He thought it was funny as hell we had him down as a possible dealer and we hung around some after that."

"When Harry died, I called Chuck." Lek went back to speaking softly again, and the four men—one by one—leaned toward her, straining not to miss anything. "Harry gave me a key to a safety deposit box just before he died. It was at the Hong Kong & Shanghai Bank; the branch on Silom. He asked me not to open the box unless something happened to him, but if anything did, to destroy what I found in it. When I saw what it was, I knew Harry hadn't died in an accident. Instead of destroying it, I took everything to Chuck."

All four of them watched Lek as she bent down and pulled several sheets of paper from a purse on the floor by her chair. Eddie noticed that the purse was a Chanel. At least he thought it was. The fakes they sold in Thailand were so good he was never sure if things like that were real or not.

Lek was an attractive woman, and she had that combination of confidence and vulnerability Eddie had always been a sucker for. As she fumbled in her purse, she shifted in her chair, and her short, straight skirt hiked up. Eddie's eyes slid over her slim, bare legs, all the way down to what may have been the sexiest, most feminine ankles he had ever seen in his entire life.

What could a guy married to a woman like this be doing at a massage parlor? Was it just a coincidence that Austin's body had been found outside the Little Princess?

Straightening up, Lek put the sheets on the table, squaring up their edges in an unconscious gesture. "These were in the box."

Eddie reluctantly pulled his eyes away from Lek's ankles. Picking up the sheets of paper, he scanned them while Bar and Winnebago leaned across and looked, too. The first two pages were a list of names, some with addresses and telephone numbers next to them, and some without. Eddie's name and Winnebago's were on the first page, along with both of their San Francisco addresses.

The last five pages were photocopies of snapshots.

Two pages showed different views of Austin and about seven or eight other men in off-duty fatigues clowning around a bar somewhere. Eddie didn't remember ever seeing the place before, but it was obvious he must have. In the first photograph, he was standing about ten feet from Austin, his arm around a cute little girl with hair down below her waist. In the second, he was sitting at a table resting his chin on one fist and looking at the camera with empty eyes.

The final three pages were copies of the two photographs that had been mailed to Eddie, and the one given to Bar by the motorcyclist. They each had the same circles around the same heads.

"Oh, God," Eddie groaned.

"Yeah, first this . . . ," Chuck waved in the general direction of the papers Eddie was holding, ". . . and then Bar comes strolling into my office with the original of one of these, and a wild story about the other two winding up in San Francisco."

"That's what happened."

"Yeah." Winnebago leaned forward. "And they were mailed from right here in Thailand."

In the silence that followed, the sound of rattling dishes, snatches of music from the karaoke bar upstairs, and the sudden roar of a motorbike with a broken muffler out on Sathorn Road all seemed unnaturally loud.

"So what you're saying is that Austin got the same pictures we got before he died."

Eddie's voice sounded thin, even to him.

"That *is* what you're saying, isn't it?" He made a question out of it, but he knew it wasn't. He was looking at copies of the pictures Austin had gotten—and the only reason he was looking at them was because Austin was dead.

"Seems that way." Chuck nodded slowly. "Which brings me to the reason I called this meeting." He looked from Bar to Winnebago, and finally settled on Eddie. "The lady and I would like to know exactly what the fuck you guys did back in 'Nam that got Austin murdered here twenty years later."

Eddie mulled that over while Chuck, Lek and Bar watched him. Winnebago studied a spot on the table.

"I know you won't believe this," he finally said. "But I don't know."

"I'd stay away from this guy, Bar." Chuck yawned. "My shit detector just went off the scale."

"Lay off, Chuck." Bar's jaw pinched into a tight line. "I haven't made up my mind about any of this yet, but I'll tell you one thing right now. No asshole's gonna frighten me away with a few old snapshots."

"You're going to help us?" Eddie, surprised, turned toward Bar.

"I didn't say that. I just said nobody's going to scare me off from something I want to do with shit like this." He waved at the copies of the pictures on the table.

"I don't get it," Winnebago said. "Does that mean yes or no?"

Bar gave him a long look. "I'm not saying yes, but I'm not saying no yet either. That's the best I can do right now. Live with it."

After that, the conversation wallowed along a while longer, but Eddie quickly lost interest. All he really wanted to do was get back to the Oriental, sit down quietly by himself, and think through everything that was piling up on him. He had to be missing something, he knew now; some connection that would start to bring things into focus.

Chuck was right about one thing at least. Eddie *did* know something. He was beginning to feel sure of it.

He just had to figure out what it was.

22

When Eddie and Winnebago left the Stardust, a taxi was just unloading two wobbly Australians. Clutching cans of Fosters the size of small waste baskets, the men struggled to steady themselves on the cracked sidewalk.

"G'day, mate." One of the men fixed Eddie with a beery eye and belched loudly as he scratched between his legs. "This the place?"

"What place?"

A theatrical leer rolled across the Australian's face. "You know, mate." The man spread his arms slightly just below waist level, cupped both hands, and began to rock his hips rhythmically back and forth.

Eddie just shook his head. The Australians had left the rear door of the cab hanging open, and he and Winnebago quickly slid in and slammed it, putting an end to the cultural exchange.

"So what are we going to do now?" Winnebago looked at Eddie expectantly.

"Let's get back to the hotel." Eddie rubbed the tips of his fingers over his eyelids. "I'm still half whacked from jet lag."

The taxi driver twisted around in his seat, flashing a broad grin. "Where you come from?"

"San Francisco."

The driver looked puzzled. "Where that?"

"California," Eddie said. "America."

"America good. You want massage?"

"No massage. The Oriental Hotel, please."

"I know place," the driver persisted. "Sexy girl. You have good time."

"The Oriental," Eddie repeated.

"Massage very nice. Make you feel number one. Special price for you."

Eddie sighed and opened the back door of the Toyota. "Come on, Winnebago, forget it. We'll walk a while."

"*Pai nai!* American all old lady!" the driver shouted after them as they got out. "Germany better. Germany like lady. Much party animal!"

The Stardust was about fifty yards off Sathorn Road on a popular *soi* for food vendors. The haze from the cooking fires on their carts mingled with the hot, saturating air, tinting it to a wispy blue. Toy-sized tables littered the street; most dark, a few flickering with the little mysteries of kerosene lamps. A wave of pungent smells rolled over Eddie and Winnebago: charcoal smoke, exhaust fumes, boiling rice, and fish sauce. From somewhere a radio was playing a Thai pop song, and a female voice was singing, high and wailing, plaintive as a child, yet still tantalizingly sexy. It was all half familiar, half unfathomable; half discord, half sweetness. It was—Eddie thought— beauty bred to strangeness.

They walked past a large wok sizzling on a gas ring that was being fed by a dented, green gas bottle. An old woman smiled at them as she scooped a pile of something out of the hot oil with a bamboo-handled basket and dumped it into a bowl to drain.

Winnebago regarded the contents of the bowl dubiously, and Eddie smiled to himself. He knew the Thais loved to snack on fried grasshoppers. He'd even tried them once himself, and had to admit that they weren't bad. Still, he found it a little disconcerting trying to talk to someone who had a pair of tiny legs sticking out between their teeth.

Fishing some money from his pocket, Eddie stopped at a cart where prawns on wooden skewers were roasting over a charcoal fire. He bought two, handed one to Winnebago, and they went over and sat on a low brick wall.

While they were eating, another man carrying a skewer of prawns ambled over and sat on the wall near them. Eddie didn't even notice him at first. He was average and forgettable in every way—he recalled later—slim, dark hair, white shirt, and khaki pants. For some reason, Eddie thought the man hadn't looked much like a Thai. Maybe he'd been Cambodian, or even Vietnamese. Eddie couldn't be sure.

The only thing that caused Eddie to notice him at all, was the second man. That man was quite a bit taller, and he bumped into Winnebago's legs as he walked past.

When Eddie and Winnebago glanced toward the tall man, the man who had been sitting on the wall jumped up, jabbed his wooden skewer at Eddie with one hand, and tried to lock his free arm around Eddie's neck. The skewer glanced off Eddie's shoulder without doing any damage other than smearing smashed prawn on his shirt, and then Eddie must have surprised the man by reacting so quickly. He certainly surprised himself.

He jerked to his feet, ducking under the arm groping for his throat, and—slamming his right heel backward—caught the man flush on the kneecap. As he howled, Eddie pulled away and saw that the tall man was wrestling with Winnebago. He hunched his shoulders and rammed his head straight into the man's back—catching him low, just above the kidneys.

"Head for the main road!" Eddie screamed as the tall man turned loose of Winnebago and sagged to the ground. "Run!"

"What the fuck's happening?"

"Just run, Winnebago!"

After half a block, Eddie decided they'd make the road easily. He looked over his shoulder and saw that the two men who'd jumped them had pulled themselves to their feet and were just standing there rather than giving chase. He and Winnebago must have put up more of a fight than they expected and scared them off, Eddie assumed at first. But then he turned back toward Sathorn and realized that the men hadn't been scared off at all. They were merely being patient.

Two other men had emerged from the shadows and were waiting quietly near Sathorn Road. Eddie had barely started measuring the men and working out their chances when the odds lengthened abruptly. One of the men pulled something silver from under his shirt and held it dangling in his right arm. The lights from passing cars splashed sparkling patterns across it, and the barrel of the gun glinted unmistakably.

Eddie grabbed Winnebago's elbow and pointed to the men in front of them. They made a U-turn without breaking stride and headed back the way they'd come. Eddie had no idea what they'd do when they got to the men waiting at the wall, but then he saw Bar, Chuck and Lek coming out of the Stardust.

"Bar!" Eddie screamed, pointing at the two men with his left hand and holding up his right, making a little gun with his thumb and forefinger. Chuck sized up the situation quickly, and jerked a black automatic from a belly holster under his shirt.

The men looked behind them when Eddie shouted, and they twitched visibly at the sight of the beefy, no-neck *farang* pounding down the steps from the Stardust, unlimbering a Beretta.

The two men apparently decided that it wasn't necessary to stick around for introductions. By the time they passed Eddie and Winnebago, heading toward their friends, Eddie thought they were moving pretty well; at least for young guys.

Chuck sloshed Johnny Walker into the two coffee mugs with gold DEA crests and pushed them across the table. Eddie picked up one and Winnebago took the other.

"How about me?" Bar asked. "I'm all shook up, too."

Chuck ignored him and Lek studied her hands.

It was almost eleven and the embassy annex was dark and quiet. A rectangular table, the color of dead leaves, surrounded by six straight chairs with dented metal frames and black plastic seats took up most of the space in the cramped conference room. The white walls—blotched with yellow patches from the years of accumulated nicotine—were bare except for a small photograph of Bill Clinton in a black plastic frame, and a travel poster extolling the wonders of Detroit.

The harsh, white wash of the fluorescent tubes strung across the cracked ceiling tiles made Eddie and Winnebago look even paler than they felt. For a long time, no one said anything.

"It could've been just a coincidence," Bar said at last. He'd already said the same thing several times in Chuck's car on the way from the Stardust to the embassy, but he liked the sound of it, so he said it again.

"You don't think those guys had something to do with all this shit about Harry Austin?" Chuck's tone was disgusted.

"Maybe not."

"Then you figure it must have been like . . . who?"

"Muggers?"

"When was the last time you heard about four local muggers surrounding two *farangs* on Sathorn Road and waving a gun at them?"

"Thai muggers can't afford guns."

"There you go."

The door to the conference room suddenly swung open and they all jumped. A young embassy guard in a marine uniform leaned in and looked them over suspiciously. When he recognized Chuck, he came to attention and snapped off a salute.

"Sorry, Sir. I didn't know it was you. This part of the building's usually empty at night and I saw the light. I was just checking."

"It's all right, Corporal." Chuck returned the salute after a fashion. "Good night."

"Night, Sir." The marine closed the door quietly and they all listened as his footsteps disappeared down the corridor.

"Something about a marine uniform suddenly makes me a little tense." Bar's voice cracked.

Chuck pushed his chair back, folded his arms, and swung his feet up onto the table. Propping his left ankle over his right, he twisted his head around until he was looking directly at Eddie. "You sure you're okay?"

"Yeah."

"I'm okay, too, in case you're interested," Winnebago put in, but Chuck ignored him. Winnebago finished his whiskey in one hit and fumbled for his Camels.

"Somebody wants your butt, Dare."

Eddie just shrugged.

"Any idea who it might be?"

"Sharon Stone?"

Chuck mimed a laugh, but his eyes didn't move.

Eddie took another sip of the whiskey and rubbed at his face. "You going to help us here, McBride, or just keep practicing your hard-ass routine?"

"What's really going on, Dare?"

"I don't know."

'Sure you do." Chuck smiled unpleasantly and rubbed his palms together.

Eddie looked away, then back. There was something like a sudden flash—like sunlight on water—when his gaze crossed McBride's. The chair squeaked as he shifted his weight. Still, he didn't respond.

Chuck watched him with a half smile. His eyes were cool and judging. Then he turned away from Eddie and spoke to Lek. "Let me see that stuff from the safety deposit box again."

Lek rummaged in her purse and handed Chuck the papers she had shown them at the Stardust. He leaned against the table on his right elbow and smoothed out the stack with his left hand.

"And this is all there was in the box?"

Lek nodded, and Chuck slowly lifted up his head and looked sideways at her.

"No bank statements or investment records? Nothing like that."

"No."

'But you said Austin had a lot of money at Bangkok Bank when you met him. What happened to it?" Eddie asked.

"I don't know." Eddie thought Lek looked uncomfortable about something, and he noticed she didn't meet his eyes. "After I stopped working there, he never mentioned it anymore. I didn't think it was my business to ask."

Chuck didn't look up, so Eddie decided his suspicions were probably misplaced. He let it go.

"Are you sure you don't know any of these other guys on the list or in the photos?" Chuck asked her.

'No. No one.''

Chuck tilted his head toward Eddie and raised his eyebrows in a silent question. Eddie held out his hand for the papers.

He studied the list again and stared at the pictures while he made a little whistling sound between his teeth. The smell of the past was coming up to him distinctly from the stack of pages. It was a worrying smell—alarming even—and he didn't know what to make of it.

"These may have been the guys in our company, but I'm not sure. It's been a long time."

He looked down at the photographs again and saw, not the past, but a blurry message from the future. Eddie could sense a door swinging open somewhere. But where did it lead? He had no idea.

Chuck took the papers back from Eddie, swung his feet flat onto the floor, and put the list of names on the table in front of him. Then he started to run his finger carefully down it.

"Thomas Mark? Ring a bell?"

"No, I don't think so." Eddie reconsidered briefly. "No."

"Marion Morris?"

Eddie thought about it for a moment. "I think he might have been a guy we called Bang-Bang, but I'm not sure."

"Heluska Jones?"

"That's me," Winnebago spoke up and everybody looked at him.

"So how'd you end up named after an RV?" Chuck's voice seemed genuinely amused.

"Don't worry about it." Eddie pointed to the list. "Why are we doing this?"

Chuck ignored him and kept reading. "Effrun Carter?"

"Wasn't that Donkey?" Winnebago asked Eddie.

"Could've been. I think his name was Carter, but I never heard of anyone called Effrun before."

"Patty O'Connell?"

"No, but he sounds like a black guy."

Chuck gave Eddie a long look. "This list doesn't really interest you a lot, does it, Dare?"

"It's bullshit. I already told you. I'm not sure about anybody on that list other than Winnebago."

"That's not true. You're sure about at least one other guy." Chuck smiled and tapped his forefinger on the top sheet. "Rupert Edward Dare. There's even an address and telephone number here: 469 Grant, San Francisco. 415-555-7104. Those both right?"

"Yeah, they're right. What's your point?"

"My point?" Chuck reared back in his chair and folded his arms. "You're connected to Harry Austin, Dare. Nobody hired you to find out what happened to him. That's crap. You're after something here yourself."

"That's not true."

Well, maybe it is.

Chuck flipped his palms open. "Suit yourself. But I'm not going to sit here all night and let you blow smoke up my ass. I'm done."

"So you're not going to help us?" Eddie asked.

"Hey, I'm an agent of the United States government, not a fucking PI."

"You're a cop—a public servant—and I'm an American citizen who needs a little service. Isn't that the way it works?"

"Nah, that's not the way it works. I'm not a cop. I'm just the DEA's observer out here. I got no jurisdiction. I *observe*." Chuck drew the word out as if he really enjoyed the sound of it.

"That's it?" Bar was taken completely by surprise. "You're not going to do anything at all for them."

"Sure. I'll do something for them. I'll tell them what this is about. Dare already knows, I figure, but maybe it'll help him out to understand that I know, too." Chuck spread his hands and leaned forward in a gesture of mock confidentiality, lowering his voice. "This has something to do with money."

"*Everything's* got something to do with money," Bar snorted.

"Yeah, but this has something to do with a *shitload* of money."

Chuck shot a look at Lek that Eddie caught but couldn't read. Lek didn't seem to notice. She continued to stare expressionlessly at the tabletop.

"I think Austin was involved in some kind of scam while he was still in the service. Maybe a few other people were in on it, too."

Chuck looked pointedly at Eddie for a long moment, then he went on in a casual voice.

"Now it seems like somebody has worked that out besides me. These pictures here. . . ," Chuck waved toward the papers stacked on the table, ". . . were obviously a warning to Austin that the game was over; that the time had come for him to give up the money he'd scammed."

"Are you saying that somebody murdered Harry over money?" Lek's voice seemed to come from a distance, and everyone looked at her.

"Yep." Chuck's nose twitched.

"What about the other pictures?" Bar demanded. "The ones we got."

"Whoever sent them . . . well, they must figure that Dare knows something; maybe even how to get at the money now that Austin's dead. The first two pictures were a warning to Dare that he and Jones better stay away and leave the dough to whoever killed Austin. The picture you got means you'd better not get involved either." Chuck paused, measuring the impact of his words. "How does that sound? Pretty sensible?"

"Who are these people you're talking about?" Eddie asked.

"How the fuck should I know?" Chuck's eyes were hooded; a shooter's eyes. "You want to know who's after you? Don't come crying to me. Kick some ass and take some names."

"Forget it," Eddie answered, his throat suddenly as dry as paper. "I'm just a middle-aged lawyer from San Francisco. Soldier of fortune stuff is way over my head."

Chuck looked pensive, but he didn't say anything. He reached down with his forefinger and sketched a little design on the tabletop as if he were drawing a map.

"So what now?" Bar finally asked him.

Chuck stopped drawing on the table and yawned, stretching in a way that Eddie found particularly unconvincing. "I'm tired. I'm going home."

"That's fine with me." Eddie pushed back his chair and stood up. "I'm sick of all this attitude, McBride. I'm out of here."

"What?" Bar was puzzled. "You just had four guys try to grab you on the street and now you're just going to walk back outside?" He turned toward Chuck. "How about getting them some protection at least?"

"Oh, jeez, sure." Chuck nodded. "I almost forgot. I'll just call Bubba right now and get you covered around the clock. Maybe the Secret Service will take you on. How about that, Dare?"

Eddie examined Chuck's face closely, but he quickly decided that irony was beyond him, and he dismissed his reference to the Secret Service as nothing more than a coincidence.

"I'm serious, Chuck," Bar went on. "Somebody may be waiting outside right now. What do you expect these guys to do?"

"I don't have the first fucking clue, Bar." Chuck stood up and held the door open. "Don't get lost, Dare. Just follow the hall all the way to the left and it'll take you out to the main gate."

"Oh, man," Winnebago said, as he stood up to follow Eddie. "Like I *asked* for this shit or something."

Eddie glanced back when they got to the door at the end of the corridor. Chuck McBride was still standing with Bar and Lek at the conference room door. Bar was talking and angrily chopping at the air with his hands, but Eddie sensed Chuck was only pretending to listen. Instead, his eyes followed Eddie and Winnebago intently over Lek's shoulder. His face nearly glowed with excitement.

All at once, Eddie saw what McBride was about.

McBride had probably known for a long time that Harry Austin had hijacked the Bank of Vietnam's reserves in 1975. He just didn't know how Austin had managed it, or what he'd done with the money.

Eddie was willing to bet that McBride had been hot on Austin's trail once. He had probably gotten so close he could almost taste it—but he'd been pushed out of the game when someone killed Harry, and he wanted back in.

Just when McBride had almost given up on finding a way, Eddie had appeared to him—like a sign. McBride didn't know if Eddie had been part of Harry Austin's scam or not, but he knew for sure that somebody *thought* he had been. Best of all, whoever that was, seemed to be closing in on Eddie fast; looking to get at whatever was left of the Bank of Vietnam's money through him. Just as they had once, no doubt, tried to get at it through Harry Austin.

Eddie knew now he wasn't going to get any help from the embassy. McBride wouldn't let it happen. McBride's game was to use Eddie to draw the opposition out into the open. He wanted to keep Eddie dangling out there—a hopelessly conspicuous white man stumbling around Bangkok; a slow-moving, easy-to-hit target. McBride was setting a trap, and he had nominated Eddie as his cheese.

Opening and closing his fists, his gaze lingering on McBride, Eddie felt transported for a moment by righteous anger. But it quickly faded.

Keeping his eyes locked on McBride's, Eddie slowly lifted the middle finger of his right hand until it pointed straight at the ceiling.

Then he turned away and walked out the door—disappearing into the languid, pungent soup of the Bangkok night.

23

Flagging down the first taxi that passed, Eddie slid in, closed his eyes and tilted his head back against the seat while Winnebago convinced the driver to take them to the Oriental Hotel instead of a massage parlor.

Eventually the taxi pulled away, turned right into Rama IV Road, and immediately bogged down in heavy traffic. Eddie concentrated on the flaking paint of a green and white bus that was wedged in next to them, until he managed to will himself into something approaching a hypnotic trance— one that soothed the uproar around him to background hiss and left him on the edge of sleep.

He teetered contentedly until Winnebago gently shook his arm.

"You awake?"

"Mostly," Eddie yawned as he straightened up and yawned.

"My new friend here. . . ," Winnebago tilted his head toward the driver, ". . . has offered to show us some of the . . . ah, sights around town."

"I'll bet."

"You coming?"

Eddie fumbled at his sleeve until he could tilt his wristwatch up into the light from the street. It read a little after eight-thirty and that immediately confused him. How could it be eight-thirty? They hadn't even gotten to the Stardust until nine.

As the cobwebs cleared, it occurred to him that he probably hadn't reset his watch to Bangkok time, and that it must be eight-thirty in San Francisco. But was that morning or night? He tried briefly to work it out, but San Francisco had become such a vague concept for him that he suddenly realized he didn't care.

"Many number one girl!" the driver sang out jubilantly. "Give you good price. Two for one deal."

Eddie looked around and noticed that they'd barely covered a mile in the crawling traffic. He saw the Dusit Thani Hotel on their left and knew that they were just edging into Silom Road, a few hundred yards north of Patpong. It would still take another half hour at least to make it back to the Oriental through the traffic. Maybe more.

"What are we doing in this hole, Eddie?"

Winnebago's question had a wistful sound to it, and Eddie glanced over.

"Why don't we just get laid a few times, eat some Thai food, and go back home?"

Eddie didn't know exactly what to say to that—the idea had an undeniably sensible ring to it, he had to admit—so he settled on a vague nod, and closed his eyes again.

It had all started out as a frolic—an adventure to be played for laughs—a harmless, middle-aged lark in exotic Bangkok. The General had waved a big bag of money at him, tossed in the romantic lure of far-away places, and Eddie had gone gaga. Now here they were, hip deep in something scary and out of control; something that had an unfathomable momentum all its own. Worse, Eddie knew they were sinking fast.

Winnebago was right, of course. He had no doubt at all about it. The only sensible thing for them to do was to get the hell out of there while they still could, and head for home. And yet . . .

"What are you thinking, Eddie?"

"Nothing." He paused, trying to decide. "Everything."

Winnebago chewed that over.

"Look, maybe you're right about going back," Eddie finally said. He glanced at his watch again and then out at the bedlam of Silom Road. "Let me out here. I'm going to wander around a little and think about it. We'll decide tomorrow."

"You going to be safe on your own?"

"I think the fireworks are over for tonight. Besides, Patpong's so crowded that Bill Clinton could be out there cruising and no one would notice."

"Then you think it's okay if I . . ."

"Go on," Eddie cut in. "We'll catch up at the hotel later."

Eddie waved the driver to the curb and got out. Before he closed the door, he bent down and fixed Winnebago with a stern look.

"Don't forget about protection."

"Don't worry, man." Winnebago gave him a double thumb's-up sign. "My new friend here will take good care of me."

"That's not the kind of protection I meant, Winnebago."

As Eddie slammed the door, he watched Winnebago's face slide into puzzlement. After that he could even have sworn that he saw him redden a little, but the taxi pulled away quickly, and he couldn't be sure.

Silom Road was a carnival. Sounds, sights and smells battered Eddie until he felt nearly weightless. Shouldering through the tourists in the street market, and the expats looking for action, he couldn't help but think back to the graceful ease with which Bar had moved through the same crowds—and he allowed himself a moment of envy at his friend's mastery of such an intense and overwhelming world. That made Eddie think of Lek again; and then he remembered that she was probably still with Bar. He wondered if he ought to envy Bar that, too.

A vendor's display of copy watches caught Eddie's eye, and he stopped and picked up a black Casio that had enough knobs on it to do everything but tune in CNN—and for all he knew it did that, too. Perhaps he'd get it for Mike, he thought. But that made him remember the call to the States that morning, and left him feeling flat.

He weighed the Casio in his hand, idly thinking how good it looked for a fake, and then realized that the old woman behind the stand was peering hard at him. She had the puckered, sad face of someone who has lived far longer than they'd ever expected—a peasant's face, brown and flat, with the skin pulled down her cheeks and hanging in flaps under her neck. The woman's eyes tightened and Eddie tried a smile, but she would have none of it. He laid the watch gently back on the table, and she glowered at him as he walked away.

When Eddie resumed his slow progress down Silom, he could feel eyes following him as he walked. He was certain of it. A half-dozen teenaged girls eating sticks of satay around a small table on the sidewalk whispered to each other as he passed. An old man slicing chunks off a watermelon stopped cutting and followed him with narrowed eyes. An Indian tailor hovering in his shop watched him through the front window, playing hide-and-seek with him behind mannequins wrapped in tight, shiny suits.

Or perhaps he was just imagining it all. Maybe the teenagers were whispering about their boyfriends. Maybe the old man looked at everyone like that. Maybe the tailor was just hoping for a customer. It was impossible to tell.

Eddie understood well enough that Caucasians were useless in Asia. They were too big, too white, too awkward, and too hairy. A round-eye could walk Silom Road for the rest of his life and never know for sure if an Asian was watching him.

Eddie felt like he might as well be wearing a helmet with a red light on top—like the fire chief's hat with the flashing, red beacon that he'd given Michael for his fourth birthday. The damned thing had nearly driven Jennifer crazy until the battery finally ran down and the beacon stopped working. She told the kid that the light had died and gone to heaven.

Jeez, what would Jennifer tell Mike if my *light went out?*

Even raising the question left him feeling decidedly uneasy, so he pushed it into the back of his mind and walked on.

Being chased by guys with guns had left him ravenous, it suddenly occurred to him. He turned away from a place that appeared to serve only Chinese food, and then rejected another that looked like a Thai restaurant from Fisherman's Wharf—all neon and fake, funky glitz. Shortly after that, an unassuming but promising-looking sign on the other side of the street caught his eye. In red and green neon it flashed a straightforward message: NICK'S KITCHEN.

That sounded just about right, and Eddie bolted across Silom without taking any more time to think about it. Dodging a minivan that was doing its best to occupy two lanes at once, he reversed direction briefly; and as he did, he caught a flash out of the corner of his eye of something that shouldn't have been there.

A *farang* wearing a tan suit was just behind him. Although it was nearly midnight, the temperature was still well over ninety, and the humidity was reminiscent of a particularly efficient steam bath.

A suit?

Eddie jumped up on the sidewalk and stood for a minute studying the display in the window of a leather shop. Tan Suit stopped further up Silom, appearing equally absorbed in the window of a tailor shop. Eddie decided at once that it had to be the same guy Bar had spotted outside Popeye's.

When Tan Suit decided it was safe to risk a quick glance up the street, he saw that Eddie had somehow disappeared. He began to walk quickly toward the spot where he'd last seen him, scanning up and down both sides of Silom. Tan Suit knew he was rapidly approaching the entrance to Patpong, and he started to worry. If Eddie had made him and had somehow gotten into the thick crowds there, he'd have no chance at all of picking him up again.

Another fifty paces and Tan Suit was standing at the big arch over the entrance to Patpong. He shook his head. The little sucker really had given him the slip, he knew now—although whether by accident or by design he wasn't absolutely sure. Anyway, he guessed it amounted to the same thing. He dreaded having to explain how it had happened.

Tan Suit felt a gentle nudge against his arm, and he moved aside for a thin Thai boy—apparently blind, judging by his dark glasses and metal stick. The boy limped by, pushing a cart with clattering wheels. A very old man, also blind, tagged along behind him. The old man held onto the boy's belt with one hand and carried a small accordion in the other.

"Pretty much says it all about this place, doesn't it?" Eddie strolled up and stood next to Tan Suit as the two blind men led each other away.

Tan Suit hated doing surveillance on smart-asses like this. They always thought they were so clever when they made you, and you could never convince them that you didn't give a flying fuck.

"I'm here for your protection, Mr. Dare." Tan Suit shaped his features into a disinterested, dead-eyed stare. "You should be grateful."

"Grateful to who, or should it be 'to whom?'"

This one's a real beauty all right.

Tan Suit pulled an identification wallet from his jacket, cupped it in his hands at waist level, and flipped it open, just far enough for Eddie to get a quick glimpse. "I'm Agent Morris. United States Secret Service liaison officer at the American Embassy."

Morris put his identification away with more care than was warranted, and Eddie assumed he was using the time to compose an explanation for his presence that would fall somewhere between the entirely unenlightening, and a total *non sequitur.*

"My instructions were to keep you under close surveillance from the time you left the embassy in order to prevent anyone from harming you."

Yeah, that was useless enough to meet even the toughest test.

Morris scratched uncomfortably at his cheek. "Look, I'm just doing my job. Go on as you were, Mr. Dare, and don't worry about me."

"Who are you supposed to be protecting me from?"

"Patience, Mr. Dare. Everything in good time. That's something Asia will teach you."

Eddie looked at Morris, shook his head, and turned away.

What an asshole. What an incredible asshole.

"You won't see me again unless I'm needed," Morris called after him.

"I will unless you get a lot better at following people," Eddie called back.

Still shaking his head, Eddie continued down Silom to Nick's Kitchen. He pushed through a metal door and found himself on a concrete staircase that smelled faintly of urine. Climbing up one flight, he reached the gloom of the second-floor entrance, and walked into a dining room that looked exactly as he would imagine the best restaurant in Sioux Falls must have looked in 1964—dark-paneled walls; straight, wooden chairs with plastic seats; red table cloths; candles stuck in wax-covered bottles; a collection of neon beer signs over the long bar; and elderly waiters in short, white jackets carrying large napkins over their arms.

As his eyes adjusted to the dimness, Eddie selected a table near the door and looked around. The restaurant was almost empty. There was a young *farang* couple near the back; four Japanese girls at a big, round table; and several men sitting separately at the bar. What eventually caught his eye, however, were the two people who had come in right behind him.

For a moment he told himself he had to be mistaken—but of course, he knew he wasn't.

The two Secret Service agents who'd come to his office in San Francisco—Shepherd and the woman with the amazing headlights—were standing in the restaurant's entrance, watching him with expressionless faces.

Holy shit. What next?

When they saw that Eddie had recognized them, they walked over to his table, pulled out chairs, and sat down without a word. Eddie didn't say anything either. He just folded his arms and glanced from Shepherd to Headlights and back again. He tried to remember the woman's name, but couldn't come up with it. He wondered for a moment if referring to a federal agent by the size of her front porch was a criminal offense. Nothing specific came to him, but he thought it was pretty undignified anyway, so he gave the woman a polite smile.

"I'm sorry, but I've forgotten your name."

"Does it matter?"

"Trust me," he said. "It would be better if you reminded me."

Shepherd and the woman exchanged looks while Eddie waited.

"Sanchez," she finally snapped at Eddie. "Agent Valerie Sanchez."

When Eddie didn't respond, Sanchez glanced at Shepherd again. He nodded, and she lifted a black briefcase with gold clasps and balanced it on her lap. She unsnapped the locks and removed a large, brown envelope. Then she closed the case and put it the floor. Shepherd took the envelope from her and laid it on the table in front of Eddie.

"We brought you a present."

"All the way from San Francisco?"

"No. It's a little something we picked up not far from here."

"You shouldn't have."

"Yeah, you're right. We shouldn't have."

Eddie picked up the envelope, ripped open the flap, and pulled out its contents. He was mildly surprised to find himself holding a small stack of 8 x 10 glossies—black and whites. He looked up at Shepherd with a quizzical expression. Shepherd just pointed back to the pictures, so Eddie twisted the stack around so that he could see the top one clearly.

When it registered that he was looking at a nice shot of the General wearing a lovely, little black dress, he struggled to keep a straight face.

Shepherd and Sanchez watched him without expression as he shuffled through the rest of the photographs.

There was the General on a horse dressed like a cowboy; the General wearing a police uniform; the General sitting at a large desk in a dark business suit with a crowd of Chinese men around him; the General in a baseball uniform, looking strangely like a slim Tommy Lasorda; and then back to the General in the dress—a slinky, black number with an amazing bust-line. Eddie's eyes flicked involuntarily toward Agent Sanchez.

He tossed the stack of pictures onto the table. "So he likes to dress up. What's that supposed to mean?"

"It means he's dressing up like a general, Eddie."

Eddie must have looked confused—which would have been easy, since he was—so Sanchez jumped in helpfully.

"The man's an *actor*, Eddie, not a general. He's a Dutchman who's lived in Hong Kong for the last eight years, and before that in Singapore. He makes his living doing bit parts in Asian movies, usually as the token European—male or female."

Shepherd wiggled his eyebrows up and down a couple of times when Sanchez finished talking. It was such a stupid gesture that Eddie almost laughed out loud. Instead, he reached out for the pictures and flicked slowly through them again, just to have something to do while he was trying to think.

"You haven't even heard the best part yet, Eddie," Shepherd went on.

"Better than the General in a dress?"

"Oh, a lot better."

"Cut the crap, Shepherd. What are you trying to tell me?"

"The guy's nothing but a broken-down actor." Shepherd waved at the stack of photographs Eddie was holding. "He didn't hire you to track down Harry Austin's stash."

"Then who did?"

Shepherd smiled very slowly, and the way he did left Eddie in no doubt at all that he wasn't going to like what he heard next.

"He's fronting for Vietnamese Intelligence. Now that Austin's dead, they're pinning their hopes of finding out what he did with the money entirely on you."

"Really?" Eddie said after a moment of silence, mostly just to be saying something.

Shepherd leaned close to him. "Yeah, Eddie, *really*."

"You're not telling me all this just to help me out, are you?" Eddie switched his eyes back and forth between Shepherd and Sanchez. "I get the feeling you still haven't gotten to the real bottom line here."

Now Sanchez leaned close to Eddie, which he found a far more appealing proposition than when Shepherd had done the same thing.

"Good guess, Eddie. You want to hear it now?"

"Yeah, sure. Now's good."

"Then here's the deal." Shepherd took over again, and Eddie decided they thought the tag-team routine somehow gave them an advantage. Actually they were welcome to it, he thought, if only they'd get to the point.

"We have a better offer for you than the Vietnamese."

Eddie was about to ask Shepherd how he knew that the General had offered him anything, let alone what it was, but Shepherd kept going before he could raise the point.

"We want you to locate the money from Operation Voltaire, just like they asked you to, and then turn it over to us."

"That's not a better offer."

Shepherd mimed disappointment, shaking his head slowly. "You mean patriotism really *is* dead, Eddie?"

Eddie waited him out.

"Okay, then here's the rest of it. In return for your cooperation, you'll get one percent. That could be as much as four million dollars, the way we figure it—a hell of a lot more than the lousy mil the gooks offered you."

Eddie thought he saw Sanchez flinch slightly at Shepherd's choice of words, but if she did, she covered it quickly.

"And then there's the bonus that comes with our offer."

"Bonus?"

"Yeah. We won't kill you."

"What's that supposed to mean?"

"Come on, Eddie. Don't be a jerk. You don't really think you could just turn that money over to the Vietnamese and then wait while they type you up a check for a million dollars, do you? Get serious. You'll never see anything from them. They'll just shoot you when this is all over."

"But of course I can trust you absolutely, huh?"

"Hey, man." Shepherd flung his arms open with a grin so wide it threatened permanent damage to his face. "We're your *government*. If you can't trust your government, who can you trust?" And then he winked.

Eddie winked back, but he didn't waste it on Shepherd. He aimed it straight at Sanchez, and then he smiled as her upper lip curled in disdain.

"I already told you I can't help you. I told them the same thing."

"I think you know a lot more than you're letting on here, Eddie."

Shepherd's grin was turning into something unpleasant.

"Yeah? Why's that?"

"Harry Austin liked you. He would've cut you in on whatever he did. You took a bullet for him, and he never forgot it."

"Where'd you hear that?"

"A lot of people know about it."

"Oh, yeah? Do they know it wasn't a VC bullet? Do they know it came from a little .22 some bargirl had stuck in her bra, and that she was just drunk and pissed off that Harry wouldn't buy her out for the night?"

"Doesn't matter."

"Do they know I caught the bullet in my ass scrambling to get the hell out of her way so she could get a clean shot at him?"

"Cut the bullshit, Eddie. Harry Austin always thought you saved his life. The two of you were friends and he trusted you. We think you know what he did with the money. Or at least you can make a pretty good guess." Shepherd shrugged. "It's that simple."

"I'm glad you think so." Suddenly Eddie pushed back his chair and stood up. "How long do I have to decide?"

"Take all the time you want, Eddie. All the time you want." Shepherd reached out and clapped him on the arm. "Just as long as you do it before the gooks get sick of all your fucking around and burn your worthless ass."

"That probably won't be very long," Sanchez added flatly, ignoring Shepherd's vocabulary this time. "I'd say the end of next week would be pretty much it for you."

"Yeah, that sounds about right, Eddie." Shepherd switched his campy grin back on, and tweaked it up a little. "The end of next week, buddy. The end of next week."

24

B ar stood on the sidewalk outside the front gate of the American Embassy, shuffling his weight from foot to foot. "I don't get it," he said to Lek. "What the hell just happened in there?"

"Maybe Chuck's tired," she ventured. "It's late and I guess he wanted to go home."

"Chuck doesn't get tired. And he hasn't been home since 1994."

"What happened in . . ."

"That was a joke."

"Ah. . . ." Lek looked confused.

A taxi crawling slowly along the curb pulled up next to them. The driver racked the engine to get their attention as he pointed toward his rear seat with a hopeful expression on his face. Bar checked him out and decided he didn't look dangerous, but he shook his head anyway. The driver flapped his hand up and down, not willing to give up, but Bar ignored him and turned his back.

He was going around in circles trying to figure out what Dare was really up to. It was starting to give him a headache. If he had any sense, he'd follow Chuck's lead and just go home, too. But he was way too wired for that.

The obvious thing to do was just call up Dare and ask him, wasn't it? What did he have to lose? If Dare didn't come up with a story that made sense, Bar could just wish him a nice life and go home to bed. But if he told him a really good story . . . well, he'd wait until he heard it to decide.

Still Bar hesitated, tapping his foot on the sidewalk and chewing on his lip until he noticed that the young marine guard behind the gate was eyeing them suspiciously. Grabbing Lek's elbow, he towed her up the sidewalk, away from the embassy, and toward the heavy traffic on Rama IV.

"Did Harry really have a pile of money when he died?"

"He was well off, I guess, but I don't think he was rich."

"Didn't you say he warned you that he had a lot of money and people might come after you because of it?"

"I don't know what he meant by that. I already told you."

"Has anybody ever done it?

"Done what?"

"Come after you. Come around asking you a lot of questions about Harry."

"Like what?"

"Like . . . I don't know . . . what he did or who he hung out with. Things like that."

Lek shook her head.

Bar wasn't certain he believed her, although he couldn't off-hand see any reason why she'd lie to him either. Still, it didn't make sense.

There was quite a crowd out there with a serious interest in the life and times of Harry Austin, and he didn't see how it was possible that no one had ever gotten around to talking to Lek. Dare had even asked *him* about Harry Austin, and he didn't know the guy from a bar of soap. Lek had been married to the man, for Christ's sake. Why hadn't anyone ever taken a run at her?

"Where are we going?" Lek asked while Bar was still pondering all that.

Bar hadn't thought about it when he pulled her away from the embassy gate. He just wanted to get away from the place and shake off the queasy feeling it always gave him.

But now that she'd asked the question, the answer popped right into his head—and he was absolutely sure it was exactly the right one.

Twenty minutes later, Bar and Lek got out of a taxi under the high portico in front of the Oriental Hotel. Bar smoothed back his hair and nodded obligingly at the young boy in crisp whites who swung open the lobby door for them.

With Lek trailing behind him, he headed straight for the registration desk, where a tiny, prim-looking Westerner in a morning coat stood sorting through a stack of papers.

"Could you tell me what room Mr. Edward Dare is in, please?"

The little man looked up slowly. His puffy cheeks and small, black eyes made Bar think of an offended frog.

"I'm sorry, sir. We don't give out that kind of information." He scrutinized Bar and Lek carefully. "Our guests' privacy is paramount to us."

Bar nodded a couple of times, as if he was glad to hear that.

"I'm Bar Phillips. You probably read my column in the *Bangkok Post.*"

The little man looked at Bar without a flicker of recognition.

"It's called 'Bar by Bar.'"

Nothing.

"It's that page every week that has . . . ah, you know, entertainment tips, that sort of thing."

Still no response.

Bar swallowed the temptation to lean across the desk and twist the little bastard's nose off. Instead he went on in a tone he hoped fell somewhere between the professionally detached and the cravenly unctuous.

"My assistant and I. . . ," Bar tilted his head toward Lek and ignored the man when he hoisted one eyebrow slightly, ". . . are interviewing Mr. Dare for the *Post*. But of course, if you won't tell me where to find him, that's not going to work out very well, is it now?"

The frog lifted his arm and contemplated his wristwatch with exaggerated care.

"You have an appointment to conduct this interview after midnight?"

"The man's a real night owl."

"What would the gentleman's name be again, sir?"

"Eddie Dare."

The man tapped briefly at a computer keyboard and peered at the screen.

"And your name, sir, was. . . ?"

"Phillips. Bar Phillips." He cleared his throat unnecessarily. "The *Bangkok Post* columnist."

The frog watched the screen for a moment, then tapped some more keys and returned his eyes to Bar's. When he reached for the telephone at his elbow, he kept them there.

"Would you like me to see if Mr. Dare is available, sir?"

"That would be ever so kind of you." Bar gave the desk clerk a supercilious smile, and got another in return.

The man glanced down and dialed a number as Bar watched. He couldn't have dialed it any more slowly, Bar was reasonably certain—no matter how hard he tried—but that was fine with him.

"Mr. Dare is apparently out," the man said after listening a moment. "May I leave a message for him?"

"No thanks. I have another appointment. I was just checking to see if he's here."

As Bar and Lek turned away and crossed the lobby, the desk clerk caught the eye of a plainclothes security man who was posted near the entrance. He gestured toward them with a tilt of his head, and the security man pointed at their backs and raised his eyebrows in a silent question. The desk clerk thought for a moment, and then he shook his head and went back to his paperwork. He wondered if he'd just been had somehow, but he shrugged it off. It wouldn't be the first time.

The doorman snapped a salute as Bar and Lek emerged from the hotel. He lifted his arm toward a taxi, but Bar waved him off. Looking around briskly, Bar turned right and walked down the driveway with Lek close behind him.

At the bottom he turned right again into a narrow, brick-surfaced path that led to the hotel's boat landing. After a dozen paces, Bar turned right a third time, threaded his way through the lush gardens, and circled the deserted swimming pool. Within five minutes, Bar and Lek re-entered the Oriental through the rear door and were in an elevator on their way up to the seventeenth floor.

"How do you know what room he's in?" Lek asked.

"I saw the number when that shithead dialed the phone."

"But isn't he out?"

"Yeah."

"Then why are we going up to his room?"

"I have no fucking clue."

When the doors slid open, they stepped smartly onto the deep carpet of the hotel corridor, and Bar lead the way to Eddie's suite.

"Are you going to break in or something?"

Bar just turned his head and looked at Lek without saying anything. *Now there's an idea.*

They stopped at the polished teak door, and he side-glanced at Lek. "I'd better check first. Maybe Dare wasn't answering the phone."

He lifted his hand to knock, but Lek reached out and cupped it in hers before it made contact with the door.

"There's a bell," she said, pointing to a white button centered in a filigréed brass plate.

"I knew that."

Bar quickly pulled his hand away from Lek's, and poked at the button with his forefinger.

◗●◗

Silom Road was still throbbing with life when Eddie emerged from the dim interior of Nick's Kitchen. He stood briefly in the lights from the street—blinking away the patterns they splashed over his face—and then he began to walk. For no particular reason, he turned to the left. He didn't know where he was going, but for the moment at least, he didn't care.

Hands jammed deep into his pockets, he adopted a measured, deliberate pace. All at once, the colors of the street seemed to have become unnaturally bright; the sounds unexpectedly loud; and the smells unusually pungent. The alchemy of it tantalized and terrified him at the same time.

It was obvious now, he guessed. Both the Asian man following them when he pulled the elevator trick, and the four men outside the Stardust, were probably Vietnamese. At least, he supposed, he'd found out who he was up against. But he wasn't all that sure what good it was going to do him.

As he walked, the Thai lettering in the signs overhead became a cryptic lattice of confusing, contradictory counsel. Music blared from everywhere and nowhere at the same time. Faces lurked in the half darkness: cigarette peddlers behind wooden trays heaped with counterfeit Marlboro boxes; dark-faced hawkers displaying sliced fruit in tiny glass cases lit with dim, yellow bulbs; *tuk-tuk* boys smoking as they sprawled across the seats of their improbable vehicles; a shriveled woman with a pale face thrusting out a baby with one hand and rattling a can with the other. Eddie floated through it all, suspended in a cocoon of fatigue and disorientation.

Abruptly, he felt something else start to push those things aside. A vague exhilaration was sprouting somewhere within him—he could feel it—but it had a sense of alarm attached to it, too. He felt like a man contemplating an oncoming attack of nausea.

A short way down Silom, he stopped and turned back toward Nick's Kitchen. Tan Suit was standing at the doorway with Shepherd and Sanchez, his hands on his hips. He was nodding slowly at whatever Shepherd was saying, but he was looking directly at Eddie.

Eddie turned away and resumed his slow, methodical pacing. When he glanced over his shoulder again and saw Tan Suit about a half block behind, he stopped and pretended to look through some video cassettes a vendor had spread out on a folding table.

Tan Suit stopped, too, but didn't bother to pretend he was doing anything. He just slouched against a wall about thirty yards back, a half smile on his face, obviously figuring that the time would soon come when Eddie would make up his mind about where he was going next.

Yeah—it came to Eddie all in a rush—Tan Suit had hit the nail right on the head.

It sure as hell is *time for me to make up my mind where I'm going next.*

"I figured we'd just wait for you down in the lobby, but then . . ." Bar looked a little sheepish and cut his eyes at Lek who was focusing somewhere across the room. "Well, your door was open, so we just came in and waited."

Eddie had walked back to the Oriental, turning everything over and over again in his mind. Tan Suit kept thirty or forty yards behind him all the way, but Eddie stopped paying any attention to him. He didn't make it back until well after midnight, and when he did, he spent another ten minutes talking to the concierge before he went upstairs.

When he thought about it later, he supposed finding Bar and Lek waiting for him inside his suite should have made him suspicious—but coming on top of everything else, that development had seemed relatively minor league at the time.

"The door wasn't open, Bar."

"It was after Lek did some little trick with a credit card."

Eddie nodded. "I wonder what other little tricks she knows."

Lek's eyes flicked briefly to Eddie's and then away—registering the hit, but saying nothing.

"Come on, man. Don't go hard-assed on us just because McBride pissed all over you." Bar tried for a jovial tone. "It's not like we tossed the place."

"You should have. You might have found something."

"Well. . . ," Bar motioned vaguely off into the air, ". . . Lek wanted to, but I wouldn't let her."

"Are you kidding?"

"No."

Before anyone could add anything else, the door opened and Winnebago came in.

He glanced around, and then his eyes fixed on Eddie. He studied him closely, like a man searching for clues. "You don't look so good," he concluded.

Eddie just nodded. He could certainly understood how that might very well be true.

25

"**A**nybody else hungry?" Eddie scratched at his ear and scrutinized the overhead light fixture. "I've been trying to feed myself half the night without getting it done yet."

"I could eat something," Bar answered.

Winnebago, putting a cigarette into his mouth and rotating it between his fingers, just nodded. Everybody looked at Lek, and she nodded, too.

Eddie called room service and ordered four club sandwiches and two large pots of coffee. He often wondered if anyone actually liked club sandwiches, or if they'd just been invented to put on room service menus so people in hotels could order something in the middle of the night that didn't require any thought. But then he'd just ordered four club sandwiches himself, so maybe that answered his question.

After Eddie hung up, he gave Lek another long look, and then turned to Bar.

"What are you doing here?"

"I want you to tell me the truth about why you're so interested in Harry Austin."

"I did tell you the truth."

"If you did, you didn't tell me all of it."

Eddie dropped into a big chair across from Bar and hauled one leg up over the arm. He let his eyes drift across to Lek again, but she was looking at the wall just above his head and apparently didn't notice. His eyes wandered down her bare, brown legs—folded together and tucked at a graceful angle under her chair. They came to rest, as they had at the embassy, on her trim ankles. What was it about Lek's legs that kept giving him this little tweak? Surely living in San Francisco he wasn't *that* starved for the sight of smooth calves and slim ankles; or was he?

"What really put you onto Harry Austin?" Bar's voice interrupted Eddie's musings.

Eddie forced his eyes away from Lek's ankles for the second time that night and back to Bar. "I already told you. I was hired to find out what happened to him."

Bar's face was perfectly still, and there was the look in his eyes of a decision being made.

"If you tell me the whole truth, Eddie, I can help. If you don't, I'm just going to get up and walk out of here." Bar lifted his eyebrows, raising ridges of skin over his forehead that looked like ripples of sand spreading over a beach. "I want to help you. I really do. Especially after what happened tonight. But I can't do it unless you tell me everything."

Eddie's face took on the look of something rooted, and the long silence that followed wasn't broken until the doorbell rang. Winnebago opened the door and a waiter in a starched, white jacket wheeled a room service table into the room with a flourish.

The four club sandwiches were elaborately quartered and arranged under glass domes with sprigs of greenery. The heavy, silver coffee pots looked like they had recently been stolen from the Louvre. The young waiter started fussing about unfolding the table and gathering chairs, but Eddie grabbed the check off the table, signed it, and hustled the boy out as quickly as he could without flinging him bodily into the corridor.

As soon as the door closed, Bar started in. "Your story about Austin's family hiring you sucks, Eddie. If anyone actually did hire you to dig up Harry Austin's past, it's for some reason you haven't told us. Or maybe no one hired you. Maybe you have reasons of your own. Either way, if you don't tell me, I'm out of here."

Eddie passed out the sandwiches and poured coffee. He took his own over to a chair by the window and ate the first quarter in silence.

"I think you ought to tell them," Winnebago finally said in a low voice.

Bar and Lek watched Eddie weigh Winnebago's advice. He tried to think his way logically through all the different scenarios that had developed over the past few days, but he gave up quickly. The possible combinations of interests and alliances were just too confusing and contradictory to rationalize into anything coherent; or maybe he was just too tired to see what made them all fit together.

Sometimes you just had to throw everything up in the air without knowing what you were doing, he knew. Just throw it up and see how it all comes down.

Eddie took another sip of coffee, wiped his mouth with a napkin, and leaned back in his chair. Then he swung his legs up on the coffee table, put his hands behind his head, and began to talk.

Carefully and methodically he told Bar and Lek about Operation Voltaire and the ten tons of currency and gold from the Bank of Vietnam; about the Secret Service investigation that first led to Harry Austin and then to him; about being hired by Marinus Rupert to search for the money; about the man's transformation into someone called the General; about Lieutenant Sirapop and about the German who had seen Austin's body dragged into the Little Princess; about Shepherd and Sanchez at Nick's Kitchen; about the black and white glossies of the General in the slinky, black dress; and finally, about Vietnamese Intelligence and the Secret Service's offer of one percent of the Voltaire money to doublecross them.

Eddie watched Bar and Lek intently while he talked. He thought that Lek appeared shaken by his story—although she hid it fairly well—but he didn't think that Bar even looked all that interested.

"Have you heard all this somewhere before?" he asked Bar when he'd finished.

"Not exactly the same story, but a lot of others just like it." Bar yawned. "Look, Eddie, Bangkok's an elephant's graveyard for crap like that. About twice a month some hustler turns up here hot on the trail of the lost treasure of the Czars, or waving a map to a stash of Japanese gold from the war. I don't get too excited about it anymore."

"I'm not a hustler," Eddie responded quietly. "And this isn't crap."

"That's what everyone always says."

"This time it's different."

Bar's eyes flickered for a moment, opening and closing, and then they met Eddie's. "They always say that, too. But I'm still listening."

"Think about it, Bar. The Secret Service spends a year chasing this story around and then ends up offering me a deal to help them find the money. The Vietnamese organize an elaborate plot to trick me into helping *them* find the money. Why would they do that unless there was something there? They can't both be *that* stupid."

"Don't forget the pictures," Winnebago added.

"Yeah, those sure as hell didn't come from the Secret Service or the Vietnamese. Whoever sent them to the three of us . . ."

"Four," Lek interrupted, and everyone looked at her. "Don't forget, Harry got them, too."

Eddie let his gaze linger briefly on Lek before turning back to Bar. "Whoever sent them thinks I know something, and they've gone to a hell of a lot of trouble to warn me off. That's three separate crowds tracking the Voltaire money with only one thing in common. They're all looking at me. Now why the hell do you think that is, if this is just bullshit?"

Bar took a deep breath and rolled his tongue slowly around in his cheek. When he spoke, he measured his words carefully, like a man doling out medicine.

"You're telling me there really *is* ten tons of money out there somewhere?"

"Looks like it. Maybe not ten tons of it anymore, but probably still one hell of a lot."

Bar rubbed at his face with one hand while he tried to grasp the concept of hundreds of millions of dollars just lying around in Bangkok. He quickly gave up. "Even if it's true, Eddie, why does it matter anymore?"

Winnebago looked at Bar like he had belched in the middle of the Lord's Prayer. "I don't know about you, you old fart, but I think a few hundred million dollars matters a lot."

"Look, whether Austin was murdered or it was an accident, the man's still dead. If he knew anything, you'll never find out now what it was. Not unless . . ." Bar trailed off.

"Unless what?" Eddie asked.

"Unless you've already guessed."

"I haven't."

There was a short silence, and then Lek collected her purse and stood up. "Could I use the bathroom?"

"Try the one in there." Eddie pointed to the door across the suite that led to his bedroom. "It's probably cleaner than Winnebago's."

As soon as he heard the door click shut, Eddie leaned forward and rested his elbows on his knees. He looked hard at Bar. "What do you know about Lek?"

"Don't go paranoid on me, man. You heard what Chuck said. You know as much as I do."

"Then what do you know about Chuck McBride?"

"Don't worry about Chuck. The DEA guys out here are solid."

"Yeah? How do you know that?"

"Know that the DEA guys are solid?"

"No, that McBride's DEA."

"Of course, he's DEA." Bar looked at Eddie in exasperation. "What else would he be?"

"He knows too much about Harry Austin and he's too interested in him. Don't you think that's odd if he's just a drug cop?"

"What are you saying? I've been to his office at the embassy a hundred times. He's got a sign on his door and everything."

"Oh, right. Because he has a little sign on his door at the embassy that says so, he *must* be DEA."

"Come on, Eddie. How the hell do you know who your daddy is? Because your mamma told you so."

Eddie nodded slowly and let it ride. Bar's nose twitched and he sat toying with his coffee spoon. Although he didn't say anything else, a look of discomfort crossed his face before he could chase it away.

Lek came back from the bathroom and settled onto the couch. Eddie went on as soon as she sat down, his tone neutral.

"What can you tell us about Captain Austin?"

She tilted her head to one side and studied Eddie before replying. She tried to read his eyes, but she couldn't.

"What do you want to know?"

"Start with the obvious, I guess. How about his finances?"

"Three years ago he had some term deposits at Bangkok Bank—just over 12 million baht—about half a million US dollars. And he had a couple of savings accounts; you know, regular day-to-day accounts with small balances. After I left the bank, I don't know what happened to them."

"Where did that money go after he died?"

Lek shook her head slightly. "I don't know."

"Did you find any trace of it at all? Deposit books? Bank certificates? Anything like that?"

"No."

"I've got to tell you that something bothers me here." Eddie looked evenly at her, still giving away nothing. "You sound pretty cold about your husband's death. You talk about his money, but you never say anything about *him*. Why is that?"

"I'm sorry I don't meet your California standards of grief," she snapped. Her face was taut. "Harry was just . . ."

"He didn't really trust you, did he? He never told you very much."

"Harry was a peculiar man in many ways," Lek said carefully after a long pause.

Eddie thought she looked like someone walking through a minefield. Something worked at him, but he couldn't figure out exactly what it was.

"He just kept some things to himself," she finished. "You had to know him to understand."

"I did know him."

"Maybe not as well as I did."

Eddie stood up and walked over to the windows, looking down at the Chao Praya River, still and black in the moonless night. He didn't really want any more coffee, but he picked up his cup anyway and tipped it to his lips, letting the lukewarm liquid just hang there against his tongue without swallowing.

What the hell am I doing? Why am I eyeing her legs one moment, and cross-examining her like a criminal the next?

He felt like he was again standing in front of that door that had started to swing open for him when he was back at the embassy; the papers from Harry Austin's safety deposit box spread over the table in front of him.

Although the door yawned unmistakably now, standing wide open—and he saw that as clearly as he had ever seen anything in his life—he could still make out nothing at all of what waited beyond it.

Nevertheless, he returned his cup to its saucer and put them both down carefully on a table. Then he took a deep breath, and without so much as a glance over his shoulder, plunged through the door.

"I'm not going to miss this party."

He pursed his lips as if he was trying to decide whether there was anything he was leaving out—but there wasn't. It was just that simple.

"That's it. I'm in this until it's over, whatever that turns out to mean."

The room was still. Bar, Lek and Winnebago watched Eddie carefully, but no one said anything. The silence quivered around them like jelly.

"If any of you want to throw in with me. . . ," Eddie paused long enough to underline the significance of what he was going to say next, ". . . I'll divide whatever we get out of it equally with each of you. If we get anything at all."

Lek's face was blank—her eyes almost transparent. Bar stared at Eddie with a gaze he couldn't read.

Winnebago took another bite of his sandwich. Chewing on it thoughtfully, he swallowed and rubbed the back of his hand across his mouth. "In 'Nam you got me into some shit that still makes my asshole pucker, man. You know, I got to think about that."

"I understand."

"I guess . . ." Winnebago paused, thinking back. Suddenly he flashed a wide grin and punched a fist into the air. "Hey, fuck this hippie shit! Let's do it!"

Eddie nodded with a serious look on his face and glanced at Bar.

"How about it?"

"What if I say no?"

"Since I've already told you everything, I'll have to kill you."

"You're kidding."

"Yeah, but only barely."

Bar tapped his forefinger absent-mindedly against his coffee cup and then traced it around the lip. He looked across at Eddie and held his eyes for a long moment. "Okay, Eddie. What am I saving my youth for, huh? I haven't had any real fun in a long time either. I'm in."

"You won't be sorry."

"I already am." Bar laughed under his breath. "But only barely."

The three of them looked at Lek.

She lifted both hands in a mock gesture of surrender. "I'm not going to get very far on my own. Count me in, too, I guess."

"Well then. . . ," Eddie wondered, not for the first time, if he knew what he was doing, ". . . I guess we're in business."

"So, what's the plan?" Winnebago asked.

"I don't know."

"You got no plan?" Winnebago looked pained. "Nothing?"

"I've got a place to start. After that, we'll just have to see how everything works out." Eddie glanced at Bar. "Can you organize somewhere for the four of us to stay for a few days."

"What for?" He looked around the suite. "The Oriental's not good enough for you?"

"Not a regular hotel. We've got to disappear for a while. Do you know anyone who's out of town; maybe someone who could lend us a house or an apartment?"

Bar thought for a moment while they all watched him. "Okay, I know just the right place."

"We'll need it tomorrow night."

"You got it."

"I don't understand something," Winnebago interrupted. "With the Secret Service, the Vietnamese, and Christ only knows who else watching every time we take a leak, how are we supposed to get to wherever this is without them all knowing where we've gone?"

"That part I got all worked out. We'll just do something so boring they'll all lose interest for a while."

"What could we possibly do in Bangkok that's boring?" Bar looked stumped.

Eddie smiled. "Go to Singapore."

They left Bangkok a little after noon the next day on a Thai International Airways flight, each having bought a ticket to Singapore from a different travel agent and paid for it in cash. No one checked any luggage. Eddie and Winnebago left everything in their suite, other than what they packed into two small carry-ons, and slipped out the back of the Oriental to the river landing. They took the ferry to Silapakorn University, lost themselves in the crowds of students, and found a taxi to the airport. Bar and Lek each made their own way to the airport; Lek using the Thai International limousine service, and Bar on a bus.

Once at Don Muang Airport, they all checked in separately without speaking, and then scattered themselves around the three cabins of the big airbus. They gave no indication that they were traveling together. Four apparently unrelated individual passengers would be far harder for anyone to remember later, Eddie thought—and certainly a lot less conspicuous than three American men and an Asian woman traveling in a group.

Eddie had no illusions about his ability to keep them hidden for very long. He was an amateur and they were up against professionals. Neither Vietnamese Intelligence nor the Secret Service was stupid. Both would trace them relatively quickly, in spite of anything he could do. When they all disappeared from Bangkok, airport departures would be the first thing checked—and it wouldn't be particularly difficult to find out where they had gone.

Every passenger leaving Bangkok filled out a departure card, and at the immigration check just before the gates, the cards were marked with both a flight number and a destination. Within twelve hours after they dropped out of sight, those cards could easily be retrieved—either officially, or more likely, unofficially—and it would be simple enough for anyone to find out that they were in Singapore. Except, of course, they wouldn't be.

At the concierge desk the night before, Eddie had gone through the Official Airline Guide and learned that fifty-two minutes after the noon flight from Bangkok landed at Singapore's Changi Airport, there was a Silk Air flight leaving for Phuket—the Thai resort island in the Andaman Sea. Forty-one minutes after the Silk Air flight arrived in Phuket, a Thai Airways domestic flight left there for the short hop back to Bangkok. They could all be tucked away back in the city, almost before anyone had worked out that they'd left in the first place. The gambit had flare, if Eddie did say so himself. Since they'd never leave the international transit lounge at Changi—and never enter Singapore—there'd be no record left behind there. No trail at all.

That wouldn't stop anyone for very long, of course. When no entry record was found in Singapore, it would be obvious what they'd done, and all the out-bound flights from Changi after the time of their arrival would be checked. But there were a lot of them, and that would take quite a while. Even when they were finally traced to Phuket, the whole process would have to be repeated there again before anyone figured out that they were actually back in Bangkok.

Eddie figured his little subterfuge might get them two or three days to poke around discreetly about Harry Austin before they started drawing a crowd again. That is, it might if they stayed lucky.

It wasn't much—maybe it was nothing at all. Right then however, it felt like a pretty good start.

26

The loading bridge nestled snugly up against the airbus, and Eddie, Bar, Winnebago and Lek filed out separately, losing themselves in the crush of passengers thronging Terminal One at Changi.

Within a few minutes, they had assembled at a spot in the terminal next to a goldfish pond. The pond was arched by a wooden bridge which looked vaguely Japanese and led to a Planet Hollywood gift shop and the Internet Café.

Stores of all sorts seemed to stretch to the horizon inside the huge complex. Overhead signs pointed to a movie theater showing four recent Hollywood films; a gym with two jogging tracks and a swimming pool; a 24-hour children's play center; a desk providing hourly city tours of Singapore; and a nondenominational chapel with a meditation area. Eddie glanced in the direction of the chapel and wondered what kind of crowd it drew.

"Okay, listen up. There are Silk Air desks over there...," Eddie pointed past a computer shop and a florist to where a few airline signs were barely visible in the distance, "... and down there." He pointed in the opposite direction toward where a storefront displayed exercise equipment. "Split up and buy your tickets one by one. Everyone got money?"

They all nodded.

"Okay. There's supposed to be a bar around the middle of this building somewhere. Meet there when you're done. We ought to be okay waiting together here."

After they'd bought their tickets and settled in, they ordered beers all around, and Winnebago reached for his Camels. Almost before the pack had cleared his pocket, a young Singaporean in a brown blazer with a gold patch of some kind over the pocket materialized next to their table. He beamed down at Winnebago with a beatific smile.

"My apologies, sir, but smoking is not permitted here. Only over there...," the man gestured toward the opposite side of the terminal building, "... in the smoking booth."

Winnebago turned and looked in the direction the young man was pointing, but he saw nothing except milling passengers and more stores. He looked back at the guy, who was still smiling maniacally, like a Mormon on speed.

"What the hell's a smoking booth?"

The man gestured again in the same direction, nodding encouragingly.

Winnebago looked again, and this time he saw it. In a distant corner of the terminal was a glass room the size of a small office. It had a sort of airlock for a door, and inside a dozen people sat and puffed energetically on cigarettes; their bodies dim outlines through a smoky haze.

Eddie looked where Winnebago's eyes were pointing. "I wonder if there's a please-don't-feed-the-animals sign on it?"

Winnebago returned the Camels to his pocket and tossed the blazered young man a salute. "Up yours, Captain."

The man looked bewildered as he flipped quickly through his mental dictionary of English idioms. *Up yours? What does 'up yours' mean?* Eventually—still obviously baffled—he returned the salute with a military snap, and walked away.

Winnebago watched him go. "Fuck, man. That's un-American, treat people like that."

"This is Singapore," Eddie reminded him. "They like rules. You can't chew gum either."

Winnebago just shook his head some more and they all sat in silence for a while and watched a man in white tie and tails play a silver grand piano. He rippled through 'Some Enchanted Evening' and 'You'll Never Walk Alone,' and he was just launching into 'The Impossible Dream' when Winnebago quickly drained the rest of his beer and stood up. "I'm going to the gate. If I have to listen to any more of this shit without smoking, I'm gonna puke."

"I'm with you," Bar chimed in, chugging his own beer.

The corridor which led out to their boarding gate was decked out in pink and blue pastels and it stretched into the distance until it seemed to disappear from sight over the horizon. It was crowded with passengers heading in both directions, but the moving walkways allowed them to make rapid progress.

Eddie and Lek fell behind the others—cut off by a troop of elderly Japanese tourists led by an earnest-looking, young woman waving a small flag—but when they stepped off the section of walkway that ended in front of Gate F54, Bar reached out of the crowd with one hand and caught Eddie by the elbow. He pointed ahead.

It was still at least fifty yards to Gate F58 where the Phuket flight was loading, and making out exactly what was happening there was difficult. One thing was unmistakable, however. A cordon of Singapore police was blocking the entry to the gate lobby, and they were carefully checking each passenger who entered.

"That's impossible. No way anyone could have traced us that fast. No goddamn way." Eddie shook his head for emphasis. "Stay here. I'll check it out."

Working himself into the crowd, he drifted with it to the line that had formed to enter F58. At the head of the line, two stony-faced policemen in starched, khaki uniforms were questioning each passenger individually; meticulously examining their passport before another pair of cops behind a table completely unpacked every piece of carry-on luggage and searched painstakingly through its contents.

Eddie eased up next to a boy in the line who he thought looked like a good bet for striking up a conversation. The boy was in his early twenties, tall, with the deep tan and the long, stringy hair of a traveler. Eddie immediately decided he was probably an American. He guessed that partly because of his clothes, and partly because of his cocky slouch. But what sealed it was the big sticker across the worn backpack lying at his feet. It unapologetically proclaimed the boy's personal policy on foreign relations: NO FAT CHICKS.

Eddie swapped the San Francisco in his voice for something that might sound a little more down home. He tried for Texas, and made it at least as far as Oklahoma.

"What's going on up there?"

"You English?" The boy looked Eddie over neutrally.

"No, buddy. American."

"Oh." The kid didn't bother to hide his disappointment. "I'm from London."

Eddie was just working on a quick change of tack when the boy took him off the hook. He pointed to the front of the line where the cops were grilling a short, dark man and examining his passport with evident skepticism.

"Looks like the local storm troopers want somebody pretty bad."

"Do you know who they're looking for?" Eddie kept his voice casual.

The kid was just starting to shake his head when an elderly woman in the line behind him leaned forward.

"They're not looking for *anyone*," she volunteered in a voice that immediately reminded Eddie of his third grade teacher. "This is a special security flight because of the Prime Minister."

Eddie and the kid glanced at each other in puzzlement.

"The Prime Minister and his family are on the plane today," the woman went on in the same pedantic tone when it became obvious that neither of them understood what she meant.

Eddie looked her over. She appeared vaguely Chinese, although her English was perfect and unaccented. The boy had also turned around when the woman spoke and was sizing her up, too.

"Tony Blair?" he asked, obviously confused. "Tony Blair's on *this* flight?"

The woman looked scandalized. "I meant *our* Prime Minister. Prime Minister Goh of Singapore." She narrowed her eyes at the boy. "Everyone isn't English, you know, young man."

"And I for one thank Christ for it," Eddie added as he made good his escape.

When Eddie got back to the others, Winnebago was the first to demand details.

"So?"

"The Prime Minister of Singapore apparently picked our flight for a little jaunt of his own today. That's why the cops are double-checking everything. It's got nothing to do with us."

"Oh, man." Winnebago loosed a long sigh. "I guess I can start breathing again."

"Wait a minute." It was Lek. "Maybe we should still take another flight."

"What's the problem?" Eddie glanced at her and saw that she was obviously concerned about something. "They're not interested in us."

"It still makes us conspicuous. We should wait."

"Look, we can't wait." Eddie's voice was firm. "There's no problem. Let's go."

"I say we wait." There was an edge to Lek's voice and her bag remained on the floor.

"This is Eddie's show." Bar's voice was level. "He says we go, and we go. We all go. That's the way it works."

Lek glanced at Bar, then at Eddie, who was watching her curiously. She seemed to think for a moment, and then lowered her head. "Sorry. I guess I'm a little edgy."

"Don't worry about it," Eddie responded as they moved off toward the gate. "We're all edgy."

After they went through the passport checks and had their boarding passes collected, they were each passed along separately for the inspection of their carry-on bags. Bar and Eddie were through first, and stood together inside the boarding lounge waiting for the others.

"Ever been to Phuket before?" Eddie asked Bar.

"Once."

"Liked it?"

"I liked everywhere once."

Winnebago was straggling across the lounge toward them when the doors to the loading bridge opened and the rush to board the aircraft started.

Over Winnebago's shoulder, Eddie could see that Lek was still in front of one of the security tables, the contents of her carry-on bag having been fastidiously distributed into piles by a khaki-uniformed security man.

"Ready?" Winnebago asked when he reached them, shifting his bag from one hand to the other.

Eddie pointed back to where Lek appeared to be having an angry conversation with the security man, and they all turned to watch. They were too far away to hear what was being said, but the man was holding up what looked like two small books he had taken from Lek's bag, and was waving them at one of the cops.

"What the hell's going on?" Bar murmured.

"You guys go ahead and get us some seats." Eddie handed his bag to Winnebago. "I'll see."

Eddie started back across the lounge, and—with a shrug—Winnebago turned to join the crowd jostling through the narrow gate to the plane.

Bar was still watching Lek. "Go ahead," he called after Winnebago. "I'll catch up with you."

When he walked up behind Eddie, he could see that three policemen had Lek and her carry-on bag surrounded. A security officer was blocking Eddie from approaching her.

"You cannot leave the lounge, sir."

Eddie pointed toward Lek. "She's with me. I'm just trying to see what the problem is."

The policeman nearest them overheard, and moved toward Eddie, checking him out cautiously.

"Did you say you were traveling with this woman, sir?"

"Yes."

The cop held out his right hand, palm up. "Your passport, please."

"You've already checked it. Twice."

Eddie slowly and deliberately folded his arms, and watched the policeman, who was very young. A black plastic plate pinned over the left breast pocket of his khakis spelled out his name—Tan—in thick, white letters.

He continued to hold out his hand, his face expressionless. "Your passport, sir."

Eddie took his time about it, but he unfolded his arms and slowly pulled his passport from his back pocket. He twirled it in his fingers for a moment in a modest show of defiance, and then slapped it into the young policeman's open hand.

In return, Tan took his time about opening the passport, and then studied the picture with particular attention. He glanced up several times at Eddie as though comparing facial details one at a time.

"You are an American, sir?"

"That's how you get the passport."

Bar winced inwardly. This wasn't the right place for Eddie to start lobbing wisecracks. He was in Asia now, not San Francisco; and out here, if you didn't lose the attitude pretty quick, somebody would snatch it away and beat you to death with it.

"May I ask what the problem is, Officer?" Bar cut in, attempting to defuse the growing hostility.

Tan flicked his eyes to Bar for a moment. Wordlessly dismissing him, he pointed his forefinger at Eddie. "Wait here."

Eddie and Bar watched silently as the policeman walked over to an older man in a dark business suit who appeared to be in charge. They spoke briefly and the man turned his head and looked at Eddie. Eddie wasn't sure if he should smile or not, so he didn't.

After a moment, the man took Eddie's passport from Tan and walked very slowly across the boarding lounge, appraising Eddie as he approached.

"What is your relationship to this woman?"

The man appeared to be in his forties, with black eyes that gave nothing away, and a hard, unlined Chinese-looking face. The fact that he hadn't bothered to introduce himself before getting straight to the point suggested to Eddie that, very possibly, this wasn't a guy to screw around with.

"She's the widow of a man who recently passed away," Eddie replied in his lawyer voice, playing it straight. "I'm her attorney and I'm assisting her with the settlement of his estate."

Close enough for government work.

"And you?" The man inclined his head toward Bar. "Who are you?"

"He's my assistant," Eddie responded quickly, and Bar nodded at the man with a serious expression.

The man looked at Bar for a long moment, and then studied Eddie's passport some more. He folded back the first page and held it up to the light, although what he might be looking for completely baffled Eddie.

When he finally closed the small, blue booklet, he stood tapping it against his hand—as if making up his mind about something. Suddenly he flipped it back to Eddie, who grabbed it clumsily out of the air. The man wheeled and walked away, making a gesture toward the guard at the table, who immediately began replacing Lek's things in her bag.

"What the hell was *that* all about?" Bar whispered to Eddie.

He shrugged. "I guess Lek can tell us."

They both stood and watched while the guard returned everything to Lek. The last things he gave her were two passports, and Eddie realized those were the books he'd seen when the guard first emptied her bag. She snatched both of them out of the man's hand, then she grabbed up her bag and stalked away.

Lek sailed by Eddie and Bar without stopping, her mouth fixed in a tight line. They caught up with her at the entry to the loading bridge.

"Self-righteous little Singaporean pricks!" She was so angry she was almost spitting.

Eddie gave her a moment and then asked neutrally, "You gonna tell me what that was all about?"

"Bullshit." Lek's eyes were flashing. "It was all about bullshit."

"And the size and color of the bull were . . ." Eddie made an open gesture with his right hand.

In spite of herself, Lek laughed.

"Sorry."

She blinked a few times, and then moved her hand slowly across her face like a child miming a change of expression. When she dropped her hand, she was smiling again.

"My American passport has my Western name in it, and my Thai passport has my Chinese name. My mother was very traditional. These morons thought they'd nabbed a terrorist with a bunch of phony passports." Lek's anger appeared to be burning itself out quickly. "I'm sorry. Singaporeans just piss me off. They're all a bunch of damned bananas."

"Bananas?" Eddie was clearly puzzled.

"Yellow on the outside," Bar explained, sotto-voiced. "And white on the inside."

Eddie laughed to himself as the line shuffled toward the plane.

"Why'd they make such a big deal out of it?" He turned toward Lek when they bogged down in the crowd. "I thought it was common for Asians to have a Western name and an ethnic name."

Lek cocked her head at Eddie. "An *ethnic* name?"

"Well, I meant . . ."

"Yeah, I know what you meant, white boy." Lek smiled as she disappeared into the airbus.

Eddie ducked through the door behind her, straightened up, and looked around. The aisle was jammed with a gathering of mismatched humanity, frantically trying to shove into the airplane's tiny overhead lockers what might easily have been the booty from the sacking of a good-sized city.

Lek slid into the first empty seat she saw, and Bar and Eddie edged on down the aisle past her. An elderly Chinese woman hefting a large box improbably labeled DENTAL EQUIPMENT ran interference for them.

When a bemused stewardess trying vainly to separate the old lady from her box halted them, Bar glanced quickly back over his shoulder to where Lek was settling into her seat. He nudged Eddie gently in the back. "What did you make of all that?"

Eddie shrugged without turning around.

"The Singaporeans get carried away sometimes. Just standard, petty horseshit for them."

Bar leaned forward until his lips were almost brushing Eddie's ear. "I don't want to make something out of nothing," he whispered. "But I got a pretty good look at Lek's passports."

"Yeah?" Eddie was transfixed by the sight of the stewardess trying to force the elderly lady's four-foot box into a two-foot locker. The old woman blocked the aisle, shrieking and flapping around in near hysteria.

"I've seen a lot of regular Thai passports. I don't think that's what Lek has."

That got Eddie's attention and he turned his head around just as the stewardess gave a mighty heave and wedged most of the box into the overhead bin.

"What was it?"

"I might be wrong. I don't want to end up with shit on my nose here, but I think it was a diplomatic passport."

Eddie cocked his head and thought about that.

"Lek's carrying a Thai diplomatic passport?"

Bar shook his head slowly.

"No, not Thai."

He took a deep breath.

"I think it might've been Vietnamese."

Eddie absorbed that slowly as the stewardess gave the box one more shove and somehow slammed the bin door shut on it. As the line of waiting passengers started to creep slowly back through the aircraft again, he puffed up his cheeks, and cautiously contemplated the implications of what he had just heard.

When he found an empty seat, he flopped into it and dropped his bag on the floor. Tilting his head back, he exhaled very slowly in the universal sigh of deep fatigue and total exasperation.

"Well," he murmered to himself. "Fuck a goddamned duck."

27

E ddie had always noticed that if an American could name any place in Thailand other than Bangkok, it was usually Phuket.

A large, limestone island set in the Andaman Sea just off the country's south coast, Phuket had reinvented itself in a single generation from a scarred landscape of abandoned strip mines, into a famed, international beach resort. On the other hand, after the churning maelstrom of Bangkok and its ten million or so souls—lost and otherwise—nowhere else in the country actually counted for anything anyway, so being the second best-known place in Thailand didn't really amount to very much.

After the Silk Air Fokker whistled in over the steep sea cliffs of the island's barren north coast and taxied to a stop at the small terminal building, the passengers were herded quickly through a cursory immigration and customs check, and then let loose.

Lek went to look for a rest room, while Winnebago lit a Camel and strolled off in search of a beer.

Eddie eyed the other passengers carefully as they got off. No one was paying any attention to them, he was reasonably sure. That was what he had expected of course, but nevertheless he felt a twinge of relief to see that it was true.

When he emerged into the terminal building, he glanced around to get his bearings. The structure looked fairly new, but it was already well down the road to shabbiness. The concrete floors were cracked and stained, and orange plastic chairs were bolted into groups of five here and there throughout the building. Most of the arrangements featured either a large dead plant or a wooden rack with a few old newspapers. There was a dreary-looking shop of some kind, and near the front doors, a few plastic tables seemed to harbor ambitions of becoming a coffee shop.

Eddie spotted Bar sitting alone in an orange row at the back of the waiting room, his head buried in a small book. He walked over and put a hand on his shoulder. "So, what do you think?"

Bar looked up. "You mean about Lek?"

Eddie nodded, and Bar chewed it over as he closed his book.

"You think Lek's playing for the other team, don't you?" Eddie prompted when Bar didn't say anything right away.

"Don't get all wound up yet. I may have been wrong about that passport."

"But if you were right?"

"Maybe it still doesn't mean anything. There're a lot of Vietnamese in Thailand, Eddie. They're not all after you. At least probably not."

"Don't you think we'd better find out about this one for sure?"

"How you going to do that?"

Eddie sat down without answering, his eyes on the door and his back to the wall.

"What are you reading?" he asked after a moment, glancing toward the thin book Bar was holding.

"It's a Thai phrasebook. Somebody left it in the seat pocket on the plane."

"But you speak Thai. What do you need that for?"

"I saved it for you. It's pretty good. None of that 'Your pencil is on the table' shit. Want to hear some of the phrases?"

Eddie shrugged noncommittally and then looked at his watch, losing interest. Where the hell were Winnebago and Lek? Maybe they'd wandered off for perfectly ordinary reasons; but then nothing ordinary seemed to have happened for a long time, and Eddie couldn't keep himself from worrying a little.

"It starts with, 'Can you find me a hotel?' That's *'Ga roo na chuay pom ha rong raem noi krap?'*"

Eddie fidgeted, his eyes flicking around the terminal, searching for Lek and Winnebago.

"Then comes, 'Can you get me a woman?' *'Ga roo na chuay pom ha pooying noi krap?'*"

Eddie glanced at Bar.

"After that, 'How much do you cost?' *'Khun ra ka . . .'*"

Eddie held up his right hand, palm out.

"Wait a minute. That's not in there. You're making this up."

Bar shook his head solemnly. "No shit, Eddie. It's all right here."

He tapped the book with one finger. "Then, 'That is too expensive,' so I figure this thing was probably printed up for Chinese tourists."

Eddie tilted his head back and started to chuckle.

"Anything else?"

"'I think you are beautiful,' and 'I love you.'"

"Those are real useful."

"There's one more," Bar added.

"I can hardly wait."

"Want to hear it?"

"Sure."

"'Will you marry me?'"

When Eddie saw Lek and Winnebago coming across the terminal, he stopped laughing long enough to lean toward Bar and whisper a few words into his ear. Bar nodded, glancing up at Lek, but then grinned again in spite of himself.

By the time Lek and Winnebago slid into two of the orange chairs, Bar and Eddie were both laughing so hard they were wiping away tears with the backs of their hands.

●━●━●

The flight to Bangkok left a half hour later and was uneventful. Since it arrived at Bangkok's domestic terminal, Eddie wasn't overly concerned about being spotted. Anyone looking for them would have been working the international terminal building, not domestic arrivals. Their return therefore went unnoticed—at least as far as Eddie could tell—but just to be on the safe side, he hustled everyone outside and into a taxi as quickly as he could.

The Forty Winks guest house was in Chinatown, at the end of a dimly-lit lane that dead-ended at the river. There was a small sign next to the green metal gate. It was a tiny, yellow-lit glass pane with one line of Thai characters and one line of Chinese, but nothing at all in English. It wouldn't have been an easy place to find had Bar not hunched forward from the back seat and given directions to the taxi driver in staccato whispers as the little Toyota whipped through a maze of tiny, twisting streets.

When their headlights flashed across the gate, set back into a concrete wall, two white-shirted boys in dark trousers and black bow-ties leaped quickly from folding metal chairs and pushed it open. Backing inside, they flicked on flashlights, and—directing the taxi with frantic but completely silent motions—led it through the gate like an airport ground crew guiding in a jumbo jet.

The narrow alleyway inside was lined with concrete parking bays, each hung with a green vinyl curtain. Above every bay was a red light bulb; some of them lit, and others dark. The attendants stopped at a bay about halfway down where the light was off, and motioned the driver toward it.

After he pulled inside, the curtain was quickly shut, leaving the taxi and its passengers hidden from view.

"Okay, boss?" One of the attendants bent down close to the window. Bar nodded and the boy bowed deeply before stepping back and opening the rear door.

"Back in a minute," Bar murmured to Eddie. He then spoke quickly to the driver in rapid-fire Thai and stepped out. Slipping through a crack in the curtain, he disappeared.

The others watched as the teenage attendant walked to a metal door at the end of the parking bay. He pushed it open, gesturing for them to enter. Lek and Winnebago glanced at Eddie, and when he got out of the taxi and followed the boy inside, so did they.

They each examined the room in silence while they waited for Bar to return. It contained a large, round bed with yellowed sheets; a single, brown naugahyde chair with a jagged rip across its seat; a metal stand opposite the bed with two thin towels, two tiny bars of soap, and a plastic comb; and a small, black-cased television with a crack down one side on which music videos with Chinese subtitles flickered soundlessly. On the ceiling above the bed, mirrored tiles were arranged in a square with tiny, white lights around it.

Before anyone could say anything, Bar came back and beckoned them outside. They followed him out past the taxi, through the curtain, and around behind the building.

A weathered deck was pitched up there like a pier, hanging just above the brown waters of the Chao Praya River. Hidden out of sight, behind the parking bays, it was narrow and almost rotted away in places, stretching along the river for thirty yards or more.

A large table and four wooden chairs were arranged at one end where the boards appeared to be the most solid. Two young girls had just finished setting out bowls of food, and one of them was spooning rice from a large, silver serving dish onto the plates set at each chair.

Eddie looked amused. "Just part of the usual service, Bar?"

"I've got a few friends here and there."

They were tired, and ate quickly without much conversation. After dinner, they all filled coffee mugs from a big vacuum flask one of the girls had set up on a side table, and pushed their chairs around until they faced out toward the river. Winnebago flashed a match as he lit a Camel.

Across the Chao Praya was a nightspot of some sort, draped in strings of brightly-colored lights. Looking at them made Eddie think for a moment of the Christmas lights his father had made a ritual of stringing around their front door every year in New Jersey, where he had lived as a child. But that had been in a time that was now probably as much myth as real memory for Eddie, and when he tried to bring it back into focus from half a world away, he found himself wondering if it had ever really happened at all.

Pushing those thoughts aside, Eddie turned to Lek. His voice was soft and without inflection. "We have to know everything you can tell us about Captain Austin. I know you might not want to talk about it, Lek, but we have to know."

"What, exactly?"

"Who he hung out with; how he spent his time; where he went." Eddie paused. "If you don't know, somebody else must."

The implication hung there in the damp, night air. It bubbled and swirled, mixing with Winnebago's cigarette smoke, and was carried away by it into the darkness. The others shifted in their chairs, and Lek shot a quick look at Bar—but he was studying his coffee as if something totally absorbing was floating there on its surface.

"You haven't been straight with us, have you, Lek?" Eddie's voice was still soft, but it had taken on an edge.

She returned Eddie's gaze without flinching. "You'd better tell me exactly what you mean."

Across the river, a motorcycle engine coughed to life. The unseen rider played with the throttle and the engine's roar rose and fell in a wave that washed back and forth over them. The wave crested, broke, and rolled away. They all sipped their coffee and listened to the sound until it faded in the distance.

When Eddie nodded at him, Bar reached into his shirt pocket. He took out a small, red booklet, and flipped it onto the table. It hit on one corner, teetered there briefly as if trying to decide how much to show of itself, and then flopped over on its back.

They could all see it was a passport; the gold stamping easily visible even in the dim half-light seeping from the nearby buildings. On the cover was a wreath with a large, five-pointed star and beams of light radiating from it. Above the wreath were the words, SOCIALIST REPUBLIC OF VIETNAM. Below it, in smaller letters, PASSPORT— DIPLOMATIC.

Lek glanced at the passport without any expression and looked away quickly.

After a moment she spoke so quietly that it was difficult to separate her words from the sound of the river sloshing against the bank. "You saw it in Singapore, didn't you? How did you get it out of my bag?"

She glanced around. Eddie and Bar were watching her closely, but neither of them responded. Winnebago started to say something, but Eddie waved him into silence.

"I can't force you to tell us anything, Lek." Eddie chose his words slowly. "It's up to you."

She shifted in her chair, pulling her legs up and tucking them under her. As she smoothed her skirt and adjusted her tiny feet so that her body rested comfortably against them, Eddie recalled the possibilities he had once imagined; possibilities that now seemed hopelessly lost.

Lek remained silent, looking away across the river.

Finally, Bar's impatience got the better of him. "You were never married to Austin, were you?"

She shook her head slowly. "No."

Bar's face clouded and he started to say something else, but Eddie held up his hand.

"Did you ever meet him?" Eddie asked.

Lek almost laughed. "I'm good, Eddie, but not *that* good. We were together a few times."

Eddie leaned back in his chair and clasped his hands behind his head. He thought he might finally be getting on top of things, and he started to feel a little smug in spite of himself. "Why did McBride tell us you were Austin's wife?"

This time she did laugh. It was so sudden and so obviously genuine that it startled Eddie, and he almost lost the delicate balance he'd assumed on the back legs of his chair.

Winnebago flung up his hands. "Would somebody tell me what the *fuck* is going on here?"

Eddie let that pass, but he slowly lowered his chair until it was flat on the ground, and then slouched down, affecting an indifferent posture. "McBride's not DEA, is he?" Eddie watched Lek carefully. "He's CIA."

Bar shook his head vigorously and waved both his hands in little jerking motions. "No way, man. I've known Chuck for years. He's DEA."

Eddie gave Bar a look like the one the kid in the nursery rhyme must have gotten right after he told his mother he had traded their cow for a bag of magic beans.

"That's right, isn't it, Lek?" Eddie shifted his eyes back to her. "McBride's a spook."

"How did you know?"

"I took a wild shot that accidentally hit something."

Lek nodded as if that was exactly what she had already decided herself.

"Oh, man," Bar muttered, and consulted the pattern of wrinkles on the back of his left hand, studying them like they were the key to a code.

"So who the hell are you, lady?" Eddie pointed at the Vietnamese passport on the table. "And which one's the phony? The American or the Vietnamese?"

All of a sudden Bar saw exactly where Eddie was going.

"You're CIA, too, aren't you, Lek?" He pointed his forefinger at her. "McBride's using you to keep an eye on us."

"No." A trace of a smile danced across her face. "You couldn't be more wrong."

She almost seemed to be enjoying the interrogation, Eddie suddenly noticed. That unsettled him. His confidence eased off a bit, hid behind one ear, and developed a twitch. "Then why did McBride throw us together?"

"He thinks I was married to Harry. He told you exactly what he knows."

"You convinced a CIA field agent that you were married to Harry Austin without him even bothering to check it out?"

"No, he checked. Everything was in perfect order—my employment history, our marriage records, everything."

Eddie adjusted his indifferent look, turning up the volume a little. But now he knew for sure that he was either losing control again, or—far more likely—had never had it in the first place.

Maybe Lek was American. Maybe she was Vietnamese. Maybe she was one and working for the other. Maybe she was both and working for neither. How the hell was he supposed to know, unless she wanted to tell him? His self-confidence turned tail and fled, not even pausing to kiss him good-night.

"I'm sick of guessing games, Lek." Eddie folded his arms and shifted in his chair. "Just spell it out. Who are you and what do you want from me?"

Again, something almost like a smile worked at the corners of her mouth for a moment, but then it disappeared completely, leaving behind no hint that it had ever been there at all. Lek's eyes became flat as mud, and she spread out her hands, palms upward.

"I am the special deputy to the general secretary of the *Hai Ba Trung*."

She looked sideways at Bar and then back at Eddie, holding his eyes with hers.

"In English you call it the Vietnamese Intelligence Service."

Then she tilted her head away and looked off at the lights beyond the river—as if what she had just said was really quite unremarkable.

28

Somewhere across the river, a radio played a Thai love song. The mournful voice of a young girl—aching in its melancholy—spread over the black water like river fog.

The air was unnaturally still—a thick, breathless dark—and no one moved for a long time. Eventually Bar raised his right arm very slowly, until his hand was just above his head. Four of the young, bow-tied attendants who'd been at the front gate stepped out of the shadows, and two of them took up positions at each end of the deck—their movements languid, like boys walking under water.

Lek glanced around and laughed under her breath. "Don't you think this is a little melodramatic?"

"No, I don't think this is a little melodramatic." Eddie kept his voice level.

"Are you going to interrogate me now?" She seemed to be amused by the prospect. "Are these little boys going to torture me if I don't tell you what you want to know?"

"The pictures you said were in the safety deposit box . . ." Eddie broke off, wishing he didn't sound so tired, but there wasn't much he could do about it. "What was the point of sending them to us?"

"I had nothing to do with the pictures, and I don't know who sent them to you. The ones I showed you were in Harry's safety deposit box just as I told you they were. I imagine yours came from the same person who sent them to him."

"I'm supposed to believe that?"

"Believe what you want." Lek shrugged.

"And I suppose you had nothing to do with those thugs waiting for us outside the Stardust either?"

"Not really."

Eddie thought he caught a tone in Lek's voice that had not been there before; something that sounded like frustration, even embarrassment. He stayed silent until she explained it, as he knew she would.

"When we were at the Oriental, I used my mobile phone to check while I was in your bathroom." She seemed to consider briefly how much she should tell Eddie, and then finished quickly without deciding for sure. "Yes, those men were ours, but I didn't arrange for them to be there."

"Who did?"

"My superiors are very thorough men. They use many different tools for their work. I am only one."

"What about the General? Is he one of those tools?"

"Yes, but I have nothing to do with him either. Someone else is running him."

"And how about killing Harry Austin?" Eddie made a little fist and rapped it against the table. "Did that tool just slip, or what?"

Lek looked away and said nothing, but she drew in breath through her nostrils so sharply that it was clearly audible.

"How did you get on to Austin in the first place, Lek?"

"The usual way. We worked hard. Bit by bit we put it together." She gave a little shrug. "We eventually found out that Harry had devised the original security plan for moving the money. We're not sure yet how it did it, but we know he got it out of the country somehow on his own before Saigon fell. After that, he just kept it."

Eddie realized that she was looking at him now with something near sadness on her face; but he couldn't see her eyes in the dark, so all he could make out was the outline of it. Why was she looking at him like that, he wondered? He kept his eyes clear and didn't ask.

From out on the river there came the low *thrump-thrump* of a boat engine leaping to life. Lek tilted her head toward the sound, and the quickness of her motion caused her white blouse to snatch up what light there was drifting in the dimness and draw it into the fabric. For a moment, the sudden flare of luminescence made Eddie almost giddy. He could see nothing but her skin; rich honey against the radiance of the light.

"Do you really think that Austin kept the money hidden all these years?" Bar's voice was hardly louder than a whisper. He could see he was interrupting Eddie's thoughts—although he wasn't exactly certain what they were—but he was too impatient to do anything else.

Lek glanced toward him with no expression. "We know he did. Most of it at least. We just don't know where."

"So they traced Austin to Bangkok and sent you here to reel him in, huh?"

"More or less. Yes."

"That was pretty cold, wasn't it? Romancing a lonely, old guy so you could steal his money? Did you have to tell him you loved him?"

"*Steal* his money?" Her eyes flashed with anger. "I cannot steal something that he stole from my country in the first place."

Eddie watched Lek's face closely. It was a lovely face, he still thought, but suddenly she appeared to be a woman capable of great cruelties.

"That's a bunch of shit," Bar growled. "You were yanking a poor old guy's pud just to find out where the money was. If you'd found it, you'd have killed him and taken it."

"I am Vietnamese. Harry Austin took something that was ours; something that he had no right to. Returning it to my country justified whatever means were required."

"Oh, I see, and you people took . . . what? South Vietnam? An entire *country* that you had no right to?" Bar gave her a tired look.

"The Vietnamese are one people," she flared back. "We had the right to bring our nation together again."

"Knock it off, both of you," Eddie snapped. "You sound like the Larry King Show."

His eyes drifted out over the river. He pushed himself back in his chair and folded his arms, then looked back to Lek.

"Okay, let's cut the crap. What's the deal you've got for us?"

Lek was clearly startled.

"Why do you think I have a deal for you?"

"Everyone else seems to have one. Why should you be any different?"

Lek dropped her hands into her lap. Her face went blank and her voice turned toneless. "I won't haggle with you. The Socialist Republic of Vietnam has authorized me to pay you up to five million dollars if you can find where Harry Austin hid the money he stole from us. So that is my offer. Five million dollars."

At least the price is moving in the right direction.

"All you have to do is find the money and tell me where it is," she finished. "After that, we will do everything else."

"I'll bet. Then I suppose you'll just send me the five million. The check's in the mail? Something like that?"

"We would be prepared to offer you reasonable guarantees if you insist."

"I can hardly wait to find out what those might be. Maybe the same ones Captain Austin got?"

When Lek turned away and said nothing, Eddie stood up and walked to the edge of the deck. The Chao Praya looked like a painted river, not a real one at all. He leaned on the rail, his back to the table, and breathed in the Bangkok night.

After a while he turned back and sighed. "I'm too tired to think anymore tonight."

"So what now?" Lek asked, glancing at the boys blocking both ends of the deck.

"Nothing." Eddie told her. "The three of us are leaving, but you're staying. These guys will turn you loose tomorrow at noon and you can do whatever you want. I figure we're at least entitled to a little head start."

"What are you going to do if I try to leave tonight?" Lek seemed balanced between amusement and surprise. "Kill me?"

"No." Eddie shook his head. "I wouldn't do that."

"But *he* might," Bar suggested in a helpful voice, pointing to the tallest of the four boys.

The boy was standing just to Lek's right, holding a black revolver with polished wood grips. He had both hands wrapped around the gun, and—although the muzzle was pointed straight up—the expression on his face left no doubt that he could bring the weapon into action quickly.

Lek glanced at the boy. "Does that mean you're refusing my offer?" she asked.

Her tone was so stilted that Eddie found himself wondering for a moment if their conversation was being recorded. He looked back out at the water again, and realized that was ridiculous. Their conversation was rolling past and disappearing into the darkness just like the river. No one was recording it.

"No, it doesn't mean that," Eddie replied in a soft voice. "Not yet, at least."

He watched a large log drift by on the current. Spinning in a slow circle as it passed, it abruptly sank out of sight in the inky water. Eddie waited for it to bob back to the surface, but it didn't. He hoped that wasn't a sign.

Bar and Winnebago stood up, and they all walked away together without looking back. Lek picked up the passport

Bar had left on the table, and flipped open its red cover. It took a moment to register, but then she realized that neither her picture nor her name were where they should have been. She was gazing instead at blank pages.

"Where did you get it?" she called after Eddie, laughing a little in spite of herself.

"Like Bar said before," Eddie called back. "He has friends around here."

When they reached the end of the pier, Eddie glanced back at Lek, although he had promised himself that he wouldn't. What he saw caused him to stop walking and turn around.

He folded his arms and looked at her closely again. She had extraordinary features—strong, yet still delicate—and the way her long, upper lip was pushed out and drawn taut made him think for a moment of a petulant child who had been caught doing something naughty.

"You are a very clever bastard, Eddie Dare."

"Think so?"

"But there's still one thing I wonder."

"What's that?"

"If you will be clever enough."

It was a good question.

Eddie knew he'd probably find out soon enough, so he wasn't going to worry about it right then. Instead, he grinned, cut Lek the biggest wink he could, and wiggled his eyebrows. It was a gesture so silly that he laughed out loud as he did it.

Then he turned back toward where the taxi was still waiting for them, and he didn't look around again.

They didn't drive too far—only a mile or so to a wharf on the river that was next to a darkened Buddhist temple. Bar paid off the taxi, and Eddie and Winnebago followed him to the edge of the river, down a ramp of creaking planks that had been bleached by the sun to the color of paper. A half dozen or more shallow-bottomed longboats—their hulls striped in brilliant reds, greens and blues—bumped against a wall of old tires; the boatmen asleep and stretched out inside them.

Improbably enough, there was a pay phone on a post at one corner of the pier. Eddie stopped and looked at it.

"Think this thing works?" he asked Bar.

"Probably not. Use my mobile."

"I'm going to leave a message for McBride at the embassy. Maybe they've got some way to trace the call to your phone, and I'd rather he doesn't know we're together."

"What difference does that make?" Winnebago asked.

"McBride thinks I'm on my own, and he isn't taking me very seriously. He probably figures I'm stumbling around somewhere with you and haven't got a clue what to do."

"Yeah," Winnebago mumbled as he reached for his Camels. "Imagine him thinking a thing like that."

Eddie lifted the receiver and smiled when he heard the hum of a dial tone. "Where's a good place for me to meet McBride tomorrow?" he asked Bar.

"Why do you want to see McBride after the kiss-off he gave you at the embassy?"

"We need help, Bar. The CIA must be interested in that money just like everybody else is. Maybe McBride will toss in with us if I tell him what I know."

"But you don't know anything," Winnebago pointed out, exhaling smoke and adding his dead match to the other garbage floating in the river.

"I'll make something up."

Bar eyed Eddie. "What kind of a place do you have in mind? Public or private?"

"Doesn't matter. Just as long as it's somewhere McBride will have a hard time tailing me after I leave. You know he'll try."

Eddie and Winnebago watched Bar while he sorted through the possibilities. The boatmen, all wide awake now, sat quietly in their boats and watched the three *farangs* watch each other. Finally, Bar told Eddie what instructions to leave for Chuck McBride, and gave him some coins and the night number for the embassy. Then he spoke quietly in Thai to the boatmen while Eddie was on the phone.

After Eddie hung up, Bar pointed toward one of the boats—a new-looking one with a long band of red and green striped canvas over a metal frame that formed a canopy from bow to stern.

They all climbed down into the narrow shell and made themselves as comfortable as possible on its hard, wooden seats. The boatman fired up the massive automobile engine in the stern, racked the throttle a few times—for good luck, Eddie hoped—then powered away from the pier and made for the middle of the wide, oily river.

After ten minutes, the boat slowed and began a gently arcing turn into a narrow canal that flowed east, away from the river.

"This is called Klong Saensaeb, the Saensaeb Canal," Bar leaned across and screamed into Eddie's ear over the unmufflered roar of the big engine. As he did, he pulled a handkerchief out of the back pocket of his trousers. "Everyone calls it the sewer run. If you've got anything to use, I'd suggest you cover your face."

Eddie watched Bar fold his handkerchief into a triangle and wrap it over his nose and mouth like he was getting ready for a game of cowboys and Indians. He glanced down at the black muck through which the boat was plowing, and then back toward the garbage that was spiraling in their wake.

Bar's eyes looked questioningly at Eddie over his hastily fashioned-mask, but Eddie just shook his head. He didn't have a handkerchief, so he crouched down and tried to breathe as little as possible. The spray off the boat's bow misted back over him like dirty water from a shower.

For the next ten minutes they plowed steadily through the fetid canal; the high-pitched yowling of the boat's engine obliterating every other sound. Eddie watched the darkened city. It was a crazed and tangled world that rolled past his eyes—soaring towers of glass and steel; rickety, wooden shacks on the verge of sliding into the water; marble shopping palaces sheathed in lights; empty lots strewn with garbage and sleeping bodies; glittering hotels with expensive automobiles around them; massive slums of tarpaper shanties packed under bridges; and roads that, even after midnight, were still snarled with traffic and enveloped in clouds of exhaust smoke.

A giant numeral—a three sketched in white neon and surrounded by a circle—loomed on top of a dark building on their left, although Eddie had no idea what it might signify. Then he saw another lighted sign that read HILTON INTERNATIONAL float past on the right and disappear behind them in the darkness. Not long after that, the boat's engine cut out and they glided silently into a rotting, wooden platform moored underneath a concrete bridge.

Bar paid the boatman and then led them over a metal ramp and up a set of steps that were barely visible—cut, as they were, into the concrete of the bridge supports. Crossing the busy road at the top of the steps, they walked down a block, and then turned left onto a smaller street, and left again into a tiny alley. Soon, they were facing another metal gate set into a concrete wall. It looked to Eddie almost exactly like the one at the Forty Winks.

There was another group of young boys waiting outside the gate, wearing white shirts, dark trousers, and bow ties exactly like the other boys had been. They seemed to know Bar well, and greeted him with smiles and nods. When they pushed the gate open, Eddie could see more lines of parking bays hung with dark vinyl curtains. Most of the dim, hooded, red lights over the parking bays were lit.

"What's this one called?" Winnebago asked Bar.

"The Sixty-Nine."

"A hell of an improvement over Forty Winks," he observed.

They passed through the gate and stopped to glance around as it clanged shut behind them.

"Looks okay." Eddie nodded at Bar. "It seems just like the other place."

"Yeah. Probably a thousand of these in Bangkok."

"And do they know you at every one of them?"

"Pretty near," Bar admitted as they followed one of the boys down a driveway that ran between the darkened rows of vinyl curtains.

They bid each other good-night under the fronds of a scraggly coconut palm that rattled softly in the warm breeze, then they were each shown to a room by one of the boys. Nobody suggested a nightcap. They were all too drained of words and exhausted of thought.

Eddie watched himself in the ceiling mirror of his room for a long while before he slept that night, counting the longtail boats as they roared by on the canal. He drifted away sometime in the early morning, and—for a few hours at least—he slipped into a deep, dreamless sleep.

29

Eddie left the Sixty-Nine just after eight the next morning. He let himself out through the gate, noticing that the bow-tied schoolboys who had been there the night before had vanished in the daylight like apparitions. Following the directions Bar had given him, he turned right.

A string of white lights tacked along the top of the wall flickered forlornly, and in front of Eddie stretched a narrow, cracked sidewalk—empty except for a line of food vendors' carts, closed and draped with tarpaulins. Two scruffy *soi* dogs were dozing in the shade of the carts. They raised their heads as he passed, and almost immediately lost interest in him.

A few hundred yards away, he could see the main road. It was already flowing thick with traffic, and out there beyond it lay the rest of Bangkok. The gossamer warmth of the night had disappeared as completely as the boys at the gate, and now the city seemed harsh to Eddie—even menacing.

The sun had barely cleared the surrounding buildings, and Eddie was able to keep largely in their shade, but still the heat poured over him like scalding water. Before he had taken fifty strides, he was already sweating. He had to learn to walk more like a Thai, he reminded himself. Walking at a San Francisco pace in Bangkok was crazy.

That thought caused him to flash back to his mornings at the Buena Vista, eating breakfast and watching the Mason Street cable cars being rotated on the big turntable down at the end of Hyde. He could be there right then, he supposed, sipping strong, black coffee from those white ceramic mugs that looked like they had been stolen from a Mississippi truck stop. Maybe even flirting a little with Suzie just to keep his hand in. But he wasn't. Instead, he was running from Vietnamese Intelligence and the US Secret Service, hiding out in a Bangkok whorehouse, and strolling down a pot-holed alleyway to meet a CIA agent to have a conversation about 400 million dollars that had been stolen from the Bank of Vietnam more than twenty years ago. It was enough to give him a serious case of whiplash.

When Eddie got to Soi Nana, it looked just as Bar had told him it would. To his right he could see the bridge over the Saensaeb Canal and the place where they had climbed up from the longtail boat the night before. He walked slowly toward the bridge, scanning the shops and street stands across the road, and he was almost all the way back to the canal before he saw the place that Bar had described. A purple Kawasaki whined by like an angry lawnmower with an entire family of four sandwiched together on the seat. Eddie sprinted through the traffic just behind it, and entered the cool darkness of the open-fronted shop.

There were a dozen plain, wooden tables scattered around, each with three or four folding metal chairs. The place was empty, and Eddie wondered for a moment if it might not be open yet. But as he settled onto one of the chairs, an old woman shuffled slowly out of a rear door, crossed the room, and placed a cracked mug filled with coffee in front of him. Fumbling in her pocket, she pulled out a handful of paper packets containing sugar and creamer, and then she shuffled away again. She hadn't left a spoon, Eddie noticed, but he decided black coffee would be fine.

"Thank you," Eddie called after her, but if she heard or understood or cared, she gave no sign. The woman disappeared through the rear door without looking back.

The coffee was okay, but before he ha d drunk half of it, he began wondering if the old woman would reappear to fill his cup again, or if he would have to hunt her down to get more. Before the thought was fully formed, Eddie pushed it away, disgusted with himself. He was sick of looking at the world that way. It was the most annoying legacy of being a lawyer, he thought—all the constant anticipating of future difficulty. Why couldn't he just enjoy his coffee because it was good? Why did he have to ruin it by wondering where the next cup was coming from, even before the first cup was drunk?

As he was reflecting on the emotional handicaps which his legal education had left him with, a taxi pulled to the curb across Soi Nana. Eddie watched as Chuck McBride got out and crossed the road. The man hardly looked like a spy— although he supposed, when he thought about it, that was probably the general idea. McBride was wearing rumpled khakis, a white polo shirt open at the neck, dark-colored running shoes, and a black baseball cap with gold letters across the front. As he came closer, Eddie was able to read the letters. They said CIA.

Walking straight to the table, but taking his time about it, McBride pulled out a chair. He sat down slowly and peered off into the middle distance as if Eddie hadn't been there at all.

Almost immediately, the rear door reopened, and the old woman—once again unbidden—shuffled toward them with another cup of coffee. She repeated exactly the same cycle that she had gone through before—the chipped mug, the packets of sugar and creamer, and no spoon. Eddie called after her for more coffee as she turned away, but she disappeared out back as if he had never spoken.

He glanced at McBride, who was gently blowing on his coffee, his face expressionless.

"I know," Eddie said. "This is Thailand."

McBride nodded slightly in acknowledgement and sipped tentatively. Apparently finding the coffee to his liking, he tossed back a big swallow and then put the mug down on the table. He said nothing, but studied Eddie with an unblinking gaze.

"What's with the hat?" Eddie finally asked after the silence had dragged on for a while.

McBride rolled his eyes up as if he could actually see it, and then rolled them back down again. "Embassy softball team."

"Oh. Very clever."

That caused the last thing Lek had said to him to jump back again into Eddie's mind, but he barged right on through it.

"Doesn't the CIA prefer you guys to be a little less conspicuous?"

McBride looked disappointed, like a man who'd been telling a long joke and had suffered the indignity of his listener interrupting with the punch line before he was through.

"How did you find out?"

"Lek told me."

"No shit?" McBride grumbled brusquely and cleared his throat. "Okay, so what's a few initials among friends anyway?"

"Yeah, that would be true." Eddie nodded. "Among friends."

McBride shook his head a little as he sipped at his coffee again. "My, aren't we witty this morning? Put us on television, they ought to. Master-fucking-piece Theater." He smiled with his face but not with his eyes. "So what are we here to talk about, Dare? That money Harry Austin liberated from 'Nam in '75?"

"Then you know about it."

"Of course I know about it. I know everything. I'm real good at my job."

"Why didn't you tell me?'

McBride snorted, but didn't answer.

"Did you know who Lek was, too?"

McBride held up his right hand and wiggled it, although what that was supposed to signify, Eddie had no idea. Then he grinned and made a circle with his thumb and right forefinger, pumping his left forefinger in and out of it several times. "Are you . . . ?"

Eddie just looked at him.

"Yes? No?" McBride prompted. "Well, whatever. You'd better keep a close eye on her either way, Dare. She's . . ."

"Vietnamese Intelligence," Eddie finished.

McBride blinked at that. "You got that out of her all by yourself?"

Eddie nodded.

"I'm impressed." McBride bobbed his head around briefly, making Eddie think of one of those little football-player dolls with a spring for a neck that he sometimes saw glued to the dashboards of '67 Chevys.

"I live for that."

McBride ignored the wisecrack. "What else you get? You find out she's a hitter?"

"A *what*?"

"You know. . . ," McBride made a little gun out of his thumb and forefinger and pointed it at Eddie, ". . . bang! bang! They use her mostly for the subtle stuff; when they need to slice something out of somebody before they put them away."

The casual violence in McBride's voice startled Eddie, leaving him momentarily speechless.

"Anyway, I'm glad you called me," McBride went on quickly, changing the subject and nodding like a car salesman whose prospect had just unexpectedly returned to the showroom. "I want to know what you and Tonto are up to."

"I thought I called this meeting."

"Yeah, that's right, you did. But I don't give a shit."

McBride leaned forward, resting his forearms on the table and lowering his voice slightly. Eddie gathered it was mostly out of habit, since there was no one else anywhere near them.

"You don't know where Austin stashed the loot, do you?"

Eddie looked away and didn't answer.

"No, of course you don't." McBride bubbled air out through his lips, making them pop. Then he leaned back in his chair.

Eddie started to say something, but McBride interrupted, holding up his hand like a traffic cop. "Before you even ask— no, I don't know where it is either."

Eddie responded with a suitable noise. He was anything but surprised to hear McBride say that.

"So then tell me. Why are you fucking around here, Dare? You don't really think you can just wander around Bangkok like an idiot until you just stumble over it, do you?"

"Maybe."

"And you somehow figure Lek would leave you alive to enjoy it, even if you did?"

"I don't think she's . . ."

"Oh, I know," McBride interrupted again, raising his voice over Eddie's. "You're a big, tough white guy. You're not afraid of a cute little Asian chick with a tight ass, are you?" McBride clicked his teeth together a few times and slapped his open palm sharply against the table. "I think you'd better come to Jesus here, Dare. Let me give you a little background. Lek's father was Chinese—a Red Pole in some triad, if the stories around are true—and she learned her trade from him. Everyone's shit scared of her—and they should be, Eddie. Shit scared. She's the meanest little cunt you'll ever meet."

McBride shook his head theatrically. There was a lot of the ham actor in him, Eddie could easily see, but it didn't quite cover the hardness. He was like a lot of American diplomats and intelligence people who'd hung around Asia longer than was good for them. On the outside, they seemed to have become nothing but flabby drunks. On the inside, they were as tough as street whores.

"She learned to use choppers from her daddy. You know, things like those long butchers' knives with the little notches on the edge that make such a fucking mess going in and out. She's good with them, I hear—so quick, that she can cut just the muscles in your arms or your legs, and then there you are." McBride made a gesture of helpless submission. "You're alive, but you can't move. You just lie there while she cuts on you some more. You bleed while she asks you questions and you'll tell her any fucking thing, Eddie, just any fucking thing she wants to know to make her stop."

"Guys like you always have to dig up a monster from somewhere just to get the kiddies into bed, don't you, McBride? Lek's not going to kill me. She thinks I can find Austin's money."

"And what if you can't, Eddie? You think then she's just going to let you go back to Frisco and forget all about it?"

McBride let that sink in, and then went on.

"Of course, I hear she really hates white guys, you know. That's why she flashes her ass around, just to taunt us." McBride spread his hands again. "We came into that piss-poor little country of hers with our big money and our loud mouths and just took it over—fucking the women and sneering at the men. Hey, it's no wonder she hates us, huh? So now that I think about it, she probably *wouldn't* kill you, Eddie, even if she got sick of waiting for you to dig up the dough. Probably she'd cut off a few parts of you, just for laughs."

Then, just to make sure that the point hadn't been lost on Eddie, McBride leaned back, dropped both hands to his crotch, and gave a long, low whistle.

"Subtle's just a little too hard for you, isn't it, McBride?" Eddie slid forward in his chair. "What do you expect me to do now? Piss all over the floor in sheer terror and then jump into your arms and make you promise to take care of me forever?" He threw his hands in the air. "You guys are such assholes."

"Hey, Dare, don't bust my hump here." McBride seemed more amused than irritated by Eddie's outburst. "I could be your best friend, you dumb shit. You have no idea at all what you're up against."

"I may have a better idea than you think,"

McBride loosed a disgusted sign and stretched his arms behind his neck. "Goddamned tourists. You're all alike. Two days out here and you all turn into Lawrence of fucking Bangkok."

A black motorcycle pulled to the curb in front of the shop and the driver slowly turned his helmeted head in their direction as he racked the throttle. It might have been Eddie's imagination, but he thought he saw McBride tense and slide his hand toward his waistband. Just as Eddie was about to fling himself to the floor underneath the table, a little girl in a pink dress appeared from nowhere, jumped on the back of the bike, and locked her arms around the driver's waist as he roared off.

Eddie focused on a spot high on the wall and willed his breathing to return to normal. He kept his face empty and didn't look at McBride until it did.

"Is it my turn now?" he eventually asked into the relative silence that fell after the motorcycle sped away.

"Yeah, sure." McBride seemed to yawn slightly, although whether it was real or just an affectation, Eddie wasn't sure. "What's on your mind, Dare?"

"I want you to watch my back while I look for the money."

"You want . . . *what*?" McBride sputtered, caught genuinely off balance. "Why the fuck would I do that."

"I knew Captain Austin better than anyone. Given some time and a little luck, I can find that money—I know I can— but I can't do it with people hanging all over me trying to take it away."

Chuck McBride looked as if he was having a hard time keeping a straight face. "And why would I help you find Austin's stash?"

"Because then I'd turn it over to the CIA. All except for five million, which is exactly what Lek offered me. I think that's a fair deal."

"Yeah, it's a hell of a deal, Dare." McBride's eyes were twinkling now, and Eddie didn't know what to make of that. It was anything but the reaction he'd expected. "On the other hand, I think you may be laboring under a false assumption here. You obviously think we give a shit about that money."

"You don't?"

"Nope. Not even one tiny turd."

"I don't understand."

"Look, Dare. That's a can of worms nobody in his right mind ever wants to open up again. We start scratching around about what really happened in Saigon back in '75 and Christ only knows what kind of bogeymen are going to come out of the closet. It took us long enough to get the fuckers in there and slam the door. We sure as hell aren't going to be the ones to open it again."

"Then why is the Secret Service looking for the money?"

"Window dressing. Standard government bullshit. That's all it is. And of course, Shepherd's an idiot who thinks he's going to make his career on this. There's that, too, but that lame jackass couldn't find his butt with both hands and a floodlight."

"So that's it then. You're not interested in helping me."

"Shit no. I already told you that back at the embassy."

"I didn't realize then that you knew about the money."

"Well now you do, and the answer's still the same. I wouldn't touch it—or you—with the old barge pole. You're on your own, Dare. You want my advice, you better go home, tuck yourself into bed, and hope for the best. Leave the big game to the big dogs."

"Work on controlling your excitement while I take a leak, McBride. There are a couple of things you don't know that might make you change your mind." Eddie stood up and disappeared through the door at the back of the café, while McBride played with his empty coffee cup—wondering what the hell there was that he didn't know.

When Eddie hadn't come back after ten minutes, he went looking for him.

The door, McBride quickly discovered, didn't lead to a toilet at all. It went straight through the back wall of the café and out to a concrete ledge that ran along the edge of Klong Saensaeb. A few yards to the right, a set of steps led down to a wooden pier where longtail boats were moving in and out in a steady stream, picking up and dropping off passengers. Another twenty yards away, up on the road, taxis were passing continuously over the bridge. Dare could have been in either, McBride realized unhappily, within a few seconds of going out the door.

Okay, he'd give Dare that one. Maybe he'd underestimated him, at least a little. But if he was thinking he could handle Lek on his own, he was still one dumb bastard.

McBride glanced again at the boats passing on the canal, and then sadly tilted his head up toward the taxis flowing over the bridge.

Damn. That boy could be halfway across Bangkok by now.

30

Trying to get back to the Sixty-Nine, Eddie made a wrong turn and wandered the side streets around Soi Nana for an hour before he finally spotted a familiar building and straightened himself out.

Wonderful. I'm hiding out from the Secret Service, a Vietnamese assassin, the CIA, and Christ only knows who else, and I can't find a whorehouse in broad daylight. This ought to be good.

Bar and Winnebago were waiting when he got there, sitting on a pair of molded plastic stools in front of his room. Winnebago smoked two Camels while Eddie told them about his conversation with Chuck McBride, and Bar just sat and listened without doing anything at all.

Bar glanced at his watch when Eddie was finished. "The boys have probably let Lek go by now. What are you going to do about her?"

"Let's see what she does first."

Bar wasn't sure exactly what that was supposed to mean, but he nodded anyway.

"I always had a bad feeling about that woman." Winnebago flicked his cigarette butt away. It arched down the driveway and landed in a puddle.

"You never mentioned that before." Eddie glanced at him, but didn't quite catch his eye.

"Every time I started to, I'd see you looking at her with

those big old cow eyes and I figured maybe I'd better keep my mouth shut."

"You were seeing things."

Bar and Winnebago just looked at each other.

"Don't start," Eddie warned, raising his right forefinger and pointing it first at Winnebago and then at Bar. "Neither of you."

There was a silence, and Winnebago filled it by shaking another Camel out of his pack and lighting it.

Bar fidgeted in his chair, glancing at Eddie, and then looking quickly away. "You think maybe you should let this slide?" He studied one of the vinyl curtains as it swished back and forth in the light breeze. "You haven't really gotten anywhere. You don't know any more about Harry Austin now than you did before you started. All you're sure of is that he's dead."

"Why do you think the Vietnamese and the Secret Service want to give me millions of dollars to tell them where Austin stashed the money, Bar?"

"Because they're desperate and stupid?" Winnebago exhaled slowly and watched the smoke drift away.

"We've got to be closer to it right now than we think."

Eddie's voice sounded confident, whether he was or not, so Bar contented himself with a skeptical grunt and let it go at that.

"We need to find out who the foreigner was who grabbed Austin's body." Eddie tapped the side of his leg impatiently with his open palm. "We'll hit that massage parlor as soon as it opens tonight."

Winnebago's eyes lit up. "I'm for that."

Bar shook his head a couple of times and then consulted the backs of his hands. When he finally spoke, it was in a voice so low that Eddie almost missed it. "You don't have to wait until tonight. Most massage places open all day, but not many people know that. There'll be somebody at the Princess by now."

"Okay, that's good." Eddie nodded. "There's one more thing. Can you get us some hardware? That's not too difficult around here, is it?"

"Hardware?" Bar looked genuinely puzzled.

"Nothing heavy duty. Just some hand guns—.9 millimeters or .45s would probably do it—and a hundred rounds or so. Also a few grenades if you can find them."

"Actually I'd recommend at least one bazooka," Bar joined in the fun. "That's generally what well-dressed folks are wearing in Bangkok this year."

"Just the small stuff will be okay. Can you do it?"

"You *are* kidding, yes?"

"I am kidding, no."

Bar started to get a queasy feeling and glanced sideways at Winnebago. "Is he serious?"

"Don't ask me. I can't tell anymore."

"It's no big deal." Eddie kept his tone casual. "I just want to be prepared."

"The way I see it," Winnebago mused, "keeping a box of rubbers around is being prepared. Getting some .45 automatics and a pile of grenades is more like jumping into deep shit."

"You're way out of my league here, Eddie." Bar looked down at his feet and folded his arms across his body. "I can't believe this."

"Sure you can. You know what we're up against. Besides, you handle a gun pretty well. I've heard the stories."

Winnebago looked interested. "What stories?"

"He sent two guys to the hospital a few years ago with some pretty fancy shooting. Some disagreement about freedom of the press."

"It was self-defense."

"They cornered you in an alley in Patpong one night, didn't they? You only fired two shots, the way I heard it. Put one in each guy's kneecap. That's pretty good self-defense."

Bar looked over Eddie's left shoulder and his eyes flickered briefly. "That was a while ago. I'm a lot older now. Smarter, too." He rubbed at his face. "Or maybe not. There's a guy I know who lives a couple of blocks from here. I'll see what I can do."

Eddie glanced at Winnebago. "You okay with this?"

"Oh, sure." Winnebago bobbed his head. "I can hardly wait to have my ass shot off by a bunch of Vietnamese assassins. I'm fine. Great."

Eddie decided to quit when he was ahead, and abruptly changed the subject. "Do you know how to get to the Little Princess from here?" he asked Bar.

Winnebago grunted. "Does the Pope shit in the woods?"

"It's not far. You can walk." Bar delved into his shirt pocket and came up with paper and a pencil stub. "I'll draw you a map."

"Will you see what you can do about that stuff while we're there?"

Bar nodded slightly and drew in silence. Then he passed the map to Eddie. "By the way, you mentioned the Little Princess to Lek, didn't you?" he asked while Eddie was studying it.

"I don't . . . yeah, I think so." Eddie looked up. "But wouldn't she know about it anyway. Austin was killed right in front of it."

"You'd think so. On the other hand, she didn't know anything about what happened to the body. Maybe she didn't have anything to do with Austin getting killed." Eddie looked doubtful and Bar shrugged. "Anyway, she's sure as hell going to shake the place down now that she knows you're interested in it."

"Okay," Eddie nodded. "I see your point. How long will it take you to get that stuff together?"

"Not long. It's not like I have to search Bangkok for an honest man or something."

"Just put together whatever you can quickly and don't worry about the rest. Meet us with what you've got at the Little Princess in an hour or so. Can you do that?"

Bar tipped his chair back against the wall and stretched out his legs.

"Yeah, I can do that."

By the time Eddie and Winnebago made it to the first turn on Bar's map, it was well after noon and they were both sweating heavily. The morning heat and a thick, nearly opaque blanket of humidity hung over the city like a shroud. Their shirts were soaked through by the time they found their way to the Little Princess.

They stumbled on it from an unexpected direction, and were crossing the parking lot almost before they realized where they were. A chrome stool had been positioned in the tiny sliver of shade thrown by the door canopy, and a bony-kneed girl in a dirty green miniskirt sat on it with her legs swinging. Three *tuk-tuk* boys, their vehicles standing idle nearby, ate at a wooden table so low it looked like it had been made for children. A few stray dogs circled them, darting in and out, lunging at the scraps hitting the ground. The dogs scrutinized Eddie and Winnebago warily, but the *tuk-tuk* boys ignored them.

The girl in the green skirt pasted on a smile and pushed back the heavy, red curtain over the doorway as they approached. Inside, they stood and scanned the room. It was large and surprisingly well lit, but the smells of stale cigarette smoke, fish sauce, and spilled beer mingled in unpleasant accumulation.

In the center of the room was a large, rectangular bar with stools around three sides. There were a few shabby chairs and two old couches scattered around the walls—all angled to provide a clear view of a glassed-in area to their left that looked something like a huge aquarium. Eddie knew it was where the girls sat on carpeted risers, watching television and waiting for the numbers pinned to their dresses to be called by customers, but it was empty.

They slid onto stools at the bar, and a tired-looking woman in a shapeless smock of indeterminate color pushed bottles of Singha in front of them without being asked.

Winnebago pulled out a handkerchief and rubbed the sweat off his face. Then he downed half the bottle in one pull.

"Where's the pussy?"

Eddie gestured silently, inclining his head toward the stool on the other side of the bar where the girl who'd brought their beer perched. Her legs were doubled-up under her, and her head rested against thin arms folded on the damp, wooden counter. Then he nodded the other way, toward the back of the room where there were a few scattered formica-topped tables. A woman of thirty or so was sitting alone at one of them, shoveling noodles into her mouth with a big spoon. She wore wrinkled, black shorts; fluorescent purple flip-flops; and a dingy, white T-shirt with bright, red lettering across the front that said, TOO DRUNK TO FUCK.

Winnebago looked dubiously at both women.

"You're shittin' me. Right?"

"Nope, but come back tonight. There'll be a hundred of them and they'll all be that 17-year-old at your senior prom who wouldn't give you the time of day."

Winnebago gave him a sour look. "Indians didn't have no fuckin' senior proms."

Eddie made a sympathetic noise and sipped at his beer. Neither girl appeared to pay any attention to them at all. Nearly a half hour passed in relative silence and no one else came or went. The girl eating noodles did disappear briefly, but when she returned, her plate was filled again, so Eddie gathered she had just gone out for more food.

When Eddie got tired of waiting for something to happen, he reached for the plastic cup on the bar where the girl had tucked their check. He folded a purple note end to end, pushed it in, and left it protruding just far enough above the rim to be seen. He sat back and waited. Almost as if an alarm clock had gone off somewhere, the girl slumped on her arms at the bar jerked upright, slid off her stool, and shuffled slowly over.

As she reached out for the cup, Eddie covered it gently with his hand.

"Speak English?"

"*Nit noi.*"

"You the mamasan?"

The girl snorted.

"I need to talk to mamasan. Get the mamasan and I give you the money."

"No problem." She pointed at TOO DRUNK TO FUCK and Eddie and Winnebago swiveled their heads in her direction. "She there."

"What's her name?" Eddie asked without taking his eyes off the woman. She continued to eat, apparently oblivious to the attention.

"She called Short Time."

"What kind of a name's 'Short Time?'" Winnebago asked in a voice that suggested he could guess.

Eddie lifted his hand away from the cup and the girl scooped it up. She gave him a graceful little inclination of her head, pocketed the note, and returned to her stool.

When Eddie crossed the room and sat down at her table, Short Time ignored him at first. He pulled out his money clip and laid two purple notes on the table, then she glanced up—continuing to chew—and looked him over. "You come back tonight," she mumbled through a mouthful. "Better then. More lady."

"The money isn't for a girl. It's for information."

Short Time didn't reply, but she put down her spoon and smiled slightly. "Either cost more than that, baby."

Eddie pulled his clip out again and peeled off three more purple bills, dropping them on top of the other two. He put the clip back, covered the stack with his left hand, and held Short Time's eyes with his. "There was an accident out in the *soi* a month or two back, right in front of this place. A *farang* was hit by a car and killed. Do you remember?"

Short Time blinked at that, and slipped away like a submarine settling beneath the waves.

"Look, you're not going to get into any trouble," Eddie soothed, keeping his voice low. "The body was brought in here by another *farang*. I have to know who it was. I need to find him."

The girl went back to eating, but she began to smile a little, and Eddie knew exactly what that meant. He easily recognized the particular smile that Thais gave when they received confirmation—if any were really needed—that *farangs* really were as crazy as they thought.

"You're not going to tell me anything, are you?"

"Tell you anything you want." Short Time looked up from her noodles, but didn't quite catch Eddie's eye. "But know nothing about *farang* killed in *soi*. Want me make up story? Then you be happy and let me eat without your bullshit maybe?"

"You ever heard of Harry Austin?"

Her manner changed abruptly. Eddie couldn't be sure exactly what it was he saw in her eyes, but he knew immediately that it was something.

"He was American. Did you know him?"

When Eddie asked the question, he expected guardedness; some continued reticence in her response—in spite of the money on the table and the look in her eyes when he mentioned Harry Austin. He expected what always happened when *farangs* in Thailand tried to deal with locals. He expected that almost ritualistic closing of ranks against the intrusions of foreigners that had been the hallmark of Thai culture for hundreds of years.

That was what he expected. What he got was a girl who wouldn't shut up.

"Khun Harry? You want give me 5,000 baht tell you I know Khun Harry?" She seemed to balance herself somewhere between disbelief and laughter. "Why you give me all that money just talk about old man? What I know about Khun Harry worth 5,000 baht? I think I know nothing worth all that money about anybody. What can I know worth 5,000 baht to you, mister? Anybody tell you about Khun Harry. Maybe 100 baht. Maybe nothing. But you want give me 5,000 baht tell you."

Eddie checked the bills under his hand. There were five, just as he thought—2,500 baht, not 5,000. He raised his eyebrows and looked at Short Time.

Short Time shrugged. "Whatever."

She pulled in another mouthful of noodles with a sucking sound so resonant that Eddie's crotch gave an involuntary twitch.

"Who you, baby?"

"A friend of his."

"Friend?"

"Yeah. An old friend."

"How I know?"

This wasn't going the way Eddie expected. He was the man; he was talking to a bargirl; and he had the money on the table. But Short Time was ignoring the money and asking *him* the questions. How had that happened?

He had brought the two photographs that had been sent to him in San Francisco. Hesitating only briefly, he reached into his shirt pocket and pulled one out, laying it on the table in front of Short Time.

"We were in the marines together. That's Harry Austin in the back."

Short Time bent forward and studied the picture.

"Why you draw round head?"

"Look, are you going to tell me what you know about Captain Austin or not?" Eddie's patience had run out. "Or maybe you're just jerking me around and you don't know him at all."

Short Time grunted, spraying little pieces of noodle all over the table.

"I know."

"How well?"

She moved her head in a gesture that could have meant almost anything, but Eddie knew that whether Thais just moved their heads around or actually spoke words, anything could always mean almost anything.

"How long since you saw him?" Eddie pressed.

Short Time chewed thoughtfully. "Two, maybe three week."

The mirage popped like a soap bubble. Eddie stood up and wearily collected the photograph and the money from the table.

"Hey!" Short Time's eyes flashed. "What you do? You say you give me money if I tell you about Khun Harry!"

"Look," Eddie snapped. "I don't need your bargirl bullshit. You don't know Harry Austin. You don't even have any idea who the hell I'm talking about."

Short Time seemed genuinely confused. "Why you say that?"

"Harry Austin's been dead at least a month. He was the man who was killed in that accident in the *soi* you don't know anything about."

"He look okay when he come see me few week ago."

Eddie just shook his head. "You're saying he came here? To see you?"

"Sure. Why not?" Short Time peered at her plate. It looked empty.

"Why would Harry Austin come to see you?" Eddie was exasperated and his voice rose.

Short Time looked at Eddie briefly before she answered. Eddie tried to read her expression, but he couldn't.

"Man come see wife. What wrong with that?"

"You're his *wife*?"

She somehow scraped another noodle off the plate and popped it into her mouth.

"No more, I guess. If Harry dead."

Jesus Wept. Eddie slumped back in his chair, shaking his head. *Here we go again.*

31

After Eddie gave him the slip, Chuck McBride went back to his office and made some calls.

He wanted to keep an eye on Eddie without getting too close, so he put out four of his locals to quietly shake the short-time hotels; not an inconsiderable task given the number of them in Bangkok. He was pretty sure Bar was helping Eddie and Tonto, wherever they were, and if he knew Bar—and he was sure he did—he'd have them all holed up in one of those whorehouses he hung around. They sure as hell wouldn't be in a suite at the Grand Hyatt.

Almost as an afterthought, he had also sent his best pair of Chinese bone-crushers to turn over some of the classier massage parlors as well. There were plenty of beds in those places, too—didn't he know it? McBride thought with a grin—and maybe Bar had been a touch more imaginative than he was giving him credit for.

Either way, Bangkok was a small town when you came right down to it—at least it was for *farangs*—and his people probably wouldn't have any trouble finding Dare pretty quickly. Yeah, when the big dog got off the porch, McBride chuckled contentedly to himself, there wasn't much anybody could do but throw down a bone and haul ass.

Certain he'd soon have everything back under control, McBride kicked off his loafers and sprawled on the couch. He'd never liked Bangkok very much when he'd been with

DEA—not really—although he'd pretended to for the sake of the job. But as he lay on his couch with his hands under his head, he thought about all the fun he was having now.

The problem when he'd been DEA, he knew, was that no place was any fun when you were nothing but the town fool. Every major drug dealer in Asia operated openly in Bangkok, and either no one could, or—perhaps—really wanted to change that. Even Khun Sa—probably the most famous heroin dealer on earth—would turn up every few months, fresh from his labors in the Golden Triangle, get his teeth cleaned, and have lunch at the Hilton with his stockbroker. After he left town, McBride would inevitably discover that absolutely no one had seen him. Not the dentist, not the stockbroker, not even Mrs. Khun Sa—who lived in a lovely home not far from Chitrlada Palace that was complete with a goldfish pond, a white picket fence, and a bunch of other stuff McBride figured she must have seen in reruns of Leave It To Beaver or some shit like that.

McBride's job in Bangkok when he had been DEA was basically to show up every day and look mean. He operated as conspicuously as possible from a building on the grounds of the embassy, and his function was officially described as intelligence gathering.

The truth of it was that he didn't do jack shit. He was just there to show that no one, by God, could run the United States of Fucking America out of a jerky little third-world, rat-turd place like Bangkok. But of course someone *could,* and—as a matter of fact—*had.* Nothing was keeping Uncle Sam's tattered anti-drug banner flying anymore but a few fat, dickless, middle-aged losers driving around in dented Jeep Cherokees, wearing counterfeit Ray-Ban's, and trying to keep their polo shirts down over their paunches.

McBride hauled himself off the couch after a while, listening to his knees crack, and stumbled into the bathroom. After going to the toilet, he stood and examined himself carefully in the mirror; something he noticed he'd been more and more inclined to do recently. He wondered briefly how much time he had left in life. He wasn't being morbid about it. It was just a question of fact as far as he was concerned. He sighed and splashed water over his face.

He'd jumped at the chance of going over to CIA when it was offered. After six years as a DEA scarecrow, he wanted to do something while he could still enjoy it. When his desk officer at Langley had gotten a hard-on over a bunch of rumors that a pile of money left over from the fall of Saigon was floating around Bangkok somewhere, he'd laughed himself silly at first. But then he had found out that the rumors just might be true. That put a whole new spin on things.

What kind of middle-aged guy could resist a hunt for lost treasure in a place like Bangkok? It was all too goddamned romantic for words. Fuck those poor DEA bastards pretending to track down drug dealers. Chuck McBride was out there now looking around for ten tons of missing cash money.

When he stumbled onto Harry Austin—almost entirely by chance—and made the connection between him and the last days of Saigon, it started to mess with his mind. Harry Austin had been sitting on all that money for twenty years now. He couldn't prove it, but now that he was CIA, he didn't have to prove a goddamned thing. He just had to know it. And he *knew* it.

Still, there was something he just couldn't figure. How could any man have a pile of cash like that—hundreds of millions of dollars in untraceable currency—and not do a fucking thing but bury it in the ground or something, and then live in a crappy little apartment for the rest of his life in a shithole like Bangkok?

McBride was sure he'd have been on a beach in Australia the day after grabbing the loot. And that would have been that. Doing anything else was plainly nuts, so he guessed

Austin must have been nuts. Occasionally he wondered if it was just having all that money that had driven him mad, or if it was something else.

Austin had probably been planning to let things cool off and then split, McBride had finally decided. But since twenty years of cooling off hardly seemed necessary, he guessed Austin had just never gotten around to doing it. It was, no doubt, one of those things he was always going to do real soon—and then there he was lying in the mud in some crummy street, his skull half crushed, and bleeding to death. McBride would have bet his last dollar that Austin started wondering right then how it was that he'd never done it; that he'd been wondering exactly that—right at moment he just lay there and died.

Most people did that with their lives, McBride had realized a long time ago. They kept on putting off the good part until they were dead—and then there *was* no good part anymore. He'd always done a lot of putting off himself, but his jump to CIA had flipped on a light; and then Harry Austin and his buried treasure had appeared to him like the Christmas star. Sure as shit, he vowed, he wasn't going to put anything off anymore.

When Harry checked out, McBride was certain he left something behind that would lead him to all that loot. And he *was* going to find it, whatever it was.

Austin's hot little wife had seemed a good place to start looking at first—but there'd been that gnawing feeling he'd had that there was *something* about her. She was sure as hell too old for McBride, so that wasn't it. It had taken a while, but he'd finally worked it out. She was not only a hitter for the Vietnamese, she was running her own treasure hunt.

After that, everything went quiet for a while, and McBride hadn't been sure what he was going to do next. But then Bar Phillips fell into his lap—sniffing around without a fucking clue like he always did—and this clown Eddie Dare and his faithful Indian companion turned up. Suddenly he was back in business.

McBride ran a comb through his hair and looked himself over again in the mirror. Better, he thought. Not so decrepit after all; still plenty good enough to get the babes in Bangkok—where the male mating cycle lasted considerably longer than it did out in the real world. On the other hand, it suddenly occurred to him, maybe Australia was a different deal altogether. Maybe the young guys got all the chicks there. He pushed that horror aside with a shudder, and went back to thinking about Eddie Dare and Harry Austin's secret stash.

He still didn't have the vaguest idea how everything would come together, but he was sure that if he hung close to Dare, something good would happen. The money was close now—he could smell it—and he was almost sure Dare was going to find it, even if that dickhead didn't know it yet himself.

Yep, McBride told himself, *that was just the ticket.* Boogie on down the road right behind Eddie Dare, keep his eyes open and his zipper closed, and eventually he'd come to the magical city of Oz. He was still working on exactly what he'd do when he got there. And that was the hard part.

He wondered what looking at ten tons of cash money really did to a man. More to the point, he wondered what it was going to do to *him.*

Maybe it would do the same thing it had done to Austin, it had crossed his mind more than once. Maybe it would make him crazy and he'd just grab all he could carry and disappear forever. On the other hand, what was so crazy about that? Maybe when you were looking at a pile of money that big, it was the only rational thing for any man to do.

Anyway, he decided, patting his cheeks with his open palms, he wasn't going to worry about that yet. McBride's daddy always said that the hen was the smartest animal in the world—because she never clucked until *after* she'd laid her egg.

McBride held that thought as he opened the bathroom door. He returned to the couch for a quick nap—while his guys shook down Bangkok, looking for Eddie Dare.

When Bar came into the Little Princess, he was empty-handed, and Eddie wondered if he had flopped getting the hardware. But then a taxi driver staggered in just behind him, struggling under the weight of a dark blue duffel bag, and Eddie smiled. The man dropped the bag where Bar pointed, next to Eddie's stool, and after he left, Eddie unzipped it, pulling it open until he could inventory the contents without taking anything out.

"Three army surplus .45s, three almost-new Berettas, and a hundred rounds for each. That's more than you asked for, but . . ." Bar shrugged and trailed off. "Anyway, you owe me 29,000 baht plus a couple of hundred for the taxi. Make it 800 US and we'll call it even."

"Grenades?" Eddie searched the bags with his eyes.

"They take two days. The samples he gave me looked good, but I figured that was too late, so I passed."

"What's the shotgun for?"

"For looks. Mostly."

Bar settled himself on a stool and called out for a Carlsberg while Eddie closed the bag and pushed it up against the bar with the toe of his shoe.

While Bar was drinking his beer, Eddie told him about the conversation with Short Time and they both swung around to look her over. She'd pushed her empty plate aside and had her head down, resting on her folded arms. She looked like she had gone to sleep.

"What do you think?" Eddie asked Bar.

"Beats the hell out of me."

"You think she's telling the truth about Captain Austin?"

"Yeah. And Richard Nixon was just misunderstood."

They looked at Short Time some more, but there wasn't very much to see, so they turned back to the bar and leaned on their elbows, resting their chins on their clasped hands.

There was a long, uneasy silence until Winnebago finally broke it.

"What the fuck are we doing here, Eddie? We're stuck in some broken-ass, third-world craphole 10,000 miles from home; we're drinking beer in a whorehouse with no whores; we've got a bag full of guns under our feet; and we're running away from a bunch of people who'd kill us in a second for something we haven't got and don't know where to find. Does any of this make sense to you?"

"Did you ever hear the old saying about having to be there when your ship comes in?"

"Yeah, but I've also heard the one about it not being over until the fat lady sings—and the bitch is doing scales in my ear right now."

"Well," Eddie shrugged. "There you have it. It's what life usually comes down to—a choice between clichés."

Bar shook his head and pushed back his stool. "This is getting us nowhere. I'm going to take a leak."

"Me, too." Winnebago followed Bar toward what he gathered was the bathroom. When he went inside, he saw that it was the kind of toilet that just begged people to piss on the floor. In fact that was the only option, since it was nothing but an empty room with three holes in the stained concrete. He noticed that each hole was surrounded by what looked like a broken toilet seat stuck to the floor.

"What the fuck is this?"

Bar unzipped and began relieving himself into one of the holes. "Squat toilets."

Winnebago followed Bar's example and relieved himself in the nearest hole. It felt a little weird to piss into a hole in the floor, but then he supposed a piss was a piss. Something else bothered him though. "You mean you got to sit on the floor to take a dump?"

Bar shook off and zipped up. "See those little footrests?"

Now that Bar mentioned it, Winnebago noticed that there were indeed tiny footprints imprinted on the seats—like the kind children made with their feet in drying concrete.

"You squat with one foot on each side and let go."

Winnebago watched his urine filling one of the little footrests and shook his head in disgust.

Finishing up, he zipped his pants and had just turned around to leave when he realized that Bar was looking at him with an odd expression.

Holding one finger over his lips for silence, Bar cracked open the door and nodded toward it. Winnebago squinted out, and—although his field of vision was limited—it was easy enough to see what had spooked Bar so badly.

Two very large men were right up in Eddie's face, their backs toward the toilet door. Both were wearing leather jackets, even though it must have been ninety degrees outside, and while Bar and Winnebago couldn't see either man's hands, their postures left little doubt that they had weapons in front of them. Eddie was saying something, but Winnebago couldn't make out what it was because they were too far away.

Bar nudged Winnebago and gestured with his head to the opposite side of the room. Short Time had risen from the table where she'd been slumped with her head down, and was moving slowly toward the corner of the bar furthest from the men. At first, Winnebago thought she was just getting her butt out of there, but then he saw the beer bottle she was holding down out of sight against her leg.

When she reached the other side of the bar, she leaned against it, as if paying no attention to anyone. One of the leather jackets glanced toward her briefly, but quickly dismissed her and returned his full attention to Eddie—who was still talking and gesturing vigorously.

When the man had turned away completely, Short Time flipped the beer bottle very deliberately across the room. It crashed against a wall and both men pivoted quickly toward the sound. When they came around, Bar and Winnebago could see that they both were holding AK-47s with long banana clips curving inward toward the wooden stocks.

"Oh *fuck*," Winnebago breathed. "I thought that spook said the Vietnamese used *knives*."

"They're not Vietnamese," Bar whispered. "They're locals. Thai-Chinese, I think."

"Locals? Then exactly who the fuck's after our ass *now*?"

Bar just grunted and didn't bother to answer. Out of the corner of his eye he saw Short Time's hands dart under the counter while the two men were distracted. When they reappeared—to his surprise—they cradled a pump-action 12-gauge, sawed off just in front of the slide. In a single, fluid motion she took a few quick strides down the bar, dropped out of sight beneath it, and racked the weapon's action to chamber a round.

The ragged *clack-clack* of the pump was an unmistakable sound to anyone who'd ever heard it. The leather jackets apparently had. They reacted instinctively, spinning toward the sound, knowing now that the crash had been only a distraction. They split apart and crouched low, scanning the room for the real threat.

When the man closest to Eddie turned, his feet shifted automatically into a wide stance—both knees bent and ready to roll to the floor in either direction. It wasn't the best posture for defending himself, and Eddie reacted quickly. He gripped the sides of his stool with his hands, cocked his right leg, and drove his heel into the back of the man's exposed knee.

As Leather Jacket lost his balance and fell sideways, Eddie sprang from the stool, clasped his hands together, and clubbed him hard behind his left ear. The cracking of hands against bone and Eddie's screech of pain came almost simultaneously;

followed soon after by the thump of the man's heavy body hitting the floor.

Winnebago and Bar were out the toilet door and hurtling across the room as soon as Eddie made his move. Scattering tables and chairs, Bar broke for the man Eddie had put on the ground, and Winnebago launched himself at the other one—but he need not have bothered. Short Time had already popped up from behind the bar and the muzzle of her sawed-off shotgun was poking him in the belly.

The man looked Short Time over, weighing his chances, but her eyes left no room for doubt. Slowly he lowered his gun, placed it on the floor, and clasped his hands on top of his head. Short Time came around the bar, kicked the AK across the room, and slammed the barrel of the shotgun across the side of the man's face. He evidently knew the drill, because he quickly went flat on the floor, his hands behind his back.

The first man was beginning to get up, and Bar hurled himself through the air. But Eddie's foot lashed out and caught the man squarely in the head, crashing him against a rank of stools. By the time Bar landed, the body had shifted to the left—so he hit nothing except the floor. Bar howled in pain as his kneecaps smashed against the hardwood.

Eddie bent over and grabbed the AK.

"Serves you right," he said as he straightened up. "Was that the world's longest piss you were taking out there or what? Even *I* was starting to run out of bullshit."

Bar pushed himself up and looked at Leather Jacket lying crumpled on the floor with two stools over his legs. He kicked the guy in the head just for the hell of it, and then rubbed at his knees.

"You come with me." Short Time tugged insistently at Eddie's elbow. "All you. Come with me."

Eddie shook his head. "We're going to get some straight answers from these clowns first."

"No! Now! With me."

She whispered something in Thai to the girl who had been tending bar, and handed her the sawed-off shotgun. Motioning urgently for Eddie to follow, she trotted quickly across the room and disappeared through a back door Eddie hadn't noticed before.

Bar and Winnebago followed her with their eyes and then turned to Eddie.

"What do we do?" Winnebago asked.

"We go."

When they followed Short Time through the door, they found themselves in a narrow alley behind the Little Princess. Garbage was strewn everywhere, and water from an outlet pipe dripped into an open sewer. Short Time was waiting for them, sitting astride a red Suzuki with the engine already idling. She revved the motor and pointed toward another motorcycle propped against a dumpster piled with Singha boxes. The bike was muddy and the make unidentifiable, but it looked serviceable.

"Who drive that one?"

The three of them looked at each other until Winnebago shrugged, climbed on, and kicked it over. Eddie settled himself on the Suzuki behind Short Time and they all looked at Bar— who didn't seem all that happy.

"I should've taken my chances with the guys inside."

"Yeah, well," Eddie said. "That's still an option."

"Oh fuck! The bag's still in there. I gotta go back for the artillery."

"No! Go now!" Short Time began to walk the Suzuki out of the alley toward the main road.

"Forget it." Eddie shook his head at Bar. "She's right."

Looking miserable, Bar slipped onto the back of Winnebago's bike and wedged his hands as tightly as he could into the small handle behind the seat.

Winnebago racked the motor a couple of times and grinned back over his shoulder. "Hold on tight, baby."

"I can see it all now," Bar sighed, tilting his head back and closing his eyes. "After forty years of beautiful Thai women, I'm going to die with my arms around an Indian named after a motor home."

"You crazy fuckers," Short Time observed. Then she gunned the Suzuki hard and squealed down the alley, blasting brown fountains of water to both sides as she cleared the sewer. Looking neither left nor right, she shot straight across traffic, dodged a slow-moving bus jammed with school children, and screamed into a hard right turn.

A small army of Korean tourists—their names printed on cards pinned to their chests—filed through a crosswalk, and Short Time aimed the big Suzuki right at them. Eddie was just wondering whether the name tags would help in identifying the bodies, when the Koreans scattered in terror.

Winnebago and Bar took off right behind her—and they just tried to stick as close as they could.

32

The outer wall was old and cracked. Some of the large sandstone blocks that had been locked together to form it on a day long ago forgotten, had given up entirely—yielding gracefully, perhaps even gratefully, to time and gravity's pull—and become only piles of loose sand again.

The breaches they left in the wall were of no real importance, since the structure only marked a boundary of sorts. It had never been meant to keep anyone in or out. Still, the crumbling wall made access to the compound particularly easy.

Its outer courtyard was outlined with seated Buddha figures—every face frozen eternally in benign tranquility. The images were larger than life, and the bright saffron of the cloth sashes draped around them was luminescent against the cool white of the stone. Deeper inside, there were walled pathways over which other ranks of Buddha images stood watch. These pathways were arranged geometrically, forming a series of concentric boxes like ordinary rectangles.

It was exactly at the center of those boxes—at the very core of the compound—where something almost indescribably extraordinary stood.

The Buddhist temple—the *wat*—looked nothing at all like the dour edifices with which Western religions browbeat the docile. It was more like something straight from a child's drawing of heaven. Its golden spires sparkled with light; its roof was tiled in vivid orange and green; its lines arched steeply to an impossible peak; and its blindingly white-washed walls seemed to pulse against the glazed cobalt of the sky.

Beyond the flamboyance of the *wat* were the simple, wooden huts where the Buddhist monks lived. They were arranged in modest rows, each structure raised above the ground on short stilts and bare inside except for a sleeping mat and a small chest.

Every *wat* had a complement of monks who lived in huts such as these—caring for the temple and its grounds, and occasionally conducting funeral rites or dispensing blessings. Some of the men had been monks since they were children. Others had chosen later in life to flee the terrors of the world and had retreated to a *wat* to live for a few months, or sometimes even years.

The afternoon—like most afternoons—was hot. There was little movement in the compound other than freshly-laundered robes flapping in the breeze, and a few scrawny dogs searching for shade. There would have been no other sign of life at all, had a nondescript man—thin and stooped—not begun slowly, even painfully, edging his way down a short ladder from one of the huts to the ground.

The man did not wear the cloak of a monk, but instead was dressed in the drab clothes of a Thai peasant with a wide-brimmed straw hat pulled low over his face. From his size and build, and the deep tan of his skin, he looked like a farmer on his way to the rice fields.

When he reached the ground, he raised his head and stood absolutely motionless for a moment—almost as if he were an animal sniffing the breeze for something that should make him uneasy. If that was what he was doing, he evidently found nothing, because he soon lowered his head and began to shuffle slowly across the courtyard.

When he reached a gap in the wall between two of the stone Buddhas, he paused respectfully. His hands formed a *wai*—a graceful gesture in which the palms of the hands are pressed together, almost as if in prayer—and he bowed his head briefly to each of the images.

Then, displaying an agility he had not seemed to possess before, he slipped though the wall, and was gone.

●●●

Short Time maneuvered the motorbike skillfully through Bangkok's narrow *sois* for the first few kilometers, then—after making a sudden left and an equally sudden right—powered up a short, sharply-inclined ramp, and emerged on what looked to Eddie exactly like the sort of nondescript interstate highway that looped around most American cities.

All he had to do was squint slightly, it occurred to him, and he could have been back in San Francisco, wheeling onto the Bayshore Freeway from the Van Ness on-ramp, heading for Candlestick Park on his way to a 49ers game. On the other hand, if he had been in San Francisco, he seriously doubted he'd be hanging onto the back of a Suzuki driven by a middle-aged Thai whore who'd just used a sawed-off shotgun to rescue him from two heavily-armed Chinese thugs. That was an important point to keep in mind, he decided

He bent forward and shouted over the noise into Short Time's ear. "Where are we going?"

She didn't respond, so Eddie cautiously unhooked his right hand from the handle on the seat and wiggled it in front of her. "Where are we going?" he tried again, speaking as distinctly as he could into the powerful slipstream.

Short Time shot a quick smile over her shoulder—a rather kind smile Eddie noticed—gave a brisk nod, and then returned her full attention to piloting the bike. As they slalomed around the tailgate of a dark blue van that was slowly backing right at them—into the oncoming freeway traffic—he decided that she was probably making a sound choice as to what she should be concentrating on, at least for the time being.

But he couldn't help but wonder what the nod was supposed to mean.

The man walked to a dusty road near the *wat,* and he stood patiently until an old bus came rattling along and lurched to a stop. The bus was crowded, as it usually was; people pressed into every crevice of its interior. But if that bothered the man, he gave no sign.

Climbing the steps, he dropped several coins into the driver's out-stretched hand, and then worked his way back along the aisle until he found a spot that was—at least comparatively speaking—unoccupied.

One or two of the other passengers glanced at him, clearly wondering for a moment if the man was a Thai or a *farang,* but because of the way he was dressed—and the likelihood that no foreigner would ever be on such a bus—they soon lost interest.

As the bus bounced away, the man made himself as comfortable as he could, rocking forward slightly and shifting his weight directly over his center of gravity—the way a man did when he was accustomed to standing. And he remained that way, hardly moving, during the entire two-hour trip into Bangkok.

When they reached the city's Eastern Bus Terminal, the man climbed down from the bus and slapped the circulation back into his legs. Then he set off up Sukhumvit Road, walking steadily. A little less than an hour later, he turned right and almost immediately left again—entering a short *soi* from which traffic had been blocked off at both ends.

Neon tubing outlined many of the buildings along the *soi,* and huge signs stuck out from most. Names like LOVE

SCENE, TOY BAR, AFTER SKOOL, LONG GUN and SUZIE WONG hinted at the delights to be found inside—but it was still early. A smoky, mango-colored sunset washed the little street in a wan light, and the neon was dark and motionless.

Here and there, small groups of women—and a few men as well—lounged at broken tables or on the curb, eating while they chattered among themselves. A girl who looked like a teenager sat side-saddle on a parked motorcycle, jiggling a sleeping baby in the crook of her left arm while she smoked a cigarette. A man in rubber boots wielded a garden hose against the accumulated grime around the entrance to one of the closed bars, and when the stream of water splashed too near, the girl shouted at him in machine-gun Thai. He grinned and kept sweeping the water over the concrete. The baby never stirred.

The man in the clothes of a Thai farmer seemed to be well-known in this little village—and he acknowledged each greeting with a small smile or a nod. When he had passed, some of the girls laughed self-consciously, as if embarrassed to have been surprised by him at such a mundane moment.

When he reached an ordinary shophouse buried deep in the *soi*—a gray, bunker-like building between two darkened bars—he ducked quickly inside and disappeared.

The occupants of the street returned to their eating and chattering; all except for two young Thai men. They slowly stood, picked up their bowls of noodles, and moved to a pair of metal chairs flanking the door through which the man had just passed.

Neither was particularly impressive physically—both being small and rather slightly built—but the way they moved and sat made the message unmistakable. Anyone else wishing to pass through that door would have to deal with them.

It was the third time they roared past a Holiday Inn when Eddie finally got the idea—and after he did, he kicked himself that it had taken so long.

Just as he was thinking how odd it was to find three Holiday Inns on the same stretch of road, he suddenly realized that there weren't. It was the *same* Holiday Inn he was seeing for the third time. Apparently they were on a freeway that looped the city—and they'd just been circling around it for nearly two hours.

Before Eddie could think of a diplomatic way to ask Short Time if she had any idea at all where she was going, she swung behind a bus, shot diagonally across three lanes, and blasted down an exit ramp. From the angry chorus of car horns that broke out immediately behind them, Eddie gathered that Bar and Winnebago were still close.

Back in the rutted streets of the city, Short Time slowed to an inconspicuous speed and drifted along with the evening traffic. She still seemed to be riding without any clear direction, Eddie thought, and it was starting to make him fidgety. Finally, he put one hand on her shoulder and pointed to the curb in an obvious suggestion that they stop and talk things over. She shook her head and kept going.

Soon, however, she was forced to slow the bike to a crawl, working it through a narrow bottleneck where a fruit vendor was jostling for sidewalk space with two blind men selling lottery tickets. Eddie saw his chance, and he grabbed it.

He reached around her and flipped off the bike's ignition. Palming the key, he vaulted off. The motor died immediately and Short Time had to drop her feet quickly to balance the bike. She twisted around on the seat and held out her hand for the key. Eddie shook his head.

Winnebago and Bar caught up and stopped just behind where Eddie was standing with his arms folded across his chest. Beyond Short Time, a crowd of Thais had already started to gather, sensing that something interesting was about to happen. When the attraction was *farangs* pushing around a Thai, the dog packs formed fast.

"You give."

"You tell me where the hell we're going first."

Bar eyed the gathering crowd nervously. His skin had never in his life felt quite so pale as it did at that moment.

Winnebago glanced around. "Where are we?"

"I'd say about a mile from where we started," Bar whispered.

"You mean we've just been riding in circles for two hours?"

"That's about the size of it."

"You figure she's setting us up?" Winnebago called out to Eddie, giving Short Time a hard look.

The crowd momentarily shifted its attention to Winnebago, and Bar tried to make himself as small as possible.

"I save your ass!" Short Time snapped.

"Yeah, but maybe just because you're going to hand it over to somebody else," Eddie suggested.

Short Time's eyes blazed. "What you want we do after Little Princess? Check into Sheraton maybe, and go for swim?"

"I want to know where you're taking us," Eddie repeated, his voice even.

"After we leave, other girl call someone meet you. I keep you move until he get there. Seem smart to me, but you fuckers smarter maybe. That right? You smarter fuckers than me?" Her voice rose to a scream. "Maybe you just told me your better idea we all be happy now!"

The crowd continued to grow, drawn by the spectacle of three white guys apparently picking a fight with a Thai girl. A few of the young toughs started edging toward the front, spoiling to be the first to take on the loudmouth *farangs*. Four boys split away and slipped behind Eddie.

Bar recognized the signs all too well. "Either make up fast or we'd better get the fuck out of here right now," he called out, keeping his voice as low as he could and still be certain it carried to Eddie.

Eddie glanced at the boys behind him, and he quickly saw Bar's point. After a second's hesitation, he flipped the key back to Short Time.

She caught it, and Eddie cut his eyes behind him and then back to her. She grinned and snapped at the boys in Thai. They immediately went quiet and shuffled around elaborately until their backs were to Eddie. As far as they were concerned, he had just ceased to exist.

"So you scared of skinny Thai boys, huh? And I think you big, tough marine." She shook her head in disgust. "Shit."

"Where are you taking us, Short Time?"

"You no tust me?"

"I no tust anybody."

And for some reason that seemed to mollify Short Time completely. "Okay. No problem."

Short Time returned the key to the ignition and fired the starter. The Suzuki turned over immediately and settled into a gentle rumble.

"I take you see someone fix everything. Someone you tust." She goosed the bike a little and raised her voice just enough to be heard over it. "Another five, maybe ten minute. No more."

Bar and Winnebago looked at Eddie.

"You go with me, or you go fuck yourself," she snapped. "Same same to Short Time."

Eddie compared the alternatives briefly. Then he let out a long sigh and climbed back on the Suzuki behind Short Time. "We've come this far," he called back over his shoulder to the others, only half turning. "A little further can't hurt anything."

"The fuck it can't," Winnebago mumbled, but he was firing up the bike as he said it, and no one else heard, or seemed to.

Short Time rode steadily for another ten minutes, then coasted the bike to the side of a quiet, tree-lined street, and stopped. She killed the engine, hopped off, and locked the Suzuki to a metal ring cemented into the front wall of a shophouse. With everyone trailing close behind, she walked briskly down the side of the building until they emerged on the sidewalk of a wide, crowded thoroughfare. The pavement was lined with vendors carts and piles of dented, metal chests—all of them pushed against the curb and covered with plastic sheeting.

"Where the fuck are we?" Winnebago whispered to Bar.

"Soi Asoke, off Sukhumvit Road. Up that way. . . ," he pointed in the direction Lek was walking, ". . . is Soi Cowboy."

Winnebago gave Bar a long look, lifting an eyebrow.

"No, really. That's what it's called. It's another bar zone," he explained. "The tourists go to Patpong. Most locals come to Cowboy."

"Oh, fine. At least maybe I can get laid before anybody else shows up to kill us."

Short Time turned left, slipped through a scattering of folding tables and chairs set up by a sidewalk food vendor with ambition, and walked quickly down the same narrow *soi* along which the man from the *wat* had walked not long before.

About halfway down, she approached the doorway through which he had disappeared, and spoke softly to the two boys sitting on the folding chairs. One nodded immediately—reaching over to open the door—while the other watched the *farangs* suspiciously as they trooped through behind Short Time.

Inside, the room was mostly in darkness, and it took a few moments for their vision to adjust enough for them to see clearly. When it did, they realized that they were in an abandoned go-go bar, and—from the dust and grime everywhere—it had apparently been abandoned for quite a while. There were tables and chairs shoved around; a darkened stage ringed by flaking chrome poles; stacks of cardboard beer cases along the wall; and a long bar with a dirty mirror behind it.

It wasn't until Eddie started walking slowly across the room, threading his way among the tables, that Bar and Winnebago noticed the man who was sitting alone on a bar stool, studying them in the mirror. When Eddie stopped directly behind him, they held each other's eyes in the mirror for a long time—and when the man on the stool eventually spoke, it was to their reflections.

"It's been a long, strange trip, hasn't it, Eddie?"

The man studied Eddie in the mirror a little longer, drank deeply from a bottle of Singha cradled loosely in one hand, then pushed himself around on the stool until the two of them were face to face. Winnebago and Bar waited silently, their eyes shifting back and forth between Eddie and the man at the bar.

"I'd say you look pretty good, especially for being dead and all, Captain."

The man seemed to consider that for a moment.

"I've looked a fucking sight worse, I guess." He nodded thoughtfully a couple of times. "Yeah, I sure as shit have."

Then he reached back and put his beer bottle on the bar behind him. The slapping sound it made against the worn, wooden surface added a kind of exclamation point to what he had just said—and that seemed to please Captain Harry Austin quite a lot.

33

Chuck McBride spent most of the afternoon parked just up the road from the Little Princess, sitting in a new, white Volvo that he'd checked out from the embassy motor pool. He watched the place carefully, waiting for something to happen—but nothing much did. McBride didn't notice anyone he recognized going in or out, and when it started to get dark, he began to fidget.

He thought at first that he might have caught a real break, but now he wasn't so sure.

Shaking down the short-time hotels, one of his locals had stumbled over an attendant at a place called the Sixty-Nine who thought he might remember Eddie and Winnebago from the night before. Juiced up with a couple of purples, the kid quickly became certain of it. He also claimed that he'd overheard them talking to some old guy about the Little Princess massage parlor earlier in the morning. After that, he said, all three *farangs* had left—and none of them had come back again.

When that clicked with McBride's memory of where Harry Austin's corpse had turned up, he knew it had to be them. And the old guy would have been Bar Phillips. It all fit perfectly.

McBride tried to find out whether the Chinese muscle boys he'd sent around the massage parlor circuit had been to the Little Princess yet. He called their mobile telephones over and over, but all he got was that stupid recording that said they weren't answering—which he already knew—so he decided he'd better hustle over to the Princess and take a look himself.

He'd been sitting there a couple of hours already, and he wasn't sure anymore that he'd made such a wise choice. He was getting way too old for this surveillance crap, he sighed as he watched two Japanese men tumble out of the Little Princess, laughing and bumping each other around in that fake-macho way that made him sick to his stomach when he saw Orientals doing it.

What was he doing sitting in a car, watching a cathouse, and peeing in the bushes? That was the kind of stuff the kids got stuck with. He'd earned a lot better by now. McBride shook off his irritation and leaned forward, examining the Little Princess again.

Jesus Christ, if it turns out Dare's just in there getting a hand job, I'm going to feel like a monkey fucking a football out here.

Two women crossing the street in front of his car suddenly pulled McBride out of his reverie. They wore short, straight skirts, and form-fitting silk jackets. Both were probably in their early twenties, he figured—but with Thai girls, who could ever tell?

He followed their progress appreciatively as they threaded their way nonchalantly through the traffic, dodging puddles and casually leaping cracks in the concrete. Their smart pumps clicked crisply against the pavement, and the unselfconscious grace with which they moved nimbly from heel to toe and back again made his crotch ache. The day he stopped being awed by Thai women, he figured, was the day he'd be stone cold dead.

Strangely, that was exactly what Chuck McBride had been thinking at the moment the hand grenade rolled underneath his car.

It made a couple of lazy circles—tipping from side to side like a child's top slowing down—and then came to rest just underneath the Volvo's gas tank. For a moment after it stopped, it rocked gently—but then, when the last of the energy from its momentum was spent, there was one brief instant in which it lay completely still.

A second later—two at the most—it exploded.

Lek's eyes followed the hand grenade as she backed away and crouched behind a cement truck parked a dozen yards behind the white Volvo.

Hand grenades bewitched her. They were almost beautiful, she thought—elongated, steel teardrops with symmetrically-spaced dimples animating their colorless surfaces. When one exploded—when the steel of the casing was shred into microscopic slivers by the power concealed inside, and needle-like shards were hurled outward with a symmetry as perfect as a sky rocket bursting on Chinese New Year—it had always seemed somehow right to her, as if an object like that *should* explode.

It had taken her only a few hours to find out where Eddie, Bar and Winnebago had gone after they left her at the Forty Winks. By three that afternoon, her people had not only flushed out a boy who knew where they had stayed overnight, he even knew they had all left around noon—and where they had gone.

That was something *farangs* never seemed to understand. They could never hide anywhere in Bangkok. There would always be someone, somewhere who watched where they went and who heard what they said. More important, that information was always for sale. That was one thing she truly loved about Bangkok—the joyous, unrestrained way anything could be bought. There was no hole so deep that money couldn't pull you out of it.

Lek cupped her hands over her ears as the grenade did its work—quickly and efficiently transforming the Volvo, and Chuck McBride, into a column of fire and smoke. Then she stepped out from behind the cement truck and watched the spreading flames clean up the mess that had been left behind.

She'd had an uneasy feeling about the Little Princess for a long time—suspecting there was some connection between it and Harry Austin—but she'd never been able to nail down exactly what it was. When Harry's body had been found nearby, she sent some men around to talk to the girls, but nothing came of it. They'd reported back that the woman who ran the place was stupid and drug-addled, and that none of the girls knew Harry Austin.

This morning, when Lek found out that Eddie Dare was snooping around the Little Princess, she got a sinking feeling that she might have been careless. When she got there and found Chuck McBride sitting outside in a car watching it, there was no longer any doubt in her mind. She should have been more exact, more rigorous, after Austin's body was found so near there.

But watching the Volvo burn comforted her. She was making up ground fast.

Killing a CIA field agent was not something to be taken lightly, of course—she knew that. But what else could she do? Besides, everybody in Bangkok thought McBride was DEA anyway—and the grenade would cause them to assume that some desperate heroin trafficker had been responsible. That was the standard procedure when the local lads needed to thin out the competition a little.

Langley would put it all together differently some day, she had no doubt—but that day would not be soon. And even when it came, what would they be able to do about it?

Everything was coming down around her like a rock pile. There were no prizes for subtlety anymore. All that counted now was who got to that money first. And she would do what she had to do.

McBride's death would not interest anyone much, she was certain enough. And once the money was back in Vietnam where it belonged, it wouldn't matter at all.

R.I.P. Chuck McBride.

Eddie, Winnebago, Bar and Harry Austin were lined up in a row on stools, drinking from bottles of Singha so cold that the condensation had formed four little pools on the wooden surface. Although the place looked like it had been closed down a long time, Short Time had still managed to produce the ice-cold beers from somewhere before she quietly disappeared.

"How do you like my club, boys?" Austin asked. "Got a few others just like it, too."

Eddie glanced around at the dusty room. "I hope they're doing better business than this one."

"This used to be the Green Latrine," Bar spoke up. "Air America and United Press had their offices over there . . . ," he waved off in the direction of the main road, ". . . but this was where you found their guys most of the time. Every other reporter, spook, hustler, and ex-military hard case in Bangkok hung out here, too. Until about the mid-eighties this was the hottest place in Southeast Asia—a legend with the old hands. It was where the elephants came to die."

"That's right." Austin nodded. "Finally closed it down about eight years ago. Ran out of elephants."

"You sent the pictures to me, didn't you, Captain?" Eddie's voice seemed to float in the dim room. "And the one to Bar."

"Yep." The Captain nodded without looking at Eddie. "Sure did."

Winnebago looked even more bewildered than he already was—if that was possible.

"How did you know that?" he asked Eddie.

"Process of elimination mostly. Who'd do something like that? Maybe not someone who wanted to scare us away at all—but someone who wanted to get our attention." Eddie watched Austin closely. "How am I doing?"

"No better than I expected."

"So, you've got our attention, Captain. Now what?"

Austin sipped lightly at his beer. He thought for a moment, as if deciding how best to work up to it, but then he gave up and just went at it head on.

"I need your help real bad right now."

"You could've just called me, Captain. I'm in the book."

"Oh, yeah," Austin snorted, his voice gathering strength. "I can imagine ringing you up San Francisco one day and saying, 'Hey, Eddie, been a long time, huh? And by the way, I've got a big pile of money over here in Bangkok that I need you to give me a hand with.' You'd have thought the old bastard had fried his brains on booze and pussy, then made some soothing noises to shut me up, and that would've been that."

"Then it's true? You really have the money?"

"We'll get to that."

Austin chugged the rest of his beer and slammed the empty bottle onto the bar.

Short Time materialized and put fresh bottles of Singha in front of each of them as Winnebago fumbled for his Camels.

"There's no smoking in here." Austin waggled a finger at Winnebago. "We're just as full of shit as California is."

Winnebago glanced around in disbelief and then reluctantly pushed the cigarettes back into his shirt pocket.

"What about those Secret Service agents?" Eddie asked. "Were they real?"

"What Secret Service agents?" Austin looked genuinely surprised.

"The ones that followed me from San Francisco." Eddie saw that Austin's surprise had turned to bemusement, but his expression didn't give all that much away. "It must've been a lot of trouble for you, arranging all that, Captain."

"Wasn't no trouble at all. I had nothing to do with it. Probably *was* the Secret Service. I always said it was better to be lucky than smart."

Bar couldn't hold back any longer. "I'm completely lost."

"Hush up, boy," Austin snapped. "Eddie's got it figured out, and that's what matters."

"All except the part where you died," Eddie disagreed gently. "Whose body was that?"

"Some poor tourist, I guess, but I don't know for sure. A taxi driver came running into the Princess one night and said a *farang* had gotten all busted up in the street. I went out there and . . . well, when I saw how much the guy looked like me, the whole idea just kind of came to me right then."

"You were the man who identified the body as yours, weren't you?"

"Yeah, and I arranged the cremation, too. I needed to lie low until you turned up. All kinds of shit was starting to come down."

"You mean the government was on to you?" Eddie asked.

"Yeah, but not *ours* as far as I knew then." Austin popped his lips a few times, thinking. "It was the woman the Vietnamese sent who scared the piss out of me. She went around claiming to be a Thai who was married to me—except she ain't Thai, and I ain't ever been married to nobody. Not really."

Bar leaned forward until he caught Eddie's eye. "Where do you think Lek went after you left her at the Forty Winks last night?"

Austin snorted so loudly they all jumped.

"So that bitch got her hooks into you, too, did she?"

"It's not that way, Captain."

"How much did you tell her about what you've figured out?"

"Not much." Eddie tried to look nonchalant, but then when Austin fixed him with a hard stare, he confessed. "Well . . . a little, I guess."

"Do you know who she really is?"

"Yeah, I found out."

Austin lifted both hands in a gesture of exasperation, and Eddie changed the subject as quickly as he could.

"Don't you think dying was a pretty dramatic way to disappear, Captain?"

"Nah . . ." For a moment Austin hesitated, but then plunged on quickly. "I was just practicing."

Eddie slowly turned his head toward Austin, but the sudden pitching sensation in his stomach told him he knew exactly what was coming next.

"The big C's blown the bugle for me, boys. Another few weeks, the quack says, then that's it." He took a long pull on the Singha, draining the bottle. "Man, that is *so* good."

Winnebago started to say something, but Austin quickly waved him down.

"I don't want to hear any horseshit about how sorry you are. It took me a while, but I'm okay with it now, so don't fuck me up again." He looked rueful. "I wouldn't have told you at all, but it explains why I need you now."

Austin chewed on his lower lip briefly while they all waited.

"I don't want that money to go back to any of the bastards who had it before. None of them. They'd just find a way to use it to kill people again—theirs, ours, somebody's." He was looking at Eddie now, but not looking at him. "It doesn't really matter if it's their government or ours that gets it. Same thing would probably happen either way. It's blood money, boys— ashes to ashes, dust to dust."

Austin's eyes were still on Eddie's, but his mind seemed to be focused somewhere off in the middle distance.

"I've spent twenty years trying to wash that money up a little." He nodded to himself, but it was hardly noticeable. "Put some of it around here, some up in Laos to build schools and hospitals. Make up for some of the damage we've done to all these nice people."

"You mean you've been giving away millions of dollars for twenty years and no one was even curious about where you got it?" Eddie asked.

Suddenly Austin snapped back into focus.

"Shit, man, this is Bangkok—the capital of the unknown world. Everybody thinks I'm the biggest drug dealer in town." He burst into a cackling laugh. "Ain't that the damnedest thing? Here I am giving away money as fast as I can—just trying to do right and help people—and the reason no one asks any questions is because they think I'm a heroin dealer. The world's real fucked up, ain't it?"

Eddie made some kind of a gesture, but even he wasn't sure what it was supposed to mean.

"Anyway," Austin continued, "I've only got a few weeks left, and I'm still stuck with more than half the money. I can't let any of those bastards get it after I'm gone, and that's why I sucked you boys in. I want you to take it before that happens. I want you to get rid of every last dollar I haven't already managed to give away."

Austin stopped talking and looked so hard at Eddie that it was almost as if he was willing him to say something. When Eddie remained silent, Austin went on in a sad voice.

"But you think about it before you agree to anything, son. Think about it real careful. I'm not sure I'm doing you any favors here. Not sure at all. Money has a way of fucking people up. And a lot of money just fucks people up a lot."

Winnebago and Bar shifted back on their stools and watched Eddie. He had a strange expression on his face, and neither of them could quite figure out what it meant.

"Maybe you'd better tell us the whole story, Captain," he finally said.

"That's fair. When you want to hear it?"

"Any time you're ready to tell it, Sir."

Austin nodded crisply.

"Now's good."

34

About a dozen people appeared right after the Volvo went up—drawn from the Little Princess and the other buildings in the area by the sound of the explosion. Lek noticed that no one seemed particularly alarmed by the event. The spectators stood casually in a ragged half-circle and watched the car burn—as if a Volvo bursting into a fireball wasn't remarkable enough in that particular neighborhood to inspire any overwhelming excitement.

Together with four Vietnamese men—all of them slim, fit-looking, and dressed nondescriptly in dark trousers and short-sleeved, white shirts—Lek strode briskly across the parking lot and into the Little Princess. She paused just inside, standing quietly in the doorway while the four men split up and covered the big room from each of its corners.

As she watched the men take up their positions, Lek thought to herself how much she hated being drawn into macho posturing. Her reputation for finesse—a cleverness that usually got her what she wanted with only the most surgical application of violence—was something she was proud of. But it hadn't done the job yet, and she was running out of time.

Everything she had worked for was slipping away from her—she could feel it. Worse, an American was gaining the upper hand.

If Eddie Dare got to that money before she did, the loss of face would be devastating. Westerners didn't understand face, Lek knew. They seemed to regard it as something like a credit rating; a record from which black marks could always be erased, if you knew how to do it. But face just didn't work that way. Once lost, it was gone forever. You had to live without it for the rest of your life.

It was time to forget finesse—something she knew her superiors often dismissed contemptuously as too feminine anyway—and to adopt the only approach to solving problems that men ever really respected.

It was time to pile weight onto things until they snapped.

Behind the bar of the Little Princess, a skinny girl in a short, black dress wiped at dirty beer glasses with half-hearted swipes. Two other girls sat in straight chairs at a formica table in the back of the room, eating fried rice. The rest of the Little Princess was dim and empty. It was too early for many customers, so few girls were around either.

"Where is the mamasan?" Lek asked the girl at the bar.

The girl in the black dress shrugged listlessly. "Go out."

"Where?"

Another shrug as she placed a glass on the shelf.

"Alone?"

Now no response at all, not even a shrug.

"Did you know a man named Harry Austin?"

When the girl began silently wiping down the bar top with indifferent strokes of her towel, Lek turned away without another word. She walked to the table where the two girls were eating, but neither looked up.

"I want to know where the mamasan is."

One of the two girls attacked her remaining rice, ignoring Lek completely. She looked very young, not more than seventeen, and had a thick cascade of glossy, coal-black hair that hung around her tiny shoulders like a nun's habit.

The other girl briefly glanced sideways at Lek with a nervous twitch in her eyes, but then she too went back to eating.

Lek pointed a finger at the closest of the four Vietnamese men, and he covered the distance to the table in a few quick strides. With a movement so smooth that it seemed at first not to be occurring at all, he pulled a matte-black automatic pistol from under his shirt, and buried the muzzle in the young girl's cloak of shiny, black hair.

Then he pulled the trigger twice. Very quickly.

When the two rounds exploded in the girl's head, they shattered her skull. Blood and bone sprayed over the wall, across the table, and into what was left of the two plates of rice. The other girl began to scream hysterically, writhing frantically in her chair and slapping both hands over and over against her face.

Ignoring her, Lek turned and walked with deliberate steps back to where the first girl was frozen in place behind the bar, her towel motionless on the wooden top.

Lek raised her voice just enough to be heard over the screams.

"I asked you if you knew Harry Austin."

The girl behind the bar began to tremble uncontrollably. Her body convulsed with sobs, and she desperately tried to draw breath through the bile rising in her throat.

But she nodded quickly.

◌◌◌

The Green Latrine was still and quiet, and the perpetual twilight that shrouded its interior made it seem to Eddie that they were drifting in a place that was outside time.

"Why me, Captain?" he eventually asked. "There must be someone else."

"You saved my life, didn't you? Took a damned bullet for me."

"Don't bring that up again." Eddie sighed. "You know that was just an accident."

"I'm not so sure." Austin poked his tongue into his cheek and rolled it around. "But what difference does it make? Either way, I figure I wouldn't be here if it weren't for you. Besides, you're the only man I know who's decent enough to trust with something like this. At least you used to be. You still a decent man, Eddie?"

The word sounded exotic—almost antique—the way Austin said it.

"I don't know," Eddie finally replied when he realized that Austin was waiting for an answer. "I haven't thought about it much."

But he *had* thought about it, and when he glanced up and caught Austin's eye, he saw that the captain knew he had.

"Did you ever wonder why I called it Operation Voltaire?" Austin suddenly asked.

The question caught Eddie by surprise, and he hesitated.

"I'll bet you thought that an old hick like me never read anything more intellectual than Zane Grey, didn't you, Eddie?"

Eddie picked his words carefully. "You always had a reputation as an unusual man, Captain."

"Maybe that's just another way to say crazy, huh?" The Captain laughed and Eddie wondered where this was going. "Anyway, sometimes it worried me that I might have gotten a little cute, sticking the operation with a slick name like that, but nobody's ever caught on as far as I know."

"I have," Winnebago spoke up quietly, and Eddie twisted around and looked at him with a surprised frown.

"Thanks for telling me."

"It didn't occur to me until just now." Winnebago leaned forward until he caught Austin's eye. "It's because of *Candide*, isn't it?"

Harry Austin pointed his forefinger at Winnebago, and winked.

"Voltaire wrote a novel in the eighteenth century called *Candide*," Winnebago looked at Eddie, explaining.

"I *know* that," Eddie snapped. He glanced at Austin, but the look in the Captain's eyes was too gauzy to make any sense out of, so he turned back to Winnebago. "What's that got to do with anything?"

"*Candide* was about a man who wanted to learn how to live," Winnebago went on in a voice like a junior college lecturer. "He journeyed the world trying to find out. Sometimes he wondered if it was all worth it, but he never quit looking for the right way."

Bar threw Eddie a look. Eddie ignored it.

"By the end of the book, he'd found it—the right way to live," Winnebago continued.

"I'm holding my breath." Eddie made a beckoning gesture with his right hand. "What's your point?"

"He decided that men who *acted* were always happier than men who only observed. A valuable life came from trying to do something, rather than doing nothing, and only waiting for others to act."

"You've pretty much got it," Austin nodded.

"Got *what*?" Bar flung his hands up in exasperation.

"Look at it this way," Austin explained patiently. "The South Vietnamese who were left at the end were mostly a bunch of useless candy-asses. They were going to sit there and let the North grab all that money just to make themselves look true-blue. I had a way to save it from *all* of them. So I did."

"The Voltaire money was in that shipment we took from the embassy to Thailand just before Saigon went down, wasn't it? It was on that run where the other plane crashed. The one with the CIA guy on it."

"That's right. How'd you work it out?"

Eddie told Harry Austin about the General, but went on quickly before the captain could start asking questions.

"It all went into the Air America warehouse at U-Tapao Airbase, didn't it, Captain?"

"Yep."

"So how did you wind up with it?"

Austin scratched his ear and pushed his stool around a little.

"It was just lying around in that warehouse after everybody hauled ass out of Saigon, sealed up all nice and safe in those steel cases inside a bunch of unmarked crates. Nobody but me knew it was there. After I was evacuated to Thailand, I just borrowed a truck and got some guys to load it up. Then I gave the kid in charge of the place some old orders I had from somewhere. He never even looked at them. I just drove away. It was no big deal."

"You just loaded up a truck and drove away? With ten tons of money?"

"Yeah." Austin nodded. "That was about it. I parked the bastard for two months in a garage. Didn't even unload it. Once I had all that money, I didn't know what the hell to do with it."

So what *did* you do with it?" Winnebago blurted out, never one to mince words. "It's not like you could stick it under your bed."

"Come on," Austin said, standing up and starting for the door. "I want to show you something."

When they got outside, the sun was down. The last traces of the day glinted from the ring of glass office towers that encircled Soi Cowboy like adults standing guard over a children's playground. There was a strong scent of bougainvillea in the languid, gray-brown dusk, and a child wailed off in the distance. Thai music started to play from a radio somewhere—a woman's voice hovering halfway between discord and sweetness.

In daylight, the forest of neon signs over Soi Cowboy had looked shoddy and lifeless to Eddie. Dirty glass tubing and shabbily-rigged electrical connections dangled grotesquely out of holes that had been hastily chopped into the fronts of the buildings. The whole place looked like a half-finished demolition site.

But now, in the fading light of early dusk, Eddie could sense a transformation taking place. As the colored lights on the signs flickered tentatively, and snatches of garish animation twinkled in the dimness, the real Soi Cowboy started to appear before his eyes—like Brigadoon rising from a pile of dirt.

"See that building over there?" Austin asked, pointing across the rooftops of the three-story shophouses to where a glass-clad office building soared forty or more floors into the night. Without waiting for an answer, he swung his finger across the bars and restaurants, and pointed off the other way—to a forest of towers that loomed in the far distance down Sukhumvit Road. "And that? You see that hotel down there with those other buildings?"

Eddie glanced at the others as they grouped around Harry Austin, but their expressions were as off-center as he supposed his must be.

"I bought a lot of land over the years, mostly around here. I kept the *soi* pretty much like it always was because I like it that way, but I built that shit out there because it makes money."

Austin glanced around and a softness came into his face.

"You want to know where the Voltaire money is?"

The question was clearly rhetorical.

"This is it, boys. This is it right here." He flung his arms open, seeming to embrace everything within his sight.

Bar gaped, slack-jawed, at Austin. "I always heard some shady Chinese guy owned this place."

Austin reached up to his face with both hands, extended his forefingers, and very deliberately pushed the outer corners of both eyes upward until they took on a decided slant. "Yeah, I always heard that, too."

"Oh, man." Bar could only shake his head.

"Anyway," Austin released his eyes and went on. "I've given all this away now. Signed most of the little places over to the people who worked in them, and the rest to a trust some big-shot lawyers in Singapore set up. I don't have the first fucking idea how it works, but all the income goes to a foundation that operates hospitals and orphanages up north."

Austin pointed to the Thais drifting into Soi Cowboy to begin another night of work.

"You don't see anything but a bunch of whores and thugs, do you? That's all I saw for a long time, but most of them got shitty lives because of where they were born, not because of who they are. They work hard, they love their kids, and they deserve a better shake than they've gotten up to now. They're good people, mostly."

Austin patted his open palms against his thighs a few times, his eyes darting among the faces in the *soi*. Eddie, Bar and Winnebago searched for some way to respond, but no one knew exactly what to say.

"You boys think I'm just a romantic old fool who's gone all soft in the head, don't you?"

"No, Sir, I think . . ." Winnebago began, and then stopped. "Actually, I got no fucking idea *what* I think."

"Don't worry about it." Austin smiled sideways at Winnebago. "That's not such a bad way to live."

There was a pause that lingered until Austin finally gave up waiting for someone to say something.

"Anyway, all this used up a lot of the money, and I gave some more away upcountry. But there's still quite a bit left. Probably about 200 million US—maybe a little more. I can show you where it is, but I don't know what I can do to help you from there."

"Are you saying you're *giving* us 200 million dollars, Captain?" Eddie heard himself asking the question out loud,

THE BIG MANGO

but it didn't sound like one that made any sense—even though he listened carefully to the words as he pronounced them.

"That's about the size of it."

"*Giving* it to us?" Eddie asked again. He cleared his throat, which had suddenly gone very dry. "Just like that."

"Sure am." Austin grinned. "But first you have to promise me something."

"Uh-oh." Bar glanced at Eddie. "I knew there'd be a catch."

Austin briefly engaged each man's eyes and held them a moment, as if he wanted to reassure himself of something before he went on. When he spoke again, it was in a firm and resolute voice.

"You can divide the money up among yourselves or give it to the Little Sisters of Charity. You can do any fucking thing you want with it. But you've got to promise me one thing— that you'll get it out of here right now and make it all go away forever."

Eddie considered that a minute, and then told Austin about the bounty the Secret Service had offered him for turning the money in.

"No!" Austin snapped. "No fucking way. You promise me that you're *not* going to do that—or this is over right now."

Austin reached over and took his wrist. Eddie could feel the urgency in his fingers.

"Look, you'd probably be better off if you burned most of it—that's my opinion—but I don't reckon you'll do it. The important thing to me is this. No government can ever have it again. Not ours. Not theirs. Not anybody's. You understand that?"

The silence that fell was heavy with anticipation, and it was left to Eddie to break it. When he did, his voice sounded thin and scratchy, even to him.

"Okay, Captain, so where is it?"

329

When the girl in the black dress had told Lek everything she knew about Short Time and about Harry Austin; when she had told her about the closed-down bar once called the Green Latrine that was where Harry Austin ran his Soi Cowboy empire from; when she had told her all that, Lek was done with her.

One of the Vietnamese men shot the girl where she stood, and then another shot the one who'd been screaming—putting each of them away with a professional double tap angled upward from the back of the skull.

After that, the four men made a quick but thorough search through the massage rooms upstairs. One found two girls and a fat German entwined together in a big bathtub, and shot them all without hesitation. Another found the two Chinese men tied up together and dumped on a round bed, watching themselves in the mirror on the ceiling. When he also found the duffel bag of weapons lying on the floor at their feet, he called Lek.

She considered the possibilities as she rifled through the bag. She was pretty sure she recognized the Chinese as McBride's men, but the question was, what were they doing tied up there in the Little Princess? Had Eddie done it? Was he making his run for the money and left them there to get them out of the way? But then why had the bag of weapons been left behind? Had Eddie decided he didn't need guns at all, or had he just left the small ones behind, taking only heavier stuff?

She could probably roast the Chinese until they told her, but that would take a while, and they might not know very much that was useful anyway. No, there wasn't time for that. Eddie Dare was too far ahead already. She'd just have to keep moving and take her chances.

Lek sighed and beckoned one of her men over. They had a brief, whispered conversation, and when they all left the building a few minutes later, the flames were already beginning to bite through the pasteboard-thin walls of the massage rooms, flowing over the cheap carpeting on the stairway like water rippling down a terraced creek bed.

Another five minutes and the crowd that was beginning to drift away from the remains of McBride's Volvo would have a fresh source of entertainment. Another fifteen, and there'd be nothing left of the Little Princess but moist memories— and nothing at all of the bodies scattered around inside it.

"I was wondering how long it was going to take you to ask where the money was." Austin chuckled as they trooped back inside the Green Latrine, past the two young Thais still sitting on either side of the door.

"I figured you'd tell us when you were ready, Captain," Eddie said.

"I'm ready now. I just need your word that neither the Vietnamese nor the Americans will ever see any of it again. I want to know that you'll destroy it if you have to before you'll let that happen. Do I have your word on that, Eddie?"

"You have my word."

"You boys okay with that?" Austin's eyes darted first to Winnebago, then to Bar.

They both nodded.

Austin whooped loudly and bounded across the room. "Then let's get to it!"

With a half-dozen lively strides, he rounded the end of the bar, reached underneath, and produced a fire ax. He raised it over his head with both hands and swung it straight down with all his weight behind it. The bar top splintered from the impact of the heavy blade, and—after a second swing—it split into two separate pieces. Austin gave the ax a twist as he pulled it back, sending half the top sliding sideways and crashing to the floor.

He turned the ax over, holding its head down like a clock pendulum, and dropped it into the open cavity beneath where the top had been. He slammed the flat of the blade forward and backward until first the rear, and then the front, collapsed in a ruined heap around his feet. Kicking some of the pieces aside, he extended the ax out at arm's length, pointing with it into the rubble.

"There you go."

Clearly visible where the bar had been ripped down was one end of a line of wooden crates. They were each sitting on two-by-four skids and bolted to shipping pallets. Eddie could only see one of the crates in its entirety from where he stood, but that was enough.

Stenciled across its side in large, white letters was something in Vietnamese. Below that, English had been added with black paint in what looked like a hasty, hand-done job. The Vietnamese meant nothing to Eddie, of course, but he could read the English easily enough—and it meant everything.

The black words leaped at him from the light-colored wood of the crate . . .

FROM—US EMBASSY, SAIGON.
CONSIGNED TO—U-TAPAO AIRBASE.
DATE—APRIL 3, 1975.

35

S oi Cowboy wasn't much more than a short, dusty lane
from which most of the automobile traffic had been
chased away. The street was inconsequential in daylight, but
after sundown it flowed with the lifeblood of night-time
Bangkok.

It was only about 100 yards long—running straight through
from busy Soi Asoke on the west, to quiet little Soi 23, the
next *soi* on the east. For its entire length, it was lined solidly
on both sides with narrow, dilapidated shophouses that had
been turned into bars. The wide porches along the front of
most of the structures made the whole place look vaguely
reminiscent of an old western town straight out of a
Hollywood movie. All it needed was hitching rails.

Lek entered Soi Cowboy from the east—the Soi 23 end.
Two of her soldiers trailed a dozen paces behind and kept
her in sight. The other two sealed off the *soi* from the opposite
end and watched them approach.

It was still early and there wasn't much going on. Some of
the hardcore locals nursed drinks at tables on the front
porches, and a few knots of curious tourists were already
cruising—mostly Japanese and Taiwanese men grouped into
packs for mutual courage and giggling nervously whenever
they encountered any Thai woman not yet sixty.

Lek picked her way carefully by an open-air beer bar
where dented stools were stacked upside-down on the

counter. A skinny, shirtless old man wheezed raggedly as he dragged brown cardboard cartons of Singha behind it and piled them up one by one. Here and there, women sat on the tiny stools provided by the street's food vendors; perched on the parked motorcycles; or just squatted in the street, eating, gossiping, or inspecting some of the skirts and T-shirts that hawkers hauled up and down the *soi* in big, wicker baskets.

Most of the women looked plain to Lek—plump little peasant girls straight out of the family rice fields in the Northeast, dried mud still under their fingernails. It was something she would never fully understand. At night, *farang* men paid money to rub the bodies of women they would probably avoid passing too close to on the street in daylight. It made no sense to her at all.

She walked by the gray, shuttered building which the girl at the Little Princess had described, glancing toward it. She noted the two men flanking the door, and continued walking.

When she reached Soi Asoke, she stepped into the deep shadow of a tall concrete wall and turned around to survey Cowboy again. All four of her men waited patiently while she considered her plan of attack; weighing carefully what they might be up against in the darkened building. The girl had claimed that the mamasan had gone there with the three *farangs*. But why had she done that? *She had to be taking them to meet someone*, Lek told herself, answering her own question.

Although the two men at the door were young, Lek could tell they were professionals. Their eyes were wary, hard and unblinking. Men like that were not there to guard three fumbling Americans and a middle-aged whore—she was sure of that. There would have to be someone of considerably greater importance inside to merit that kind of attention. But who?

It was then that the possibility of Harry Austin still being alive crossed Lek's mind for the first time—and she toyed with the idea, trying it on, turning it this way and that. She doubted it, when she thought about it. But still, if it were true, it would explain a lot. It certainly wouldn't be the first time that a foreigner in Bangkok had faked his own death in order to disappear.

One of Lek's men ducked quickly away at her signal, and—in only a few minutes—was back again. He reported that the two rows of shophouses lining Cowboy backed up to large buildings on both sides. There could be no rear exits from any of them. That suited Lek perfectly, and she could feel the tension began to drain away. She was back in control again. The only way out of the gray building was through its front door and right out into Soi Cowboy. And the only exit from Soi Cowboy was to walk out through one end or the other. Whoever it was inside there with Eddie Dare, he was now completely in her hands.

Lek sent two of her men down to the opposite end of Cowboy, where they found an empty table at a food vendor's stand and pulled up two red plastic stools. The old man who owned the stand started toward them, but they waved him away. Glancing quickly into their eyes, he retreated without protest. Both men lit cigarettes and settled in.

Lek found a wooden box for herself and pushed it up against the wall. She sat down on it—while her other two men squatted watchfully a short distance away—and studied the gray shophouse, thinking.

They had surprise on their side, she eventually decided. It would do no harm to wait and watch for a while before they made their move—just to be on the safe side.

◗◗◗

Austin chopped away the rest of the bar while Eddie, Winnebago, and Bar stood and stared. Within minutes, eight wooden crates—each about three feet square and four feet high—sat lined up on their pallets, making a neat row in the middle of the wreckage.

"I hope you had a lot of fire insurance," Eddie said, looking at the crates.

Austin pushed the blade of his ax into a tiny crack at the top of the crate nearest him. Putting all of his weight on the handle, he wrenched the lid upward with a cracking sound, and pulled the ax out. With two sharp, chopping uppercuts, he split the lid away. Then, using the ax handle, he rapped on the box inside the crate—the top of which was now visible. The sound was solid and metallic.

"These things are waterproof and fire resistant to a temperature of 2,000 degrees. It wouldn't be any safer buried a mile under Wall Street."

Eddie wasn't so sure about that, but he didn't argue.

"Believe it or not, there're no locks on any of the cases," Austin added. "We figured that anyone who wasn't authorized would never be able to get close to them, so we didn't bother."

Dropping the ax, he reached into the crate, put both hands flat against the top of the metal case, and curled his fingers into hidden recesses on its sides. He rotated the two handles inside a half turn clockwise with simultaneous twists of his wrists, and lifted the top away. There was a slight *pop* as the watertight seal separated, and Eddie, Bar and Winnebago all leaned forward together, straining to see inside.

The bundles of American currency were all bound with identical yellow and white paper wrappers—each of them printed with the legend, '$10,000'—and they lay in perfect, neatly-aligned rows. The symmetrical blanket of Benjamin Franklins looked like a Warhol print.

There was a full minute of utter silence.

Eddie's first reaction, he was surprised to notice, was no reaction at all. The money seemed more like a movie prop— or maybe stacks of that play money sold at novelty shops. He wasn't really sure *what* it looked like, but it didn't look like real money.

Then the smell hit him the way the smell of a new car spills out when you open the door. It made him dizzy, and he reached out and held onto the edge of the wooden case to steady himself. It was only the odor of paper and ink, he supposed, but the aroma was still unmistakable, even after so many years—and it left him feeling a little drunk as he breathed it in.

Fuck . . . it's real.

"I sold the gold a long time ago," Austin eventually said in a voice that was not loud, but made them all jump in the silence just the same. "What's left is mostly American currency, but there might be some foreign stuff mixed in there, too. All I've found so far is some yen, although I could've sworn we put marks and pounds in somewhere, too."

He thought about it for a moment.

"I just can't remember where it is anymore."

His voice sounded like a man trying to recall what he had done with his car keys.

"Anyway, be careful if you find it. The old US currency is still in circulation, but I think the foreign stuff has been replaced. You'd be pretty conspicuous if you tried to pass it."

While Eddie was still pondering that, Winnebago tugged at his elbow.

"Shit, man. What are we going to do now? We can't just call a taxi and pile this in the back seat."

Austin disappeared briefly through an interior door and returned with a sturdy-looking cart that had been rigged with an electric motor. He rolled it up to the first of the crates, wedged its long steel lifters underneath, and hit a button on the handle. There was a brief buzzing sound and the lifters ground steadily up and back until they stopped with a snap.

Eddie realized that he was probably looking at over a half a ton of money, just waiting to be wheeled away.

Austin slammed the metal top back onto the case and

twisted the handles. There was a *whoosh* as the seals locked back together.

"Let me show you something else," he said, as he rolled the cart back out through the same door.

Eddie looked at Bar and Winnebago. Both of them seemed rooted to the spots where they stood, but as he trailed along behind Austin, he felt them close behind him.

Through the door, they found themselves in what looked like a large storeroom. A pile of empty Carlsberg cases was heaped to one side, and a collection of bar furniture was up against the wall. Austin pushed the cart straight across the dim room, hauled it around until it was in front of another door that was in the far corner of the right-hand wall, and then pulled a heavy ring of keys out of his front trouser pocket.

"You can't exactly push shit like this down the middle of Soi Cowboy." Austin sorted through the keys, selected one, and inserted it in the door's handle. He seemed to drift away for a moment—almost as if he had suddenly thought about something that was too personal to mention—then he shook off whatever it was, flicked his wrist, and clicked the lock open.

On the other side of the door was a long, well-lit hallway. It looked like a corridor in a modest office building—plain, white walls; black linoleum floor; and ordinary doors set at irregular intervals along the right-hand side. The corridor ended about 150 feet away, at a door that looked just like all the others.

"This runs behind some of my bars. I put the heads back here. Saved me a lot of money not to have to build separate toilets in every place."

Eddie involuntarily glanced toward the packing case on the cart. He wondered how many bathrooms Austin could have built with its contents.

"That door up at the end. . . ," Austin pointed down the corridor, ". . . will take you out into another building of mine. Used to be a Tex-Mex joint called Poncho's, but I couldn't get me a decent cook so I finally closed it. Anyway, you won't have to go out onto Cowboy to get out of here. You can go right down there, open the front door of old Poncho's, and you'll be on a sidewalk five feet from Soi 23.

"What do we do then?"

The floor squeaked as Eddie shifted his weight.

"Fucked if I know. I can't do everything for you, boy. I'll cover your ass as well as I can from here, but once you're out this door, you're on your own."

Darkness had taken over Cowboy, and the crowds were beginning to roll in. A steadily growing river of sweaty, white flesh sloshed up and down the short lane, eyeing the action.

A glitzy neon sign near the gray shophouse flickered on—AFTER SKOOL—and a wave of unidentifiable rock and roll suddenly boomed from a loudspeaker system somewhere inside.

Lek took another slow walk by the gray shophouse. The men guarding the door were watching a very fat man slumped on a stool at an open-air beer bar, and paid no particular attention to her as she passed close by them. A thin girl who looked no more than eighteen unwrapped a white towel from a plastic bag and wiped the fat man's face, starting with his forehead and working her way gently down his cheeks to his neck. The man suddenly shouted something at her in Swedish, waving his beer bottle in the air, and the young girl backed away, confused.

One of the men at the door screwed up his face as he said something to the other that Lek couldn't hear. Then he pulled out a cigarette and lit it, curling his lip and flipping the match off in the direction of the Swede.

Lek stopped not far away and surveyed the doorway. It would be easy enough to take them now, she knew, but it would probably be better to wait just a little longer. In another hour, Cowboy would be running full. The street, the go-go bars, and the food stands would be crammed with the kind of customers who wouldn't be distracted by a little ruckus. There could probably be bombs going off and small-arms fire rattling in the street, she thought to herself, and the old *farangs* who hung around Cowboy would just keep on swilling beer, buying drinks for the girls, and searching the night for a little hope.

Another hour, Lek decided. *Give it another hour, and we'll go in.*

"Couldn't you let us have a couple of days to get the logistics worked out, Captain? I'm sure we'd find a way to move this stuff without any problem, but we've got no way to do it right now."

"Jesus Christ, you still don't get it, do you?" Austin waved a finger at Eddie. "Those guys at the Little Princess weren't the fuckin' welcome wagon. You stand here much longer farting around and somebody's going to be so far up your ass you'll need a grappling hook to get them out."

Eddie winced at the image, but it was very persuasive.

"We'll have to find a truck or a couple of vans somewhere."

"I've got an old Nissan out there some place," Austin volunteered. "It's a van, but it's a piece of shit. Won't take any weight."

Eddie looked at Bar. "What do you think?"

"The Ambassador Hotel's near here, and the resident manager's a friend of mine."

Bar chewed the idea over. "I think they've got a couple of Toyota Hiaces they use for hauling tour-group luggage. But he'd lose his job if they were gone more than a couple of hours."

Eddie glanced toward the top of the metal case that was sticking up out of the open crate, and then back to Bar.

"Ah. . . ." Bar nodded. "I think I see your point." He pulled out his mobile telephone and began to dial, slowly walking away toward another corner of the storeroom. The outlines of a negotiation were already beginning to form in his head.

Eddie turned back to Austin. "We can all go, Captain."

"No thanks, Eddie. I've been here so long I might as well stay a little longer."

"If Lek finds you, and you're right about her . . ." Eddie left the thought unfinished.

"Doesn't matter." Austin shrugged. "There's not much she can take away from me anymore."

"She'll hurt you, Harry."

"Not if I see her first."

Bar came back, snapping his telephone shut. "Done deal. He and another guy are going to drive the vans around and pull them up on the sidewalk outside Poncho's. He says he knows the place."

"What did you tell him?"

Bar grinned. "Told him I was repossessing the fixtures from a club that owed me money."

"And he believed that?"

"Shit, no. But I said I'd give him 5,000 dollars to park the two vans on Soi 23 with their keys in the ignition and not report them stolen till tomorrow. He believed *that*."

Lek checked her watch again. It had been almost an hour and no one had entered or left the gray shophouse. The two men flanking the door were still there, smoking and waiting patiently, doing nothing until somebody gave them instructions. It was something Lek knew the Thais were particularly good at.

It hadn't taken long after dark for Cowboy to soar into full flight. A man in baggy shorts passed by wearing a tiny, black bra wrapped around his bald head like a sweatband. Two young girls with golden skin watched him, laughing out loud. They wore red, pleated school skirts, black and white saddle oxfords with white socks, and white blouses unbuttoned to their waists. They had nothing on underneath.

Across from where she sat against the wall, Lek counted the *farang* men pushing through a curtain into a bar named Long Gun. Each time the curtain swung open, she caught a flash of the young girls inside. Most were slim, dark-skinned, and naked except for G-strings. They twirled through a forest of silver poles on an elevated stage, shuffling their feet to uncertain rhythms. Rock music throbbed into Soi Cowboy—its volume rising and falling as the heavy curtain opened and closed.

Abruptly, Lek decided she'd had enough.

So much for the legendary Asian virtue of patience which Westerners loved to mythologize. It was time to do some damage. Stealth and guile had their place, but maybe her male counterparts were right. When you came right down to it, violence and pain were what you could count on to deliver the goods.

She nodded at one of her soldiers who squatted nearby. He stood up and walked toward the gray shophouse, and one of her men sitting at the other end of the *soi* mirrored his movements. After they had both worked their way into position, dawdling at a vendor's cart near the building's entrance, Lek approached the men sitting by the doorway.

She appeared hesitant and confused. One of the men flipped his cigarette away and snapped something at Lek as she approached—but she pretended not to understand, and addressed him slowly and carefully in English, as if speaking to a child.

"I lost maybe." Then she looked at the other man. "Is this right place?"

"What you want?" he snapped.

"I see Harry Austin."

The mention of Austin's name surprised the two Thais—as it was meant to—and they looked at each other, neither knowing quite what to do. But since the Vietnamese men moved so quickly, they didn't have long to worry about it.

There were two almost simultaneous noises—hardly louder than coughs—and each of the guards took a single, silenced round in the head. The Vietnamese swept both boys from their chairs, folded them onto the ground as if they were drunk or sleeping, and quickly filled their places. In the uproar of Cowboy, no one even seemed to notice.

Lek was moving through the door even before the two Thais were down. She crouched in the shadows just inside, and silently drew a long-bladed knife with a serrated edge from a scabbard under her blouse. Remembering the bag of weapons she'd found back at the Little Princess, she waited—silent and motionless—letting her eyes adjust to the semi-darkness.

36

It had taken barely a half hour to wheel all the crates out of the Green Latrine, down the back hallway, and into the empty shell of Poncho's. Within a second half hour, they'd been loaded into the two white Toyota vans, marked AMBASSADOR HOTEL LUGGAGE SERVICE.

Before they started working, Bar had found Harry Austin's old Nissan and pulled it up on the sidewalk in front of the Toyotas—blocking the line of sight between them and the eastern entry to Soi Cowboy. In most cities, Bar knew, parking on the sidewalk made you conspicuous. In Bangkok, it just caused you to fit right in.

Eddie and Bar had talked about where they'd take the crates while they hoisted them up into the Toyotas. After considering and discarding several possibilities, Bar had suggested a motel that a friend of his owned in Pattaya—a moldy beach resort on the Gulf of Thailand about seventy miles east of Bangkok. Eddie eventually agreed that it sounded fine, at least for starters. It would be a place where no one asked too many questions, and they could hide the vehicles in two of the traditional, curtained parking bays until he figured out what to do next.

Eddie knew that cash in large amounts was a major headache to deal with. You couldn't exactly wheel a few million bucks in hundreds into Citibank and open a checking account without drawing a fair amount of undesirable attention.

With a couple of good nights' sleep and a little time to think, however, he was pretty sure he could come up with something cute. He'd handled enough money laundering cases in his career to have picked up a few tricks of the trade. Actually, he had a couple of ideas kicking around in the back of his head already.

Eddie wanted to take one more try at persuading Austin to go with them before he called it quits, but when he looked around, he noticed that the captain had disappeared. He had apparently slipped back inside sometime while they were loading, so he walked back through Poncho's, and up the hallway to the Green Latrine.

When he discovered that Austin had locked the door to the storeroom behind him, he was a little surprised—but he assumed it must have happened by mistake, so he went back outside. While the others hooked the security straps around the crates and then cinched them to the U-bolts welded into the frames of the vans, Eddie walked up Soi 23 to go around to the Latrine's front door

He slipped past a food cart from which a smiling woman was doing a brisk business selling plastic bags filled with an unidentifiable yellow liquid, and then he turned right into Soi Cowboy. He took a few steps, slowing while his eyes searched out the front of the Green Latrine. Then he stopped abruptly, and blinked quickly a few times, trying to absorb what he was seeing.

Lek was pushing gently with one hand against the Latrine's door, while two Vietnamese—with the unmistakable look of pros—took up positions on either side to seal off any escape from the building. Eddie was pretty sure he could pick out at least two more soldiers hovering not far away; their eyes also fixed on the Latrine.

He slid carefully back into the crowd, and hastily retraced his steps.

It hadn't taken long for Lek's eyes to adjust to the darkness, and as soon as they did, she took stock of the room. The place was thick with dust; tables, chairs and bar stools had been shoved haphazardly around; and the floor was littered with debris. Splintered wood, nails, dirt and broken bottles were everywhere.

Her caution kept her motionless in the shadows, but when no threat materialized, her curiosity finally got the better of her. She rose slowly from her crouch and began to edge across the room, poking carefully at the wreckage with her foot. Her eyes scanned methodically for an explanation as to what might have happened, but she found none.

She was almost in the middle of the room when she heard a *click* that made her freeze. A male voice spoke from somewhere behind and off to her right.

"Hey, Lek. What took you so long?"

Instinctively, she dropped to the floor, rolling away from the sound even as she registered that it was Harry Austin's voice she was hearing. He *had* faked his death. *The clever old bastard.*

Lek crashed against a chair and felt her shoulder hit the wall furthest from where the sound had originated. She pushed herself up and edged along—her back pressed against it—looking for cover.

It was only a few seconds before she felt the cold metal against her neck. Knowing immediately that it was the muzzle of a gun, she stopped moving without a word.

"I'm right here, honey. These remote-control tape things are slicker than owl shit in a greased tube, ain't they?"

Austin grabbed Lek by the hair with his free hand, jerking her head roughly backward and to the side. She grunted, but did not cry out.

"Let it go, baby doll."

She opened her hand and the knife clattered to the floor.

"Now there's one more thing I need for you to do, darlin'," Austin announced in a cheerful voice. "Scream real loud a few times, would you?"

Lek didn't respond right away, trying to work out what Austin was up to.

He jerked hard on her hair again, this time slamming her head against the wall.

"You didn't come alone, did you? Your goons are outside and I want them in here. That's simple enough, ain't it? So, a nice loud scream, please—or I'll shoot you through a kneecap to get it."

Underscoring his seriousness, he snapped her head against the wall again. Harder this time.

Lek couldn't see what harm it could do her, so she gave Austin the long, wailing scream he wanted.

Almost immediately, the two Vietnamese covering the front door burst into the room—followed quickly by the two who'd been hovering out in the street. Keeping low and clearing their weapons smoothly, they split apart until they had Austin and Lek covered from four widely-spaced angles.

"Okay, Harry, we're all here. Now what?"

"Only four?" He sounded almost amused. "You're traveling light these days, baby. I'm not worth anything heavier than that?"

"Fuck you, Harry."

If Lek could have seen Austin's face, she would have realized that he was smiling. But she couldn't, so she tried the obvious tack.

"We can make a deal, Harry. You can still save yourself."

She could feel Austin shaking his head.

"It's the others I'm worried about now, Lek. I got no chance anymore. No chance at all."

"You're dead if you hurt me, Harry."

Austin laughed. "No, honey, I'm dead anyway."

Before Lek could work out what Austin meant by that, he told her—in a matter-of-fact voice.

"It's cancer, they say. If I shoot you now, I just get dead a little sooner, that's all."

Suddenly, unmistakably, Lek knew exactly why Austin had wanted her to scream and pull her men inside. And she saw, in a flash of total clarity, just what he was going to do.

She lunged desperately away from him, dropping toward the floor and groping at the place where her knife had fallen. It was a hopeless gesture.

Harry Austin's old .45 was loaded with hollow points—rounds that tumbled and twisted on contact, chewing into bone and tissue alike, ripping away everything in their path. He'd wedged the pistol's muzzle solidly into the flesh under her chin, and her weight falling toward the floor only jammed it tighter.

When he felt Lek begin to move, Austin squeezed the trigger twice in rapid succession. The roar of the .45's detonations echoed deafeningly in the small room, and all four of the Vietnamese instinctively opened fire. In an angry counterpoint of silenced coughs, they emptied their clips into Austin—but the shots came far too late to do Lek any good.

Both she and Austin were dead before either of them hit the floor.

37

The two Toyotas were parked about fifty yards up Soi 23, facing away from Soi Cowboy. By the time Eddie got back to them, Bar had finished strapping the crates down in the closest one and was just closing the back doors. Winnebago was still working inside the other.

Eddie took Bar by the elbow, towing him quickly through Poncho's and up the hallway toward the Green Latrine—describing to him as they walked what he'd just seen. He'd barely finished, when they both heard a woman scream—followed shortly by an unmistakable explosion of gunfire.

"Oh, Christ," Eddie shouted as he leaped toward the back door of the Latrine. "We've got to get the captain out of there!"

Bar grabbed Eddie's arm and pulled him away from the door. His eyes were flat.

"Didn't you see that he sent Short Time away?"

"What's that got to do with . . ."

"He was protecting her, Eddie."

Bar pointed to the locked door, still holding onto Eddie's arm with his other hand.

"When he went back in there and locked the door, he was doing the same thing for us. He knew Lek was coming. He was buying us time."

Eddie shook off Bar's hand and stared at the locked door.

"He's dead, Eddie. That's the way he planned it. Now we've got to get the fuck out of here before we're next."

Eddie took a deep breath and started to say something—but Bar was already pulling him away. Reluctantly, Eddie allowed himself to be led back up the hallway in silence. He knew Bar was probably right.

As they stepped out of Poncho's, there was a *ching* on the wall next to Eddie's cheek, and brick dust showered his face. Eddie and Bar dived behind the nearest Toyota, hugging the concrete as more shots ricocheted off the buildings along the sidewalk and *pinged* into the van.

Eddie glanced back over his shoulder. He saw Winnebago's eyes go as big as saucers, and he waved him to cover behind the crates of the second van. Whatever else a steel case full of money was good for, it ought to stop bullets, he thought.

The shots came from the direction of Soi Cowboy, and since he had heard no audible reports, Eddie gathered they were from silenced weapons—probably handguns. He guessed it could have been worse. They could've been staring down the wrong end of a rocket launcher.

When he risked a quick bob of his head toward Cowboy to reconnoiter, the movement drew a second volley of shots. They missed, and Eddie got a clear look at Lek's soldiers.

Two were edging carefully into Soi 23, and the other two were providing cover from behind a parked motorcycle. Beyond them, Cowboy seemed to be partying on as usual. A few faces had turned toward the Vietnamese, but they looked more amused than frightened at the antics of the four men.

"I don't see Lek." A tight smile crossed Eddie's face. "I'll bet the captain got her."

As the sound of the second volley died away, Winnebago's old reflexes took over. He high-stepped his way smartly up from the second van—drawing more shots that went high and wide—and flattened himself between Eddie and Bar.

"We're loaded," he said without preamble. "Let's get the fuck out of here."

Winnebago didn't ask about Captain Austin. Eddie figured that he'd already guessed what had happened.

Glancing over his shoulder and measuring the *soi* behind them, Eddie shook his head. "We'll never make it. They'll cut us up before we get out of range."

"They aren't sure if we're armed, and they'll hang back until they decide. How could I have left those guns at the Princess?" Bar slapped his cheek with his open palm a couple of times. "Stupid. Fucking stupid."

Eddie glanced up and down the *soi* again. Then he scanned the walls of the buildings that lined both sides. He sighed deeply and made a hopeless gesture with his open palms. "We could always throw rocks at them, I guess."

Bar thought about that for a second, and then shoved his hands down into the deep side-pockets of his fatigue trousers. "Or these might be better," he suggested.

And like a magician dipping into a top hat, he produced two hand grenades—one from each pocket.

Eddie couldn't believe it. "Where the hell did you get those?"

"The guy I bought the guns from gave them to me. They're the samples I told you about. I forgot I had them until something just reminded me. Can't imagine what."

Eddie took the grenades from Bar and hefted one in each hand. "Oh man, oh man. Aren't these the most beautiful things you ever saw?"

"Ah . . ." Bar broke in reluctantly. "Don't get too carried away." He pointed to a smear of red paint on one of the grenades. "That one's not real."

Eddie closed his eyes.

"It's a dummy?"

"Not quite. But it's only a smoker."

The Vietnamese had begun working their way cautiously up the *soi* in a two-by-two cover formation. The lack of any return fire was making them bolder.

"Well, hell." Eddie shook his head, bouncing the grenades up and down in his hands. "I guess you work with what you got."

He switched the live one to his left hand and rose into a half crouch. Pulling the pin on the smoke grenade in his right, and clinching the spoon tightly, he duck-walked his way around the van, staying down out of sight as long as he could.

When he reached a spot where he was sure he'd be in the clear, he bobbed up with his arm cocked, and launched the smoke grenade in a perfect arc over Austin's old Nissan— right down the middle of Soi 23. By the time it hit the concrete, the Vietnamese were already reacting as Eddie knew they would—falling back into Soi Cowboy and flattening themselves against a wall to ride out the explosion.

But there was no explosion.

The grenade hit the concrete with a solid *cling* and bounced a couple of times before it lay still. After a moment, it gave out with a long, slow *hiss*, and began emitting a thick cloud of yellow smoke which quickly filled the *soi*.

On the downwind side of the smoke, part of the Cowboy crowd had worked out that something nasty was happening— and a few people were starting to scramble away, without being certain what they were running from or where they were running to. The Vietnamese ignored them, as well as the hysterical screams of two girls who'd seen the grenade hit.

The four men peered cautiously around the corner into Soi 23, trying to decide if the smoke was the only thing that was coming at them—or if something much more unpleasant was just behind it.

On the upwind side of the smoke, Eddie was busy. As soon as he let the smoke grenade go, he had sprinted back to where Bar and Winnebago were crouching.

"You take the first van, Bar. . . ," Eddie pointed at the Toyota that was furthest away up the *soi*, ". . . and you can lead us out of here to the main road." He twisted his head toward Winnebago. "You get this one started and sit tight until I get back."

Eddie shifted the live grenade to his right hand and looked back at Bar, who hadn't moved.

"Take off, man! Do it now!"

Bar and Winnebago glanced uncomfortably at each other, neither wanting to leave Eddie alone to do whatever it was he had in mind.

"Do what I'm telling you!" Eddie snapped. "Move your fucking butts!"

And they moved.

Within a few moments, Bar was powering the first van up Soi 23, away from the Vietnamese, while Winnebago fidgeted at the wheel of the second, its engine idling.

By then, Eddie had sprinted forward again and jerked open the back doors of Austin's old Nissan van. He climbed through the cargo space and vaulted into the driver's seat. The engine fired on the first try, and Eddie let out a thankful sigh. He yanked the shift lever into drive, and accelerated down the *soi* toward the yellow smoke.

When the Vietnamese heard engines turning over, and the unmistakable sound of vehicles moving, they quickly abandoned their cover positions and plunged out of Cowboy, zigzagging through the swirling smoke and firing as they ran. They were now certain that the smoke had been only a diversion—that nothing else was coming at them.

It was a miscalculation on which none of them would have long to dwell.

As the Nissan hit the edge of the smoke, Eddie made the steering wheel as steady as he could. Then—in one quick motion—he rolled over the seat and out through the flapping rear doors. When he hit the ground, he staggered slightly, but kept his feet and turned halfway back. He pulled the pin from the live grenade, and lobbed it underhanded into the Nissan's open cargo space.

The driverless van wobbled from one side of Soi 23 to the other—but it kept going toward Cowboy. It crunched over a pile of empty cardboard boxes, grated against the front of a building, and then nosed into the thickest part of the smoke. Shots from the four charging Vietnamese thudded off its front and sides, and Eddie heard the windshield go with a *pop*.

Scrambling back to the Toyota where Winnebago waited behind the wheel, Eddie was screaming, *"Go! Go! Go!"* even before he wrenched open the passenger door and dived inside. As Winnebago slammed the accelerator to the floor and popped the clutch, the sounds of two separate and distinct explosions punctuated their departure.

The hand grenade went first, and then—a split second later—the gas tank of the Nissan.

As the two sounds rolled up together, they reverberated back and forth between the buildings that lined Soi 23, amplifying themselves into an awesome, guttural rumbling.

In the background, Eddie was sure he could also pick out another sound, too. He was certain he could hear the higher-pitched, staccato rhythm of the rounds carried by the four Vietnamese. They were going off one by one, tapping out a minor key counterpoint to the bass roar of the explosion.

When they closed up on the other van, Eddie leaned out his window far enough to give Bar a thumb's up and a big wave. Winnebago thumped the horn a couple of times for emphasis—scaring the hell out of two schoolgirls who had been puttering peacefully along the curb on a motorbike until the three *farangs* flew by in the Ambassador Hotel vans.

Eddie felt his surge of adrenaline fade as quickly as it had come—and he slid back inside the van, rolled up the window, and settled heavily into his seat.

Winnebago glanced over. "You couldn't have done anything for the captain. This was the way he planned for it to end."

Eddie just nodded, keeping his eyes straight ahead. He knew Winnebago was right, but he was still going to have to live with it for a while.

The two vans fell into convoy through the early evening streets of Bangkok, winding their way toward the Pattaya highway. Winnebago focused his attention on following Bar, and didn't say anything else for a long time.

Eventually he glanced over at Eddie and wiggled his eyebrows up and down a couple of times.

"Pretty good moves for an old guy."

Eddie smiled a little at that, and then he leaned his head back and closed his eyes.

He wondered briefly if he should start trying to put everything that had happened to him over the last few weeks into some kind of perspective; to begin trying to understand exactly where he had ended up, and how he had gotten there.

But it was too soon and it wouldn't come—so he didn't dwell on it. Anyway, he decided, that was thinking like a lawyer again. He really *was* going to have to stop it.

Inhale and exhale. Don't try to hold your breath. Not in this air.

Suddenly Eddie smiled to himself. There was at least one thing he knew for certain—and he didn't have to think about it at all.

His future was out there in front of him again.

It was back where it belonged. Back where, by rights, it should always have been.

And so it began.

NOTES AND ACKNOWLEDGEMENTS

Although many of the places described here are real, the characters and events are not. This is fiction. The story is entirely a product of the author's imagination and does not portray actual persons or events. Any resemblance to either, is entirely coincidental and completely unintended.

The lines at the end of Chapter Seven are quoted from *A Visit from St. Nick,* written by Clement Clark Moore in 1822.

There are three people without whose support and encouragement this book would never have been written. My gratitude to them all is immeasurable.

Jess Taylor, my agent at Endeavor in LA, was bold enough to believe that even a screenwriter could construct enough complete sentences to wind up somehow with a novel. You're a great man and a gentleman, Jess—even if you *are* an agent.

Richard Baker, my editor at Asia Books, labored tirelessly to make sense out of those complete sentences after I had constructed them. Whatever they're paying you, Rich, it's not nearly enough.

Most of all, I am forever and always grateful to my wife. No matter how good she makes my life look, I have to honestly admit, it's better.

Just imagine this. She never even snickered—not once— when I said to her one day, "Darling, I think I'll write a novel."

Jake Needham
San Francisco
June, 1999